C0-ANB-987

3 4028 07899 7013
HARRIS COUNTY PUBLIC LIBRARY

Mystery MacDow X
MacDowell, Rose
The lost book of Mala R. :
   a novel

                    $15.00
            ocn692288259
               01/11/2012

THE LOST BOOK OF MALA R.

BANTAM BOOKS TRADE PAPERBACKS   NEW YORK

The Lost Book of Mala R.

A NOVEL

ROSE MacDOWELL

The Lost Book of Mala R. is a work of fiction.
Names, characters, places, and incidents are either the
products of the author's imagination or are used fictitiously.
Any resemblance to actual persons, living or dead, events,
or locales is entirely coincidental.

A Bantam Books Trade Paperback Original

Copyright © 2011 by Rose MacDowell

All rights reserved.

Published in the United States by Bantam Books,
an imprint of The Random House Publishing Group,
a division of Random House, Inc., New York.

BANTAM BOOKS and the rooster colophon are registered
trademarks of Random House, Inc.

LIBRARY OF CONGRESS CATALOGING-IN-PUBLICATION DATA
MacDowell, Rose.
The lost book of Mala R. : a novel / Rose MacDowell.
p. cm.
"A Bantam Books trade paperback original."
ISBN 978-0-385-33858-5—ISBN 978-0-345-52927-5 (ebook)
1. Romanies—Fiction. 2. Outcasts—Fiction.
3. Family secrets—Fiction. 4. Identity (Psychology)—Fiction.
5. Texas—Fiction. 6. California—Fiction. I. Title.
PS3613.A27147L67 2011
813'.6—dc23   2011018171

Title-page and interior art: © iStockphoto

Printed in the United States of America

www.bantamdell.com

9 8 7 6 5 4 3 2 1

Book design by Dana Leigh Blanchette

THE LOST BOOK OF MALA R.

One

*N*obody liked to revel in another's misfortune, not publicly any-way, but there hadn't been a trial at the camp in almost two years, and the fact was, it was overdue. People were hankering for some-thing to talk about. You couldn't go too long without a scandal; life didn't work that way, and thank God. It was one thing to enjoy your own happiness; another to be bored to death when your neighbors were quiet and content for months at a time. It got old. Sooner or later there had to be a break in the monotony. Mala—barely nine-teen, daughter of a mental case and a drunk—was providing that for them, doing something useful with her life at long last. After years of bringing shame and hard times to her clan, she would finally have to answer for herself at two o'clock in the dusty clearing that served as courtroom, marriage hall, and place to prepare the dead for what came next.

The trial would be nothing like going to city hall on a vagrancy charge, head bowed before a judge you'd never met, your feet pinched in borrowed shoes, the proceedings so orderly and respectful you nodded off halfway through. Mala should have it so easy. The *kris* was more like being prosecuted by your entire family, your ex-husband, his mother, and some people you owed money to. Not a very impartial jury, but they knew you. They had an intimate understanding of what you'd done because they'd been watching from behind a tree. Each of Mala's victims would have the chance to tell their story, and then she and whichever idiot dared to defend her would speak on her behalf. Even now, with only a few minutes to go before the trial started, bets were being collected. They wagered with a cast iron pan, a matchless earring, a planishing hammer with a loose head. It wasn't every day a woman was tried, let alone a young one, but the list of Mala's transgressions had grown too long: speaking her mind, flouting tradition, and last week, reading a book out in the open with no attempt to hide it, just sitting there by the river with children in view as if betraying her culture was the simplest thing in the world.

The council and witnesses gathered under a clump of mesquite trees whose branches bent east with the wind. It was a nice day for a trial: sunny, cool for May, with bluebonnets and purple horsemint sprouting up wherever there weren't fire pits and garbage and rusted trailers. A bright sky, Mala thought, at least there was that. She sat at the edge of the clearing on a rock that had previously been occupied by an adulterer, an exceptional liar, and a man who'd invited a plague into the community by keeping a stray cat named Darling, and then denying its existence after it bit his cousin. Her father, Beni, stood beside her kicking at a half-buried root and swearing to himself, not because of the injustice being done to his child, but because he was still drunk from the night before and believed he was the defendant. "Done nothing," he muttered, hands plunged into the pockets of his only pair of trousers. "Nothing but suffer my whole life and eat shit."

"Calm down, Daddy," Mala said. "They're after me."

He thought for a minute, lids blinking slowly over bloodshot eyes. "What's the difference?"

"Go back to bed. You'll know what happened soon enough."

"The trouble you've caused? If I don't stick up for you, nobody will."

"I'll do it myself."

"Nobody believes a word you say, they're gonna start now?" He coughed and spit into the grass. He looked so frail and wobbly, Mala wondered if the trial might be the thing that finally killed him.

"I'm sorry I brought this on you," she said.

"My fault. I could have tried to change you but I didn't." He sat next to her, his bony hip digging into the side of her leg. "Ask me, we been stuck in one place too long. This is what happens when you stop moving. Things freeze up. The balance ain't right anymore. We done this before, thirteen years shackled in one place and for what?"

"We've only been here since October."

He nodded. "Like I said. Turn over any one of those wagons and you'll find worms been there all winter and spring. Weeds growing up to the trailer windows. Light coming at a different slant now but nothing else has moved. It's not natural."

Beni was right; it was the longest they had lingered since losing their storefront seven years ago. Through the thirties they'd been the scourge of Pecos County, the mercurial nuisance no sheriff or vigilante could round up and be rid of. They had tried for stability, the women telling fortunes, first in tents stuffed with bright rugs and wildflowers and later in a tiny rented room, the younger men day-laboring for pennies on nearby farms and ranches, laying irrigation pipes, swinging tools whose handles had been gnawed by locusts. So much toil, but in the end it was useless. The storefront was plundered and times changed, one modern tractor throwing ten men out of work. Mala had been twelve when they unchocked the trailer tires and moved on, the only time she could remember Beni praising God.

Now it wasn't hunger for money or respectability keeping them grounded, but something no one could name. Weariness, maybe. The trouble of getting thirty-four people to agree. This field, one of two dozen Mala had learned the smell and contours of and turned her back on, had become so repetitive she could have walked it blindfolded. Maybe that was all home was, just a place where you never sat up in bed on a moonless night and whispered, "Where am I?" Little by little she'd become accustomed to the arthritic tree out her window and the stove and boiler parts that made a corroded pathway around camp, all the broken valves and heat vent covers and thumb pads the men had collected on odd jobs and kept, because owning something useless was better than owning nothing. Here was the thistle patch, there the dented gas can Beni used as a water jug. She could close her eyes and see it all laid out, as familiar as a worn floor. The wind had scrubbed the field flat, and the river was filled with cattle carcasses and barbed wire, but the land didn't appear to belong to anybody, and if it did, the owner didn't care. Right there was reason to stay. It wasn't that life was turning out so well here, but that moving on took money and prospects, and both had run out. Thanks to Mala, some people would say.

If the trial went the way most did, it wouldn't last long. An hour or two at most, and then the council—the male heads of seven families, including the father of a boy Mala had kicked when she was nine—would deliberate and hand down the verdict. Mala had no doubt she'd be found guilty, it was just a matter of what happened after. Though the adulterer had been declared unclean and ordered to give his car to the husband of his mistress, he'd offended only one person, and okay, provided him with a bastard son. But in Mala's case, there wasn't anybody she hadn't crossed or scared the hell out of. Her clear green eyes terrified the children, who blamed her for everything from bad dreams to scorpions in their shoes. Her old friends—sitting across the circle, a marriage-crazy bunch of girls in long, grubby housedresses, their braids pinned loosely behind their heads—had stopped talking to her around the time she started wearing a pair of men's pants bound at the waist with a scrap of rope. Even her aunt Drina, a three-time widow who dyed her hair with kitchen bleach and sold sedatives she made from powdered hemlock, had not forgiven her for watching helplessly as her mother bubbled down into Canyon Lake, where she hung suspended with her skirt around her shoulders until she was hauled up by fishermen a week later.

Drina stood in Mala's line of sight shaking her head, still beside herself though it had been fourteen years.

The trial started late, so by the time the oaths were taken and people began to speak, there was a sense that everyone had been pent up too long. It was as if they'd all just had tape ripped off their mouths. "Here we go," Beni muttered. "Business in the gutter, that's what this is about."

One witness after another came forward to detail Mala's shortcomings. Long story short, they said, the girl had always been trouble. She talked back to her father, refused to marry, and frightened off the townspeople with relentless visions of disasters, when all they came to her for was a palm reading and a little hope. She had ruined herself by bobbing her hair, and no one could say if the impulse would be contagious. She sat with her knees apart, came up behind you when you least expected her, and fed birds of prey from her own plate. Every spell she cast had a twist to it, a trapdoor that fell open under your feet. Ask for love, and you, a handsome young man, might find yourself pining for an old crone for whom you would eventually hang yourself. Come to Mala for money and it would appear in the form of a rich husband whose wheezing laugh would make you pray for the peace of poverty. There was no sense in it. Whatever she touched turned puzzling, like something viewed through the haze of a high fever. Sure, her spells brought you whatever you wanted—shortly before they turned and bit you on the ass.

But worst of all, Mala had single-handedly destroyed her clan's livelihood and optimism. It was fine if she wanted to empty her own pockets in the name of honesty, but what about the rest of them? Did she think the local people drove to the outskirts of town and paid good money to hear the truth? It didn't matter if her predictions were accurate (and this was a matter of dispute—was she predicting these dismal events or causing them?), they were bad for business. Not that she cared about business or anything practical, so consumed was she with reading books about things that had never happened, written by people she would never know. That was Beni's fault from years back, for letting an outsider teach his daughter to read while he mucked stalls for a lousy wage. It was tragic that Zina had drowned when her daughter was just four, but everyone had hardships. It was no excuse.

"What does my father have to do with this?" Mala asked, rising to her feet. Twenty-odd sunlit heads swiveled in her direction. Her cousins, Joseph and Rosalia, stared like strangers who happened to share the same steep jaw slope and copper skin. All six of the camp's children watched her, open-mouthed, their feet bare and their dark hair stiff with dirt. Only Chester the Spaniard—who had English and Romanian blood but spoke a few wretched words of Spanish, which he misused at every chance—refused to look up. He kept his eyes on the stick he was whittling, showing no sympathy for the girl who had spurned him in such a loud and public way.

Beni yanked at Mala's hand and forced her down next to him. "Let me talk. You'll just cause more damage."

"I don't care."

"For once in your life pay attention to what I tell you," he said, straightening his cap. "Trust me. All right?" He stood up on quivery legs and stumbled to the center of the circle, his cracked boots kicking up puffs of dust.

He raised a hand and swore to tell the truth on the memory of the father he had barely known, but a moment later lost his train of thought and started complaining about his bad back. Eventually he remembered his purpose and began to cry loudly, an act that fooled no one. His daughter was an orphan, he said, too young and impressionable to be held responsible for her impulses. This was such an obvious falsehood that the crowd began to laugh and throw clods of dirt at him, but Beni plowed on even as pebbles and twigs collected at his feet. Mala's foresight had left them destitute, he agreed, but had also prevented the camp from being swept away when the river flooded its banks. Didn't anyone remember that? Her spells might be a bit unfocused, but at least they worked, which was more than he could say for the slop most people practiced these days. Look in the mirror, he said, every man here was a storyteller. They were all con artists who created tales from thin air, and sometimes they created them from less than that. Why single out his daughter, who with her books was only carrying on tradition, albeit in a perversely modern way? Besides, he had nothing else to live for. Send Mala away and in a week he'd be dead, a stain on the conscience of everyone present.

Chin high, trembling from exhilaration and alcohol, he returned to the rock and sat down. "We've almost got them," he said between hard breaths. "You ready?"

She didn't answer. The entire circle waited, watching her in silence.

Beni nudged her with an elbow. "Aren't you going to speak?"

"Why?" she said. "There's nothing more I could say."

It took just twenty minutes for the council to reach a decision. Mala would be banished for one year—a light sentence, considering the harm she'd inflicted on the community. No one would be allowed to communicate with her, the books would be buried, and if Beni wanted to die in protest, so be it. He could be entombed in the same hole.

Beni was sober when he walked Mala down the dirt road to a flat strip of pavement that ran to the horizon in both directions. He handed her a woven cloth bag containing some coins he'd stashed away, enough food to last three days, and the books she had been rereading since she was twelve. "I got to them before anybody else could," he said. "I guess I'll be going in that hole by myself."

"Don't talk that way."

"No point in denying it. One year is a hundred at my age."

"What'll you do when I'm gone?" she asked, so worried for him there was no room to worry for herself.

"I'll wait." He fixed her with damp eyes, one speckled brown, the other blue. "Damn me. I wouldn't have let Ruth teach you if I'd known how it was going to turn out."

Hearing that name gave Mala the sick, hollow feeling of missing something she didn't want to admit was gone. "It turned out okay."

"This is okay?"

"I had no mother. It was better than leaving me with Drina every day."

"Yeah, well. Who would think a housekeeper on a ranch would know so much. Should have made you work alongside me, little as you was. You'd be ignorant but at least you'd talk like the rest of us." He looked up and down the road. "Not many people traveling today. Might be hard to get a ride."

"It always is."

"I'm not one to give advice, but here it is. Your reputation precedes you, so don't go tracking down another clan. If I was you, I'd hitch to Midland, find a job, wait it out. Tell folks you're Mexican or

Indian. With your looks it won't be easy, but you'll have to try. Things at camp'll settle down. When life's still lousy in a year, they'll know they were wrong about you."

"But you'll all be gone by then."

"Who knows, growing roots like we been doing," he said, the wind buffeting his shirt. "I envy you, going on the road. I should come along."

"On foot? You wouldn't make it two miles."

"No, I suppose I wouldn't. I'll just wait with you awhile, then."

He sat down on the gravel shoulder and hooked his skinny arms around his knees. Mala was beginning to wonder if he'd gone to sleep that way when he got up and started pacing slowly from one side of the tar to the other, his eyes aimed at the ground like he'd lost something. When she couldn't stand the sound of his boot heels anymore, she reached out and caught his wrist. "What are you doing?"

"I'm thinking."

"About what?"

"Nothing."

"How does a person think about nothing?"

"I've been doing it half my life. Trying, anyway."

For several minutes he looked straight into the ebbing sun. "I got something to tell you," he said at last.

"Take your time. I could be here for days."

"I mean it. Listen to me, okay?" he said, turning and grabbing her upper arms. "The rumors you heard all these years ain't lies like I said. Your mother was with another man from town. I only married her so nobody would know. Because I didn't want to see a pregnant woman do what you're doing now, walking off into the world by herself."

Mala squinted at his gaunt, wrinkled face. She hadn't heard him right.

"You understand what I'm saying?" he said louder. "Zina was no good. You ain't my daughter, you never have been. For a long time I been meaning to . . ." His voice broke and petered out.

What must have been the only truck in Texas rumbled by, but it was too late to try to wave it down. For the first time since she was a child, Mala started to cry. "Why are you saying this now?"

He dropped his hands to his sides. His arms stretched almost to his knees. "I don't know."

"There has to be a reason."

"To make going away easier on you, I guess."

He kissed her, slipping a stale piece of bread into the pocket of her pants to ward off *bibaxt*, bad luck. "You don't need any more of that," he said, and gently pried his sleeve from her fingers.

He was a scarecrow walking back toward camp, a bowed, worn-out figure in a plaid shirt with thin wisps of hair whirling around the top of his head. Mala thought she would never lose sight of him, but the sun went down all at once and he disappeared with it. Because there was nothing else to be done, she headed west, plodding along in the work boots Beni had discovered the previous winter in an abandoned shed. The light in the sky lasted for fewer than thirty steps, then she walked as well as she could from memory.

The city was out there somewhere, it was simply a matter of continuing until she found it. Keeping Mala company were flocks of silent bats and exactly seven stars. What had happened to the rest of them, she didn't know. She was hardly half an hour from camp when the bag Beni gave her became dead weight on her shoulder and had to be unloaded in a ditch. She dug a shallow hole with a rock and carefully placed the books inside, burying them after all. She couldn't see them but she knew each one by its weight and the smooth feel of its dust jacket. *The Great Gatsby. Light in August. The Adventures of Huckleberry Finn*. She hoped an animal would find them and tear them apart with its claws, using the pages to sleep in or hide under. Too late—a mile or so down the road—she wished she had kept one of the books, to read when the sun saw fit to rise again.

No matter how bad a situation seemed, it couldn't be called a tragedy until it was all played out. That's what she had told all the people whose futures she'd forecast, not because she was good at predictions, but because you only had to look at a person and what they'd done to know what was in store for them. It was simple. A man who didn't mend his fences would find his cows gone in the morning. But the tale didn't end there. Most of his livestock would be stolen or slaughtered by flash floods and hunger, but one calf would find its way to a sun-beaten house that hadn't been visited in decades. The house would belong to a woman whose blind daughter had spent her entire life in the same room, knitting blankets and looking out at nothing. When the man came to collect his only surviving cow, he would see the beautiful blind girl through the window and think of his dead animals as blessings and his hardship as fate.

It had always been a comforting notion, but tonight, with the darkness absolute and coyotes calling to each other in the fields, it seemed to Mala like something she'd made up a long time ago to help herself sleep.

Two

*M*id-morning, sunny and warm. In this part of the world there seemed to be no other kind. Linda Fredrickson had just peeled the plastic off her husband's dry cleaning when her friend Audrey called from down the street and, with the inappropriate excitement common to those delivering bad news that doesn't really affect them, said, "They found a dead body on the other side of the hill behind the rec center. A woman, strangled. Turn on your TV."

"What?" Immediately Linda's mouth went dry, force of a strange reflexive habit. Whenever anything went wrong, anywhere, she always had the sensation that she was in some distant way responsible for it.

"She'd been there for days," Audrey said. "They have no idea who did it."

Linda reached across the counter, groped for the remote. The television hummed on above the kitchen table. "Oh, my God. How did you find out?"

"Christine called. She was up early and saw flashing lights." Audrey paused for a second to gasp. "They're showing her picture now. Are you seeing this? She was only twenty-two."

"Who was she?" Linda asked, flipping through channels.

"She worked for a family over in San Andreas Meadows, taking care of their twins. Can you believe they didn't even know she was missing? The whole time, they thought she was visiting her mother."

"Was she from around here?"

"Nevada somewhere. This country's gone crazy. I'll never let Jonathan out of the house again."

"He has to go to school," Linda said.

"No, he doesn't."

When Linda finally clicked onto a local news station, a male voice reverberated through the room and her television brimmed with a picture of the dead girl, Jennifer Guthrie. Her face left the impression of having only three parts: round cheeks, a broad smile, straight dark eyebrows, a composite of features so unremarkable she could have been anyone; she could have been Linda. Linda had an overwhelming desire to go back in time—just to last week, and only for a few minutes—so she could warn the girl and save her life, but even as she pictured rushing up to Jennifer in a mall or restaurant and pulling her out a side door to a different fate, it was absurdly painful to recognize that she couldn't.

"This has always been my worst nightmare, and now it's getting closer," Audrey said. "Literally my own backyard."

"Think about it. What are the chances a murder would happen here again?"

She could almost hear Audrey's mind bouncing from worry to

worry, trying to find something that couldn't be refuted. In the six months Linda had known her, there wasn't an anxiety Audrey hadn't entertained at least once. "For all we know, somebody in the development did it," Audrey said, "and if that's the case, you know who the real victim will be—our property values. They'll probably make a spectacle of it and question everyone in the neighborhood. The poor Shermans. Their house will *never* sell now."

"Question everyone?" Linda shut her eyes, sick with her failure to have seen what was coming. A sweeping investigation. The police probing every resident of Golden Hills Estates, including her, though for years she had been so careful, never jaywalking or overdrawing an account, avoiding any tiny breach that might call attention. Everything she'd done for the last eighteen years had been meticulously planned, every foreseeable effect mulled over before she ate out or applied for a job. She'd hardly allowed herself to have memories, for fear that she would somehow telegraph her crime to a person standing nearby. Yet in the back of her mind she'd known she could be defeated by the mere proximity to trouble. Once somebody took a cursory look into her background, it wouldn't take much to find the thread that led back almost twenty years. She could imagine how it all might unravel, so many secrets compressed into a few ruinous days.

"They can't investigate all of us, right? How many people live in this development, two hundred?" Linda thought of her suitcases upstairs, stored away only last November. Practically still warm.

"Oh, I don't know. The state's so broke, maybe they won't question anybody. We'll be lucky if they don't file this with the cold cases and forget about it."

"Let's hope not," Linda said, but the idea of sloppy investigators and understaffed police departments gave her a twinge of relief.

And as the days passed and the killing remained unsolved, and their book group chose the April novel, and Audrey's son returned to seventh grade, and no one bothered with even a perfunctory visit to Linda's house to ask if she'd seen anything suspicious, she began to think that the murder of Jennifer Guthrie would only graze the surface of her life, leaving no trace. The hill where the body had been found wasn't technically on development land anyway—ironically, it belonged to a competitor of Linda's husband's company, an investment firm specializing in "the sensitive utilization of green space for the modern commercial enterprise," a discovery that gave the occupants of Golden Hills Estates both a soothing feeling of detachment and the dread of a mall going up in their backyards. Soon, Jennifer became the second headline on the news, then the third, and then she was hardly mentioned. It had been just two weeks since her death, but it seemed to Linda that she was the only one who remembered her. While everyone else returned to their barbecues and the home improvement projects that shouldn't have been necessary in houses so young but were, she scanned her computer every morning for updates, feeling aggrieved on Jennifer's behalf when she found nothing. There was something about her she couldn't let go, this lost young woman who for no particular reason reminded her of herself at that age, who in her last moments had probably wondered what she'd done wrong, why she'd been given so few chances.

Then the family strife began, and Linda had to push the dead aside to make room for the living. And although Jennifer Guthrie was buried in a vast urban graveyard three hundred miles away, she lingered over the streets of Golden Hills Estates, returning that spring and summer to hover around the lives of Linda and her neighbors like a question, something started but left undone.

Linda had always known there was a remote but appalling possibility that her husband's ex-wife, Margaret, would die or become clinically depressed or go *Eat, Pray, Love* on everyone and leave her offspring in the lap of their father so she could flit away to another continent and find herself, but it had never occurred to her that one of Peter's children might beg to move in with him because of a family quarrel, or that Peter, who was still straining to adapt to a world in which he was a person of limited means and consequence, would agree to it. Seem positively excited about it, in fact.

Eight months earlier, his company had closed the New York branch where he was managing principal, slapping him with the meaningless title of VP of Accounts and exiling him to the home office near Rancho Alegre ("Incorporated: 2003"), an inland nowhere between L.A. and San Diego. If Linda hadn't been so busy resisting her new life and finding quiet ways to express her aversion to it, she might have seen what was coming. The signs had been there for weeks: teary phone calls from her husband's ten-year-old daughter Paige, texted blow-by-blows of stepsibling battles, even a long-distance fatherly chat between Peter and Paige's stepfather, who had two young sons and a daughter and therefore plenty of skin in the game. "I think the blended family thing was fun for a while, but the novelty's worn off," Linda heard Peter say through the closed door of the den. "She's not one of two anymore, she's one of five, and her brother always takes the side of the other kids."

At first the cross-country squabbles and negotiations had been a welcome distraction from unpacking and taking in surroundings that were unfamiliar but not in the exciting way of new beginnings. The house was a six-year-old suburban monstrosity with garishly grand rooms, each one accented with an architectural detail from a different epoch. To enter the kitchen, it was necessary to walk under a Tuscan brick arch. Ionic columns propped up the living room ceiling, while the exterior had been violated with a Victorian turret and the kind of dark wood siding normally nailed to mountain chalets in Switzerland. Linda found herself looking forward to Paige's distraught calls—"Hi, it's an emergency, is my dad there?"—because her stepdaughter would be calling from Connecticut or her grandmother's apartment on the Upper West Side, and this gave Linda a fleeting feeling of connection to the places where she had recently been happy. It was as if her old life were calling to remind her that it soldiered on in her absence, and to stay strong.

On the advice of their realtor, they had priced their Manhattan apartment to sell, and it was gone in a week. The weekend home near Darien hung on for two months but eventually succumbed to the full-price offer of a more fortunate couple. Linda wanted to rent when they got to California—it was only a matter of time before Peter found a new position in New York, so better to keep one foot out the door—but Peter had never rented in his life and would not start now. The house in Golden Hills Estates was the top-of-the-line model on the best street in the development, and it was discounted thirty percent. It had every possible convenience except proximity to a grocery store or major city, and it was close enough to Peter's office that he could see his bedroom window if he stood on tiptoe behind his desk and peered across the freeway through binoculars. "No commute," he told Linda. "I could even come home for lunch." This gave him the cozy, old-fashioned feeling of working in the same neighborhood he lived in, though he had actually lived a quarter mile closer to his office back in New York. Linda looked it up on the Internet, carefully calculating the distance and adding up every block lest California should come out ahead by a few feet.

In the end, New York won easily, but after all that she didn't have the heart to mention it.

For a while it had seemed as if Paige and her older brother would be too absorbed by their boisterous home life to be bothered by Peter's absence. They had taken the news of his transfer the way they usually took an adult announcement: with looks of vague disappointment that it wasn't more interesting. They matter-of-factly reclaimed the possessions they kept at their father's apartment and stood with brave smiles beside their mother in the airport—no tantrums, no tears, just muted, grown-up farewells and immediate immersion in their cell phones as soon as Peter broke from their embraces and joined the line at security.

"It's a front," he told Linda, slipping off his shoes. "They don't want me to know they're upset."

This turned out to be true, at least for Paige. Her brother, Brooks, was thirteen and enjoyed the power he'd recently gained from the company of a stepsister, also thirteen, who played wicked queen to his heartless king, giving them full and capricious control of all decisions while the adults were preoccupied or out of the house. Yes, his father was three thousand miles away, but there was always Skype, and spring break and Christmas, and he would have to spend a lot of time on the lacrosse field at his day school if he wanted to make junior varsity. He wouldn't have been able to see much of his father even if Peter had stayed in New York. Paige, however, followed up her stoic performance before the move with increasingly shrill cries of despair.

"Are things worse at home?" Peter asked her one night in May. "Or are you just sad that I'm far away?"

Paige insisted it had nothing to do with him being gone, although of course she missed him constantly. The real problem was everybody she lived with, including her mother, who talked on the phone to her friends all the time, and the stupid names of Neil's kids—Fiona, Walker, and Kipton—and Fiona's cruel streak, and the constant noise and the Ping-Pong on the deck under Paige's window when she wanted to study, and the competition for a place to sit, for the Xbox, and for snacks, which vanished as soon as they went into the refrigerator. The problem was that her mother wanted another baby now that she was married to Neil, but she was too old for it and might adopt from Ethiopia. Paige had no say in the matter, or in anything else. She was certain that her emails had been opened while she was at chorus. She desperately wanted a cat, but Walker was allergic.

Linda peeled carrots in the kitchen, listening to her stepdaughter's grievances blare from the speaker phone in Peter's home office across the hall. At times like these she wondered whether her impression of Paige had ever been accurate, or if it was just something she'd whipped up from bits of paranoia and the remnants of an unhappy childhood. Paige could sound so wonderfully ordinary. Simple, even. Right now, from here, there was no reason to believe that she'd ever been particularly clever or insightful, or had singled out Linda to goad with terrible little observations imperceptible to everyone else. "You don't like being in big groups of people, do you?" Paige had asked when they were suddenly left alone in Margaret's kitchen the previous Fourth of July.

Linda had to swallow before answering. "What do you mean?"

"It's okay. Neither do I, sometimes." This should have made her feel better, but hadn't.

While spending the night in the city one weekend, Paige had walked in on her in the master bathroom. "Looking for a Band-Aid," she said distractedly, rooting through the medicine cabinet while Linda struggled to zip her jeans. Later Paige had come up as she was accepting a delivery and said in earshot of the doorman, "Sorry about earlier. You should do what my mom tells me and *always lock the door.*"

Consulting Paige about Peter's birthday gift—it would be from Linda and the children, and with luck might become a yearly tradition—had resulted not in a rush of shared excitement with her stepdaughter or a whirlwind shopping trip followed by lunch and ice cream, but in Paige saying, "I'm telling you, he hates getting clothes for his birthday. It won't be any different just because they come from you."

Paige was too young to know all the possible interpretations of her remarks—that's what Peter would have said had Linda brought it up. But he took for granted Linda's ability to adapt to troubled stepchildren and phone calls at all hours because she was afraid to highlight what he must already suspect: his second wife had no maternal feeling at all. It wasn't a dislike, it was a nothing, a part of her brain, or heart, that had failed to form. When they still lived in New York, he had seen her interact clumsily with Brooks and Paige on holidays, and steal glances at her watch while she mouthed "Happy Birthday" and "Silent Night," her smile a product of practice and too much red wine. He wasn't an idiot. Two months before their wedding he had asked if there was a reason she didn't want children of her own. "I'm just so happy with you," she'd answered. "I really don't need anyone else." This seemed to satisfy him, and he hadn't brought up the subject again.

Linda was running the food processor when Peter came into the kitchen, so she didn't hear him until the blades whirled to a stop. "I want your opinion on this," he said, "and please be honest because it affects you."

"What is it?" she asked over her shoulder. She busied herself with scraping out the pureed carrot, turning on the faucet full force, and dropping utensils into the sink with such a racket that only disembodied fragments of Peter's words survived: "Summer. After exams. Defuse things. Best for everybody."

Finally, when the last spoon had hit the stainless steel, Linda turned to face him. With his slender, athletic frame and thick brown hair, her husband normally looked younger than fifty-one—people often took them for the same age, mid-forties—but tonight there was a weariness in his eyes that made him appear almost grandfatherly.

"Margaret's okay with this? I mean, her daughter will be thousands of miles away."

"It'll be temporary," he said. "She wouldn't have agreed to it otherwise. You know, it's not like she's sending her daughter to live with strangers."

"Of course it isn't."

Peter reached out and took her still damp hands. "I'm not signing you up for full-time parenthood. She'll be back home in three months, maybe less."

Linda scrambled to think of a way to dissuade him. "But what about that girl they found a few weeks ago?" she said. "Jennifer Guthrie." It felt distasteful to bring her up, but the alternative was to give in with barely a whimper.

"What do you mean? What about her?"

"They don't even have a suspect. And with Paige coming—I don't know. That doesn't make you nervous?"

"I thought they were looking at the boyfriend."

"Audrey said they let him go."

"Well . . ." Peter shrugged. "It's a horrible thing but it happens everywhere. It happens in Connecticut all the time."

"I would think you'd have more of a reaction, considering that your daughter would be living just down the road. You can see where they found her if you go up Gardenia Boulevard. There's still yellow tape on the trees."

Peter brought his hands to Linda's shoulders and let them rest there. His soothing palms could tranquilize her into almost anything: eloping after four months of dating, moving out West, mothering his daughter while his ex-wife coddled stepchildren with stupid names. "Paige is a pretty sophisticated girl. She's spent half her life in the city." He smiled, a gentle, apologetic smirk that indicated he was about to back Linda into a corner. "There's a crime every two seconds in New York. I don't remember you saying she shouldn't visit."

Linda turned away and flipped on the faucet. "Well, she has no friends here and there's a good chance she'll be bored out of her mind. What will I do with her all summer?" There had to be a way to avoid spending weeks alone with the girl while Peter was at work. Linda couldn't imagine returning to professional catering, but there were other options besides a job. She could develop a mysterious fatigue that confined her to bed. She could volunteer with the homeless. She had friends in New York who had substituted entire careers with occasional phone banking for political candidates and children's hospitals. An I Voted sticker could buy a woman a year of lunching with friends.

"Do with her?" Peter laughed. "I don't know, what do people do in Southern California? Go shopping. See a movie. Walk on the beach." Peter didn't do any of these things, so he couldn't possibly know what he was recommending. To shop in this part of the country was to walk for miles through refrigerated chain stores crawling with underdressed teenage girls with orange skin and lousy grammar. The beach, an hour of traffic jams away, was overrun by the same teenage girls from the mall, only here they screamed at the top of their lungs and wore even less.

"I'll teach her to cook," she said without looking at her husband. "You wanted your boss to come for dinner, right? I could use the help." She expected Peter to resist—Paige needed to be indulged, not forced into service chopping vegetables—but he seemed to realize that agreement on this small point would deflate her resistance and end the discussion.

"Perfect," he said. "Anything to make her feel important."

The plans were set in concrete by the following afternoon. As soon as Paige's exams were finished, she would be free to escape her overpopulated white colonial in Westport and the incessant crack of Ping-Pong paddles. She would have the summer to relax and enjoy her solitude, and in August everyone would reevaluate the situation.

August, which Linda had discovered meant nothing in California. It was just March with longer days.

Nine days before Paige's arrival, Linda went to buy a lamp for the room that would be her stepdaughter's for the summer. She decided to try one of the garage sales in the development before going to the mall, not because it was the practical thing to do, or as a gesture of support for less fortunate neighbors, or because Peter's income had dropped by half, leaving them less than a hundred thousand in savings. Linda could hardly admit it to herself—she gave the thought only an instant's recognition before brushing it away—but buying a used lamp for Paige would be a small way of expressing her irritation with how things were turning out. Paige wouldn't know that the lamp had sat for years in a spidery basement or on the desk of an unpopular teenage boy, but Linda could lie in bed at night while Paige slept obliviously down the hall and feel a little bit in charge.

The closest garage sale of the day was on T Street, seven blocks away. All of the streets in Golden Hills Estates had been organized by letters of the alphabet, a blandly efficient way of doing things, and one that made it impossible not to know where you were in the development or how far you were from your own house. Even if you wanted to get lost, you couldn't. Linda and Peter lived on M Street, a treeless asphalt curve overlooking a range of mountains whose starkly beautiful slopes were always catching fire. The beginning of the alphabet, which was closer to the security gate and therefore the busy road that led to the freeway, was reserved for starter homes, while the alphabet after Q featured houses nearly as large as the Fredricksons's but without stained glass and gazebos. It was in this part of the development, where upper-middle-class families had spent years stockpiling junk, that most of the garage sales took place under a permanent haze of U-Haul exhaust. In eight months of Saturdays, Linda had bought only a tiny porcelain rabbit, which no one else seemed to notice was smiling. A few weeks earlier she'd come across a framed watercolor, some housewife's attempt to give her days meaning with pastel paint and a freeway median filled with wildflowers. It started the day propped against a fireplace screen and ended on the curb under a stack of *National Geographic*s. Driving by at twilight on her way back from the grocery store,

Linda nearly stopped to rescue it until the person behind her leaned on his horn. Her neighbor from across the street, Tim, who had thrown her a friendly wave once he realized who she was.

The tattered box in the front yard at 18 T Street might have gone the way of the watercolor had Linda not wrenched her ankle on what had been smooth green grass before Susanna Marsh's husband left her and stopped paying the landscapers. As she stood speculating about the robustness of Susanna's homeowner's insurance policy, Linda noticed the box—upper flaps gone, corners collapsed and bulging—sitting on a folding chair next to the garbage cans. It wasn't the bedside lamp she had come for, but any item that couldn't be identified from five feet away was worth a look.

She walked up and peered inside. On top were several layers of red fabric so old the fibers crackled and broke in her hand. Below these was a tin tray filled with tarnished costume jewelry, a ribbon-wrapped stack of old letters, and under that, some kind of notebook. She pulled it out and turned it faceup. It was nothing, a warped, ugly, water-stained scrap, cracked along the spine and smelling like a musty library. The thin cardboard cover was curled at the edges and resisted the pressure of her fingers. She wasn't going to bother with it, but then the book fell open to pages covered with a strange, slanted script.

How to Get Blood from a Stone. Prayer for Youth Preserved. If You Must Achieve the Impossible.

She carefully flipped through the notebook, expecting it to tear apart and flutter away in yellowed pieces. Page after page was filled with bizarre little incantations, but not the sort Linda had ever heard of. Under their titles were lists of strange ingredients—the fetlock of a mare, a word torn from a dictionary—and precise instructions for what to do with them. Filling every corner and margin were the faded remains of what seemed to be random thoughts and observations. *Haven't seen the moon in a week. To lower fever, shake a young tree.* There were faint pencil sketches of plants and animals, and on one page a roughly drawn map, its lines wavy from water damage. Pressed in the back of the book was a sprig of something that had long since decomposed. Before Linda could touch it, it blew away, leaving behind a hooked gray smudge.

She beckoned to Susanna, whom she'd first met at an emergency meeting of the homeowners association after illegal immigrants were discovered squatting in two foreclosures on B Street. Susanna was downsizing to a rented condo, and the contents of her once idyllic life were scattered around as if the house had coughed them up. Even her estranged husband's underwear was for sale, three for a dollar. Susanna's son Ethan stood near the driveway, miserably staffing a table covered with his own toys.

"Where did this box come from?" Linda asked.

"It must have belonged to somebody who lived in my mother's place in Bakersfield," Susanna said. "We found it behind some boards in the crawl space when we sold the house a few years ago. You want it?"

"I don't think so."

"You can have it for nothing. I was going to throw it out."

"All right. Only the notebook, though."

"I didn't know there was a notebook," Susanna said, frowning, suddenly interested.

"Just some old recipes, I think," Linda said quickly.

"It's all yours."

Linda went to her car and tossed the notebook onto the passenger's seat. Now that she had it, she wasn't sure what to do with it. Obviously its contents hadn't worked very well, because it had ended up in a place where the closest anyone got to magic was Tarot Night, a monthly gathering attended by half the women in the development and a couple of slutty card readers. At the urging of Audrey, whose house was the runt of the block and perched on a viewless corner, Linda had attended her first Tarot Night a few months before. The whole point was to be entertained. Everyone eavesdropped on each other's readings, and if you didn't drink and laugh to excess, you weren't invited back. There wasn't a lot of gray area at these things. If you had a health problem, you would be cured. If your husband had left you for another woman, he would regret it via herpes or a feminist judge. If your finances were a disaster, you should call the card reader's sister, who made five grand a week selling a diet drink from home and could show you how to do it, too.

Linda had known the whole thing was ridiculous but nonetheless felt a glimmer of excitement when her turn came. For a few minutes she had actually wondered if it was possible to crack the code of her own life. Even when her future came spilling from the mouth of a rough-voiced blonde wearing decals on her fingernails, part of her surrendered to what the woman said ("You're trying to win a battle that isn't worth your time and energy") because she had nothing else to go on. She left the party feeling a little thrill of hopefulness and intrigue, but there was too much reality outside—cars filling the driveway, the smell of dryer sheets in the air—to keep up the illusion. Laughing about it later with Peter, describing the card reader running outside to smoke between sessions, she'd felt like her skeptical self again. "The only battle I'll have is with Audrey," she said, "when she tries to drag me to the next one."

To atone for her impulse to retaliate against Paige with a used light fixture, Linda skipped the other garage sales and drove to Rancho Alegre's four-block "business district," where she spent a thousand dollars on an Italian table lamp. She looked back on her thoughts of a few hours ago with embarrassment and shame. No matter what her stepdaughter did after she arrived on Tuesday, she would give the behavior no more notice than it deserved. If Paige put her on the spot, she would change the subject without answering. If Paige made a smart remark, she would muzzle her with food, DVDs, and shopping. Three months of getting everything she wanted in large and unhealthy quantities wouldn't kill her, and might very well cure her.

The new lamp was as perfect as one could be in the featureless white rectangle of the guest room, though it made the area rug look cheap. Linda buried the receipt at the bottom of her bedside table drawer, leaving only the book she'd discovered at Susanna's to find a place for. She was about to put it in the den on the shelf reserved for half-read novels and Peter's childhood encyclopedias when she noticed the slight impression of words pressed into the cover. She stepped to the window and raised the blinds in one sharp tug. As she turned the book toward the early afternoon light, the words appeared like a figure emerging out of fog. The old pencil marks were gone but their imprint remained, written in the same antique hand as the lines inside.

Mala Rinehart, 1948.

These were the only clues, then, a name as strange as the book, and a year that hardly made it an ancient artifact. It was probably worthless. Still, it managed to survive more than half a century while the relics of her own youth—school photographs, drawings, third-grade art projects—had vanished into the tar pits of childhood before she turned twenty. She created space on the shelf between two paperbacks, but remained standing there with the book in her hand. There was something about its faint personal touches that made putting it away impossible. It had been buried in a box for years, and, unsentimental as she was, she couldn't bring herself to sequester it again. She pictured the long wait the book had endured in a dark crawl space, decades of muffled living going on one floor up. It wasn't rational, but she felt that by jamming it between two immense old classics, she would be depriving the book and its mysterious author of air.

She took it to the breakfast nook—a flimsily built solarium, really, with a view of the street and the neighbor's recycling bins. Seeing the book in the kitchen's stainless steel glare made it look not less peculiar, but more so. It was no bigger than the scratch pad she used for grocery lists, the stiff cover bound with fraying gray linen. The paper inside was rough, not the mechanically smooth reams she was used to, but something she imagined being pressed and cut by hand. While the first page contained only a single nonsensical phrase—*Latcho drom*—the rest were crowded with curvy, ornate handwriting, every F like a music note, the Y's drawn out with elaborately long tails. It was obvious that the book had been written in no particular order. Incantations were haphazardly thrown together, sometimes sideways, occasionally misspelled, their words nearly obscured by drawings of birds and remarks without punctuation. There were several strange proverbs—*you cannot walk straight when the road bends; a dog that wanders will find a bone*—followed by an entry that claimed an entire page to itself.

Everything as It Should Be.

The meaning of it had hardly registered when Linda felt a tiny but insistent glint of curiosity. Of course there was nothing to it, but of the titles she'd seen so far, this one seemed most relevant to her life. It took only an instant to envision how it should be—her happiness restored, Peter's position returned to him, her stepchildren a trivial concern and soon grown-up and moved away. With her hand resting lightly on the stained page, she tried to imagine the shifting of events that would make such an outcome possible, the rapid rewinding of time, the strokes of luck, the premonitions that would let her make this decision instead of that. When she thought of all that had gone into the present moment, years of striving helped or thwarted by chance, it felt too large and complicated to understand, let alone change. There was what you could do, and then there was everything else. In almost all cases, everything else prevailed.

Linda looked up as Peter's car pulled into the driveway and vanished into the garage. She had plenty of time to get up, slide the book onto the shelf, and position herself in front of the computer before he walked in with grassy shoes and a sunburned forehead. She intended to tell him about the book over dinner, but by then she'd forgotten about it. For the second time in a year her life was about to change. There were windows to wash, New York friends to call with sanguine reports of abundant sunshine and storage space, and summer duvets to buy for the beds. To top it off, she would need at least two days to carry off the dinner for Peter's boss, a rough-around-the-edges California native who held all things East Coast and educated in contempt.

There wasn't time to worry about how things should be. This was the way things were.

Three

*O*dds were that the latest pregnancy would turn out like the others, so Christine and her husband Tim decided to assume it was already over. It was the only way to get through it. No matter what happened, they wouldn't be heartbroken and they wouldn't blame each other, they would simply have "another woman's body ready to go," as Tim crassly put it—but then one of his best traits was that he didn't beat around the bush. In the past they had made the mistake of giving each tiny, unformed life a name; now they gave them numbers, like death row prisoners or remote galaxies that were visible only with a high-powered telescope. This time they didn't smile at each other over breakfast, they sat divided by a carton of milk and read emails on their iPhones. Christine took walks without Tim there to protect her in case a truck jumped the curb. Neither of them claimed to have a good feeling about it, and they didn't tell anyone, not even Christine's parents. They just got in the car three days after the test came back positive and drove to Riverside as if the need to find a surrogate were a foregone conclusion.

It was a Tuesday afternoon in May, unseasonably hot. Following the commands of their navigation system, they drove down a street of decrepit houses and pulled into the sort of driveway that seemed destined for crime tape and chalk outlines. The garage door had been damaged by a fender, or maybe an earthquake. A dog was barking from behind a cement wall next door, and somewhere down the block a woman was shrieking hoarsely in Spanish.

"Scenic Riverside," Christine said.

Tim kept the engine running and his seat belt on. "This is where she lives? I thought you said she was from Eastern Europe."

"She is. I guess they don't have much money."

"Not the ideal place to carry a child for nine months, is it?"

"No," Christine said, "but she's cheap."

He sat for a minute, staring at the slumped little house with its torn window screens and blistered blue paint. "I don't like you being here. You still have a baby growing inside you."

"Nothing's going to happen, Tim. It's two in the afternoon."

"It doesn't make a difference in an area like this," he said, with the bitter certainty of a realtor who'd once specialized in luxury property but now specialized in whatever might sell. "They shoot at each other all day long. Look what just happened in our neighborhood with that girl getting killed. No place is safe."

"For God's sake." Christine leaned back in her seat, suddenly so exhausted she wasn't sure she could stand. "What if I start bleeding while we're in there? Should we have some kind of sign?"

"You never bleed until after the sixth week."

"Okay, but if I do."

"I don't know, text me. Or better yet, just tell her she's hired."

Christine smiled slightly and leaned her head against Tim's shoulder. "I feel like throwing up."

"Go ahead. I brought paper towels."

Five years of being injected by Tim with hormones and losing baby after baby had mutated their relationship, laid them open to each other like people who were always crossing paths at funerals. That they had little in common didn't matter. Grief had welded them together after an impulsive marriage that Christine was certain would have collapsed under happier circumstances. Their connection had been forged in doctors' waiting rooms, in bathrooms with blood-speckled towels, in rumpled beds, drugstore aisles, and the pews of ugly suburban churches. At times Christine felt that she and her husband were too close, that they'd uncovered too much about each other. She would have liked to take back some of her screams and sobs, to not have her red, twisted face fixed in Tim's memory the way his was fixed in hers, but it was too late. They knew everything about each other.

A curtain parted and a pale blond head appeared at the window. "That must be her," Tim said. "What do you want to do?"

"We can't just leave. If this doesn't work out, we'll have to get somebody in India or Mexico, and I don't know if I can stomach that."

"How's it different, though?"

"This woman lives here," she said. "We can visit her every week. She's not working for one of those third-world baby mills so she can buy food. I mean, imagine all the diseases in those countries. You think Riverside's a dump."

"You heard good things about her, right?"

"I heard good things about her from somebody on a message board. She sounded nice on the phone. That's all I know."

"How many times has she done this?"

"I told you," she said quietly. "Twice, twins the second time. What happened to you? You were fine until we got here."

"It's not what I pictured, that's all."

"Is anything?"

"No." Tim switched off the engine, making a show of his disappointment, sighing heavily as he pulled the keys from the ignition. "All right. Let's get this over with."

The surrogate, Sofija, threw open the front door with a burst of excited chatter and ushered them into a slope-floored bungalow that smelled of something cooked too long in the microwave. In one quick glance Christine had seen almost all there was of the place: brown-tiled fireplace, small yellow kitchen, dining area, and two short hallways that led to the bedrooms. The living room was decorated with drooping old furniture and several shelves covered with crystal figurines. With its paint-crusted crown moldings, wood beams, and built-in bookcases, it was the kind of house Tim might have advertised as a "Craftsman-style classic with fabulous historical details," while he and his fellow realtors called it "that shitbox on West Highland."

They accepted Sofija's offer of coffee and sat on the sofa with their backs to a barred window. Christine couldn't help but feel like they were hiring a prostitute. It wasn't much different, was it, renting someone else's internal organs for a task you couldn't quite manage on your own? Sofija didn't see it that way, apparently; it was her "privilege" to give "the gift of living" to "not very fortunate people," and of course, her husband Arso was "super supportive" (no doubt he was, he worked as a limo driver and made probably eighteen thousand a year). Both of them hailed from villages in Bosnia, and they valued children above all else, in no small part because they had each lost brothers and cousins during the war. Within ten minutes of meeting her, Tim and Christine knew that one of Sofija's cousins had been found beheaded, while another was starved and tortured. "Now he is music teacher in Belgrade," she said. "Very successful." Her husband had an uncle who was still missing more than fifteen years later.

"What a tragedy," Tim said, crossing his ankles. The space between his eyes crinkled, giving him an almost theatrical look of sympathy.

"Maybe because I see the bad part of life, I indulge my children too much," Sofija said.

This was "obvious, right?" from the way her three very American kids ran unchided through the living room with noisy plastic weapons, their homemade capes flapping behind them. Sofija reached out and grabbed the oldest, a six-year-old named Benjamin, and covered his squinting face with kisses. If her intention was to demonstrate that she was a warm, loving mother, it worked. Tim's face softened and he seemed to have completely forgotten his extensive list of questions: *Do you now or have you ever used illegal drugs, alcohol, or tobacco? Would you consider selective termination if more than two embryos become viable?*

Christine sat in the floral grip of the couch, assessing Sofija like a house at auction. She was small but sturdy, with wide hips and a shapeless midsection, not surprising given that she'd had six children, three of them for paying customers. With her short forehead, pale hair, and high cheekbones, it was easy to imagine her trudging up a hill carrying laundry or wailing over a coffin. But Christine had to admit that she was better than the other surrogate they'd interviewed, a no-nonsense former teacher who'd asked them to meet at her lawyer's office and bring a year's worth of bank statements. Sofija didn't want to discuss the issue of money; she blushed when Tim brought it up and said, "Doesn't matter now, okay? Please. Later." Tim had wanted to hire an American through the best agency they could find, but since he couldn't pay for the best of anything these days, they would have to settle for what they could get: any healthy woman who would agree to have their baby for thirty grand or less.

He wouldn't even consider adoption, which he was afraid would result in a child with attachment issues who would kill them in their sleep in ten years.

Sofija's husband Arso came home to bedlam—his wife in the kitchen sweeping up a dropped coffee cup while his children pummeled each other in the hallway. "I'm sorry to be late," he said, slipping off worn wingtips and leaving them on a mat in the entryway. Bald, with small hands and delicate features, he was the opposite of Tim, who had long limbs and a prominent chin and kept his wavy hair out of his eyes by perching a pair of polarized sunglasses on his head. Arso wore a drab working man's uniform of a wrinkled black suit and athletic socks, while Tim dressed in the style he'd adopted during the boom years: wildly patterned Italian shirts, jeans with buttoned back pockets, expensive loafers. Snapping his fingers, Arso sent his kids scattering to their rooms with three quiet words Christine couldn't understand, then shook hands with Tim and sat beside Sofija on the love seat. For a few moments they all exchanged smiles and exhaled as they settled back into cushions, but no one said anything.

"Sofija was just telling us about Bosnia," Tim finally piped up.

"Uh-oh." Arso patted his wife's round thigh. "I hope she wasn't making you to sleep."

"Not at all," Christine said. "It's been very interesting."

"Ah, well. She likes to remember, I like to forget."

No one seemed to know how to respond, and for several long seconds they were silent.

"How long you lived in the U.S.?" Tim asked in the booming voice he used only when he drank too much or met new people.

"Eleven years."

"Citizens?"

"For a long time."

"Not that it matters," Christine jumped in. "He's just wondering."

"It's okay," Arso said, shrugging. "You need to know who we are."

Tim slurped from his second cup of coffee. An air conditioner rattled on in the window across the room, ruffling Christine's hair.

"Anyway, down to business," Arso said. "When did you want to begin?"

"Begin?" Christine said.

"The baby. The reason you are here."

"Soon!" Tim said. "As soon as possible, right, Chrissie?"

"You know about the surrogacy, how it works?"

"I've done some research," Christine said. In fact, she had spent weeks combing websites, reading about the pitfalls and trying to be practical and clear-eyed about it. Even so, it had been much too easy to picture something wonderful, an immaculate conception occurring in an all-white medical setting, the egg retrieval stressful but nothing she hadn't done before, the surrogate pregnant with twins on the first try. She had imagined feeling a deep connection to humanity in the months before the birth, when the surrogate would call just to talk because she felt so *close* to her, but now that Christine was here, she realized that the teacher they'd interviewed hadn't been a fluke. Sofija's love for children, Christine's primal desire to link herself across time with the mothers of the world—all that was a sentimental sideshow. As with nearly everything else, what really mattered was the money.

Arso looked at Christine and Tim in turn. "The reason I ask is, we have other interest, okay? A family from San Diego comes last weekend to talk to us. Very nice people. Anxious to start."

"With Sofija?" Christine asked.

"Yes. Same story like yours. They think they have all time in the world and one day the woman is too late."

"We've been trying for five years," Tim said with a touch of defensiveness. "The doctors say it might have nothing to do with her age."

Christine laughed abruptly. "Wait a minute. What does that mean, another family? Is there going to be a bidding war or something?"

"No, no, nothing like that," Arso said, raising his hands. "Forgive me. I only want to tell you, to be honest about it."

Tim's mouth twitched. He didn't like being pressured. He pressured people for a living and was very good at it, or had been when he had clients. "Obviously we can't decide right now. We need to look at medical records and references and all that."

"Of course, and we will make a contract, the four of us. You have a lawyer, I'm sure."

"Oh, yeah, absolutely," Tim said, although they didn't and had hardly discussed it.

Arso took a manila envelope off the end table and held it out toward Christine. "Everything is here. All information, doctors, phone numbers. Something is missing, you tell us and we get it for you."

"Thank you." Christine held the envelope on her lap, not opening it.

Sofija, who seemed to have faded into the cushions since her husband had come home, suddenly said, "I have easy time with labor. No C-section, no epidural."

"Do you usually keep in touch with the families after the birth?" Christine asked.

"If they like, yes. Your decision. You live close by?"

"In Rancho Alegre. About forty minutes from here."

"Very nice," Arso said, and turned his eyes to Tim. "I hear you work in real estate?"

"Been in the business twelve years."

"Maybe you can give a little advice. We want to make another property investment, a duplex or a small apartment building for a good price."

Tim glanced at his wife for only an instant, but his thoughts were as plain as if he had spoken. In addition to all the career reaming he'd endured over the last few years, here was another injustice, blindsiding him in a situation he'd expected to dominate. It had always been his dream: to quit the brokerage, fix up houses and rent them out, to be a developer, an entrepreneur, a person who did things his way. But his dream was sitting across from him in stocking feet and a thrift-store suit, with a mouthful of crooked teeth and a wife who'd made a cottage industry out of her reproductive system. This was what he got for working so hard? For doing what he was supposed to do his entire life?

"What do you think, house or apartments?" Arso asked. "My wife says apartments will be too much work, but we can always hire a manager."

"How many units?"

"Eight, maybe ten."

"I usually get paid for information like this." Tim forced a chuckle. "But you might want to start small. Don't get in over your head. Buy a duplex and see how it works out."

"We have already duplex in Fullerton with good tenants, but maybe you're right. One more is not so much headache. We can do apartments later, when I don't work two jobs."

"Sounds smart." Tim began to bounce his legs up and down the way he did when he was agitated. "Well, listen," he said. "We need to talk this over and look at the packet you gave us, but I'm hoping there's a way to—you know, reserve our place here."

"Yes," Christine said, leaning forward. "Just for a few weeks."

"This other family—they haven't given you a deposit or anything, right?"

"No," Arso said.

"What if we did?" Tim said. "Ten percent or so to give us a little extra time. I can write you a check right now."

Christine looked at him. He hadn't thought this through. It was one of his impulses, a way to save face with Arso.

"Whatever you want," Arso said, looking less surprised than Christine thought he should. "It is up to you."

"Chrissie?" Tim said, but he was already reaching into his back pocket.

"You brought the checkbook?" she asked in a low voice. "Shouldn't we think about this?"

He gave her a puzzled look, as if she were diverting from a well-rehearsed script. Which she supposed she was. She couldn't let Tim down now, they had already agreed. They'd discussed the matter for months. Sofija had an empty womb, lived locally, and was willing to have their baby for next to nothing. What was left to do but miscarry and draw up the contract?

Tim wrote a check for three thousand dollars and gave it to Arso. Now that money had changed hands, they talked casually about unrelated things, gas prices and local politics. Sofija gave Christine a frank look of complicity—let their husbands negotiate, the women would focus on what had to be done, the difficult and important part ahead. But even this silent exchange felt like something that had been orchestrated from the start.

"I'm sorry," Tim said when they got in the car. "For all I know, this alleged couple from San Diego doesn't even exist. I just can't take another setback."

Christine shook off his hand and looked out her window without speaking. She couldn't help thinking that none of this would be happening if her father, a son of privilege who'd used his inheritance to fund a kind of perpetual migration when she was young, had just given her the money she'd asked for. "I've got nothing left but crumbs from Social Security," he'd said over a crackly connection from a cabin in British Columbia, the latest in a lifetime of half-baked projects and obsessions. "You don't think I'd send you money if I had it? I'd do anything for a grandchild, you know that."

Tim mumbled something and flipped down his visor.

"What?" Christine said.

"Nothing. There's been a car behind us since we left Riverside."

She turned around, but all she could see was the backseat and the roof of a black sedan. "Who is it?"

"No idea."

"Are you speeding again? You've had so many tickets lately it's like you're trying to make a point."

"Going forty in a forty, hon. I'm just saying, it's a little strange."

"That a car is going the same direction we are?"

"No, that a car with tinted windows has been on my ass for four miles."

"Maybe you cut him off."

"Or maybe it's one of Arso's goons, finding out where we live and what we're up to."

Christine leaned her head back and laughed. "Goons. Are you serious?"

Tim pulled his sunglasses out of his hair and slipped them on his face. "You didn't think there was something a little KGB about him?"

"Arso? He's not Russian."

"So? He looks like he could put a radioactive isotope in some-body's salad and not lose any sleep over it. Sofija was all right, but her husband was—I don't know. I'm supposed to believe he's buy-ing houses because he works hard and saves his money? Please."

"Then why did you give him a deposit? So you could prove we have it?"

"Because we can't afford to be picky right now. Anyway, he's not the one having the baby." Tim's voice thickened slightly. "And I honestly thought—I know it sounds ridiculous—that if I gave him the money, maybe you wouldn't miscarry this time. You know? Like it was a bribe or something."

"To who?"

"Whoever. The all-seeing jerkoff upstairs."

Christine frowned at him. "Don't say that, Tim, even as a joke. You don't know what you're inviting."

"Come on, Chrissie. You don't believe in God any more than I do. And why should we, after what we've been through? I mean, it requires suspension of disbelief on all levels to keep going back to church and begging the guy who's kicked sand in your face for years on end. If he even exists."

"People go through wars and still have faith."

"People are morons." Tim looked in the rearview mirror. A line of sweat had formed along his hairline, and his neck was covered with red blotches.

"Are you honestly worried?" she asked. "Turn off at the next exit. Get some gas."

"No, you're right. It's nobody. I'm not going to get all paranoid because of Arso—what was his last name? Ceric."

Christine put her hand on Tim's knee. It seemed to shudder under her fingers, or maybe it was just the vibration of the car.

"The only thing I want is to make you happy," he said. "Nothing else in our lives has worked out. This has to."

"Some things have worked out. I've got a career going after about ten false starts." All the business cards she'd printed up over the years—for party planning, closet and office organization—sat in the backs of drawers at home, mementos from ambitions that now seemed timid and ridiculous. After eight months in practice it was still strange to think of herself as a marriage and family therapist, to see the plaque on the door of the space she rented in a mini-mall between a dentist and a nail salon. So far, none of her clients seemed to care about her qualifications, which consisted of a dubious online degree and a brief internship at an underfunded methadone clinic.

"The one bright spot," Tim said. "I'm proud of you."

He turned onto the road that led to Golden Hills Estates, then drove through the open gate and past the security booth that had sat empty for months. "They should just tear that down," Christine said. "Stop pretending and be done with it."

"They're still sucking dues out of us. I guess they have a lot of pools to drain." They were coming up on their neighbor Linda's house, whose wrought-iron Juliet balconies Christine admired but didn't really want. Though her own five-bedroom neo-Tudor was one of the simpler models on M Street, she couldn't imagine living anywhere else. She would be happy if she never moved again, if she died in her bed and was buried under the floor. Since she and Tim owed more on the house than it was worth, she supposed that might be exactly what happened. Secretly, she had been relieved when Tim admitted how much equity they'd lost. "A hundred and seventy grand down the shitter in two years." The house had seemed to solidify around her after that like a protective husk, each of its oversized rooms conspiring with her so she would never have to leave. In spite of Tim's desire to continually move up, she would get to have a family here, watch the walls gradually buckle, let the basement gather newspapers and dust. Every time she went downstairs and saw the collection of clutter growing toward the ceiling, she wanted to raise her arms in victory.

"What the hell," Tim said, striking his hand against the steering wheel.

Startled, Christine glanced over at him. "What?"

"There's that car, parked in front of our house. They must have taken Gardenia Boulevard and beat us here." He pulled into the driveway too fast, nearly running into the curb. He put on the parking brake but didn't get out.

"What's going on?" Christine asked, worried now.

He didn't answer. A moment later two men got out and walked across the lawn. They were wearing dress shirts, ties, and badges clipped to their belts.

"Oh, Tim," Christine groaned, dropping her head back. "Was it another school zone?"

"No."

"Did you hit somebody?"

"Of course not." He stared straight ahead at the house.

"Then what is it?" she asked. "What have you done that you haven't told me about?"

"Nothing! Would you relax?"

She threw open her door, turning her head to glare at him before she got out. "You see?" she said. "This is what happens when you say terrible things about God."

Four

The problem with big extended families was that bad things seemed to happen all the time. To Audrey, it made sense. The more of you there were, the more likely it was that somebody would poison a coworker, change their gender, die in an accident that made the papers, serve jail time, marry a schizophrenic, or go missing in a Middle Eastern country. And that was just in the last ten years. The oral history of the Reaneys, who had traveled in ragged groups from northern England to settle in Atlanta, Georgia, went back to the late 1700s and included cholera and shipwrecks, stolen religious icons and suicide, and of course a lot of sleeping around. Still, the survivors had outnumbered the dead forty-to-one. All human and pathogenic attempts to kill off her bloodline had failed, resulting in two dozen living nephews as well as nine elderly aunts, each capable of driving through a stranger's living room on her way back from the drugstore. With that many relatives, disaster was just a matter of being patient. Rack up a certain number of cousins and eventually one of them would bring a rifle to Thanksgiving dinner.

It was no wonder that she'd hightailed it to California the second she turned eighteen, shed her accent, dyed her hair, and married the first man who asked her so she could change her name to Cronin and call two people she hardly knew "Mom and Dad." Audrey's own father was living comfortably off an income stream of embezzled cash, while her mother spent her days going to funerals and bail hearings and filing restraining orders, her manners and dress impeccable, her fender dented from hitting a dog. Not that some of Audrey's relatives weren't successes, but for every action in the Reaney clan, there was an equal and opposite reaction, for every college scholarship, a baby born in the bathroom at the prom. It had taken forty-two years and the discovery of a body a quarter mile from her house, but Audrey had finally figured it out. Living on the West Coast wouldn't protect her—she carried her bloodline wherever she went. She'd passed it on to her son, Jonathan (one of thirty cousins), who sat in front of her eating toast and texting a friend, oblivious to his flawed lineage.

With luck, Jonathan would end up like his father. Well, maybe not exactly like his father, who stood at the kitchen counter pureeing his daily breakfast of supplements and leafy greens. "Anybody want some?" he shouted, giving the blender one last, deafening pulse.

"How about some solid food, Mark?" Audrey asked.

"None for me. Though I will take a little applesauce." He reached for a bowl and the muscles in his arms stood out like snakes.

Audrey sat at the table, watching him with a combination of irritation and anxiety. Her once strapping, handsome husband looked small and shrunken, and the skin around his mouth was loose, as if all the air had been let out of his face. Scrawny though he was, he had an energetic bounce in his step that was so light and cheerful it was almost offensive. What did he have to be happy about? Besides the fact that he weighed less than his wife.

This had been going on for seven months and Audrey still didn't know whether to force-feed Mark or divorce him. The loss of his IT job to an Indian national on a temporary visa combined with an episode of double vision, diagnosed in the ER as a migraine, had shocked him out of his "meaningless existence" and into a quest to beat back time and work on something of real importance. "Singularity," the next big thing. The high-tech blending of man and machine. Audrey hadn't even heard of it and suddenly her husband was a full-fledged convert. Instead of job-hunting, he set up an office in the spare bedroom and parlayed his once-lucrative software skills into a blog aimed at the tiny part of the population who thought death was optional. It would have been funny if Mark hadn't been so earnest about it. "All the billionaires in Silicon Valley are investing in this," he said. "Immortality. Superior intelligence. It'll make caloric deprivation look like the eight-track tape." He was done being a corporate drone. He wanted to support his wife and son, but he literally couldn't survive in a career that crushed his spirit and exaggerated the importance of money.

Mark always knew how to make her bend. Make her imagine the tragedy of widowhood, his funeral and the desolate aftermath, and she wouldn't say another word.

"Listen, Dad," Jonathan was saying. "It's coming in, like, twenty years, and when it hits Earth it's going to take out an area the size of France."

Both Mark and Jonathan had scientific minds, which meant that the conversation often revolved around blind fish that lived in total darkness, or rare disfiguring diseases that sounded made up but weren't. If even half of what they said was true, Audrey would never set foot in Africa.

"*If* it hits Earth," Mark said, pulling out a chair.

"It will. But by then I'll have this amazing weapons system I invented that can take out meteors and vaporize people I don't like."

"Jonathan, please," Audrey said, her mouth full of Danish. "I hope you won't talk that way around Paige. Linda's worried that she'll get here and have nothing to do. I told her you'd be her friend this summer, introduce her to some of the kids in the neighborhood."

"How old is she?"

"Ten, but very mature from what I hear."

"She's a child, Mom."

"So are you."

"But not like he was when he was ten, right?" Mark said, winking at his son. Mark was a better parent than Audrey, if only because he knew how to manage the complex mind of an intelligent twelve-year-old. "Just be glad the kid's not autistic," he'd said once when Jonathan was being especially difficult. "With a mathematical brain like his? We dodged a bullet." That seemed to be where they were these days. Their blessings were in the things that hadn't happened, not in the things that had.

As she drove Jonathan to school, Audrey kept an eye out for signs. Ever since Jennifer Guthrie's murder, omens had been appearing every time she turned her head. Last week, a plastic bag had blown into the house and wrapped itself around the face of the cast iron rooster she used as a doorstop. Then a sparrow had smashed into her office window, only to regain consciousness and stare at her accusingly when she went outside to bury it. The next day, she'd stepped on a shred of paper on which were scrawled the words "when was the last time." This in particular had made Audrey uneasy, and for days afterward she'd been unusually careful while driving and walking down stairs. Though she'd felt a little silly taking cues from a scrap of trash, years of family misfortune had taught her that life was too tricky to be handled in a straightforward way. It couldn't be lived, it had to be outsmarted.

"Go straight home this afternoon," she told Jonathan when she dropped him off at school, a low cement block building with a panel of brown sod out front. "Your father will be waiting for you. No detours, and you know not to get in anybody's car. They haven't found that murderer yet."

"He killed a girl."

"That doesn't mean he wouldn't kill you if he had the chance. The wind is supposed to pick up later, so be careful of falling branches. I read about a boy who died that way up in Petaluma. He never knew what hit him."

"What branches are you talking about, Mom?" Jonathan said. "There aren't any trees." He grabbed his backpack and got out of the car without saying goodbye.

Two days earlier, Audrey had begun sleeping with one of her clients in an apartment that looked onto the back of a big box store. She worked at an agency that helped returning veterans find affordable housing, and that particular morning she'd taken a young man to look at vacant one-bedrooms near the rehab hospital. It was a bad day from the start. At breakfast she and Mark had squabbled over a seminar he wanted to attend in Florida, something cultish that was supposed to teach you how to create an explosively successful business from home. He would be kept up late, his bathroom breaks would be limited, and he'd be expected to do a lot of shouting in unison, and for this he would have to fork over two thousand dollars, which he wanted to put on their last open credit card. Then Jonathan claimed on the way to school that he was about to throw up, so she had to go home and wait with her suspiciously cheery son until Mark returned from a ten-mile jog. By then the wildfire that had been burning for days closed part of the freeway, forcing her to take clogged back roads all the way to work.

Waiting for Audrey in the reception area was her nine o'clock appointment, William, whose left leg had been shattered by a road-side bomb in Afghanistan. They had met twice the week before to discuss what he needed, which, because he had no family living nearby, was simple: a cheap place to live where he could use his housing voucher from the VA and look for a job. He began to rise when Audrey came through the door, but she waved him back down. "I'll be ready for you in a minute," she said in the harassed tone she normally reserved for the last client of the day.

She dropped her insulated lunch bag, purse, and car keys on her desk and went to the bathroom. Her face was pouchy and red under the merciless fluorescent light, which appeared to have been installed specifically to highlight the dark roots of bleached blondes. She had recently gained another ten pounds, bringing the total to 171. Her hips were accentuated by a pair of pocketless pants that always left a deep purple crease across her stomach. But it didn't matter, not here. She was like everyone else in the office, except she had no illusions about it. For years she had listened to her coworkers—usually older, chronically unappreciated wives and mothers—make wistful and occasionally explicit remarks about the men who limped and wheeled themselves through the office, as if to prove that menopause, routine, and sexual neglect hadn't yet killed them in their cubicles. A few times a week a hor-monal smoke signal would go up from one desk or another—Paula the office manager would wear a plunging top that revealed the wrinkled cleft between her breasts, or Lily of the support hose and recent bunion surgery would arrive with gleaming maroon lips and a hair extension bolted to the back of her head. Audrey always wanted to sit them down and say, "I've got some bad news for you. You're getting old."

Audrey and William went to see three apartments, each worse than the last. It was hard to like a job that involved following a griev-ously injured person through a series of depressing dumps, and Au-drey no longer tried. What had begun six years before as an attempt to give back and get out of the house had quickly morphed into a way to curry favor with God, and thereby protect herself and her son from such things as cancer and random shootings. If she turned her days over to veterans in need, she and Jonathan might be spared. She had no proof that this was true, but since she had no proof that it wasn't, it seemed best to continue on as usual even if it meant she was alone with men who had annihilated scores of people in distant deserts. On the rare occasion when she examined this point, it didn't seem like a particularly airtight line of reasoning.

"So, what do you think?" she asked after they'd toured a furnished one-bedroom on the ground floor. The place was made uniquely awful by dark, tunnel-like hallways and a handicapped shower stall with cracked plastic walls. It seemed like the perfect apartment if William's intention was to give up hope.

"It's all right," he said from the linoleum corner that served as the kitchen. He'd leaned his cane against the stove and was dutifully opening cabinets and peering into their grubby depths. He looked utterly out of place, a rangy, rough-featured kid with disheveled blond hair and a vague aura of importance about him, standing in a hovel that Audrey happened to know had just been vacated by two drug addicts and their iguana.

"They'd probably paint if you asked them to."

"It looks okay as it is."

Audrey yanked open the short stiff drapes above the sofa. "It's close to everything. Target's right there, and you can drive to rehab in about ten minutes." She couldn't believe she was trying to sell him on the place, it was so obviously the worst of the bunch. But that was her job, wasn't it, to make what was unthinkable feel like a brand new start.

"I guess I'll take it, then."

"Are you sure?" she said, relief leaking into her voice. Her legs ached and she wanted nothing more than to get to her car and devour the half-empty bag of pretzels that had been sitting in the glove compartment for a month. "There are other places to see, you know."

"This is the cheapest, though, right?"

"Your voucher will just about cover it."

A smoky wind slammed the front door shut, and William jumped, his cane slipping and clattering to the floor. "I got it," Audrey said, but he shook his head before she could move. "Please don't." He limped a few steps, gripped the edge of the counter with one hand, and after several tries snatched up the cane with the tips of his fingers. The effort seemed to instantly exhaust him. He stood staring at her, breathing through his mouth, his flushed face gradually returning to a bedridden kind of gray. The entire episode lasted less than ten seconds, but Audrey had trouble looking at him after that. She had never been good at papering over uncomfortable moments, but for some reason this was especially horrible; she honestly wondered if she could stand the job after today. Regular life, where people weren't maimed and emotionally ruined, was bad enough. Couldn't it be argued that she was constantly surrounding herself with the very misery she was trying to avoid?

After another look at the small concrete patio, William decided to put in an application. She walked slowly in front of him to the rental office, careful not to get more than a step or two ahead, and helped him fill out the paperwork. He sat beside her in a frayed fabric chair, leg extended, writing with his left hand and jotting down question marks in place of his rental history. "They'll want to call at least one landlord," she said. "You can't remember any addresses? Even the last one?"

"That was two tours ago." He seemed sullen, as if the cane incident was slowly working its way into his damaged memory. At one point, she glanced over to find him considering her with hooded brown eyes. Who was this woman? he seemed to be wondering. Didn't she have anything better to do than sit here and prod him in her reedy voice to remember pointless details? "I'll put down a friend I stayed with for a while," he said. "Will that work as a reference?"

"It'll have to."

After walking him to his car, she went back to the office and slumped at her desk, wishing she were a person who knew how to make things easier. Growing up, she had never known what to say—what *could* you say to a second cousin's death from leukemia or a drunk uncle throwing a Christmas tree into the street, ornaments and all—but she'd been a child then, and now there was no excuse. Paula might wear inappropriate tops and eat three cinnamon rolls before noon, but she took the happiness of her clients personally, she didn't roll her eyes when her extension rang or store her closed files in a soda-streaked trash can under her desk. Audrey was about to email William with an invitation to contact her if he had questions or needed anything at all, day or night, when the rental office called. At the agency's request, William's application had been expedited and approved. He could pick up his keys anytime before seven.

She phoned William and they met outside the apartment just after six. "That was quick," he said, making his way toward her over the cracked concrete walk that led up from the parking lot. It was the first time she had seen him smile.

"I asked them to rush it since you've been living in a motel," she said, opening the door and stepping inside. "Did you have time to check out?"

"Yup. Took me five minutes to pack."

She handed him the key, which dangled from a dented metal ring. "I hope the place works out. It's simple but it's better than where you were."

"You're leaving already?"

"Unless you need help with your luggage."

"This is it," he said, pulling a black duffel bag off his shoulder and dropping it to the carpet.

"I'll let you get settled, then."

"Hey," he said, looking at her so directly her stomach turned. "Thanks for getting me here."

"Of course." Because she didn't know what else to do, she hugged him. It was awkward, and he was much taller than she was, but it was the only way to escape his gaze. She was patting him on the shoulder blade and breathing in the slight detergent tinge of his shirt when he pulled back, lowered his face, and kissed her. After an instant of stunned paralysis—she hadn't been kissed by anyone but Mark in twenty years, and the sensation was so strange she barely recognized it—her impulse was to replay every conversation with William, searching for the thing that could have tipped her off. His sullenness, his forceful way of looking at her, her need to stand in the bathroom that morning and castigate herself. What else? Had two decades of marriage put her to sleep? Were her instincts so blunted she couldn't have seen this coming?

"I can't," she said, because resistance seemed obligatory. But when he led her to the couch, a cheap hulk of plaid pushed against the wall, she went willingly.

He held her head in his hands, his palms tight against her ears as if he were afraid she would pull away. It was an all-encompassing feeling she didn't get from Mark, who gave stiff hugs and pecks with pursed lips because one of them was always on their way out the door, and said "Love you" so often and absentmindedly it was now a rote stand-in for "Goodbye" and "Good night." These thoughts flickered through her mind and receded. As soon as they were gone, she realized that William could feel her pounding heart and labored breathing, and that was why he wasn't stopping. If he started to undress her, she would be incapable of saying no. As if he knew this, he didn't try.

It was twilight and her phone had rung twice before Audrey extricated herself and stood up. "I have to go," she said, pulling her shirt over her stomach. "That was probably my husband."

"Sorry," he said.

"I'm not," she said.

"Really?"

The youthful insecurity in his voice made her smile. "Really."

"Stay ten more minutes," he said. "Please? I'll be right back."

By the time he came out of the bathroom, she was sitting on the bed, her shoes off and her hair fluffed around her shoulders. If she was going to stay ten more minutes, she wanted to do something significant with it. For all she knew, this was the last exciting thing that would ever happen to her.

"Audrey?" he said from the hallway. She had never heard him say her name before.

"In here."

He came into the dim bedroom, stood silently, then began to unbutton his shirt. There were no sheets under the blue bedspread that had come with the apartment, but Audrey pulled it back anyway, the mattress slick against the soles of her feet. The situation was so unfamiliar it gave her a sense of calm detachment, as if she were lying in her tub at home imagining the scene in great detail.

"You don't want to look, okay?" William said, stopping before he uncovered his leg.

"I don't mind."

"I do."

His self-consciousness had the effect of eliminating hers, and she began to undress too.

At a stoplight on her way home, Audrey took a quick breath and looked at herself in the rearview mirror. She was sure she'd see something contemptible, but all she saw was a vaguely sexy woman with crow's-feet and bruised lips, her dark circles giving her an alluringly soulful expression. It was a face in a black-and-white photograph. A faded French character actress on the wrong side of forty, smoking at the window of a cluttered hotel room, her mascara smeared, her young lover asleep in the tangled sheets.

For nearly two hours she had existed without the fear that she would be broadsided or that her son would contract something that would kill him at sixteen. She had forgotten to worry, which felt a lot like not needing to. There had to be a connection between her disastrous behavior and this oddly invulnerable mood, which she expected to pass at any moment. But it only increased as she merged onto the freeway, sliding in between two trucks, practically daring them to crush her. It seemed impossible for something bad to happen now, after what she'd done.

"Sorry I'm late," she said to Mark as she walked in from the garage.

"You're late?" he said, barely looking up from the stove.

"Isn't that why you called?" She kissed the back of his shoulder. "I was helping a client move."

"Nice of you. I've been looking all over for the turmeric. Are we out?"

"It's in the cabinet behind the salt."

"If I didn't know better I'd think you were hiding all the healthy stuff."

"Better than throwing it out. That's next." She gave his arm a brief squeeze.

"By the way," he said as she headed toward the stairs, "our son is a terrible liar. I took him to school at noon. He's upstairs studying and he's in perfect health."

"*Is* he?" Audrey said, barely able to hide the satisfaction this news gave her.

"And I already got four responses to my last blog entry, some really thoughtful feedback. All in all, not a bad day."

The three of them were having dinner when Audrey noticed an unfamiliar car pull up in front of Christine's house down the street, followed a few minutes later by Tim's SUV. Two men got out, spoke briefly to Christine and Tim in the driveway, then all four went inside. "Who's that at Christine's?" Audrey said, peering through the window behind Mark's chair. "A couple of men I've never seen before."

"Maybe they've come to repossess something," Mark said distractedly.

"Mm," Audrey said, with a sympathetic tilt of her head. "Maybe."

But the next day, the news that detectives had questioned Tim about Jennifer Guthrie's murder was spreading in deliciously horrified tones throughout the neighborhood. The gossip was particularly gratifying because Tim had once bragged endlessly about his jet skis and his cars, before he'd had to sell everything to pay for his bloated mortgage and Christine's fertility treatments. No one honestly believed he was a killer, but the possibility made for excellent conversation. When word arrived at the Cronin household, even Audrey, who considered herself Christine's best friend, couldn't help but feel he'd gotten a little of what he deserved.

Five

MAY 21, 1948

Mala had always assumed that if you don't fit somewhere, then you fit somewhere else, but the last five days had proven she was no more part of the world than of the clan that had shunned her. She'd been lucky to travel two hundred miles. Some people saw her tattered clothes and peculiar eyes and picked her up out of curiosity, or because they didn't know any better, but most of the time she was forced to walk. In some ways she didn't mind. She had little experience riding in cars, and the accelerated view of the landscape made her dizzy. It was the hottest May she could remember. Her feet blistered and bled before going numb. She used her money for meals and stuck to the highway, not because she was going someplace in particular but because she had no map and wouldn't know how to use one anyway. Straight ahead was west, whatever that meant. She had always pictured the rest of Texas as an enormous navy blue sky filled with billowing flags, and below that, a grid of well-swept sidewalks and Spanish missions. But it was easy for an imagination to get things wrong. Contrary to the stately sound of their names, Big Lake and Rankin turned out to be grim and suspicious places where dust whirled down the middle of the street and faded flags spun limply on their poles.

In a general store in McCarney, she bought a notebook and pencil. Only three days of her year had passed and already she'd begun to forget the things she knew. What she'd always stored in her head, snippets of family history, the formulas she had come by through instinct and experimentation, now felt like keys to the life she'd left behind. Lose them and she might never get back in. On desolate roadsides, in rattling truck beds with her hair swirling, she chronicled all the things she'd invented or altered, wondering even now if they were just offshoots of traditional nonsense, like the rule forbidding a woman from walking between two men. She had seen Drina's herbal cures heal the sick and kill them, too, and often as not, a prediction came true years late, in a way that could as easily have been accident as destiny. Still, she wrote everything down, pages of detailed instructions along with drawings to pass the time.

Had Drina known about the book, she would have burned it. It wasn't just that Mala was recording clan secrets, though that was insult enough. You didn't tell strangers your business, especially if you wanted money from them. Share what you knew with outsiders and they would harm themselves with it and blame you for their ignorance. This was the nature of mankind. From the time Mala was a motherless little girl, Drina had repeated these adages again and again. Don't write, don't read, speak your own language. Trust no one, and tell them nothing.

Wise advice, which Mala had been scorning since she was twelve years old.

It was 1942, the middle of a distant war they'd heard of on a radio somewhere. In the aimless months after Ruth went west and the storefront closed, when they wandered across the Edwards Plateau to a deserted valley of thorns and scrub on the edge of Fort Worth, there was nothing else for Mala to do but tinker with the established order of things. If she couldn't study, she could experiment with techniques that hadn't changed in centuries. While Madame Drina, Herbalist and Psychic, was off delivering custom sleep remedies to well-paying insomniacs, Mala had free run of her trailer, cluttered with every imaginable type of dried leaf, semiprecious stone, bird feather, and exoskeleton. Endless possibilities and no chaperone. Each tiny tin box held something that could be combined with nightshade stem or fool's gold. Nothing happened at first, except Mala felt dizzy after mixing metal shavings with an unlabeled powder that gave off steam when stirred. Then, on a cloudy June afternoon when Drina went to Killeen to make deliveries, Mala found a chunk of desiccated *Sanguinaria* wrapped in black cloth and the skin of a corn snake in a drawer with Drina's worn-down lipstick. Mala's objectives were lofty—she wasn't interested in treasure or true love, but in getting blood from a stone, something she'd heard could not be done. Two hours after she told Beni to follow her instructions, his sworn enemy, Nic, came to apologize for an argument they'd had in 1930.

With this success as impetus, Mala set about transforming a bunch of reliable and unassuming formulas into little explosives that turned ordinary life on its ear. After half the men contracted vertigo, she tried at Drina's insistence to undo her work, but without success. With no remedy and no idea which experiment was the cause, the clan descended into chaos. It would become known as the Year Without a Summer, when a dry fog settled over the camp and flakes of snow drifted down in August. Furious at being blamed for the weather, Mala persisted until three children were born in one night and Drina put a padlock on her trailer door. It took until October for the fog to clear and for the men to walk without clutching their heads.

"Just because something is old doesn't mean you should meddle with it," Drina told her. "So you create it yourself, so what?"

"But you make medicines the same way," Mala argued. "You grind up poison and sell it to people."

Drina gave her a dismissive pat on the head. "Talk to me when my medicines bring snow in August."

A sad family of drifters picked up Mala near Crane, dropped her in Midland, and continued on. They were too beaten down to be fearful of an unusual face, and had shared their lunch—rye bread and part of a hen they'd snatched from a farm and strangled—before settling into silence. They drove away in a ticking station wagon Mala was certain she would see again, hood steaming on the shoulder, no one in sight. She stood in the middle of the sidewalk, surrounded by more people and automobiles than she had ever imagined could converge on one spot. It seemed impossible that the same sun should be overhead, but there it was, burning at a sharp angle over the clock of a bank building. Or maybe there were two suns? The thought had never occurred to her before, but she didn't have time to examine it. The crowd had thinned out and she could see a narrow path through. Any sense of triumph or fear accompanying her arrival would have to wait. It was nearly three in the afternoon on a Friday, and if she wanted to eat, she had to find work.

She was waved out of the first place she entered, a dressmaker's shop. "No, no, you don't come in here. I don't want what you're selling."

"I'm not selling anything. You have a sign in the window, and I can sew." Mala wasn't good at it, but desperation would change that.

"I don't care."

"I'll work for almost nothing."

The woman grabbed her arm and pushed her out to the street. "Don't let me see you again."

It was the same at a small grocery, though there were black and brown faces stocking shelves and scrubbing floors. It was no surprise, Beni had repeated this truth for so many years he'd nearly made a fable out of it. Everybody else had a place, even if it was under the boot heel of another person, but there would never be a place for people like him and Mala. Try as you might you didn't undo a thousand years of wandering.

"Anybody can make grand statements about choosing their lot in life," she had argued. "It's easier than getting up and doing anything about it."

"But there's nothing to be done," he'd replied in the intensely philosophical way he had when drunk. "If you can prove otherwise, wake me up. I'm going to bed."

He hadn't seemed to realize that a person with no place would be impossible to find after a year of exile. Which field would she look in first? Which state?

Mala had missed Beni before, but at the moment it felt like an illness, something she had to quickly get rid of. She'd adjusted to him not being her father simply by not believing him. He had done a lot of outlandish things to protect her, but this was the worst and the most charming. Most fathers wouldn't think of it at a moment like that, but Beni had sent her off with no ties to worry about. During that first night, barely asleep in a roadside gulley, Mala had come out of a dream with a smile on her face. Of course it was a lie; had Beni ever dealt in facts? Her heart went out to him in gratitude. The lie hadn't worked for long, but at least he'd tried. He had given her something to ponder for a few hours.

The manager of a dime store had no job for Mala, but he felt sorry for her and fed her at the end of the counter after the other customers left. His name was Robert and he stood at the soda fountain and stared at her while she ate. She tried to make herself very small, the way she had when she was a child and Beni was looking for her, but felt monstrously conspicuous even though the store was empty. Beni loved marching into the lunch counter in San Angelo and causing pandemonium with his bedraggled clothes and unshaven face, bringing employees running to collectively hurl him outside. He struggled and shouted the same way every time, with the hysterical joy that came from being the object of so much attention. "Heaven's sake, I only want a sandwich. Is that against the law in this town?" Apparently it was; the last time he'd done it, he spent a night in jail.

Mala looked up from her plate, which now was nearly empty. The wall in front of her was lined with mirrors. Her black hair was flat and shiny, and her skin had turned the color of dirt after days in the sun. Her eyes glowed unnaturally under the buzzing lights. It had taken only two hours of being in the city by herself to realize her own strangeness. There in her face she could see about five foreign countries, as well as all of the relatives who had traveled over on ships from England and Romania, hauling flimsy steamer trunks, measles-infected babies, and wild bears on chains. She saw her kin rioting at Ellis Island, and if they were lucky enough to escape immediate deportation, fanning out under cover of night to squalid tenements and distant states, not starting new lives so much as continuing the old ones in a different place. She was the product of these hopeful journeys, and it made her sad to think she had it no better than they did back then. Some might argue that being alone like she was, she had it worse.

She caught Robert's eye in the mirror and he smiled. He was young, with round cheeks and a high white forehead. There was something funny and a little frantic about him, he couldn't stop wiping things down. Mala swallowed large, solid chunks of her ham sandwich so she could be finished with it and go. Her stomach roiled after days of unusual and tasteless food.

"How's your lunch?" Robert asked. It was hard to hear him over the song on the radio, wild violins and a man who sounded like he was singing through his nose.

"Fine. What do I owe you?"

"You're new in town. My treat."

"Are you sure?" She reached into the pocket where her last few coins lay buried. She didn't want to pay him, but she had to make the gesture. If she didn't, he might insist.

"On second thought, let me ask you this. Do you dance?"

She stopped chewing. "What?"

"Girls like you know how to dance," he said, flushing to his ears. "I've seen them."

"I don't. Sorry."

"I like this song," he said after a pause. "Bob Wills."

"Oh. It's nice." She wished someone would come in. Anything to give her a moment to think.

He stepped closer and started wiping what was already clean. "Won't you even try? It's the Texas Swing and the song is almost finished."

"I should be going." She stood up and took her bag off the stool beside her. It looked filthy against the immaculate green seat. The last time she'd bathed was three days ago in a muddy river, a little ways upstream from a herd of wading cows. The water had tasted like dead leaves in her mouth.

"What's your name?" Robert had come out from behind the counter, leaving his rag in a wet gray bunch by the cake display.

"Mala. Thanks again for lunch."

"That's a queer name. Never heard it before. For future reference, Mala—you'll be glad to know this—these are the first couple of steps of the swing."

For the first time in her life a man who wasn't her father put his hands on her. She didn't fight because it would give him the opportunity to call the police. He could say whatever he liked: that she'd tried to steal from him or walk out without paying. She told herself that it wasn't so awful, it wasn't like he was trying to kiss her. He clasped her hands and placed them on his shoulder and bare arm, then haltingly stepped back and forth out of time with the music. His face was so close it looked blurry.

"I've never danced with a girl wearing boots," he said.

"They're all I have."

"You're pretty. I bet nobody tells you that."

Mala hated herself for being flattered. Though maybe it was okay, because in some ways the situation was like a scene from a book. An overlooked girl gets noticed and picked to dance by a man from a higher standing. The parallels should have been thrilling, but Robert smelled like a woman, scrubbed and fragrant, and his soft arm was cold under her fingers. His hair stuck to his temples. There were no urns of flowers or feathered masks, just a wall of mirrors showing a scene she would try to forget as soon as it was over.

"Robert?" The bell on the door jingled and a woman with a cap of stiff white hair stood on the threshold, her eyes lit up in disbelief.

Robert pushed Mala away and straightened his apron. "Hello there, Mrs. Fowler. How are you?"

"How am I? How are *you*?" She didn't look sorry to have stumbled onto something scandalous; on the contrary, she looked delighted. "What's happening here?"

"What do you mean?"

"What's that person doing in your father's store?"

"I don't know, she was hungry. She just got to town this morning."

"How is that your problem to solve?"

He stared at Mrs. Fowler defiantly, like a child. "The church tells us to care about our fellow man, *that's* all."

"She's not what the church was referring to."

"Mala's a nice girl," he said, turning back to the counter and grabbing his rag. "She's been keeping me company on a slow afternoon."

Mrs. Fowler shook her head slowly. "Well, I don't know what to say."

"All right, then. How about a cold drink?"

"No, thank you." There was a long pause. The voice of the radio announcer blared so loudly his words were garbled.

"Maybe a malted?" Robert said.

Mrs. Fowler went on as if she hadn't heard him. "I guess I'm not surprised. You've always embarrassed your father. And for your information, your reputation among the young ladies is of someone with no sense. I used to think they were being cruel but I'm not so sure anymore."

Mala moved slowly toward the door.

"Why, that hurts my feelings, Mrs. Fowler," Robert said, but his voice was hard and sarcastic.

As Mrs. Fowler stepped aside to let Mala pass, she drew in a sharp breath and held it. Mala plunged through the doorway and out to the street with a quick glance back at Robert, who stared after her with a pitiable look, as if he were being deserted by the only person who understood him. She hurried toward the bank with its large and amazing clock, or was the bank in the other direction? She almost laughed, thinking of the imagined powers heaped on her by people she'd known since she was born. They'd need only to see her here, wandering around in a helpless and confounded state, to realize the limitations of her talents. Otherwise, wouldn't she know exactly where to go and what to do? Wouldn't she have foreseen this outcome and avoided it? As if to demonstrate the depth of her ignorance, she wandered blindly and with mounting exhaustion until it was dark and the streets were nearly empty.

The city's fortune-tellers were stuffed together in a shabby, one-block area near the bus station. A few women leaned in doorways, their slender figures lit dimly by lamps burning in interior rooms. On the opposite side of the street, Mala walked back and forth, watching their heads turn as they followed her movements. She might not be able to sew, but she could read cards, and that was worth something, wasn't it? A meal and a place to sleep for a year?

Mala knew exactly how it would go. She would flatter one of the readers, speak her language and find people in common (done properly, there might even be tears), and then, against her better judgment and grumbling as she did so, the woman would invite her in. There would be tea and negotiating, and simple food if there was any to spare. Mala would sleep on the floor on a jumble of musty coats, and in the morning would begin a series of days that played out in a shuttered back room. A deck of worn cards, tragic predictions, people in search of communion with their unreachable dead. Every night from her moldy pallet she would stare into the same corner and look for the tiny spider that lived there. On the evening when she found the web snapped and the spider gone, she would count the days and discover that only two weeks had passed. Her fate was a riddle, but that much she could foretell.

Mala was at the bus station in five minutes. Without a thought for her next meal, she spent the rest of her money on a one-way ticket to Bakersfield, California. She realized as she did so that the thought had been lingering in her mind for days, waiting to be recognized.

The last time she saw Ruth, she'd been so consumed with reading books she would have gladly chosen it over speaking. The only trouble was the shock and disappointment she felt when she looked up from a page and discovered that she wasn't sitting in the shadows of an English garden, but in a noisy ranch kitchen that smelled of bacon and hot iron and floor polish. Every weekday morning from the time she was seven, she'd come to have her spelling and addition corrected and be reminded again not to get in the way.

"I have a household to manage," Ruth always said. "Mrs. Nolan is a tolerant woman, but if you interrupt the work of these girls, that's when her tolerance will end." It was easy to believe that Ruth was heartless—she smiled when she was angry and her heels made a rapid knocking sound that sent the maids and cooks scattering when she approached—but when Mala watched while Ruth peeled vegetables, she saw a gentle face that gazed absently out the kitchen window, eyes fixed on the fields with a longing, faraway look. When no one else was around, Ruth would touch her shoulder with a rough hand and say, so quietly it was as if she were embarrassed to reveal evidence of a tender heart, "There should be more like you."

Long after Mala had begun to take her time with Ruth for granted, Mrs. Nolan dismissed Ruth for taking books from the house library and giving them to Mala to read.

"Such a scandal, stealing Mrs. Nolan's property," one of the maids, Annie, whispered that morning with barely contained glee. She wasn't more than nineteen but had been dusting banisters and sweeping floors in the main house for as long as Mala could remember.

"She loaned them to me," Mala said.

"A loan without asking is stealing. She got what she deserved. Only yesterday she was ordering all of us around and now she can't step foot in this house."

"She's not coming back?" Mala asked, queasy with guilt. "Ever?"

"She's gone to California. Bakersfield, I heard. You won't be welcome here either, and the same goes for your father. Mrs. Nolan will make sure of it."

Annie was right. That morning, the foreman gave Beni his wages and told him not to return. Beni and Mala walked hand in hand down the long drive toward the highway, faces high against a stinging wind. "Keep your head up and don't look back," he said. "That's the only right way to go."

...

It was an outside chance, but tonight, it was all she had. The bus to Bakersfield left early in the morning, and she had no money to pay for lodging, so she lay on a bench near the ticket window and rolled her bag under her head. Against the back of her neck she could feel the notebook, already half filled, and so much more still to write. She closed her eyes and tried to call up all the sunsets and spring-times, the tails of comets and flakes of snow that had fallen on rare winter mornings, but all she could see was her mother's rickety wagon on the night of the funeral, standing at the edge of the desert in flames.

Six

When Paige bounded into her father's arms at the airport on Tuesday afternoon, she looked so sweet and gangly that Linda wondered if her memory of the girl was skewed. But then she said, "Hi, Linda!" in her chirpy, self-possessed voice, her pale blue eyes glimmering, and Linda knew she was the same brutally perceptive child she had always been, the one who'd wished her bon voyage six months earlier by saying, "I bet you can't wait to have my dad all to yourself in California."

"Hello, sweetheart!" Linda said.

Peter, clutching an airport kiosk teddy bear in one hand, grabbed his daughter and buried his face in her hair. Linda tried to hug them both, wrapping her arms limply around their backs, but they didn't seem to notice and after a moment she stepped away. "Excuse me for a minute," she said. "I need to find a restroom."

By the time Linda returned, Paige had collected her suitcases and was chattering to her father as if she'd been released not only from the claustrophobic clutches of an airplane but from a vow of silence. She waved with the bear when she saw her stepmother approach, but in a way that seemed a little impatient. "Where have you been?" she seemed to be saying. "I'm here to upend your life and I'm anxious to get started."

People noticed Paige as she walked hand in hand with Peter out of the airport; it was difficult not to. She was small and slender, with olive skin, a dark pink mouth, and the huge, plaintive eyes of a daguerreotype orphan. Linda had a wholesome American look—strawberry blond and unthreatening, the kind of beauty men responded to but women found empty and easy to duplicate. Her height was the only reason she'd modeled way back when, a hundred years ago now. Paige wasn't wholesome, she was something out of an English novel where the houseguest drowns in the pond and there's a ghost wandering the estate. Her dark hair, normally a mass of smooth curls, went frizzy during storms. She gave proper burials to dead butterflies and played cribbage on her cell phone, all further evidence that she belonged somewhere else, in another time. Every few weeks she would give up another food group, and if sunflower seeds or Pop-Tarts weren't available, she would stop eating until her collarbone stuck out and her eyes turned to sinkholes.

Paige had never been to California before. She sat in the front seat at Linda's insistence and jabbered about the scorched hills and skinny palm trees and putrid brown air, all in the same fascinated tone. She rolled down her window and poked her head out so she could see better. Mouth agape, she looked back at the wide intersections with their oversized street signs as if she'd just whizzed past the Eiffel Tower or a particularly gory car wreck. When Peter pulled onto M Street and into the garage, Paige shrieked, "Wow! It's giant!" like such a typical kid that Linda smiled.

"A pretty good start, I think," Peter said as Paige ran upstairs to see her room, which only this morning had been a peaceful, closed-off appendage of the second floor.

"Margaret will be happy to hear it."

"You okay?"

Linda grabbed Paige's suitcases from the trunk before Peter could. "Do you see any indication that I'm not?" she said, though her uneasiness was so consuming it seemed ridiculous to protest. Why couldn't Peter's son Brooks have come to stay? He was thirteen and a show-off, but there wasn't anything penetrating about him, he didn't have anyone all figured out.

"Why don't you let me carry that?"

Linda let the suitcases thud to the garage floor. "They're very heavy," she said, walking into the house. "It seems to me she brought everything she owns."

The day before, with Paige's arrival imminent and no act of God or Margaret on the horizon to stop it, Linda had waited for her husband to leave for work, then gone to the den and pulled out the book she found at the garage sale. For more than a week it had been sitting between James Baldwin and Alexandre Dumas, its slender spine flush and nearly invisible. Peter had even poked around for one of his home repair manuals without noticing it, and she hadn't pointed it out. She had waited too long to tell him, and now it was too late. She wouldn't have known how to explain it, any more than she could explain why she was taking it into the kitchen and flipping through the pages, looking for the only words she remembered. *Everything as It Should Be.* They were there on the page the book fell to when allowed to open by itself, written in such a flamboyant hand they were almost illegible. It was a ludicrous thing to be doing on a day when she had to buy groceries and make a dessert for her book club, but nothing else was offering such a propitious outcome, and, with her stepdaughter coming in a matter of hours, it seemed almost reckless not to try to do something about it.

Though the instructions were simple, they had the script's same romantic, slightly outdated flourish. The page was gritty with dust that left tiny red streaks on Linda's fingertips as she traced each line.

> *white flower petals*
> *enough water to drown an insect*
> *salt*
> *as many stones as one hand can carry*
> *a broken button*
> *a true photograph*
> *patience*

She read the list twice. What had this woman—Mala—meant by a true photograph? And what miraculous development was supposed to occur when Linda put all this stuff together?

It didn't matter—the point was to get it over with quickly, hope it had some effect, and not torment herself for having done it. It was just a lark, anyway, a way to release stress before she turned her home and her summer over to a ten-year-old. Which reminded her that she still hadn't bought pillows for the guest room—Paige refused to sleep with her head on the fluffy remains of a dead or tortured goose—giving Linda even less time to waste on pointless flights of fancy. Leaving her half-finished cereal on the counter, she took the book upstairs and ripped a broken button from one of her husband's three-hundred-dollar shirts, leaving a raw and unfixable hole. She plucked five small rocks from the garden and filled a cup of water at the sink of the downstairs half bath Peter often forgot was there. She put these objects in the center of the breakfast table along with a fashionably grim-faced picture from her brief and humiliating career as a catalog model, a ramekin of salt, and several white petals, pilfered from an exploded peony in the yard. All together, the objects made Linda think of what the house might look like after an earthquake—a bunch of unrelated scraps thrown into a sudden and bewildering heap.

Order the objects by color. Then order them by size.

There was a kind of freedom in doing what she was told, even by an unseen person directing her through the written word. Her actions weren't completely her own. She shifted things around the table, separating them into three parts. What hadn't seemed to go together was now beginning to look strangely harmonious, the flower petals the same color as the broken mother-of-pearl button, the dish of salt the same circumference as the rocks, the cup of water as reflective as the mirror in the photograph. Everything as it should be, maybe, if she looked at it from the right perspective.

Close your eyes. Think only of the objects in front of you and your future as it should be.

Linda sat meditatively in the chair with her hands in her lap, picturing the petals and broken button and salt, and beyond that, her ideal future, shimmering off in her left field of vision. But almost immediately these apparitions were crowded out by distant voices, clinking bottles, an endless series of dark rooms linked by a long hallway. This wasn't a glimpse of her future, it was her past, carrying on by itself in some isolated region of her head. At first she thought it was a shadowy scene from childhood, her mother dead, her father out past midnight, the whole world smelling of wet snow and ashtrays and the Goodwill store she passed every day on her way to school. But a moment later, with a queasy feeling of recognition, she realized it was a memory fragment from the murky and chaotic years before she met Peter. Before she'd wiped her life clean of fingerprints and flushed all the evidence.

She had been hurtling toward thirty, her modeling career finished, her brother struggling through college, both of them broke and living in the city. It was the time of terrible things, as she thought of it, when the weather was always cold and rainy, the neighborhoods slummy, the people loud, drunk, or sobbing. Surely the sun had shone during that two-year period; it must have been summer and she must have seen her old friends on occasion, but none of those memories had survived. Eighteen years later she'd succeeded in sealing off all but the most persistent images, which would crop up occasionally during a bath or at a stoplight, flickering across her eyesight in a disorienting flash like a migraine aura. For some reason, she almost always saw herself opening the door of a hotel room for one particular man, though she'd forgotten his name and had never seen him again. You couldn't choose what stuck with you, apparently, and once it was in your mind there was no getting it out again.

As if she'd stumbled into the screening of an avant-garde film, the frame changed from one disjointed sketch to another. This time the images came in stills drenched in lurid color and detail. She was sitting in a chair, young and unspeakably bored, wearing an expression of weary and bemused acceptance. Whatever happened, she appeared to be thinking, would happen. Each change of scene featured something different: a fringed lamp, a shoe, the long, suicidal view from a hotel window down to the dark street. She was standing at the door in a tight dress she didn't remember, letting someone in and laughing a laugh she had never used again after that night, as if it were a coat she had left in a cab. The frames accelerated to a strobe-like pace—her hand, the lamp hitting the back of a man's head—stopping only when she gasped and opened her eyes, shocked to find herself in her living room on a bright Monday morning.

She stood and began grabbing everything off the table. The

flower petals, photograph, and button went into the garbage, the stones were thrown back in the dirt, and the ramekin and glass dumped of their contents and hidden in the dishwasher. She was supposed to be patient and repeat the words—*everything as it should be*—for one week until they became habit, but she was no longer interested in the outcome. She wished she'd never tried it. Let things be what they shouldn't instead of what they should, just leave her memories undisturbed in the silt of her brain where they belonged.

She was frantically searching for her handbag so she could take refuge in a department store when Christine rang the doorbell.

"I'm on my way to the office, but please tell me you're coming to book group later," she blurted when Linda opened the door.

"Hi. Of course I'm coming."

"Good. I'm only halfway through what we're supposed to be reading, and if you weren't there and I had to listen to Susanna monologuing all night, I think I'd scream. She's also an awful cook."

"You haven't finished the book?" Linda asked. "Didn't you like it?" She finally spotted her purse in the corner of the foyer. It was all she could do to refrain from lunging at it.

"I'm supposed to put up with a story about nuclear disaster?" Christine said, her voice quivering. "What does it have to do with me right now? I mean, have you ever read a more depressing book in your life?"

And then she started to cry.

After helping his daughter unpack, Peter brought her suitcases down to the basement as if they wouldn't be needed again for a very long time. Paige had just finished exploring the house—walking into closets, turning the electronics on and off—when Audrey dropped by with her son Jonathan. He was a bright, good-looking kid, tall for twelve and a bit on the strange side, and Audrey adored him so much that she would shut up immediately if he began to talk so she could sit and watch him with a look of tormented pride on her face. This afternoon, though, she seemed distracted and a little giddy. She'd recently disclosed her affair to Linda at the supermarket in an exultant whisper, as if she naturally assumed that Linda would be impressed. Linda had to admit she was, simply because she'd never expected to be surprised by Audrey, whom she'd considered the most ordinary person in the world.

Jonathan sat across the coffee table from Peter and gobbled cheese and grapes from the platter Linda had put out. "I don't know if you know this," he said to Paige, "but there could be a killer living on this street."

"Really?" Paige's eyes widened and her mouth trembled with excitement.

Audrey clucked her tongue at her son. "Don't exaggerate. Tim was cleared, for the time being at least."

"No, he wasn't. They just don't have enough to hold him."

"Christine came over yesterday morning," Linda said. "She told me there was an anonymous caller. That's how the whole thing started."

"*And,*" Audrey said, "did you hear this? Somebody took a picture at a restaurant near the hill on the night of the murder." She paused, looking around to make sure all eyes were on her. "You've got a couple of people posing at an outdoor table, and in the background is a car just like Tim's."

"Seems pretty circumstantial to me," Peter said.

"They're catching hell, you know," Audrey said. "Wackos calling them up at all hours, telling them to get out of town. They've stopped answering their phone."

"How did people find out?" Linda asked.

Audrey shook her head a little, as if the answer should be obvious. "I've told everybody I know. Haven't you?"

"Yes," Linda admitted.

"Multiply that by ten neighbors, and in two days the news has spread to Florida."

"But I never said he was guilty."

"Since when does that matter? People like to draw the worst conclusion possible. It's human nature."

"Why don't we talk about something pleasant?" Peter said, sitting forward and slapping his knees. "Sounds like we've all been watching too much television."

"Not me," Paige said. "Since Mom and Neil got married, I'm only allowed to watch an hour a week. I'm like one of those Asian girls at my school except I don't play the piano." She was sitting on the couch with her bare feet dangling a few inches off the floor. She had changed out of jeans into white shorts, revealing pale flamingo legs and knobby ankles.

"You're on vacation now," Peter said. "You can watch as much as you want as long as you're still coherent at dinnertime." It was an absurd thing to say, but Linda could tell that he meant it. He seemed to be trying to sell his daughter on staying for good.

"Did you hear that, Mom?" Jonathan said.

"The only thing I heard is that if you work hard this summer and improve your algebra scores, you might be able to skip a grade. I don't think I told you, Linda. Jonathan did so well last year he might go straight to ninth grade."

"Really?" Linda said. Audrey had told her twice in exhaustive detail.

"I can't *imagine* doing that," Paige said in her toy voice, though her private girls' school was one of the most competitive in the Northeast. At ten, she already appeared to know how to use self-deprecation to her social advantage.

"It's not hard to do at my school," Jonathan said. "You just have to do your work."

"Of course it's hard," Audrey said. "Don't downplay it."

"Anybody can see you're really smart," Paige agreed.

It was clear from Audrey's expression that she would be firmly on Paige's side for the rest of the summer. Linda hadn't told her much, just that her stepdaughter could be "challenging" and "outspoken," because to use words like "cunning" and "dark-hearted" would sound preposterous. Now she was glad she'd kept her feelings to herself. No one else in the room appeared intimidated by a bright young girl who had yet to get her period or wear a bra. She just needed to change her perspective. But then the only shaft of light in the room sought Paige out, turning her skin white and igniting her eyes like two gaslights. Audrey and Jonathan were watching her talk as if mesmerized.

"She's adorable," Audrey said later, in the kitchen. "Smarter than the two of us put together."

"Yup," Linda said.

"Pretty, too. What a combination." She peered at the side of Linda's face. "Something the matter?"

"No. It's a big change, that's all."

"I know how it is, having a brilliant child around. Mark went through a period of feeling upstaged by Jonathan, with all the academic awards and everything. But he got over it and so will you."

"Get over what? How does that apply to me?"

Audrey put a piece of cheese in her mouth, smiled guiltily, and grabbed another. "It isn't easy, but we all have to make way for the younger generation."

"But I still think of *myself* as the younger generation. My life just started."

"It didn't, though, you know?" Audrey said, crunching a cracker. "It just feels that way."

Audrey and Jonathan were about to leave when Linda stopped them on the porch. "Hang on a second, I have something for you."

She ran to the den and took the book off the shelf. The best way to put it out of her mind was to get rid of it. She was afraid to court bad luck by throwing it away, but it couldn't hurt to give it to someone else.

"Here," she said, rushing to the door. "I thought you might want this."

"What is it?" Audrey said.

"I got it at Susanna's garage sale. You like antiques and old postcards and all that, don't you?"

"She's been doing our family tree since last Christmas," said Jonathan. "The incredible history of the crackpot family."

Audrey opened the book and began turning pages. "What is it?"

"A journal, I guess. I'm not really sure."

"Do you know who wrote it?"

"There's a name on the cover. I Googled it and got nothing."

Audrey went through the book slowly, pausing to take in entire passages and blurred scribbles in the margins. "Unbelievable," she said. "Have you tried any of these things? These spells?"

Linda forced a laugh. "With Paige coming? I haven't had time. It's not really my thing, anyway."

"You don't mind if I keep this?"

"No, please. Take it. I wouldn't know what to do with it."

Audrey closed the book and held it to her chest. "Well, thank you. It's amazing you should give this to me now, with everything that's been going on in my life. It seems awfully strange, doesn't it?" She was speaking in code in front of Jonathan, who had wandered down the steps ahead of his mother.

"I wouldn't put too much stock in it, Audrey. Maybe it's just a diary, written by some crazy woman."

"I don't know. I think everything happens for a reason."

"But what if it doesn't? What if it just happens?"

Audrey smiled, but there was pity and sadness in it, and maybe even a little superiority. "Oh, Linda. You could think that way about everything and then you wouldn't bother living."

Seven

How does it feel to be screwing a MURDERER I bet you knew all along.

 $\mathcal{C}$ hristine read every one of the forty-seven comments in her in-box on Wednesday morning, deleted them en masse, then shut down her blog for good. She had been writing "Babies on the Brain" for nearly two years and had a following of a few thousand sympathetic women, but since Tim was questioned by the police three days earlier, her readership had doubled. Most of the comments were signed "Anonymous" or some variation of "Disgusted," so she couldn't be sure, but it seemed that many of her new readers were badly educated men who, without any apparent sense of irony, wanted to kill Tim with their bare hands.

> He should be strangle like he did to that young woman only worse.
> If I had the chance I would do it myself.

"Are you kidding me?" Tim said, reading the last comment over her shoulder. "What the hell, they just asked me some questions. It was totally routine."

"I don't think being questioned by the police is ever routine."

"Whatever, this is getting out of hand. How did word get out, anyway?"

"The police are here for an hour and you think you can keep it a secret?" Christine said. "There's some local guy who wrote about it on his blog. He's friends with Eric and Nina down the street, and you know how *they* talk."

"Maybe we should move, then."

Christine craned her neck and looked up at her husband. "We don't have enough to deal with? Now you want to sell the house?" Her voice was taking on a hysterical edge but she didn't try to stop it. Sometimes overreacting was the only way to make Tim realize the depth of her feelings.

"I'm sorry," he said, stroking her hair. "It was a stupid thing to say. I didn't mean it."

"Somebody has it out for you at work. Now that sales are coming back, they know you're going to be the most successful person there, just like before. They don't like it and they'll do anything to destroy you."

"Maybe you're right. People are desperate. Rob Chance hasn't made a sale in seven months."

"Rob Chance, enemy number one."

This made Tim laugh. "I'm just glad you don't suspect me. As long as we're together on this, nothing else matters."

"Suspect you! I can't believe the police aren't investigating the person who tipped them off. Everybody has an agenda, even anonymous callers."

But there was no doubt about it, Tim had always ruffled people's feathers. It was the way he was wired. He'd had noisy and embarrassing altercations with housepainters, clients, the neighbors with the barking shih tzu, and the guy up the street with the loud motorcycle. He had gotten into a heated discussion about the governor with his boss at a company barbecue. Most of Christine's friends wished they knew what their husbands were thinking—this was not a problem with Tim. He would pause a movie in the middle to opine about the nonsensical screenplay, and spend hours debriefing after an argument and examining the conflict from all sides. Christine believed it was the doing of his late mother, Alice, a twice-divorced art teacher who had divulged everything to her son from the time he was old enough to speak. When he was seven, she'd begun telling him about her dates with men and asking his advice. What should she wear to a casual dinner party? Was it okay to call a man if he didn't call her? Christine had once referred to the relationship as "inappropriate" and "enmeshed," but Tim had flared up, saying he didn't want everything labeled with therapy lingo now that his wife had a degree, so she hadn't mentioned it again.

"Listen," Tim said, leaning against the desk, "do you think Sofija and Arso heard anything about this? They live half an hour away, so probably not, right?"

"If they send us any abusive messages, I'll let you know."

"Are you feeling okay?" Tim had been on her all week to eat more, to get some fresh air, to take naps.

"I can't tell anymore. My stomach's in knots on a permanent basis."

"Maybe just a pregnancy symptom."

"I think it's all this stress."

"Great. That makes me feel awful," he said in a vaguely hurt tone.

"Don't let it. It's not your fault." She went back to invoicing, hoping he would drop it. With Tim, even the slightest suggestion of blame could be enough to ignite an hour-long back-and-forth.

He spent a minute loitering in sulky silence near her desk. She was relieved when he finally turned and went back to his home office, where he had spent the last two days moping and avoiding contact with his coworkers, who had been alerted to the situation by an expletive-laced email.

Over the next week, the police phoned twice.

Both times, Christine was home, and both times she stopped what she was doing, her face going cold as she listened to her husband hem and haw and kiss ass in the next room. She knew he hadn't murdered anyone, but there was something in his manner that unnerved her. He had always been cocky and defensive, and she had expected these traits to intensify under the current circumstances. While the police had interviewed him the first time, she'd stood outside the dining room with her back pressed against the wall, bracing for one of his outbursts: "Are you out of your fucking minds?" or "You don't have one iota of proof!" or "Don't you people have a black man to beat up for no reason?" He said these kinds of things when stopped for speeding; it stood to reason that he would lose his marbles when questioned about a murder. The moment he opened his mouth he would be arrested for disorderly conduct or worse, Christine was sure of it.

But he'd been repulsively docile and polite, not himself at all. "Sure, you guys gotta job to do, I understand, absolutely," and "I don't remember exactly, except I was showing a few houses that evening." He'd even offered them coffee, fumbling around by himself in the kitchen and bumping into cabinets until Christine took over, hissing at him to get back to the dining room. The whole episode had given her the sense that for seven years she'd been tricked; she was living with someone who stood up for himself only when it was easy, when his foe was a yappy little dog or a home inspector who was just doing his job.

Tim wasn't sleeping either. He had always been the kind of person who could fall asleep upright with the television roaring and his cell phone vibrating in his pocket, but now she would awaken in the night to find him downstairs by the picture window with all the lights off, as if he were expecting assassins.

"If you did nothing wrong, what are you worried about?" she'd asked the night before.

"The truth doesn't matter in a thing like this," he'd said. "I'm getting concerned."

"About a bunch of stupid emails?"

"They're death threats, Chrissie, and now I'm getting them at work. I think we should get a gun."

She let out a bark of laughter. "How about a lawyer?"

"Even if we could afford one, a lawyer won't keep us safe. I'm getting a gun first thing tomorrow."

This made Christine furious—he seemed to enjoy exaggerating the situation and making it as violent and menacing as possible. "Why, so you can look even guiltier?"

"What are you talking about, guiltier?" he shouted, his face contorted in the glow from the moon. "I have to listen to this from my wife? The wife I supported while she waltzed through three different careers?"

"You don't remember where you were that night?" she exploded. "How can that be? You remember fights we had years ago. You remember everything your mother ever said to you when you were a child!"

"Do you remember where you go every minute of the day? Where you were that afternoon? Can you tell me that?"

She sat in silence.

His voice got very low. "You know what, I've always taken your side. I love you more than anything and I keep no secrets from you. But here I am in the middle of a nightmare and all you can do is give me shit."

"Nothing you say makes sense anymore! That scares me!"

"Calm down. You're probably giving yourself a miscarriage right now, if it hasn't happened already. But maybe that's what you want. To get away from me."

An hour later, hoarse from shouting, she had gone upstairs relieved and ready to sleep. He was back to his old self again.

But when one of the detectives called the next day to "follow up"—not a big deal, but did Tim have anyone who could vouch for his whereabouts?—Christine had overheard her husband using that simpering tone of voice, complaining about the harassing phone calls they'd received and asking if it would be possible to have an officer stationed outside the house just in case (the answer had been no). She realized how much she'd come to rely on his defiance, which had pulled them through countless bad times: the collapse of their finances, unresponsive doctors, lousy service in restaurants, past due charges on credit cards. There wasn't anything Tim's hot-headedness couldn't make better. He was so determined, so certain he deserved more than he was getting, that it seemed impossible he wouldn't eventually bend circumstances to his will.

Since being questioned, though, it appeared he had given up. If he was folding in front of the police, whom he despised, what was next? Would he take to his bed and cry the next time a package was delivered late or someone cut him off on the freeway? Was it all up to her now?

"It's a weird situation," Audrey said when Christine stopped by her house after work. "You're going to see a different side of him." They were out in Audrey's yard, which had a pool and an outdoor kitchen but ran parallel to L Street, the central artery of the development. Audrey hardly seemed to notice the steady stream of cars thundering by ten feet from her chair.

"But that side never existed before," Christine said. "I thought I knew him."

"I thought I knew Mark and then he lost his job and got a migraine. Now I'm about to celebrate my twenty-second anniversary with a man I met seven months ago. What I knew was a particular situation, and that situation is over."

"I came here to feel better, Audrey."

"I'm making you feel better. I'm saying that people change. It doesn't mean Tim is a bad guy."

"But I don't *like* this Tim. I just wish there were some way to undo it all. Go back to the way we were."

"Well, you—" Audrey stopped, her lips still parted but her mind suddenly somewhere else. "You just made me think of something," she said, getting up and starting across the yard. "I'll be right back."

She returned a few minutes later with an old book Linda had given her. "Here," she said, handing it to Christine. "I think you should do this."

"Do what?"

"I don't believe it just appeared at a garage sale by accident. Go ahead, look through it and tell me if it isn't eerie."

Too excited to let Christine draw her own conclusions, Audrey chattered on about how Linda had discovered it at Susanna's and hadn't found any information about it, but Audrey had genealogy experience and could surely uncover something, and already she had followed one of the entries, *Good Fortune from Bad*, staying up late the night before after Mark and Jonathan went to bed. With her family background and worries for her husband, those words in particular had spoken to her. All it took was a wooden match, an old letter, an object that had never been indoors, a green glass jar, and a child's toy, which she dug out of a storage bin in the garage. Using only the moon to see by, she fit all of these things together, one inside the other, and slept with them in view. When Mark awakened in the morning, he'd kicked the jar over and everything spilled across the bedroom carpet. "I hope it doesn't affect the outcome," she said. "I'm not sure how I'd know even if it did."

She had taken the book back from Christine and was flipping through it. " 'If You Must Achieve the Impossible,' " she said. "I think this was meant for you."

"I've said too many prayers. I don't want them to conflict."

"Don't worry about that. They're two different traditions." Audrey held the book in one hand and a melting margarita in the other, her bare feet propped on a planter. "Someone took the trouble to record all of this and pass it down to us. That means something."

"You think it does. You don't really know."

Audrey finished her drink and got up. "Wait here, okay? I think I have everything we need inside." She emerged five minutes later carrying two tall white candles, a slightly battered silver ring, a picture torn from a magazine (*a photograph of a stranger*), and a scrap of black cloth, probably from an old T-shirt or a sheet.

"You won't let me go until I do this, will you?" Christine said.

"Find a leaf the size of your hand," Audrey replied, waving Christine toward the fruit trees along the back fence. "It's the only thing we're missing."

"Length or width?"

"Both. If you can find it."

By the time Christine returned with a leaf only slightly shorter and narrower than her hand, Audrey had lit the candles and set the other objects in a straight line on the teak patio table. As instructed, Christine sat in a wicker lounge chair and closed her eyes. At first it was difficult to concentrate. Every few seconds a car went by, there were kids splashing in a neighbor's pool, and she could hear Audrey's son talking on his phone through an open window. But eventually these sounds blended together into a soothing and hypnotic white noise. With quiet prompting from Audrey, she thought of the seemingly impossible things she most wanted to bring about: motherhood, and a life free of the turmoil that had plagued her and Tim in one form or another since their marriage. Peace and a place to call home. It wasn't difficult to envision this life. The difficult part was that she'd been imagining it for years, and it had the vaguely sepia-toned feeling of something once cherished but long lost. A brief love affair from her youth, or an abandoned plan to travel the world.

But her instructions were to think of nothing as impossible, and to bring these visions to mind whenever she saw a burning candle, a silver ring, the color black, a stranger's photograph. After a few minutes of struggling against the idea, she felt herself gradually surrendering to it. It was harmless, not much different from guided imagery, and no worse than all the other things she had done to sway events, the aromatherapy, the meditation, all of the Chinese herbs she had swallowed and the mental games she'd played. *If I like the next song that comes on the radio, I'll get pregnant. When it's time to stop trying, God will let me know.*

When she finally opened her eyes, the sun had dropped behind the mountains. The candles had gone out and Audrey was trying to relight them, shielding them with her hand against a sudden strong gust from the north. "Spooky," she said, "the way they blew out like that, just before you opened your eyes."

"It's only the wind," Christine said. But for the rest of the night, even while she and Tim were lying in bed reading, it made her shiver a little to think of it.

She waited an hour the next afternoon to see the doctor. Usually she spent this idle time lying on her back with her feet perched comfortably in the potholder-wrapped stirrups, looking through magazines and returning phone calls, but today she paced back and forth in the short space between the mirror and the door, steeling herself for the worst. *He's going to tell you it's over. If you say you want to try again, he'll fire you like that other doctor who said you weren't facing reality.*

"Mrs. Mahoney?" Dr. Marsh knocked and cracked the door open.

"Come in," she said, sitting on the edge of the chair.

"How are you?" he said, and grasped her hand. Dr. Marsh was small and hook-nosed with eyes that were too closely set, but all these things together somehow made him look extremely competent.

"A little nervous," she said.

He bustled around, setting down her files, rolling out a stool and sitting down. "So was I until I took a look at your blood tests."

There was a long pause. "What?"

"We should schedule another ultrasound, but right now everything looks great," he said, smiling. "Believe me, I'm as surprised as you are."

Christine felt nothing at all, then she experienced a heaviness horribly akin to disappointment. Not with what the doctor was telling her, but with her own feeling about it. She should be elated—it was the longest she had made it into a pregnancy by more than two weeks—but she reflexively understood that it would add to her anxieties, and the timing was awful. Tim's troubles had managed to spoil a turn of events so wonderful she hadn't thought it *could* be spoiled.

"We're going to be seeing a lot of each other over the next few months," Dr. Marsh said. He talked for several minutes, though she was hardly able to absorb any of it. She would need to continue progesterone treatments, she understood that much. A lot could still go wrong, and of course she would have to be closely monitored, but he was cautiously optimistic that this time might be different.

"Why?" she asked. "Is it something I did?" She thought of sitting in Audrey's backyard the night before, of obediently looking for the color black and strangers' photographs in the hours since. She had even slipped on a Mexican silver ring she hadn't worn since college.

"Who knows?" Dr. Marsh answered. "If I could explain these things, I'd be a deity instead of a doctor."

Walking to her car, stunned by the gravity of the news, Christine felt an intense desire to keep the information from Tim, at least for a day or two. Telling him would be almost like rewarding his weakness and his outrageous insistence that he couldn't remember his actions. More than anything, the situation ignited her distrust in him. Part of him was growing inside her now; this vulnerability magnified the improbability of his memory lapse and made it feel even more worrisome. She drove home, her indignation spliced by flashes of guilt. If only Tim weren't so damn kind sometimes. There couldn't be many husbands who would patiently comb through their wives' hair the way Tim did, hunting down stray gray strands and pulling them out with tweezers and taking it all very seriously. "Hold still, Chrissie. I just found a grove behind your ear."

It seemed like a long time since a tender moment had happened between them, but it had been less than a week.

"We need to get the money back from Arso," Christine said when she walked in the house. Tim was sitting at the kitchen table with coffee and a bunch of contracts. Any thought of coming straight out with the news evaporated when she saw his self-pitying scowl.

"The crazies have my cell phone number. I just got three hang-ups."

"Did you hear me?" she said, dropping her purse on a chair. "Arso. The money. You need to take care of it."

"What are you talking about? How'd your appointment go?"

"Okay."

"I was going to come with you but then you were gone," he said in an injured voice. "I came downstairs and you'd just left."

"I was late."

"What did Dr. Marsh say? I tried your phone but you didn't answer."

"They don't have the results yet."

"They couldn't call and tell you that?"

"Apparently not." She leaned against the counter, the granite edge cold through the fabric of her pants. "Listen," she said. "I've been thinking about this a lot."

"What?"

"I can't—I don't know. I'm not ready to plunge into this surrogate thing. Even if I miscarry."

At first Tim's face was blank, but after a few seconds his mouth turned into a disbelieving smile. "Hold on a minute. You want to fill me in on this sudden U-turn in our lives?"

"I'm filling you in right now."

"Okay. Do I have a voice here, or is that gone along with everything else?"

She raised her arms and let them drop. "Is it that hard to figure out? We're lucky we don't have an armed mob outside our house. You need to hire a lawyer. You can't remember what you do or where you go from one day to the next. And we're supposed to give all our money to a couple of Bosnians in Riverside? Has your judgment gone completely out the window?" She watched his face carefully. She wanted fury, a screaming defense of himself and everything he'd ever done. If he could convince her, they could go upstairs and have frenzied, restorative sex after which they could celebrate their amazing good luck. If Tim only realized how close he was to this kind of outcome.

"Fine."

"What do you mean, fine?"

"Sounds like you've made up your mind," he said, looking back at his paperwork. "Nothing I say is going to change it."

"Try."

He shrugged. "Total waste of time."

"Do you realize how guilty you sound?"

He pushed back his chair and it scraped rudely across the floor. "For fuck's sake, Chris, do you honestly think I murdered that girl?"

"No. But I don't think you're being honest with me."

"Not being *honest*?" He snorted. "You've been around too many bad marriages lately. Maybe you should shut down your practice and go back to organizing people's drawers."

"You're an asshole."

"Yup," he said, flipping through papers, "I am."

"So that's it? You can't understand my point of view at all?"

"Hm," he said with an exaggerated frown and pursed lips. "Let me try to see it from your perspective. I've known my husband since college, he bought me a house, paid for my counseling degree and four stabs at in vitro, gave me everything I ever wanted when he had money, sold everything he owned so we could have a baby, puts up with my freakshow father when he flies into town, pours his heart out to me, and says he loves me five times a day, but he's not being 'honest' about killing somebody. Did I get that right? Is that the kind of demented world you live in?"

Tim was angry now, but it wasn't helping. There was a note of calculation in his words that nearly made Christine panic. He seemed to know the effect she was looking for, and was acting it out for her benefit. It struck her then that she might be imagining it, that she had a kind of prepartum psychosis that had turned everything soothing and familiar into a threat. Given enough motivation or imbalance, the brain was capable of almost anything.

Besides, if it wasn't all in her head, then she'd spent a significant portion of her life being completely mistaken.

"I'm going upstairs to change," she said calmly. "I have two clients to see, so I'll be home around seven. If you could call Arso before then I'd appreciate it."

Her composure seemed to immediately deflate him. "I'm sorry."

"Me, too," she said, turning her back. But the false relief that came with blaming herself lasted for less time than it took to reach the stairs.

Tim had made the bed as always—it was the one chore he could be counted on to take care of—but Christine could see traces of his anxiety in the way the comforter lay, slightly crooked and too long on one side. She straightened it with an angry tug. Yes, he was "a person of interest" in a revolting crime, a bunch of crackpots wanted him dead, and he hadn't sold a house in almost a month, but couldn't the small things stay the same? Could she at least have the solace of an untroubled bed?

As she changed her clothes it occurred to her that something that purported to achieve the impossible might succeed in giving her children and at the same time infect her existence with a thousand unknowns. She'd never considered all the impossibilities a life could contain (and wasn't "impossible" the same thing as "certain," and wasn't there a wonderful comfort in that?), but it was unthinkable that every one of them should come unspun at once. Of course it wasn't really happening—the sky hadn't gone black in the middle of the day. Gravity hadn't stopped. But why shouldn't it? Where was it said that even unchangeable things should continue as they always had?

Either her clients weren't aware of her husband's problems or they were too absorbed in their own to care. She sat through both sessions with her hands resting protectively over her abdomen, fighting the urge to yawn. It seemed absurd that she should have the authoritative club chair while they sat on the hard leather couch in easy reach of the tissues. Neither of them was hiding a pregnancy or living with a murder suspect, which put them miles ahead of their therapist.

On the way home she decided to tell Tim what the doctor had said, not because it was the right climate for it but because it might be the only thing that could shock him into becoming himself again. If impending fatherhood didn't fire up his instincts, he was lost. The house was dark when she pulled up to the curb. Her heart sank with the feeling that he was probably blameless, that she had been hard on him because the situation embarrassed her and because it was easy. Poor Tim. No matter how much they argued, he had always loved her more than anyone else. He would be lying on the couch with his arm over his eyes when she walked in, or standing at the window ready to drop to his knees at the sight of her. She wouldn't be surprised if he had gotten drunk.

"Honey?" Christine said, going from room to room. He didn't answer. She switched on each bathroom light with her heart fluttering, imagining him dangling from one of the shower rods.

He was gone. His car and wallet were missing, and he had left dishes in the sink and his contracts scattered on the table. She tried calling him but his phone rang in the basket by the garage door, its cheery jingle muffled by a stack of unopened mail. She went to the living room window and pulled back the curtain, hoping to see him driving up, but all she saw was an unmarked car—the police, surely—parked across the street. For several long minutes she stood there, watching the man who sat smoking in the driver's seat, watching her.

Eight

Audrey was convinced that the map in the book was of a cemetery somewhere in California. Unlike the rest of the entries, it was a stark, black ink sketch, and that alone gave it a gloomy quality. The curly marks at the edge of the page looked like trees, and the wavy line appeared to be a creek of some sort. The streets were short and circular the way they often are in old graveyards, and there were only a few buildings, which she thought might depict a mausoleum and a small chapel, and maybe a grand old funeral home with a parlor and curved mahogany staircase. It was so vivid in her mind she could almost smell the romantic decay of the place, the dark perfume of the mourners and the wilting lilies. She pictured the area as a lush forest park, strangled under ivy and patrolled by whispering ghosts. It was the kind of setting where she might like to die, when she was very, very old, perhaps from a large branch cracking off a tree and killing her instantly. The cemetery was out there somewhere, she knew it. She was almost certain that if she could track it down, she would discover Mala Rinehart buried on the grounds, surrounded by a mature stand of willows with an enormous marble angel weeping over her plot.

But Mark looked at the map the night before he left for his seminar in Florida and said that Audrey's hypothesis made no sense. First of all, she could forget the willows, as this wasn't Georgia, and ditto the marble angel, as this wasn't France. Also, nobody would draw a map of the cemetery they were buried in, since it would be pretty hard to visit your own grave. While he agreed that the jagged line looked a little like the Santa Ana mountains, that was pure conjecture, and the map reminded him more of a small neighborhood or botanical garden than anything else. Besides, how did Audrey know it wasn't just a sketch that had no significance at all?

"Everything has significance," she said.

"It could be anywhere in the state. In the country, for that matter."

"That's what I like about it."

"Well, I guess if you can find a Civil War soldier in your family, you can find just about anything. Good luck."

Though Linda had discovered nothing about the book, Audrey knew that her research had been perfunctory at best. And then she had simply given it away, pushing it on Audrey as if regifting a useless Christmas present. It was almost midnight and Mark was already in bed, but Audrey knew it would be impossible to sleep without trying to find out more. She might have had a trove of clues had Linda not tossed aside the box of clothing and jewelry and taken only the book, but at least something had survived. It was more than just a tattered little mystery to be solved—it was the most significant sign she had discovered in a lifetime of signs. It made everything that came before—the plastic bags and wrong numbers and concussed birds—seem like what Mark had always said they were: random nothings. Ordinary superstition. Now that she had the book in her possession, she believed she knew the difference.

With the printout of her family tree staring down from the wall behind her computer, she trolled the familiar resources, the websites that had helped her track down not only H. L. Reaney, loyal son of the Confederacy and recipient of the Southern Cross of Honor, but a crooked state senator and a great-great-aunt who had slept with a married preacher, a sin immortalized when the spurned wife delivered their love letters to a Tennessee newspaper. But Mala, it appeared, was more resistant to being located. Rinehart, Reinhart, Reinhardt—no matter how Audrey ordered the letters, the result was the same. If the Internet were to be believed, Mala had never existed. Census records showed small pockets of the surname scattered across the country, but the closest she could get was a Mara Rinehart born in the Wisconsin Territory in 1842 and buried in Benton County, Minnesota, fifty-one years later. There was no evidence of Mala's birth, no obituary, nothing in the Social Security database, no mention of her in any immigration archives. Whoever she was, she hadn't left a trail for a stranger to follow sixty years later. But she had left her book, which might hold the only clue to her existence.

Audrey read carefully, searching for mention of any town, state, or landmark that might place Mala at a particular location in time. There was nothing she recognized, no address or American city, but scattered on various pages, among blotches of dried ink and simple recipes for milk cake and potato soup, she found three words she had never heard and didn't understand. *Vardo. Lachto Drom.* If she could find out what they meant, she might be able to piece a bit of Mala's life together, or learn something that would lead to her.

Vardo, Audrey typed, and watched, with the thrill of discovering the bizarre and unknown, as the page filled with photographs of elaborately carved and decorated wagons. Some were worn-down, their wheels crooked, their walls made of raw wood, but others were like showpieces, with domed roofs, scrolls, brightly painted shutters, and curved stairs leading to the ground. There were as many recent photographs as there were grainy ones from the early part of the previous century. She looked back at the book and reread the sentence in full. *Burn the vardo and all belongings after death.* It had to be a funeral ritual, then, something old-fashioned and tragic, so like the cemetery of her imagination that she almost felt she'd found it.

She still didn't know where Mala was, but now she had an idea of the sort of woman she might have been. It was almost painfully romantic to imagine her wandering the country in a carriage adorned with golden birds and tree boughs, but considering the things she'd written it only made sense. Who else would fill a book with folk remedies and oddly titled spells, and who would draw so many different versions of a horizon? On four separate pages there was a straight line punctuated with trees or cliffs or mountains, and the last showed what looked to be a distant farmhouse. It was as if Mala had spent her life struggling to reach something but never quite made it.

Lachto Drom, Audrey found, meant "safe journey" in a Romani dialect, more evidence that her conclusions about Mala were right. She had never imagined that such a flamboyant culture existed in her own country. It was always something she'd associated with shantytowns and sad children begging in foreign metros, though how she had formed this conclusion she couldn't recall. Television or books. Someone else's ideas having quietly become her own.

The further back Audrey went, the more twisted and obscure Mala's history became. Tribes with strange names—Kalderash, Machwaya—crisscrossed back a thousand years to ancient groups of Indian warriors sent abroad to battle. Wherever they traveled, they picked up bits of language, leaving a hazy record of the countries they'd passed through—Persia, Greece, Armenia. Eventu-ally—the 1300s maybe, not even historians seemed sure—they had arrived in Europe, which wasn't kind to the wanderers with dark skin and a strange language. For hundreds of years they lived as slaves and outcasts, lucky to be banished instead of hanged or whipped. Though wandering was sometimes their only crime, their language and music were banned, the women sterilized, the men shipped off to remote islands to labor in fields. More than a million of them had been murdered in the Second World War. Bound by that tragic history, it seemed impossible that any of Mala's ancestors survived long enough to travel to America, but they had. Once in the United States, they adopted the names and dress of the people around them, staying on the fringes of their new culture, clustering in settlements and caravans. Generations later they still followed ritual purity laws and talked to ghosts in a language almost no one wrote down. Even Mala had written only a few words, as if it were the only secret she didn't dare tell.

Audrey shut off the computer, staring at the empty screen for a while before going upstairs and sliding into bed beside Mark. What she'd started for purely selfish reasons had become something else. There was more to the book than her own signs and superstitions, there was an entire life behind it. She knew now that it hadn't been an easy one.

She saw her husband off just after dawn. "Please don't join a cult," she said, leaning against the door frame, her eyes still cloudy from sleep.

He kissed her. "According to my wife, I already have."

"And don't forget to eat. If the plane crashes, cover your mouth and stay low."

"Okay. I'll call you if I land."

"Funny."

In spite of her nine-day-old affair with William, Audrey felt that her relationship with her husband had been improving. It was a development that bewildered her, though it made her betrayal seem, if not acceptable, then at least useful in some way. She was seeing Mark with fresh eyes. His obsession with eternal life was diminishing into one of those mystifying and humorous male preoccupations, like brewing beer or spending hours on a ham radio in the basement. Somehow, infidelity had succeeded where previous attempts at accepting her husband had failed, if only because she was now too distracted to obsess over the arcane inner workings of his mind. Every time she imagined ending her relationship with William, she decided it would hurt Mark on a practical, day-to-day level and was out of the question. She couldn't go back to governing his every move, calling him in the afternoon to make sure he hadn't choked at lunch.

"Why don't you put video cameras around the house?" he'd once asked. "If I'm going to live in a prison, we might as well do it right." While Mark would never choose to bargain away her faithfulness in exchange for his independence, he had recently noticed that she was "more relaxed" without understanding why. She wondered if she had found the solution: she simply had to split her love between two men in order not to damage them with it.

Audrey watched Mark drive away, her stomach pitching with adulterous excitement. She had three days without her husband, and Jonathan would be spending Saturday night with a friend whose parents she trusted. Though she felt terrible—underslept, nauseated, tormented by images of herself in the bed of someone nearly half her age—there was a thrilling quality to her misery. After years of humdrum conversation, she had reason to use phrases normally used by more interesting people: "I have to see you today," and "I'll try to get away as soon as I can." It was as if snatches of film dialogue came floating from her mouth the moment she started to speak.

That afternoon, she left work early and drove to William's apartment with a housewarming gift, a spider plant to hang in the apartment's only bright corner. She was afraid that one day soon he would refuse to answer the door or she would discover him in bed with a twenty-year-old Target cashier, but so far she had seen no evidence that he was getting tired of her. Every time she decided she had ruined everything by appearing too old, too grasping, or too easy, William would send her a text message asking her to come by. He never seemed to do anything but go to physical therapy, play video games, and wait for her. Whenever she asked questions—gently, matter-of-factly; she'd endured all the agency training—he shrugged and said he'd talked his war experiences to death with the social worker at the hospital. Recently, Audrey had considered the idea that her presence wasn't good for his recovery. If she stopped coming to see him, he would be forced to invite friends over or leave his apartment for human interaction, but instead a pent-up and deeply grateful woman arrived on his doorstep a couple of afternoons a week and usually brought presents.

"Welcome to the neighborhood," she said when he answered the door.

"Is it real?" he asked, holding up the plant by the plastic hook.

"You think I'd bring you something fake?"

"I don't know, I never had a plant before. I'll probably kill it."

"That's okay. Just enjoy it as long as it's alive."

He smiled, and Audrey felt she'd said something poignant and meaningful that only he could understand.

They hung the plant from the ceiling, watered it, cleaned up the brown water that poured onto the linoleum, then went to the bedroom to make love. William kept the television on in the living room most of the time, so no matter what they were doing, it was made slightly cheap or amusing by the background chatter of commercials or breaking news. Audrey had hardly noticed the noise in the beginning—she hadn't been able to hear anything over her own anxiety and ragged breathing—but now that she and William had slept together a handful of times, the television had begun breaking into her consciousness and making everything she did seem vaguely ridiculous. She couldn't arch her back without a group of televised children screaming in delight in the next room. She hoped for some sort of touching theme music, or barring that, silence, which wasn't ideal but had accompanied thousands of forbidden love affairs over the centuries and could be considered classic. But she was exhausted from years of nagging, and afraid that any effort to alter the situation would somehow condemn it. It took all of her nerve to pull back as William was unbuttoning her blouse and say, "What if we put on some music?"

He looked down at her through limp strings of dark blond hair. "All I have is a bunch of crap from the seventies. Albums."

"Sounds good to me."

She followed him to the living room, where a stereo sat on the floor in a linty corner by the sofa. William had all of his parents' old country and folk records, musicians Audrey had never heard of like John Hartford and Tom T. Hall. "You're probably going to hate this," he said, grimacing as the first crackly notes drifted from the speakers, but to her surprise Audrey found the music charming, even romantic. It wasn't Italian opera, but maybe opera wasn't suitable for this kind of affair. The music made the bed's rough sheets and William's nicotine-flavored tongue seem like bits of working-class Americana, the kind of fantasy she had never allowed herself when she was younger because she honestly hadn't realized how quickly she would age. It explained everything: William's eleventh-grade education, his clumsy grammar, the stacks of car magazines on the coffee table. She had been afraid that these things would erode her interest in him, but seen from the right perspective, they became exotic and appealing, the traits that excited her most of all. Though she hardly knew him, there were a few things about him she could say for sure. He would never keep her up late with an exhausting discussion of what his life meant and where it was going. He wouldn't sign up for a men's retreat offering nudity in the forest and drumming meant to restore his wounded masculine spirit. He would never make things more complicated than they needed to be, either because he couldn't or because he'd learned from his unspeakable experiences that it was pointless to do so. Either way, Audrey took his presence as proof that for some people life really could be simple.

By the time she left it was after six. Jonathan would be waiting to be picked up from chess club, and if she didn't hurry she would find him sitting outside the locked doors of the school by himself. She had a voicemail message from Mark, who had survived his flight to Florida, as she had been certain he would, since she'd practically assured his safe passage. Walking toward the parking lot, it passed through her mind that this was nothing but a flimsy justification for moral failings. You didn't prevent havoc by intentionally corrupting your life. You didn't distract fate. How did she know she wouldn't be doomed by some form of comeuppance that might take years to materialize? This morning her older brother Brewster had sent her an email, an unintentional reminder that while she was in California using infidelity as a cure-all, back in Georgia the slow-motion upheaval of her family continued unabated. Written in choppy, telegram-style fragments, Brewster's messages were like dispatches from a remote disaster site: *Mom back in court today—alleges inappropriate touching by the florist, hope he settles before it makes local news . . . Section of my ceiling came down last week, doing yardwork at the time, would have been killed . . . Cousin Glenn's daughter dropped out of college, became Mormon convert, first one in our family and you thought we had no firsts left, lol!*

Bless Brewster, he was the only one of them who still had a sense of humor. He was able to make light of these events because he didn't see them as part of a pattern or the precursor to an all-out collapse, this was just "the way it is," and if he broke his wrist falling in the shower or their grandmother took a drifter under her wing and wrote him into her will, it had no connection to events in years past or to distant cousins running a meth lab in Appling County.

"Audrey?"

She was five steps from her car when she heard a woman call her name. Her heart seemed to stop for a second before throbbing painfully back to life.

"Audrey?" The voice was right behind her now.

She held her breath and turned around. It was Paula, the agency's office manager, wheezing to a low-heeled stop. Today she wore, not one of her plunging shirts, but a prim white top buttoned to the neck.

"You look summery," Paula said, eyeing Audrey's bare arms.

"Thank you!" she said, so shrill her voice rang off her car window. "What are you doing here?"

"We placed two more clients at this complex this week. I thought you knew that. I was dropping off a rental contract on my way home."

"You live nearby?" Audrey asked, just as Paula asked, "Didn't you leave work early?"

They both paused, and then Audrey jumped in. "I was on my way back from the doctor when I remembered that I had a follow-up scheduled."

Paula's small brown eyes nearly vanished when she squinted. "Who'd you see?"

"William Townsley." Even his name sounded sexually explicit. Audrey had left him naked in bed, smoking and fiddling with his cell phone while a scratchy Waylon Jennings record spun around the turntable in the living room. It seemed impossible that Paula couldn't see all of this just by looking at her face.

"Oh, that's right."

"So . . ." Audrey brought her hand up to the front of her blouse and found that the top two buttons were gaping open. After a moment during which her entire low-paid and unfulfilling career flashed before her eyes, she said, "Warm today, isn't it? I'm absolutely burning up."

"You had a follow-up at this hour?"

"Yes, but—I have to go get my son," she said, as if she'd just remembered she had one. "He'll be waiting for me."

"If you're going to schedule home visits during off-hours, ask me and then put it on the schedule."

"I've been at the agency for six years. I know how it works."

"Barbara and Dee have crushes on him, you know. They think he looks like a young Clint Eastwood."

"Do they?"

"I don't see the resemblance at all, with the acne scars and that shaggy hair."

"I hadn't noticed."

"The point is, it's a safety issue. We can't have everybody making their own rules. We need to know where you are when you're on agency business."

"He's not a danger to anyone, Paula."

"He is a client, and with clients we follow protocol. We don't get personally involved." Paula had a slight smile that gave everything she said an edge of derision. It was the same smile she wore when scolding somebody for answering personal communication at the office or leaving leftovers to rot in the breakroom refrigerator, basic infractions that only idiots like Audrey committed.

"Follow-up is personal involvement?"

"It's six o'clock. You've been seen here once before in the last week. We depend on grants and donations. Any appearance of conflict could be damaging."

"There is no conflict."

"But you can see how it looks."

"Why would a twenty-seven-year-old man be interested in me?" Audrey asked, raising her arms out to the side. "Does that make sense to you?"

Paula seemed to realize that the most insulting way to answer this question was to ignore it. "As I remember, you were interested in the fundraising side of things at one point. That would be a promotion."

"I know. And I still think I'd be good at it."

"Maybe, if you could focus on the needs of the agency."

Audrey despised the words "agency" and "nonprofit" and "community outreach" because they reminded her that she'd squandered whatever money-making ability she might once have had. "I focus on the needs of the agency's clients," she said, obviously angry now. "I thought that's what I was supposed to do."

Paula's face was saturated with the glow of victory, or high blood pressure. Either way, she looked delighted with Audrey's reaction. "Of course. Well, it's getting late. I'll let you go pick up your son."

"Okay. Have a nice weekend." Audrey groped for the door handle of her car, lifting it twice before realizing that her keys were still buried in her handbag.

"You look like you're losing weight," Paula said as she walked away. "Congratulations. I have no idea where you get your motivation."

Nine

MAY 22, 1948

The bus to California seemed to stop every ten minutes. It lurched out of Midland at dawn with a rumbling sense of purpose, but this lasted only until the next depot, a tiny outpost in the desert with a stray dog sprawled out front and no real town to speak of. The motor ground to a halt with a disappointing sputter. People got off, people got on, and the bus hunkered under the climbing sun like something that would have to be coaxed into moving again, and when that failed, sworn at and kicked. They had made so little progress that when Mala craned her neck and peered through the window across the aisle, she could see the rippling haze of Midland on the horizon. She'd awakened that morning frightened for the first time since leaving camp. She had seven cents, two days of travel ahead of her, and no promise of finding Ruth. She had been stupid and impulsive, a combination that rarely resulted in happy events. When she looked up at the sky, she saw what looked like proof of her foolishness: a group of vultures spinning in slow figure eights, halfway to the heavens, their eyes glittering as they listened to her hunger pangs and the sound her thoughts made whirling through her head.

The driver seemed in no hurry at all. He smoked and talked out his window in a flat whining voice that carried all the way to the back row of seats. "Don't litter on my bus or I'll throw you off," he had said to her when she boarded, though she hadn't heard him say it to anyone else. She might have been affronted if she hadn't thought of the Greyhound trip she took to Beaumont with Beni, her aunt Drina, and Drina's two sisters-in-law when she was fourteen. The women had taken over the last few rows of the bus, chattering as if their language were a thing to be shown off, making up names for people seated nearby, and flinging peanut shells and orange skins to the floor. Several people plugged their ears with bits of cotton or buried their heads under layers of clothing. Sleep was out of the question. Though Mala had pretended to stare at the passing scenery, she was creating curses in her mind, making them up as she went along and envisioning swift and irreversible outcomes. She must have done something wrong, though, because Drina and her sisters never did turn to sparrows or find their vocal cords frozen, and when they finally skipped off the bus in a flurry of laughter, the driver spit after them and called them whores.

With a burst of black exhaust that clouded the windows and drew gasps from the passengers, the bus started up again. Mala had chosen an old drunk to sit beside in the hopes that he'd be too cross-eyed to give her trouble, but this prediction, like most of them, was proving to have two sides to it. He slept for the next hundred miles. He wore brown trousers with shiny knees and a coat that was much too heavy for this time of year. His head rolled from side to side with the sway of the coach and bumped against the window on occasion without waking him up. They weren't far past Monahans when he popped out of sleep looking cross, as if somebody had thrown him onto a moving vehicle without his approval and turned the sun so it would shine in his eyes. He appeared to look around for a person to blame, then slumped back in his seat. After taking a sip from the brown glass bottle tucked under his leg, he looked at Mala and asked, "Where are we going?"

"California."

He frowned and his whole forehead seemed to fold up. "California!" He leaned forward, asked the passenger across the aisle for confirmation, and began gathering up his things with narrow, trembling hands. The next stop was twenty minutes ahead, and he leapt off the bus the moment it pulled into the station as if escaping the worst decision of his life.

Mala slid into his empty seat, and for three hours no one took the spot beside her. Occasionally she would glance up and meet the unabashed gaze of a child who refused to sleep or color. A pale little girl in the back coughed so often that the sound became almost soothing. The sun blazed against the side of Mala's face, stupefying her with heat and putting her to sleep against her will. "Are we home?" she mumbled when she was jarred awake at El Paso. To ward off self-pity, she plunged into practicalities. She arranged the contents of her bag and brushed her hair. She washed her face in the depot bathroom, got a drink of water from the fountain, and stared with intense longing at the table of paper-wrapped sandwiches by the entrance. In a small, humiliated voice, she offered to buy one with her last few pennies but was waved off. It had always been Beni's contention that propriety and survival weren't a natural fit, so when the woman turned away to make change for a customer, Mala slipped a sandwich into her pocket and walked away, whispering a wish for the woman's good fortune.

The food made her dizzy at first, but after a few minutes her strength returned and she felt better. The bus was about to pull away when there was a pounding noise and the driver braked, throwing everyone's head forward and setting off the baby who had been an angel until that moment. The doors whooshed open to let in not the sandwich seller in search of a thief, but a young man who bounded up the steps and through the aisle toward the only empty spot on the bus. He clobbered someone's shoulder with his knapsack, stepped on a woman's toes, then sat heavily next to Mala so that his seat creaked and the person behind him grumbled.

"Made it!" he crowed, wiping his brow and grinning, and Mala knew that whatever his prejudices might be about people of her kind, they would be quickly overcome by his need to talk about himself.

His name was Billy Cunningham and he was going to California to make his mark. He had driven as far as Fort Stockton and that's where his old car just melted down in the heat and refused to budge another inch. Billy was a comedian, a crack shot, an amateur geologist, and a part-time usher at a movie theater in San Antonio. Everybody said he had the face and personality of an actor who broods and shoots his way through scenes, and this was a valuable quality for which the studios would pay handsomely. Mala knew nothing about movies—the closest she had come to seeing one was when she and Beni were caught trying to sneak through a theater's exit door—but she was willing to take Billy's word for it.

"I was doing a little Chekhov at the local playhouse and there was a talent scout in the audience," he said. "He came backstage and told me to get out to Hollywood without delay. What was he doing in San Antonio? Still a mystery, but it couldn't have been a coincidence."

Though Billy claimed to have a wad of savings that would float him for months, it took no special skill to see he was frayed around the edges. His sock poked through a hole in his shoe and his shirt strained to cover a pair of large, sloping shoulders. Though his features were regular and appealing, the grease in his hair had started to flake, he needed a shave, and one of his eyes was smaller than the other, giving his face a lopsided look.

"Why are you going to Bakersfield?" Mala asked.

"I have a cousin there, likes it all right. Not a lot of sights to see, but he's there to get rich in the oil business. He'll show me around for a couple of days and then I'm on my way to Los Angeles."

While she sat watching him, it came to her as if she were borrowing memories he hadn't made yet. He would never leave Bakersfield; he would get in trouble the first week. Believing a fortune was on the horizon, he would squander what little money he had on whiskey and bets, and his cousin, once he'd wrung everything he could out of Billy, would double-cross him with a woman or move north for work. At first Los Angeles would feel like it was just around the bend, but the city would move farther and farther away like a drifting island, until Billy stopped mentioning it and started taking jobs he felt were beneath him. He would sit through movies with a crushing sense of life's unfairness, heckling the actors, propositioning girls, and getting on people's nerves. After the show was over, he would spill his drink on the floor and leave gum for someone to step in. Billy would make his mark, all right, but not the one he'd intended. He would be known for his raging temper. He would never give up the idea that he was a person of importance, and this would leave him feeling permanently disappointed. He would pass on his jitters and his dreams to his children, who would never shake the feeling that they'd let their old man down.

"I'm sorry," Mala said.

"For what?" It was the first question Billy had asked all afternoon.

She touched his arm. "Nothing."

...

Billy finally talked himself to sleep around twilight. His knapsack was open on the floor, and inside Mala could see a few pieces of rolled-up clothing, a crushed pillow, and a movie magazine. He and Mala didn't have anything in common but they were equally prepared for what lay ahead, which is to say, not prepared at all.

He began to repeat himself near the Arizona border, and his angry streak flared up in Tucson. He returned from a visit to the depot newsstand and men's room to find a stranger in his seat. Mala, who had stepped outside for a breath of air that hadn't been passed around by a crowd of cantankerous and unwashed passengers, got back aboard just as Billy began to raise his voice. "I don't know if you've ever traveled before, but a magazine on a seat means it's reserved."

"I travel all the time," the other man said. "I'm a salesman, and a magazine on a seat means somebody left his trash behind."

Billy was incensed. "Trash! I paid good money for that magazine." He yanked it from the other man's hands. "Now I'm ready to sit down, if you don't mind."

Mala stood a few feet behind Billy, watching him rise up on the balls of his feet in a repetitive jerking motion as he spoke. No one on the bus appeared to notice what was happening; they'd been listening to Billy talk for so many miles that his voice had become a part of the coach's mechanics, like a bit of aggravating engine noise.

"Take my seat," Mala offered.

Billy whirled around. "And give in to this? Like hell I will."

All she had to do was stall him. The driver would be back any moment, and he'd make sure everyone had a seat whether they liked it or not. "I don't mind sitting in the back. It's all the same to me."

But a moment later an old woman one row ahead stood up and said, "For heaven's sake, I'll move. I've never been so put out in my life. I'd rather sit by a sick child than hear a couple of grown men argue with no regard for anybody else. It isn't good for my heart. My doctor says it could give out under any strain at all."

Both men protested, but the old woman didn't want to hear it, the damage had been done and she wanted peace. Dismissing Billy's offer of help, she wrested her overnight bag down the aisle and sat across from the coughing little girl with a resigned sigh, as if she were so tired of bus travel that death would be a welcome break.

Billy reclaimed his seat, but all the triumph had been taken out of it and he fell into a sour mood. He shared his dinner of cold fried chicken and peas with Mala because his appetite had been spoiled. He blamed the other man, who sat in the old woman's place chattering to a young couple about his position as sales manager for a company that sold parts for oil rigs. Before that he'd been in the navy and fought the Japanese in the Pacific. Mala didn't know much about where she was going, but she knew the Pacific was nearby, and the idea that she might see the same ocean as a Japanese soldier was thrilling. "Big deal," Billy muttered as the other man's stories grew bloodier and more fantastic. "I would have enlisted myself but I wasn't old enough." He'd received no apology and believed that his trip had been cursed by his contact with a barbaric country fool.

It took another whole day to get to Bakersfield. The pines and thin air of Flagstaff were a different world, a cool, bright blue place that reminded Mala of nothing but how far she was from Beni, still roasting like a lizard in the desert. How many miles had she traveled, five hundred or more? Beni was too frail and star-crossed to endure that kind of distance. Even under the best of circumstances he barely survived: his joints ached, he fell asleep with candles blazing near his head, he was tormented by thoughts of the bad endings that had come to his relatives, as well as to people he'd never known but had heard stories about. He was petrified of owls. He had lost his singing voice and ability to cheat at cards, giving him nothing to do at night except argue with his neighbors over things that didn't matter. Mala couldn't imagine how he was filling his time and who was cooking for him (certainly not Drina, who blamed Mala not only for her sister's death, but for her lame ankle), or was he simply starving in his trailer, going mad from lack of company? Mala sat stiffly in her seat, seized with the certainty that she would never see him again. But it was hard to tell fear from a prediction, and prediction from coincidence, and coincidence from a hard, aimless world with no plan behind it. "So don't try," Beni would say. "Stop thinking so much and go to sleep."

They drove into the southern San Joaquin Valley that afternoon and got to Bakersfield at nightfall. Before the driver had even braked, everyone gathered up sweaters and paperback novels and baskets of knitting and crumpled handkerchiefs and crowded into the aisle. It wasn't a happy homecoming. No matter where they'd boarded, the women looked exhausted and the men ready for a strong drink. Children who had been quiet for two hundred miles began to sob bitterly. "We're here now, isn't that what you wanted?" a young mother snapped. Mala didn't like what she saw out the window; it was like West Texas all over again except every bit of wildness had been taken out of it. The trees were low and covered with a layer of dust. The moon was a sickly yellow. Even from here she could smell the sewers, the oil rigs, and the fields spread with manure, and the greasy stench of the engine blew in the moment the driver opened the doors.

Billy sighed loudly, peering over the heads in front of him. "What's taking so long?" he kept asking, but nobody seemed to know.

A young boy was finally pulled from under a seat by his ankles and deposited on someone's hip, allowing the crowd to start moving again. Billy was halfway to freedom when the man he'd argued with leapt up from his seat and began shouting, paralyzing the passengers and goading the crying children to hysteria.

"I've been robbed!"

Sometime in the last several hours his money clip had gone missing from his briefcase, which he'd left in the aisle propped against his seat. It could have happened when he was asleep or taking a cigarette break, but it didn't matter because he knew who had done it. He glared at Billy, whose face was dark with anger and a strange look of satisfaction.

"You're crazy," Billy said. "You have no proof."

"You were sitting right behind me," the other man said. "You had a hundred opportunities to take it."

"So did everyone else."

"Nobody was behind me but you."

Billy pointed to Mala, standing a few rows behind him. "She was."

Mala had been accused countless times of things she hadn't done; it was a feature of her life no different from her name or where she was born. In the kitchen where Ruth had taught her to read, the housemaids blamed her for the china they smashed and the food they stole, and her own clan believed she brought the storms that swept through camp every spring, leaving behind knee-deep puddles and at least one capsized carriage with its occupants still inside, clinging like horseflies to the ceiling. Better she'd never been at the center of a crowd that was hoping for the worst, a crowd that, if it couldn't have bloodied noses and a struggle over a loaded revolver, would take the story of a depraved palm reader and vagrant who'd tricked everyone with her polite manner until she was unmasked by the man who'd had the misfortune to sit beside her.

She had just about concluded that jail would have its benefits when the old woman rose from her seat in the back and said she wanted off this instant. "I don't care who took what," she cried over the bedlam. "I've been on this bus two days and I'm not waiting another minute."

The driver, saved from chaos by his feeblest passenger, shouted, "All right, everybody off, one at a time, take it easy, we'll sort all this out . . ."

But Mala knew what it meant to sort things out, and she took off running the moment she stepped on the asphalt. She had tried to race roadrunners when she was a child; it was something to do on August afternoons when everyone else at camp had been felled by the heat. She'd forgotten how good it felt to run like this, numbly, flat out, over railroad tracks and down strange roads, but this time she had to find Ruth, to summon her from an ugly town and a few shadowy memories no matter how grim the odds, because she'd come more than a thousand miles to see her and had no place left to go.

Ten

*P*aige adored California, it was the absolute best thing that had ever happened to her in her entire life. She loved the swimming pool, the palm trees, every single one of the four malls she'd visited, and especially her room, which made her room at home seem like a coffin, one of those plain wood ones meant for paupers. The neighbors' kids were supernice, and she had friended a bunch of them on Facebook. She'd been staying with her father and Linda only a week, but already the mere mention of "Connecticut," "autumn," or "school" was enough to send her into a crumple-faced panic. "I'm not going back there!" she would cry, eliciting a cascade of bribes from her father that might include a water park excursion, PG-13 movie tickets (R-rated if she lowered her voice right now), dolphin petting, or an immediate trip to Sprinkles for as many cupcakes as she could consume without vomiting on the floor of the car.

Peter didn't actually say this about the cupcakes, but that's what it amounted to. Eight months away from his children had transformed him into a man who could be brought to his knees by a few minutes of shrewd whining and a distended lower lip. He parented with a combination of sentimentality and guilt, with heaps of unrestrained affection, funny noises at the dinner table, hyperbolic interest in Paige's stories, stern warnings to watch for runaway cars and strange men, and gram upon gram of sugar. Linda told him he was going to turn his daughter into a diabetic with an unseemly sense of entitlement. Peter defended himself by saying that if she loved someone the way he loved Paige, she would understand what it was like for him. "I love *you* that way," she said, but according to Peter, married love wasn't the same. If it were, she would be powerless to say no to him.

Margaret rang constantly. If she wasn't calling Paige's cell phone or sending text messages so amusing that her daughter read them aloud (*R U alive? Call me!!*), she was on the phone with Linda, giving patently obvious instructions and taking Linda into her confidence. Which was the last place Linda wanted to be.

"I wish I could say nothing's changed since Paige left," Margaret said while she grocery shopped three thousand miles away, "but it's not true. Everyone's getting along very well. Neil and I had sex last night, first time in a month. We finally had a few minutes to ourselves without one of the kids screaming the house down. How are things out there? Is Paige adapting okay?"

"Everything's fine," Linda said. "She's enjoying the change of scene and we love having her."

There were a few moments of background chatter while Margaret ordered a pound of roast beef, then she said in a quiet voice, "Peter's not letting her watch too much television, is he? An hour a week. She should be reading her classics. She'll be expected to discuss *The Count of Monte Cristo* when she goes back to school in September."

"Not to worry, Margaret. We have everything under control."

Of course, Peter *was* letting her watch too much television. The first few days, Paige watched whatever she liked—graphic crime shows, QVC, and *Little House on the Prairie* appeared to be favorites, and she would watch the local news with her father after dinner—but then she started speculating about Jennifer Guthrie and the possibility of Tim's involvement and that was the end of that. It was Peter's only hard and fast rule thus far. Of course, he and Linda talked about Tim after Paige was asleep, because Linda was getting regular updates from Christine, who for the last three days had been positive that she and her husband were under surveillance.

It was, Christine said, like living in the kind of movie she would normally walk out of. It didn't matter where she was, she was convinced that people were staring at her or communicating her whereabouts by talking into their sleeves. It sounded irrational, she knew, but none of her friends understood what it was like to have their husbands interrogated at the dining room table, the place mats sullied by dirty notebooks and the elbows of strange men. The experience had been traumatizing, and instructional. For the first time she understood what it must be like to be paranoid schizophrenic or drug addicted. In the future it might help her be more empathetic in her practice, but for now she would be much happier ignorant and unfeeling.

As if to demonstrate the veracity of Christine's fears, an ominous mood had settled over the development in recent days. The windows at the rec center had been smashed by vandals over the weekend, and a depiction of male genitalia drawn in pink chalk on the back wall of the abandoned security booth like a parting wave. There were sickening whiffs of natural gas everywhere, and no one could say where they were coming from. In a matter of twelve hours a set of Tibetan wind chimes, a breast pump, and a Smart Fortwo had vanished from G Street without a trace. Not all of it could be the fault of visiting hoodlums, which meant that a few of Linda's neighbors or their children might be involved, perhaps trying to further depress everyone's home values in some twisted impulse of spite and self-destruction. It made her wonder why the hell the police were watching Tim, while right under their noses criminals were running around pillaging the neighborhood. Peter blamed it all on teenagers on summer vacation, while Paige seemed to enjoy the upheaval, the gas grill stripped by the side of the road and the accountant from two streets over going house-to-house in search of his screen door. It was a lot better than living in Westport, she said, where the most interesting thing you could hope for was a wild animal incursion.

Her first several days in California, Paige had kept a respectful distance from Linda, minding her manners and behaving like the well-bred young lady she appeared to be. But then, as if she could sense that her stepmother was a repository of secrets, she began to ask a lot of questions. It seemed to come out of the blue. One night at dinner—the last before Peter returned to work after a week off—Paige began to probe her past as only a pampered child with a high IQ can. "What did you do before you met my dad?" she asked, a speck of mashed potato stuck charmingly to her lip. You could do anything to Paige, you could chop off her hair at the scalp and dress her in burlap, and she would still be striking.

"Well, I didn't meet your father until five years ago, so I did lots of things."

"Did you work?"

"Let Linda eat her dinner, honey," Peter said.

"I don't mind," Linda said. "Yes, I worked, I had a small catering business in New York. I was catering a party at a hotel and your father was there." She smiled at Peter but he didn't notice; he was watching his daughter chew with her mouth open.

"Were you ever married?"

"Not until I married your father. I'll never forget how adorable you were, with your flower tiara and your yellow dress." Paige had complained that the dress itched, and to Linda's embarrassment had attempted to unzip it halfway through the ceremony in front of two hundred guests.

Paige let this irrelevant bit of schmaltz pass without comment and dug into Linda further. If she wasn't married when she was younger, did she have boyfriends? Where did she live? What was her family like, and how come nobody had met anyone but her brother? Where was her mom? It went on like this for fifteen minutes until Linda expected Paige to ask if her father was indeed a drunk with dementia who'd been stuck in a nursing home by his overwhelmed children, and if she'd supported herself during a lean stretch with a brief and horrifying foray into the sex trade.

She had never been so happy to have dinner interrupted by a call. "Excuse me," she said, grabbing her phone and escaping to the kitchen. She almost hoped it was Margaret, who could occupy at least an hour talking first to her, and then repeating almost everything to Peter before asking to speak to her daughter. But tonight it was Audrey, calling to discuss the one thing that could make Linda crave a return to the dining room table. "You know that book you gave me?" Audrey said.

"Which book?" Linda asked, though she knew very well.

"The one you found at Susanna's. Christine and I were playing around with it last week, and she did the spell about achieving the impossible. Anyway, now she—well, she thinks it might have had some unintended consequences."

Linda felt a stab of alarm. "Come on. That stuff doesn't work."

"You didn't try it, Linda. Just look at her life over the last several days. If that's not the impossible coming true, I don't know what is."

"What's impossible about surveillance?"

"She's pregnant, didn't she tell you? For the first time, she's made it to eight weeks without a miscarriage. All together it's pretty strange, don't you think?" Audrey didn't sound the least bit concerned about Christine or unintended consequences. If anything, she was practically breathless with excitement.

"I'm not sure. Is it?"

"Of course it is. You got my voicemail, didn't you? About all the information I found?"

"I think I deleted it by mistake."

But of course she had gotten it, had listened for what felt like ten minutes while Audrey described the story of a countryless culture, the pictures of old wagons in England and Hungary, an entire dreadful and flamboyant history brought to life—and death—in a few hours of research. Hearing the passion in Audrey's voice, Linda almost wished that she'd been the one to investigate the book's stranger passages, but that would have meant taking it seriously. Or maybe she had taken it too seriously, letting it scare her into thinking it would make a difference. Obviously, it had made no difference at all. She took Paige's presence in her house to mean that everything was not as it should be, and therefore the book had done nothing for her. Though she had expected this result, she'd followed the instructions anyway because there was always a sliver of doubt, even with the most settled things. Now she didn't know what to think. Had she not given the thing enough time to work—patience, after all, had been one of the requirements—or had she, like Christine, exposed herself to unforeseen repercussions that might knock her world off kilter at any moment?

"I'll forward you everything in an email," Audrey said.

"Do that."

"Listen, the other reason I'm calling is because I'm planning a little trip and I want you to come."

I'd love to, Linda nearly said without thinking. If it gave her even a few hours of independence, she would have a difficult time saying no. "Where are we going?"

"We—the three of us—are going to Bakersfield next Saturday to do a little digging."

"Bakersfield? Why there?"

"The book came from there, Linda. Haven't you been listening? If we're going to find Mala, then that's where we need to start."

Equestrian camp: it was the perfect solution to the first week alone with Paige. Linda felt a tremendous rush of relief when she thought of it; not only did Paige miss her dressage lessons at home—that was all she missed, good riddance to everything else including her mother—but a day camp would limit their time without Peter to approximately one hour in the morning and one in the afternoon. Linda had it all figured out. Awkward silences and accidental meetings in hallways could be avoided if she planned in advance. The time in the car would be filled with phone calls and satellite radio, leaving only breakfast to manage and, if she was lucky, a short interval at the house before Peter returned from work. She could occupy this time with meals, television, and a hot shower for Paige. The next week and the week after that were still mysteries, but she had seven days to ponder that problem, and in the meantime California might lose its imitation gold luster, making Paige violently and irreversibly homesick. It was still early in the summer. Anything could happen.

The first breakfast without Peter was a disaster. Linda rose early to make sour cream waffles, shirred eggs, and freshly squeezed orange juice, but Paige claimed to be too nervous to eat, and after swallowing one bite at Linda's urging, she gagged over her plate. Though it might have been nothing but a performance, a reminder that Paige would determine the success of any maternal efforts, Linda had no choice but to respond with sympathy. "That's okay, go ahead and get dressed," she said, feeling a combination of pity and exasperation as she dumped an hour of her life down the disposal.

In a matter of fifteen minutes Paige's mood shifted, and she was cheerful and talkative on the way to camp. She had already done some asking around and had heard about a private school a few miles north that she'd decided would be the perfect alternative to her school back East. It was called the Brandt School, and Emily from down the block had a friend who went there. "Can we drive by it before we go to the stables?" Paige asked. She sat in the passenger seat wearing the riding regalia her mother had overnighted from Connecticut—knee-high leather boots, heavy breeches, a vest, and gloves—looking like she was on her way to a fox hunt. Her helmet and English saddle were in the trunk.

"I don't think we have time this morning. Maybe later?"

"Maybe later is another way of saying never," Paige said matter-of-factly.

"Well, the schools out here aren't really on the same level," Linda said.

"As mine?" Paige snorted. "A fifth-former got pregnant last year."

"What's a fifth-former?"

"She has a year to go before she graduates. At least she did until she had a baby."

Linda hated the lingo of prep schools, which Margaret used constantly. Her children and every member of her family down to her bipolar cousin had been to Saint this or Academy that, and holiday conversations inevitably deteriorated into recollections of beloved headmasters and crew races and freak campus accidents that always seemed to start with a harmless prank and end with an icy pond. Once, Margaret had asked where Linda had gone to school and when she replied, "Glens Falls High," Margaret pulled her eyebrows together in the middle, touched Linda's hand and said, "Really? That's wonderful," as if Linda had spent her teenage years in the ghetto teaching poor black children to quilt.

MacCallum Stables was a bucolic collection of barns of varying sizes and corrals that backed up to one of the area's "golden hills," if dead grass could be called golden. The largest barn was also the closest to the parking lot, and the entrance was clogged with young girls and the women who could still afford to spend the day shuttling them to expensive activities. The smell of hay and leather and manure was overpowering. Linda wished she had joined her stepdaughter in boycotting breakfast.

"Where do I go?" Paige said in a small voice, her saddle draped over her arm. She seemed so unusually timid, Linda wondered for a moment if she was putting it on.

"I'll find out," she said. She stopped a helmeted woman with short red braids and was directed to another barn a few hundred yards away.

"We should have left earlier," Paige said. "I bet everybody's already there."

"Maybe not. I'm sure it won't matter either way."

"You don't ride, so how do you know?" She took off walking ahead of Linda, her thin arm barely keeping the saddle from grazing the ground.

It was at moments like this that Linda wanted to ask Margaret and Peter what they'd done wrong. Did they realize their mistake? She had cooked meals for her father and brother from the time she was thirteen, she'd made her father's bed every day and tiptoed into his room when he was asleep to make sure he was breathing, she'd sat by the window on winter nights waiting for his headlights to sweep the driveway in that reassuring arc that lit up first the mailbox and then the hedges, she'd gotten nothing from him but the ability to find trouble and then claw her way out of it, yet she had never spoken to him the way Paige had spoken to her just now. It hadn't been a testament to her father's ability to command respect, but something else: her insane fear that everything hinged on her actions, every event, the movement of every atomic particle. The idea that a single thing said or done thoughtlessly might be enough to suffocate her father in his bedcovers or keep the snowy driveway dark and empty.

But what did Paige know of all that? The divorce had made her unhappy, she disliked her stepsiblings, but she wasn't expected to prop up the world, she could speak sharply to her parents and toss her mother aside, and when she was done, eat a huge helping of dessert and sleep soundly. And what was wrong with it? It was what everyone should want for her: the childlike prerogative to take everything important in life for granted.

The intermediate ten-to-twelve-year-old group was still having boots zipped and hair yanked into ponytails by mothers when Linda followed Paige into the smaller barn. "See?" Linda said. "You're early." But Paige wasn't listening. She was already asking another girl if they would be able to choose which horse they rode for the week, or if this was a decision that would be imposed on them by instructors who knew nothing about their preferences or abilities.

Linda introduced herself to the instructor, stood around for a few minutes listening to mothers talk about nothing that would matter in ten minutes time, and with a wave that Paige might have missed, she left. She ran errands, then spent the afternoon shopping, drifting through stores, trying on clothes that somewhere over the Pacific had picked up a thousand-dollar price tag. How did that happen? she wondered, tossing a wisp of a blouse onto the velvet bench in the dressing room. Who had made such a stupid decision?

All of a sudden it was time to get Paige, and she was twenty minutes away. She drove too fast but was still late. When she arrived at the stables, Paige was sitting on the curb at the end of the parking lot, minus a saddle, her boots dusty all the way to the knees. She got in the car and shut the door without a word.

"Sorry, honey," Linda said. "Traffic."

Paige pulled the elastic out of her ponytail and shook her head violently. Horse hair flew around the car and settled slowly on the seats and dash.

"How was it? Did you have fun?" Paige gave a few one-syllable answers and went silent. It seemed to take forever to get home.

After dinner, Linda was in the kitchen doing dishes when she heard Paige's raised voice over the sound of the running water, and Peter's low, insistent responses. By the time she turned off the faucet to listen, the voices had stopped and Paige was clomping by on her way up the stairs. A few minutes later Peter came in. "What happened today?" he asked.

"What do you mean?" Linda said, turning and drying her hands.

"Why did you rush off this morning? I don't know if you noticed, but Paige was upset. She wanted you to see her ride."

"It's not like I abandoned her, Peter. I left her there to make friends and enjoy herself. I thought that was the point of a day camp."

"This isn't about the day camp," he said, his clipped words the only sign of his frustration. "It's about Paige wanting to have a relationship with you."

Linda let her hands drop to her sides. "That's fine, but it would be nice if I weren't expected to read minds."

"Nobody's asking you to. Just be aware of her. I think she wants your approval."

"Honestly?" Linda said, nearly whispering. "I don't like how she speaks to me sometimes. Interrogating me the other night at dinner. Using a sharp tone of voice. She does it with you, too, and you let her get away with it."

He crossed his arms, sighing in a way that seemed to acknowledge this point. "Try to give her a break. She's had a hard time lately."

"She has two sets of parents running around like imbeciles trying to placate her. That's a hard time?"

"All right. Just do me a favor and talk to her tonight. She's only been here a week and I don't want this to mean more than it should."

"Well, it means nothing to me."

"See if you can change that." He smiled and squeezed her shoulder.

At ten-thirty Linda stopped by Paige's room and went through the motions of an apology. Paige had obviously been schooled in how to accept an "I'm sorry" without giving one in return. "It's okay," she said, turning over. "Would you leave the door cracked and keep the hall light on?"

Peter was sitting up in the dark when Linda came into the bedroom. "How'd it go?" he asked.

"She hardly seemed to care. I think it embarrassed her that I brought it up. I wish you hadn't asked me to do it, frankly."

"She's going to act differently with you," he said, sliding down under the duvet. "You haven't spent that much time together."

"Well, I'm going to watch her ride tomorrow, so that should be the end of it."

"Good."

Peter's breathing soon became deep and even. Linda lay awake, her anger slowly being eaten away by remorse. Paige had wanted to impress her, and she'd hurt her feelings. It was such a normal familial incident, it seemed almost impossible that she and Paige had been part of it. Shortly after her marriage she had developed a very specific opinion about her stepdaughter, and hadn't revised it since. Maybe Paige was changing as she got older; of course she was. But that was the puzzling thing—Linda wasn't sure she wanted her to change. It would likely mean a muddled transformation of their relationship, unpleasant talks and the divulging of feelings, and even then it might come to nothing more than confusion and disappointment. Above all, it sounded tiring. All of that effort and emotional maneuvering. The mere thought of it made Linda so weary that she finally fell into the sleep that had eluded her for an hour.

She opened her eyes in the middle of the night. By the clock, it was just before three. The room was dark and silent, but she felt instantly alert. Peter was snoring gently. Linda lay without moving, searching for whatever had jolted her awake. Was it a distant siren? A scream from outside?

She was beginning to relax and drift back toward a dream when she was struck by a thought that seemed irrefutable: it was she who was being watched, not Tim. She couldn't believe it hadn't occurred to her before. Tim was still just a suspect, but the crime she had committed was a fact. Half her lifetime wasn't long enough to escape it. Once, it had felt like something that could be erased if she straightened herself out, if she moved so far from it in thought and action that she reduced what had happened to a kind of abstract, a road not taken. What might have happened, if. But part of her had known it would lie in wait for some future decade of her life, until a quiet autumn day, or an ordinary Wednesday evening when she was preparing dinner, and there would be a knock at the door or a phone call. The passage of time had made her more complacent, but not safer. A dead person could afford to be patient. They could wait as long as it took.

Stricken by this thought, Linda turned over to find that Paige had crawled into bed sometime during the last few hours. She felt a laugh rise in her throat. That was all it was—no siren, no surveillance, just a little girl lying beside her. Paige was wedged between her father's body and Linda's, asleep on her back, her head on the second pillow Linda never used. Her mouth was open and her nightgown had twisted tightly across her narrow chest. Linda moved as carefully as she could toward the edge of the bed, but stopped when

Paige moaned in her sleep. A moment later Paige's hand drifted over and came to rest on her arm.

"Paige?" Linda whispered. "Paige?"

She didn't wake up. Linda lay still, her legs frozen in a painfully uncomfortable position until it was nearly dawn and she had no feeling in her hip. She slid down to the end of the bed and managed to get her feet on the floor without waking either Paige or Peter. She walked down the hall to a dark, empty guest room and crawled under the sheets. It felt like a hotel room—bland, cold, reassuring. She was asleep in seconds.

Eleven

$\mathcal{S}$o far Christine had none of the symptoms associated with pregnancy except mood swings, which made the situation with Tim feel alternately like a nightmare and a comedy of errors. Though she was convinced her husband was innocent of murder, her feelings about everything else felt fluid, even distorted. It wasn't only her constant awareness of the police, who made no secret of their presence, littering the street with their cigarette butts and their fast-food wrappers. She had developed a gallows humor, as well as a doleful eye that could turn the sight of a crushed snail shell on the sidewalk into a microcosm of life's savagery. She had a nearly uncontrollable urge to scold her clients for their weaknesses, yet she rooted for fictional criminals on television, hoping they would get away with it. She wondered if this warped viewpoint was related to her condition, or if she was simply trying to adapt to recent events and not doing a good job of it. Either way, she and Tim seemed to have the opposite reaction to everything that happened. Though he found the possibility of surveillance so demeaning it was difficult to bear, Christine decided it was comforting that no email vigilante would be able to follow them or break into the house without being seen. It was the silver lining of being suspected of something unspeakable: they were disgraced in front of their neighbors, their freedom and privacy had been stolen, but in practical terms they were safer than ever.

Tim's problems had given Christine the one thing she'd never consistently been able to claim during her marriage: the high ground. At least where Arso was concerned, Tim couldn't say he hadn't brought the situation on himself. The night that Christine came home to an empty house, Tim had gone to see Sofija and Arso with the intention of correcting at least one of his recent mistakes. It hadn't gone as planned. First, he had asked nicely for the deposit, then he pleaded, then he beseeched Sofija, and finally he threatened both of them with arrest, a lawsuit that would result in the loss of their properties, and deportation. But Arso was a legal immigrant with a job and American-born children. He knew his rights. He and Tim had a valid verbal agreement, and the deposit was nonrefundable. Arso remained perfectly calm while Tim spent an hour foaming at the mouth in his foyer, and then, in the most insulting send-off imaginable, wished Tim good luck and a pleasant evening.

In the days since, little had changed. Tim and Christine had shared a few minutes of untempered joy when she revealed what Dr. Marsh had told her, but Tim's worry about supporting a child had quickly taken over, resulting in a string of obscenities directed at Arso for stealing his money and at "banksters" for snuffing out the real estate business. Though he accompanied Christine to her ultrasound with great excitement, it was ruined by a glance from the receptionist, which he interpreted as knowing and hostile. Sinister emails continued to trickle in at his work address. People drove by once in a while and peered at the house. Detectives watched from drivers' seats and, as Christine noted one morning on her way to work, occasionally fell asleep, head thrown back, barrel chest nearly flush with the steering wheel. Nothing was determined one way or the other. It was beginning to feel like a chronic condition, a disease of circumstances. It had been only a few weeks and already she knew without thinking to pull the blackout shades on the first floor at twilight and to brighten everything she said to keep Tim from sinking into gloom and self-pity. For the first time, she saw what was perhaps the only benefit of moving two dozen times before she turned eighteen: she had retained a bizarre, almost mindless tendency to adapt, to take what was handed to her and carry on.

Christine was making coffee one morning when the police called Tim and asked him to come down to the station for a talk.

"About what?" she asked when he hung up.

"I don't know," he said, dropping his cell phone onto the kitchen table with a bang. "They probably want to try electric shocks to see if I'll confess."

Christine laughed, and Tim gave her a hurt look. "I'm sorry, honey," she said, her smile fading. "I thought you were joking."

"I was. It wasn't the kind of joke you're supposed to find funny."

Twenty minutes later he left, his spine sloped just enough to give Christine a feeling of desolation. "I love you," she said, with an intensity she hadn't expressed in a long time.

"Me, too," he said, and shut the door without looking at her.

She spent the rest of the morning on the phone with an insurance company over an unpaid claim and counseling two sisters who couldn't agree on the fate of their deceased father's house. In her free moments the same question kept rising in her mind, obscuring all other thoughts. How well did she know her husband, really?

How well could you know anyone? She and Tim had dated for two weeks at the end of their senior year in college and hadn't spoken again until their fifteenth reunion, where they had been among the few people who were still single. Though he had slept with scores of women, five just in their graduating class, all he wanted now was to settle down. After an impulsive marriage at a cheesy Bahamas resort, they had plunged into life together as if there were no other option but to follow two popular but unproven ideas—marriage and children—and see where they led. Although she'd had no reason to, she assumed the best would happen. Everyone did, didn't they? Nobody planned for a tragic decade. But through those troubled years, she'd always had Tim. And she *had* known him, hadn't she? There was nothing of his personality that she hadn't experienced or seen ripped open. All of those talks they'd had about the stars—how minuscule human beings were, how they might be the consciousness of the universe, each person a tiny expression of whatever strange force was behind everything—no one could say he hadn't let his wife see his soul. Through all that, what part could he have kept hidden? Of course it was possible to stop knowing someone, but could it happen so quickly, in sixteen days?

The questions were maddening. Christine was sure of only one thing: their relationship had changed. Now she wondered if their life together was wishful thinking, a script she had written for herself and Tim that imitated reality but had little to do with it. It was too late now, though, she was in it. It might be a created reality, but it was hers.

Christine had been home from work only a few minutes when the doorbell rang. She parted the dining room curtains and looked out the window. The dark sedan that had been parked at the corner fifteen minutes before was gone. On the doorstep stood a heavyset woman of about fifty wearing suit pants and a blazer.

"He's not here," Christine said when she opened the door.

"Hello," the woman said, smiling, unruffled. "Christine Mahoney?"

"You know who I am."

"Can we talk for a minute? I'm Detective Warner. I'm working on the Jennifer Guthrie case."

Christine turned and walked through the hall and into the living room, her throat tight with fear. There was that thought again, the one that flared up with every unexpected incident or bit of bad news. Why had she let Audrey talk her into tampering with her life? The situation with Tim could be exactly the same and she would at least have the peace of knowing she wasn't at fault for it.

She and the detective sat on opposite ends of the couch. Christine didn't offer her anything to drink because she wanted her to go away as quickly as possible.

"I'm very busy," she said.

"Then I'll get straight to the point. Does your husband have any children from a previous relationship?"

It was all Christine could do not to throw something. "Why don't you ask him?"

"I'd like to ask you, if you don't mind."

Christine hesitated. The way the detective looked at her—expectantly and with a hint of malicious glee—suggested a trap. She was afraid that no matter what she said, the answer would result in something terrible she couldn't anticipate.

Detective Warner grinned and raised her eyebrows. "Any children? You would know that, wouldn't you?"

"Yes, of course. He has no children."

"Nieces or nephews in the area? Either you or your husband?"

Christine shook her head.

"Okay. That's what I thought, and the reason I ask is because we have some additional information we're trying to follow up on. Someone saw a man they believe was your husband sitting in his car near the park with a young child. This was two or three nights before the murder we're investigating. Does that make any sense to you?"

Several seconds passed. Christine's throat was dry. "None."

"No ideas?"

Her mind whirled. It was as if she had just been told that Tim liked to dress in women's clothing or videotape dogfights. It was getting absurd, outside the bounds of what she could listen to without laughing or losing her mind. If the police couldn't corner Tim with the evidence they had, they probably weren't above creating witnesses and false leads and springing them on her to see what she might blurt out when Tim wasn't around to defend himself. If defending himself was possible anymore.

"What does this have to do with Jennifer Guthrie?"

"She was the nanny for two three-year-old boys. We just want to rule out any connection between the children and your husband."

"It wasn't Tim. That's the only thing I can suggest."

Detective Warner swept the room with a violating glance, as if every object she saw was hers to desecrate, toss aside, turn upside down in her search for the truth. "I know we've asked this before, but do you remember where Tim was the night Ms. Guthrie died?"

"Of course I do. He was working."

"And a few nights before that?"

"Same thing, probably. I don't know. I don't keep a log."

"Do you have proof that he was working on either night? Did he make a phone call or see anyone who could help us clear him? I know you want this to be over as much as we do."

These words, so falsely solicitous, drove Christine to a quiet fury. "There's nothing I haven't already told you. When you find my husband's DNA on that girl's body, give me a call," she said, getting to her feet.

Detective Warner stayed seated. "You don't want to talk to us?"

"I'm talking to you right now. I've told you everything I can."

"All right, then," she said. "Thanks for your time."

Christine showed the detective to the door and shut it with a curt little slam. After changing her clothes, she made tea and sat down at her desk to transcribe notes from the day's sessions. She didn't think about Tim once. But when she heard the deep hum of the garage door opening, she felt her body prepare for battle. She began to sweat and a sharp ache pierced her left temple.

"Hi," Tim called, walking through the kitchen and directly upstairs. Christine followed him to the bedroom, where he stood at the dresser with his back to her, unfastening his cuff links.

"How are you feeling?" he asked without turning around.

"Pretty good. A little tired."

"To be expected, huh? I'll give you a backrub later."

She leaned against the doorjamb, gathering her strength. "I see they didn't arrest you today," she said with a little laugh.

"Nope," he said flatly.

"What happened? You never returned my call."

He shrugged. "Nothing. Same old shit."

"Well, I got a visit from a detective a few hours ago. By now maybe you've heard about—"

"Can I have a minute to relax here?" he said, his wide shoulders going rigid. "It's been a long fucking day."

"But I—"

"I said I don't want to discuss it right now."

"You can't just talk over me. You can't shut this out."

"Shut what out?"

"Are you seriously asking that?"

He took off his watch and set it carefully on the dresser beside his cuff links. "You don't want to know how my showings went? I had two of them. I mentioned them this morning at breakfast."

"I know you did."

She almost apologized but quelled the urge. How many times had she apologized to Tim—to everyone she had ever met—without even knowing why? "But first, tell me why the police made you go down there. It's getting pretty stressful, you know, all these surprises. This should be the happiest time in our lives and instead we're being hounded."

"Complain to the cops about it, then."

He took off his tie and shirt and disappeared into the closet. A minute later he came out wearing a T-shirt and shorts. His plastic flip-flops slapped the carpet.

"She asked me if you had any children," Christine said.

"Yup. They asked me the same thing."

"And?"

Tim's entire body sagged with exasperation. "*And?* Can I go have a beer now? I've been looking forward to it all afternoon."

"Why are you so upset?"

"Christ's sake. How would you feel? You don't know me well enough, you have to ask me all these questions?"

"But I didn't—"

"Chrissie. You did."

As he tied the string of his shorts, she noticed his fingers trembling and felt a sudden swell of pity. She was tormenting him. So he couldn't prove where he'd been for ninety minutes in all the time she had known him. If asked, could she? It was true what he'd said: he had helped her through the worst of life—sickness, death, melancholy. He had never complained. The night she fell asleep on the bathroom floor during her second miscarriage and he carried her to bed and cleaned up the blood she left behind—did that matter at all? She owed him her home, her sanity, the child growing inside her, but when he needed her, she could muster only self-absorption and mistrust. What was wrong with her that she was so intensely dependent on him and in the same instant so cruel? Was this just another impossibility to add to the thousands that might pile up before she undid the book's damage, if it could ever be undone?

She rose and wrapped her arms around his broad, suntanned neck. "I won't do it again," she said. "I promise."

He felt stiff and unresponsive and his hands exerted almost no pressure on her sides.

"All right," he said, the faintest tenor of satisfaction in his voice. "That would mean a lot."

He turned and went downstairs. Christine stayed in the bedroom, fighting the feeling that somehow Tim had won and she had lost, though what she had lost, she couldn't say.

Twelve

*T*here had not been a cloudy day for weeks, which made Saturday's dark, turbulent skies and buffeting winds feel to Audrey like an unmistakable sign. She would discover something in Bakersfield today, circumstances would align to create an outcome that couldn't be retrieved if she waited. That was how events happened. One step to the left and an entire generation was killed in the womb. If H. L. Reaney hadn't survived the Civil War, then her great-great-grandfather would not have existed, and on and on through the years to include her and her son, who, in less fortunate circumstances, would have been just one of an immense number of tragically unborn children.

As she got ready, she kept expecting to electrocute herself or slip in the shower. When neither of these things occurred, she expected a dead battery and a moving van parked at the end of her driveway. But her car started right up, and she drove unimpeded into the street and down to Christine's house, where she pulled over to the curb and blasted her horn.

Christine, who felt queasy, grumbled a hello and took a seat behind Audrey. "Don't back into the cop car," she said, slipping on a large pair of sunglasses. "Actually, you know what? Go ahead. Hit him."

Linda was cheerful, happy to take a break from entertaining a ten-year-old and interested to see more of the surrounding area. "Bakersfield isn't known for its scenery," Audrey told her.

"At least it will be something new," Linda said.

Audrey had hoped that Linda would offer to drive everyone in her big white BMW, but as a poor substitute she'd made a home-made lunch: free-range grilled chicken sandwiches with garlic bell pepper spread and tropical fruit salad. Audrey had been looking forward to McDonald's or Chili's, but she thanked Linda profusely, as if she didn't get enough whole grain crap at home. The least Linda could have done was make Mala's milk cake recipe. It had taken Audrey ten minutes to type it out and email it to her, and her intention, though not actually put into words, had been clear.

"So, you know where we're going?" Linda asked.

"The Westchester neighborhood, one of the oldest in Bakersfield. I printed out a map. Not sure what we'll find when we get there, but it'll be interesting."

"Who lives in the house now?"

"I don't know. Susanna couldn't tell me."

"I hope they can tell us more about Mala," Christine said. "You found a lot of history, but we don't know much about *her*."

"Well, I think we can assume that she was a fortune-teller of some kind, although those people didn't usually write anything down. That makes the book unique."

"If they didn't write anything down, how do we know she was a fortune-teller?" Christine asked.

"Who else would write a book like that?" Linda said.

"Most of them didn't know how to read," Audrey went on. "They didn't even go to school. It was against their culture. And you could never find out who their ancestors were, because when they got to this country, they got labeled as Native Americans or Jews and they just scattered all over the place. Totally untraceable."

"I don't understand," Christine said. "This woman couldn't write, but she wrote a book. She's untraceable, but we're driving to Bakersfield to find her."

"Good point," Linda agreed.

Audrey looked at Linda, then glanced into the rearview mirror at Christine. "We have to try, don't we? Even if it doesn't work out? Anyway, how long's it been since any of us went on a road trip?" she asked, raising her eyebrows. "Right?"

Linda turned her head and stared out the passenger window at the bald hills. In the rearview mirror Audrey saw Christine close her eyes. A few moments later she dropped her head back against the seat as if she were being kidnapped and had just now decided that she wouldn't fight. She would simply give in and hope to escape when they stopped for gas. Audrey wished that she'd invited William instead—he seemed like the kind of person who would need nothing more from a five-hour excursion to Shitsville than a few minutes of wanton sex in a grimy motel. Well, if she couldn't have him along, she could approximate his presence with the CD he'd made for her. She reached into her purse and felt around for it. There it was, *70s country*, written across the disk in black ink.

The first song, "For the Good Times," succeeded in drawing Christine out of her pregnant half slumber in the back. "What the hell?" she muttered.

"You like it?" Audrey said, tapping her fingers against the steering wheel in time with the bass.

"No."

"William made it for me. We've been listening to a lot of this stuff lately. There's something kind of romantic about it, don't you think?"

She could feel Linda looking at the side of her face. "How's that going anyway? You're still—seeing him?"

"I'm awful, I know," Audrey said, failing to suppress a smile. "But it feels kind of like . . . a *reward* for everything I've gone through in my life. I've taken care of other people for a long time, now I'm finally doing something for me."

"Adultery's not a spa," Christine said, and she and Linda laughed.

"It's not adultery," Audrey retorted.

"What is it, then?"

Audrey hesitated, trying to find the words. "My own life, I guess. Something I don't have to share. Mark was at a seminar for four whole days last week and hardly called me. He has his blog and his life extension friends and I have this."

Both Christine and Linda were silent for a minute, then Linda said, "We all get through however we can."

"Yup, we do," Christine sighed, stretching her legs across the seat.

Bakersfield rose out of the desert like a junkyard of billboards and strip malls, closed off on one side by a smoggy range of mountains and on all others by feedlots and oil fields. Audrey was surprised to find it oddly charming. There was something moving about a city that had persevered in spite of a terrible location and the pervasive stench of fertilizer and industrial smoke. You couldn't help rooting for it. Every tree she saw displayed the scrappy power of nature, skinny trunks sprouting from broken sidewalks, their branches spreading lushly over graffitied bus stops and empty parking lots.

They looked like they couldn't wait for human beings to go extinct so they could confiscate the place.

The house was still three miles away, but already Audrey felt the excitement that comes with not knowing how something will turn out. Maybe it was part of being a Reaney, this ability to find suspense and interest in unsettling circumstances. Growing up, problems in her family had been so numerous that an uneventful day was viewed as a letdown. When her grandfather vanished for a week when she was nine, it had been less a family crisis than a fascinating development about which even the smallest child was encouraged to offer a hypothesis. Did the signs point to a mental breakdown? Was Granddad dead? Was there any reason to believe he'd gone hunting?

"I don't care what happened," her mother said. "What kind of half-wit wanders off without telling anybody the number of his bank account?"

"How far could he have gone?" Audrey asked her father.

"On foot, or in a stranger's car?"

Audrey thought a while. "On foot. Grandpa says never to get in a stranger's car."

"All right," her father replied with a frown of interest. "Let's get out the map and see what we come up with."

Audrey and her brothers had hoped that their grandfather had been taken to space to be used in important but gruesome experiments, and were sorely disappointed when he appeared alive and drunk and wearing a turquoise bracelet at his ex-wife's house in north Florida, about where Audrey's father estimated he would end up if he traveled on foot for a while and then rented a car. Audrey's mother lamented that he hadn't run off with a rich widow, a move that could have benefited everyone, if only he had stopped and thought of others. Years later it occurred to Audrey that she must have been raised by maniacs to harbor such unkind thoughts about her grandfather, to crave the most complicated in life because the least was too anticlimactic.

The house that Susanna's mother had owned sat four doors down from the corner on a middle-class street of bungalows, solid, humble homes where Audrey imagined people had eaten and slept and died for the last hundred years. It had felt important to come here, to respect the book and expect everyone else to as well, but the plainness of the neighborhood and the cars parked at the curb made her thoughts seem foolish. Christine must have felt something similar because she said, "Shouldn't we have talked to Susanna's mother first? She's the one who found the box."

"She's dead," Audrey said, slowing down to look for house numbers. "She only lived here for five years anyway."

"There must be public records."

"That won't tell us what happened to the people who lived here, or where they went."

"I've probably been overreacting," Christine said. "I'm going through a bad patch, that's all. It doesn't have anything to do with the book."

"But won't you wonder?" Audrey asked.

"Maybe wondering is better than knowing in this case."

"Wondering will drive you crazy. Knowing won't."

Though the house looked recently painted, the grass was overgrown and shot through with dandelions, the porch scattered with boxes and two chairs that had been left outside to rot. The hedges along the walk had tentacles growing in unruly shoots toward the sun. It was a disappointment, though Audrey knew it shouldn't have been.

She parked and turned off the car.

"We drove all this way for this?" Christine said.

"We're not here to buy it," Audrey replied, throwing off her seat belt. Neither Christine nor Linda showed any sign of moving. "Who's coming with me?"

Linda turned and looked at Christine. "Well?"

"You two go. I just want to lie here for a while."

"You really should get out and walk around," Audrey said. "You haven't budged for a hundred miles. You'll get a blood clot in your leg."

"I'm fine. If I change my mind I'll come in."

"It's up to you," Audrey said. "We won't be long."

She walked several steps ahead of Linda up the walk and onto the porch. It gave her comfort to know that the book had been found here, even if they couldn't go inside. But as soon as she rang the bell, that comfort was replaced by the same chilled feeling she'd had when she was twenty-one and living alone in an off-campus apartment, paying her way through state university and avoiding her parents' attempts to find her and drag her back to Georgia. She had come home after waiting tables at a cheap restaurant popular with students, her arms filled with books and grocery bags. After kicking the door shut, she walked down the dark hallway to the kitchen and flipped on the overhead light. It took her a minute to realize something was wrong. Then she saw her stereo sticking off the living room shelf, disconnected wires poking out from the back. Her little television was pushed to one side on top of the bookcase. She stared at it, uncomprehending. Had she been moving things this morning and stopped because she was late for class? Wouldn't she remember a thing like that?

It was only after she saw the thin white curtains sucking in and out of the bedroom window that she realized what she'd interrupted. She pulled the window shut and jammed a broken broomstick into the casing to substitute for the flimsy lock. Every closet, cabinet, and hidden space had to be checked and rechecked. She felt so close to disaster that it seemed to still be in progress. She could hardly comprehend it when she saw herself, safe and untouched, in the bathroom mirror, and for weeks after she slept with the lights on.

"Someone's coming," Linda said, and almost immediately the door opened. Standing behind the screen was a barefoot little girl, no more than eight years old.

"Hello," Audrey said, crouching down. "My name is Audrey. Is your mother home?"

"Who is it?" she heard a female voice call.

The girl blinked at Audrey and stayed silent. A moment later a woman appeared wearing sweatpants and a T-shirt, her short spiky hair dyed red.

She came out onto the porch, squinting against the bright gray sky. With a wary frown, she listened to Audrey's questions before shaking her head. She knew nothing about any book or who had lived there before. How would she? She was renting the house, which had been in foreclosure when it was bought by a man who charged too much rent and didn't even live around there. As far as the crawl space went, there wasn't one anymore. It must have been filled in and walled off when the basement was finished, not that they'd done a very good job of that or anything else. The sink leaked, the pipes made funny sounds, and her daughter was sure her room was haunted. But if they wanted to come in and look around, they were welcome to do it.

Audrey knew it wouldn't make a difference, but she went inside anyway. Linda followed. Every bit of history had been chipped off the living room walls and plastered over, and the floors were covered in beige carpet. What had probably been a fireplace, flanked by two square windows, was now a built-in bookcase. There might be some fascinating scrap of the past lying under floorboards or behind drywall, but Audrey knew she would never find it.

"The basement is this way if you want to take a look," the woman said, leading them through the kitchen and opening a white door.

"Thank you." With Linda a few steps behind, Audrey descended toward a flickering lightbulb at the bottom of the steep plywood stairs, waiting for the feeling that she was getting close to something important. Even if the house had been ruined, she might at least detect a presence, a spirit that had trailed the book to a dark corner and lingered behind after it was taken away.

The basement was cool and smelled strongly of turpentine. She had hoped to find piles of broken antiques and an ancient furnace and boxes bursting with old letters, but saw only paint buckets and a few sticks of rusted lawn furniture. A washing machine spun loudly under a high row of dirt-smeared windows.

"It looks like every other basement," Linda said, standing in the weak pool of light.

"Feels like it, too," Audrey said.

"I wonder where the crawl space was?"

"Maybe that wall?" Audrey pointed to a seamed concrete slab.

Linda, graceful in her kitten heels, went up to it and ran her fingers along the joint. "It's like a vault. We couldn't get in if we wanted to."

"So that's it?"

"I don't know. The book *is* sixty years old. It was inevitable that the house would change in that time."

Audrey turned slowly, looking from wall to wall but seeing nothing. "Somebody has to know something about this, but who? How do we find them?"

"We probably don't," Linda said. "It would be interesting to know more, but do you really have time? It's a lot of effort with no guarantee of how it will turn out."

"Yeah," Audrey said, and reluctantly trailed Linda up the stairs. "I guess you're right."

"Thank you," she said to the woman, who stood in the kitchen drinking coffee and watching a television on the counter. "We're sorry we bothered you."

"You didn't bother me," she said. "You made me wonder what kind of place I'm living in, and that's something I could do without."

Audrey and Linda were halfway down the walk when the woman called out to them from the porch. She said there was a man across the street who was practically blind and never left his house anymore, but he'd lived on the block since he was a young man just back from the Second World War. His name was Aaron Gray. Maybe he could help, if he had any memory left.

Christine got out of the car and joined them. "Did we get the wrong address?" she asked, looking sleepy and confused.

"No, we're just going to talk to somebody else," Audrey replied.

"Did you find anything in the basement?"

"A lot of paint cans."

"The crawl space is gone," Linda told her. "Completely cemented over. I wonder if the box was even found there, or if it's just one of those stories that gets made up."

"Well—now what?"

"We try something else," Audrey said, heading out into the road. "Unless you want to just give up and go home?" She saw Christine and Linda exchange a look.

The other house was white with green trim and stout brick columns framing the entry. A woman of about thirty stood outside watering window boxes. Audrey introduced herself and her friends and asked if it would be possible to talk to Mr. Gray. They were doing a little historical investigation of the bungalow across the street and had been told he might be able to help.

"Are you related?" Audrey asked.

"I'm his granddaughter, Beth," she answered.

"Do you think he'd mind talking to us?"

"I'll ask him if he's up for visitors. Wait here."

A minute later she returned and ushered them through a wallpapered living room, past an upright piano covered with photographs and birthday cards. "Just for a few minutes," she said, sliding open the back screen. "He usually takes a nap this time of day."

Aaron Gray sat on a white plastic chair in the backyard, a narrow, manicured rectangle of clipped grass, flagstones, and short potted palm trees. He had a glass of ice water on a small table next to him. Large dark glasses obscured his eyes and half of his face.

"Hello," he said at the sound of their heels on the steps. "What a surprise, a visit from three young ladies."

Audrey, who was used to holiday gatherings attended by two stone-deaf nonagenarians as well as a step-uncle known as Senile Ned, crouched by the chair and touched his arm gently. "I'm Audrey Cronin," she shouted. "Nice to meet you."

"I can hear you perfectly well," he said. "It's seeing you I have trouble with." He put out a white hand and she shook it.

"We're hoping you can give us some information about the people who used to live in the bungalow across the street. The blue one with the red roof."

"Yes, yes, I know it," he said impatiently. "Lived across the street from it now for sixty-five years."

"We're trying to find a woman named Mala Rinehart? She may have lived there in the forties. We have a little book that she wrote, and—"

"Doesn't sound familiar."

"It might have been around 1948, or the book could have been written then, but she didn't move to the house until later."

He sat for a few minutes with his face turned toward the sun. "So many people moved in and out over the years. You know anything about her?"

"Nothing, except that she might have told fortunes and things like that."

He smiled, revealing gleaming white dentures. "No neighbors I ever saw told fortunes. And an author, too?"

"Not exactly. It's just a handwritten notebook, but we'd like to find out more about it."

"Nineteen forty-eight. I would have been here about . . . two years, I suppose, just married with my firstborn on the way." Mr. Gray folded his hands across his stomach, lowered his head, and went silent. Audrey looked to Linda for help, but her only response was a quick, helpless grimace. Christine was over near the azaleas, either admiring the pink blossoms or preparing to throw up in them.

The old man had been quiet so long, Audrey considered the possibility that he had died in his chair. It wasn't out of the question—his chest didn't appear to be moving and it was impossible to see his eyes.

Suddenly, he opened his mouth and took a deep breath that shook his shoulders, making Audrey flinch in surprise. "Now, I *do* remember a woman lived in that house," he said, "might have been around the time you mention. Had no husband. She was there I'd say ten years at least. Middle-aged, kept to herself. But I don't think her name was—what was it?"

"Mala Rinehart."

"Nope. Doesn't ring a bell. Funny things happened over there, though, some of the neighbors talked."

"What kind of things?" Audrey asked.

"She had a young girl of about twenty come to stay for, oh, maybe a year, must have been before 1950 because I was still at the phone company. They didn't look related, but I suppose they could have been."

"Did you know her name?"

He shrugged. "I only met her once or twice. She had a strange way of talking, and she looked different, too. Jet black hair straight to her chin, a bit of an accent. She was from Arizona or—no, I think it was Texas. I remember because she was like no Texan I ever met."

"Did she happen to mention a book?" Linda asked.

"If she did, I don't recall it. Wish I could tell you more. I might have been able to if you'd asked me fifty years ago. Don't have long now, as you can see."

"Well, we really appreciate your help. I'm going to leave my phone number with your granddaughter, okay?" Audrey said. "If you think of anything else, give me a call."

"I probably won't, but all right. Thanks for stopping by, ladies. I enjoyed it."

Christine and Linda, obviously anxious to leave, were already walking up the back steps and into the house to say goodbye to the old man's granddaughter. With a last look at the peaceful garden, Audrey stood and went after them. Two women—one young, one middle-aged, one of them from Texas. It seemed unbelievable that she should be leaving Bakersfield with so little information. Maybe this was the sign she had been looking for, and it was telling her she was a superstitious flake who wasted other people's time. Or it was instructing her not to give up. How would she ever know? Wasn't the meaning of everything open to interpretation? At that moment it seemed better to blunder through life unaware than to be paralyzed by every crumbling old book and empty plastic bag.

They got lost on the way out of town. It was disorienting to feel so low to the ground, without a hill or familiar landmark to guide them. They turned around and tried to make their way back to the highway, and in doing so drove by a cemetery. Flat, colorless, and enclosed by a stark metal fence, it was so different from Audrey's fantasy that it felt like a blow to her imagination; still, she couldn't help but slow down and look. There were trees—palms and cypress and spindly young pines—but all of them appeared to have been stuck haphazardly in the ground without thought to how they might look when they grew taller. The clouds had blown off toward the coast, leaving the yellow grass to wither under a dry afternoon sun. But on a day when she was desperate for something to meet her expectations, this cemetery was the closest she might get.

"Do you mind if I stop?" she asked. "Only five minutes, I promise."

She parked and left Linda and Christine sitting on a low concrete wall near the car. The office was closed, and there wasn't a map of headstones to follow, so Audrey gravitated toward the oldest part of the cemetery and stayed there, drifting from grave to grave. But after nearly an hour of searching she had to acknowledge that there was no Mala Rinehart here, no grand willow tree or weeping marble angel. It had not been a good day. Both the basement and the cemetery either held no secrets or refused to give them up. Still, she had a middle-aged woman and a young girl from Texas, and she was glad for that. They might be impossible to find but they were something, an old ruin to dig through when she was the only one on the street still awake.

Linda volunteered to drive home, and this time Audrey sat in the backseat. "You can change the music," she said when William's CD began to play. It seemed like the kindest gesture of friendship when Linda said, "Why don't we leave it on? I think I'm actually starting to like it."

Thirteen

*F*inding Ruth would be practice for finding Beni when Mala went back to Texas in a year. That was how she decided to think of it. Both missions were likely to end in failure, but she might discover something from the first search that would make the second easier to endure. Still, she couldn't help but hope. Her first two days in Bakersfield, she had truly believed it was possible that someone would say, "I know just the woman you're looking for. I can take you to her myself." But it didn't happen that way. Bakersfield was a combination of buttoned-up and proper and frontier rough, and the people looked kinder than they turned out to be when you spoke to them. They weren't rude, exactly, just set on a particular course. The

Mexicans—who didn't look like Mala here any more than they had in Texas—had their work and lived on their side of town, and there wasn't the trouble of figuring out who was who. Nobody knew what to make of Mala, however, and their amiable attitudes evaporated as soon as she approached and asked for help.

"Where'd you come from?" one woman asked, her expression more puzzled than afraid. Four people might come out of the back of a feed store to gawk at her, but no one would tell her if they knew Ruth Simon.

"Depends who's asking."

"I might, I might not."

The best part of Bakersfield was that she could take food from the fields at night. Everything was out in the open, and after dark it wasn't difficult to get enough to eat if she was quiet and careful. It required a lot of walking back and forth from her hiding place in an abandoned warehouse to scattered farms and gardens, just as her feet were starting to heal from so much walking in Texas. The lettuce was a delicacy at first, but in a few days it became a chore to tear off and chew leaves that were streaked white with spray and crunchy from bits of dirt. Tomatoes, peppers plucked before their prime, hard peaches, and handfuls of mint were her midnight meals, and during the day she made do with thoughts of what she could eat later if she was patient.

One night in early June under bright stars, Mala was caught at the edge of a carrot field. A dog gave her away with its hoarse, frantic barking and the heavy rattling of a chain. There was a light, the grinding crunch of gravel, and a loud voice telling her not to move.

"I got lost," she said. "I was just leaving."

"Every one of them says that," said a young male voice. "Turn around."

"I promise I won't come back."

"That's right you won't. Now turn around."

Hands at her sides, she did. He was just a kid, maybe a year or two older than she was. He was tall and his hair was shaved almost to the scalp, but the threatening look this might have given him was undercut by his boniness and the awkward way he held his rifle. These types were the most dangerous, the most likely to aim at their own foot or somebody's kitchen window, to shoot just because their fingers were shaking. "All right," she said, with a smile meant to be calming and apologetic. "I turned around."

"You think stealing is funny?"

"No, I don't."

"Then what's the damn smile for?"

She shrugged. "Seems pretty silly, you pointing a gun at a woman half your size."

He lowered the barrel immediately. "I got no choice. It's my job to protect these fields."

"Then I'll get out of your hair. I won't bother you again."

"Can't just run off now," he said, raising the gun again. "I have to tell my boss about this. That's the rule. We don't call the sheriff, the same ones come back night after night till we got nothing left but footprints."

Mala thought about it, but decided against trying to outrun a fidgety kid with a rifle.

"Come on to the barn," he said, jerking the gun toward the dim outline of a building, "where I can get a better look and decide what to do. Never caught a girl before, surprised the heck out of me."

Mala stumbled along in front of him over rough soil, listening to his breath jolt out of his lungs with every step, mentally trying out her options. Run and hear bullets flying by her ears, pretend to faint and drop to the ground, or keep walking blindly in the direction of who knew what. Before she could decide, they were almost at the barn and an older voice called out of the darkness. "That you, El-liot? What the hell's going on?"

Reflexively, Mala stopped in her tracks and the kid ran into her, gun barrel first against her right flank.

"Nothing!" he yelled back, too quickly to have considered the answer.

"Where you been?"

"Heard something. Boars, probably. Whatever they were, I chased them off."

The voice in the darkness mumbled a reply, and a few moments later a screen door slapped shut. A light went on, illuminating a small house where one hadn't existed. The light went off and the house vanished again.

"Who was that?" Mala whispered.

"My uncle. He's also my boss."

"Why'd you do that?"

"I don't know." Elliot sounded disappointed in himself. "Should have handed you over to him when I had the chance."

She stood waiting for him to direct her. When he didn't, she said, "What now?"

"Have to get rid of you, that's what. Not sure how without somebody getting wind of it and giving me grief in the process."

He finally decided that he would drive her back to town. She would have to come with him to his truck, which was parked outside the shed where he slept. "If anybody asks, I'll say the Pruitts' dog got loose again," he muttered. "Had to cart him home before he went after the chickens. 'Course, if they see a girl with me, I'm done."

Shushing Mala with vague threats of big trouble, he grabbed her upper arm and took off toward something she couldn't see. "Where do you live?" he asked when they were out of earshot of the house.

"You can drop me anywhere."

"In other words, you've got no home, do you?"

Mala tried to yank her arm away but Elliot only clutched it tighter. "I'm in town looking for somebody," she said.

"Well, whoever it is isn't on this farm."

"Could be, for all I know."

His head turned toward her. "You're pretty young to be running around on your own, aren't you?"

"I'm not much younger than you."

"And you still don't know right from wrong. Keep walking."

The shed was just that—a leaning, old wood contraption, peeling paint, a concrete block for a step, and a crooked door with a splintered inside edge, as if the only way to gain access was to break in with a crowbar. "Wait here," Elliot said. "Take off and I promise you the next guy who finds you won't be so kind."

As soon as he went in, distant headlights turned and started down a long dirt track in Mala's direction. Somebody was coming. She slipped around the side of the shed into deep shadow, but this only seemed like a good idea for a few seconds. The headlights bounced up and down with every rut in the road, illuminating Elliot's bashed-in blue truck, a stretch of barbed-wire fence, and the littered patch of hard-packed dirt that Elliot probably called a front yard. In thirty seconds they'd be here, the whole shed and everything around it lit up, doors shutting, the scuff of boots, men's voices. Before she could think, she was at the door and inside.

Elliot whipped around. "What are you doing in here?" A single blinding bulb swung from a cord so long it dangled in front of his forehead. There was nothing in the room but a chipped table and a thin mattress on the floor. The blanket was army-issue gray wool, pulled tight and tucked in at the sides.

"Somebody's coming," she panted.

In an instant he'd plunged the room into darkness and pushed Mala down to the floor in the corner. "Keep the light off and your mouth shut," he said.

He went outside and pulled the door closed behind him. She could hear the deep drone of his voice, surprisingly soothing, but the words were absorbed by the noise of an idling engine. He wasn't gone for twenty seconds before Mala heard two doors shut and the engine noise get distant and peter out. She waited, crouched and on her toes, for Elliot to come back in. He didn't.

She had no way of knowing how long she waited, but it must have been close to an hour. The thought of finding her way off the farm and back to the abandoned warehouse took more energy than she had left. She sat on the end of the bed, then allowed herself to put her head down. She hadn't slept in a bed since leaving Beni's trailer, though that was nothing but old duck feathers stuffed into a flannel sack. This wasn't much better. She would lie down only for a minute, then get up and figure out what to do.

When she woke, Elliot was behind her, asleep. She knew it without looking because there was a line of heat at her back, an inch or two away. She could hear his ragged breathing and smell his skin—dirt, sweat, soap. She went rigid at the thought of a man lying beside her, the first time ever, and she still had her boots on. Every rumor that had dogged her in Texas seemed to be coming true at once: thief, tramp. Hours must have passed since he'd left because a wet chill had come over the room and the gaps around the door showed chinks of pale gray sky. Elliot's gun was in the corner where Mala had hid, its barrel aimed at the ceiling.

Slowly, she turned over.

His cheeks were covered with pale, patchy scruff, and his nose was a broad ridge, nothing like the narrow hawk's beak that formed the backbone of Beni's face. His eyebrows were straight slashes, darker than his hair and almost connected in the middle. There was a good amount of space between his pale purple eyelids, and his mouth was high and curved at the top, like something you could slide down in winter. It was the face of a kid up to the jaw and chin, which seemed to belong to somebody else. Not handsome, really, but hard for her to tear her eyes from. Mala watched him for a long time and still couldn't decide exactly what he looked like or how everything fit together.

It took a rooster to wake him, and even then he fought it off for as long as he could, groaning and covering his face with a sinewy forearm until the rooster came up right outside the door and crowed with shrill intention. Mala knew from the way Elliot sat up and sucked in a breath that he'd meant to wake earlier, to take care of his mistake and hers under cover of darkness.

"I'm sorry," she said, self-consciously smoothing her hair.

"Too late for sorry," he said, getting to his feet and stamping on his boots. "I'll catch it now for sure."

"Why didn't you wake me up?"

He seemed to be having trouble looking her in the eye. "'Cause I was stupid. I didn't have the heart. Can't even shoot a feral cat."

"Where did you go last night?"

He let out a huff. "What's with all the questions? It doesn't matter. We've gotta go, that's all." He took her shoulder and pushed her toward the door. "Now stay low and keep quiet. If you can."

"You're the one doing all the talking," she said.

It was brighter outside than Mala expected. The whole farm—hulking barns, fields, distant stands of trees—was blurry under a layer of mist and lit up from a sun that hadn't risen yet. Elliot opened the rusted passenger door of the truck and practically hurled her inside. He jogged around the front, scrambled in, and started up the engine by turning the key hard to the right and holding it there until the truck finally gave in and turned over.

"Are you going to be late for something?" Mala asked, hanging on to the strap over her head. The road was bumpy enough to rattle her voice and make her heart skip beats.

"I was late an hour ago." He paused, looked over, and pushed her down to the seat. "Nothing personal," he said, "but you have to stay out of sight."

For at least a mile she lay half bent on the seat, staring at Elliot's denim-clad leg and his boot flattening the gas pedal. She knew they were off the farm by the sudden smooth hum of the paved road under her ear. She looked up at the underside of his jaw and said, "Can I sit up now?"

"Sure."

She pulled at the cuffs of her sleeves. She supposed she should be furious, but being angry at the outcome of her own actions didn't make much sense. It was a lesson learned, simple as that. But what lesson exactly?

"I hope your uncle isn't too hard on you," she said.

"Aw, well, I'll blame it on a girl." For the first time, she saw the flicker of amusement around Elliot's mouth. "Where am I taking you?"

"I don't know how to get there unless I'm on foot."

"You gotta go someplace. I'm not leaving you on the street. Not that I care, but it wouldn't be right."

"There's an old warehouse not far from the bus station. I'm sleeping there for the time being. Do you know it?"

He gave her a disapproving look. "Darn right I know it, and it's no place for a girl to stay by herself. Who's this person you're looking for anyway?"

"Her name is Ruth Simon. She might be working as a housekeeper."

"I don't know any Ruth Simon."

"Neither does anybody else." The light of day made the search for Ruth seem impossible, a maze constructed of dust and dead ends. The warehouse was never particularly welcoming, but at least after dark it was hard to see the details, the padlocked doors and smashed windows. Ugly though it was, she was glad for it. It wasn't a safe place but it was big enough that a woman who kept to herself and made no sound would be difficult to find, especially at night.

"I don't feel right leaving you here," Elliot said. "You have any money?"

"Would I have been at your farm if I did?"

He stopped the truck at the corner. Leaning his forearms against the steering wheel, he looked over at her with bloodshot gray eyes. "Where are you from?" he asked. "You talk different, like you're not from around here."

"I'm from Texas, that's why."

"I know people from Texas, and you don't sound like them either." He paused, then reached into his pocket. "Here," he said, handing her a five-dollar bill. "Stay out of my fields."

"You don't have to pay me for that."

"I'm not paying you. I'm helping you."

"I don't need it."

He shook the money impatiently. "Take it. I'll cause all kinds of trouble for you if you don't."

It was nice sitting there in the truck talking to somebody, even under the circumstances, but there was more pride in taking the money and getting out than there was in staying and talking. She pretended to walk away without looking back, but when he drove off she turned to watch him, murmuring, "I have a feeling you'll be causing me trouble either way."

Fourteen

*P*eter's boss, Dennis, came for dinner on a Friday night, two weeks after Paige's arrival. Linda had met him only briefly at a company gathering, but a clammy handshake and a bit of background from Peter had told her all she needed to know. Dennis was one of those self-made men with a shirt-stretching paunch, pitted cheeks, and the indefinable accent that brands the products of western trailer parks and Section 8 housing, following them into adulthood like a criminal record. His career wasn't the result of education or connections, but of shady real estate deals, drained wetlands, and evicted children who screamed when they were dragged out to the car. He hadn't told Peter any of this, but the story had been passed around and probably exaggerated by other men at the company, all of whom despised Dennis and were despised by Dennis in return. Peter hadn't yet been lumped in with the pathetic group of legacies and crybaby leeches Dennis had to oversee, and for this reason dinner was a big deal, the most important thing Linda had done, perhaps, since coming to California. It wasn't simply a social obligation. With her food and elegant company, she had the opportunity to give Peter the glow of a kindred spirit, a future partner who could carry on Dennis's unethical policies with aplomb long after he was gone.

She decided to grill elk. It was hearty and original, and although she had purchased it mail order from a ranch in Colorado, for all Dennis would know she and Peter had driven to the Sierras one weekend for the hell of it and shot it themselves as it ambled over a jagged peak (snapshots of the wilderness had been appearing to her since Peter mentioned that Dennis owned a cabin near King's Canyon). If Dennis wasn't impressed by elk, there was no hope. It was more than meat, it was frontier food with an important subliminal message. Peter had come from nothing just like Dennis, his Yale MBA and twenty-five years in Manhattan just elitist bumps in the road on the way to his true calling: taking over West Coast operations after Dennis had a heart attack or was indicted. Both very real possibilities, from what Linda had heard.

"I'm not going to eat deer," Paige announced the morning of the dinner.

"That's right, you're not," Linda said, pounding the meat with a mallet. "First of all because elk isn't deer, and second because you'll be in bed asleep."

Paige gave Linda an interested sort of frown. She wasn't used to being outwitted by her stepmother, and this idea seemed to confuse her. "At seven o'clock?"

"Your father said you can read until you're tired."

"When was this decided?"

Linda began sprinkling a southwestern rub over the meat. Fifteen days into Paige's three-month stint in California, Linda had stopped walking on eggshells and trying to mimic a woman with a maternal instinct. She spoke to Paige the way she would to an adult who was small, crafty, and had no actual power. No dumbed-down explanation of her thought process, no softening of her tone, just the bare truth. Besides, if she was too accommodating, she might set in motion a chain of emotional events that would result in Paige deciding to stay for life.

"This is a dinner party for adults," Linda said. "One dinner out of an entire summer. I'm sure you'll survive."

"I could be dead tomorrow."

"You could be, but you won't."

"I don't understand why I can't go back to horse camp."

"Because it only lasts a week, sweetie. And you just rode yesterday." That a sixty-pound child could appear so in control and confident on the back of a huge animal was astounding. Linda had felt diminished standing at the edge of the dusty corral, cowering like a kicked dog every time the horse galloped in her direction. Watching Paige, she'd wondered what she might have done with her life if she'd had her stepdaughter's courage.

"I want to go again tomorrow," Paige said.

"We'll go on Monday. Your father wants to spend time with you this weekend."

Though Paige didn't argue, her silence reeked of mistreatment. While Linda worked in the kitchen, Paige spent the next hour stomping from room to room and looking wounded. Her earphones gave off the tinny sound of toy snares every time she walked by. It wasn't just the dinner that had thrown her into bad spirits, it was living in a household where the prospect of chaos was severely limited by the small number of residents. After much observation of her stepdaughter's moods and manipulations, this was the conclusion Linda had come to. Paige was bored of peace.

"Hey, Paige?" she said.

Her stepdaughter sat ten feet away at the breakfast table, damaging her hearing with the score of a Broadway show and kicking the wall while she looked through a catalog of equestrian gear. She flipped past the riding boots with hostile impatience, nearly tearing the pages from their staples. Only when she glanced up and saw Linda's mouth moving did she reluctantly pull a headphone cup from her ear. "What?"

"Want to help me with the biscuits? They're really fun to make." This was a lie; making biscuits was a chore she dreaded. All that measuring and mixing, waiting for things that often refused to do what they were supposed to. While Linda enjoyed the sheer physicality of snipping out chicken backs, separating snapper bones from the delicate raw flesh, and peeling pound after pound of tomatoes, baking was a black art, the kind of undertaking you could pour your heart into only to be insulted with something tough and deformed. And there was also the fact that she loved to cook alone. Sharing the kitchen, handing off tasks to people who were sloppy and distracted, having to chitchat while the thing that mattered—the pie crust or the soufflé—was turned into an afterthought—it made no sense at all. It seemed like a complete reversal of priorities.

"My mom is a bad cook," Paige said. "She's proud of it. She says it's a waste to spend so much time on something that's only going to disappear in a few minutes." But to Linda's surprise, Paige left her catalog and earphones on the table and, smacking the glass measuring cup on the counter to make everything level, measured out the flour.

She examined the giant mixer with sinister curiosity, as if it were something she might be able to modify in the time it took Linda to make a phone call or check the mailbox. "How does this thing work?" she asked. "Does it do anything else besides mix?"

"Watch your fingers," Linda said. "Don't turn it on yet, okay?"

Paige broke the eggs into the stainless steel bowl, singing, "So long, little chicken," with each crack, and dropped in a stick of butter from the greatest height possible, going up on her toes and stretching her arm above her head before letting go. She laughed when it splashed into the eggs with a sick little thud, sending droplets of yolk sailing through the air and onto the floor.

Linda said nothing. That was how you interested children in activities, or so she had heard; you stepped back and didn't get in the way. You let them explore and make up games without admonishment or rigid rules. Margaret always bragged that her children were exceptional readers for the simple reason that they'd been given free rein to maim, draw in, and weaponize every book in the house from the time they were babies. "I didn't want them to have any bad associations with reading," she'd said. "Sometimes that meant letting them throw books at each other and figure out the repercussions themselves."

Margaret was right about one thing—Paige had no bad associations with reading, or apparently much else. She had never been spanked or screamed at. She had been warned away from nothing, only reasoned with in multisyllabic language that had likely gone in one ear and out the other. As a result, everything was fodder for her curiosity: stove knobs, the contents of the recycling bin, the dryer hose, Peter's blood pressure medication, stinging beetles, dust balls, Linda's wallet. Paige was a world-class hoarder, a collector of all things colorful, fascinating, and dead. She came back from outings with her pockets full of dried leaves and her candy wrappers tied into a crinkly plastic rope that she would chew on and then use to flog the furniture. Any suggestion of "decluttering" or "straightening up" was met with derision, as if Linda were of the bottled water generation that thought nothing of discarding perfectly good objects and starting over, while an albatross on a distant atoll fed its young plastic scraps it had mistaken for food.

Paige claimed to have advanced knife skills, which she would prove right now if Linda let her chop the pancetta. "You need to trust me," Paige said, standing before her stepmother in pink flip-flops, her nails a blood red she'd slopped on at a sample counter at the mall. She had flour on her toes, and the end of one curl was stiff and pointy with egg white.

"No, I don't," Linda said.

"I have to grow up sometime."

"But not all at once," Linda said, holding the chef's knife out of reach. "Not today."

Paige squinted. "You said I could help."

"Why don't we chop it together? I'll stand behind you and put my hand over yours." There was an edge of hysteria to her voice, not only because she was afraid Paige would hurt herself, but because her kitchen had been defiled in a matter of fifteen minutes. It was as if her stepdaughter had run in, spray-painted expletives on the appliances, and run out again.

"I'm not a child," Paige said, reaching for the knife.

"You're not?" Linda said, trying to sound playful. "This knife is bigger than you are."

"You want me to be independent, don't you?" This sounded like the jaded reasoning of a girl whose mother had left too many parenting books lying around.

"Yes, but I also want you to have all your fingers. You might need them someday."

"It's not like I've never used a knife before."

"But this is a big one. Let's do it together."

"What is this, Guantanamo?" she said, turning and walking away, leaving a striped floury footprint on the slate floor. "I have no rights at all in this house."

There were thirty seconds of silence, then an upstairs door banged into its frame. Paige's earphones lay discarded on the table, broadcasting a miniaturized version of some uplifting show tune. It took Linda several tries before she managed to turn it off in the middle of a soaring chorus. She chopped the pancetta, every drop of the blade an indictment of her ability to simply act, accept the consequences, and move forward. The kitchen took forty-five minutes to clean. Somehow, egg yolk and buttermilk had petrified into cracks Linda hadn't known were there, leaving behind fossilized evidence she would be discovering for months. After covering the biscuit dough with plastic wrap, she sprayed the surfaces down with bleach, ran a toothpick along the juncture of wall and counter, scrubbed the cabinets, mopped the floor, and still there was a dusting of cornmeal as fine as fingerprint powder along the rim of the microwave door. It was going to be one of those memories she couldn't erase, which replayed at the vaguest reminder and materialized in the middle of the night when she woke to go to the bathroom.

She was removing the strings from snap peas when she heard footsteps outside the kitchen. "Paige?" Wiping her hands on a towel, she went out to the foyer just as the front door shut. Anger rising, Linda pulled the door open and strode out to the porch. Her stepdaughter was halfway down the drive, dressed in a thin, sleeveless white dress and sneakers with no socks and carrying her overloaded backpack, a child who had bumped along through centuries and gotten lost, a waif no one knew what to do with.

"Where are you going?" Linda called. She was surprised to find her voice so even, as if she were simply curious to know where a ten-year-old might be off to on a summer afternoon, her shoes untied, her narrow, translucent shoulders exposed to the blazing sun.

"To Emily's to go swimming," Paige said in a soprano monotone. Her eyes were fierce.

"Emily from down the block?"

"Do you know another Emily?"

"When will you be back?"

"Don't worry about it. I called my mom."

"What does that mean?" Linda asked, but Paige was already at the sidewalk and walking in the direction of the Preston house. "Is there an adult there? Do you have your phone?"

Paige vanished behind a palm tree and was gone. Linda went

inside and called Peter, who said he was very busy and hoped she could handle it. Anyway, what was the big deal? Paige was in one of her moods and was going swimming for the third time with Emily, whose parents were perfectly qualified to babysit even if they did rent out their basement and drive a dented minivan. Amy Preston had made it through Stanford Law before chucking it all to stay home with her kids; she was certainly qualified to keep two children from drowning.

"Okay," Linda said. "You're right." As long as Peter was aware of the situation, she was absolved of responsibility. Although who knew what he would say when he heard about the knife, how the whole silly mess would eventually become her fault?

Linda set the table. She used their everyday plates and napkins on the assumption that Dennis would view anything fancier as a knock on his humble beginnings. Peter had said she was putting too much thought into it—Dennis didn't exactly show up to work in cowboy boots, he wore silk ties—but if she wanted to psychoanalyze every aspect of dinner for maximum effect, it couldn't hurt. There were a hundred things she might want to say but wouldn't be able to; she could only hint at them with the lighting, the food, the absence of a tablecloth, flat shoes instead of heels. Instead of begging Dennis to allow Peter to rise from the corporate ashes at fifty-one, she would serve ice cream and cookies for dessert, nothing fancy, nothing French. We've fallen off our pedestal, we've learned to be humble. New York ruined us. These words would be written in the simple swirls of chocolate sauce on Dennis's plate.

Four o'clock came and went and Linda began to worry. She didn't dare bother Peter again, so she called Margaret in Connecticut and woke her from a nap. "Just checking in," Linda said, and grimaced. This was Margaret's phrase, and it always sounded to Linda like a way to let oneself off the hook for bothering somebody for no good reason.

"Why?" Margaret said, her voice hoarse from sleep.

"No reason. Paige's swimming at a neighbor's house."

"Oh. What time is it?"

"After four out here."

"I should get up. The kids are at camp this week but I have a lot to catch up on. Sleep included, I guess."

"Listen, did Paige call you?"

"Not for a few days. That's a good sign, don't you think?"

"Yes. Absolutely."

"Does she miss me?" Margaret asked sleepily. "She's far away for the first time in her life. I just hope she misses me." There was a needy whine to her voice that Linda found strangely repulsive.

"Of course she does. She brings you up all the time." It was true; over the last two days Paige had mentioned that her mother played favorites, surfed adoption websites as if she were shoe shopping, and got headaches that allowed her to abscond to the darkened master suite while Fiona drowned Paige's favorite sandals in the koi pond.

"I'm glad. I wouldn't want her to forget me."

"No chance of that," Linda said, and claimed to hear the oven timer.

Paige had lied about calling her mother, a fact that Linda now considered a gift. Her stepdaughter was secretive and difficult to manage, something even Peter wouldn't dispute once he heard the facts. Freed from culpability by Paige's dishonesty, Linda scraped the grill and emptied the dishwasher. She ironed a simple white blouse, straightened the living room, and took a shower. No one called, and there were no screams from down the block. No ambulances drove by with their sirens wailing, paramedics working feverishly in the back. And at two minutes before five, Paige walked in, stinking of chlorine, her hair wet, her mood carefree. "Guess what, I can hold my breath underwater for almost a minute," she said, thumping upstairs.

"How do you know that?" Linda said, imagining Paige suspended in the deep end, her face turning blue from lack of oxygen.

"How do you think?" she replied, and shut her door.

By the time Dennis arrived, Paige was full of macaroni and cheese and parked in front of a DVD in her room, too distracted to care about the dinner she was missing downstairs. Dennis was a jocular, saddle-nosed man who loved wine and foie gras and ate every morsel Linda put in front of him. He hulked in his chair at the head of the table—candlelight illuminating the divots in his skin, his stomach erupting from his solar plexus—and talked about golf courses and deep-sea fishing. "Not just a beauty, but a great cook," he kept saying to Linda, a compliment that somehow made her feel put down, as though he'd patted her on the ass. To her horror, he thought the elk was "exotic," though he concluded after inhaling it that it wasn't much different from beef. He didn't talk about Peter's performance at work once; a good sign or a bad one, Linda couldn't tell.

Dennis stayed too long. He went to the bathroom three times. He peered at framed photographs and leafed through books. Just after eleven, Peter yawned with his mouth closed and Linda glared at him. He was not allowed to be tired. He was barely allowed to breathe. They would nod and ask questions, stay up until dawn, offer Dennis their bed and the use of Peter's razor if they had to, but they would do nothing to make him feel unwelcome. Yes, they were demeaning themselves, but that was life, a series of sellouts that no one enjoyed but everyone took part in.

Eventually, Peter went to check on Paige, who hadn't been heard from in hours. Dennis was tipsy now and a bit slumped, the lamp casting a pinkish, feminine glow over his enormous head. Linda shifted in her chair, so exquisitely self-conscious it was like a wave of nausea.

"Come sit over here," Dennis said, patting the cushion beside him. "I'm lonely by myself."

"I don't think I can move," Linda said, feigning extreme comfort.

"Peter didn't tell me he was married to a stunner. If I was him, I wouldn't keep it a secret."

"Thank you, Dennis, but I think that's the cognac talking."

"Hell it is. Come here, just for a second."

Linda hesitated. By the time she got to the couch and sat down, Peter would be back. She had more to lose by refusing than by giving in, at least until she was lying in bed later, admonishing herself for being such a pushover.

She got up, slipped past the coffee table, and sat next to Dennis. Up close he was pathetic, a lumpy, insecure oaf who would probably give every cent he owned for an attractive woman's attentions. He put his hand on the juncture between her neck and shoulder, a moist, bungling grasp that made her think of helping her father to bed when she was a teenager. "All the other wives are scared of me, every single one," he said, sounding puzzled and a little hurt.

"I'm not scared of anybody," she said.

"I wish you worked for me instead of these grad school clowns. Every time I walk by, they just about jump out of their skin."

"You'll never find someone more loyal than Peter. Or better at what he does."

His thumb slid into the hollow of her throat. "New York's done, for better or worse. Peter didn't get what he needed from us, I understand that. But he made some investment decisions I wasn't thrilled with. I've said the same thing to his face. He's got to prove himself here and it's going to take time."

"He'll do whatever it takes, Dennis. Can you say that about anyone else who works for you?"

"I shouldn't tell you this, but no. And that's the truth."

She gave him the sort of smile she hadn't used in years, a warm, secretive look that under the circumstances felt practically adulterous. Tonight, such a smile seemed necessary, almost as essential to Peter's prospects as his education and corporate sales transactions. "You're welcome here for dinner anytime," she said. "Now, how about some coffee?"

"Why not. With a face like yours, I'd probably drink lighter fluid if you put it in front of me."

She patted the back of his hand. "I'll make it so strong you'll think I have."

Her mouth flattened the moment she stood up. Straightening the collar of her blouse, she escaped to the dark kitchen, where her phone glowed blue on the granite island. It was a text that Audrey had sent a few minutes before.

Got a lead on her. Call me when you get this.

She hadn't spoken to Audrey since the trip to Bakersfield. Dreary as the excursion had been, Audrey wasn't the only one disappointed with the lack of information about Mala Rinehart. Linda had the sense that she, Audrey, and Christine were the only people who knew of the woman's existence. To give up on her would be to condemn her to permanent obscurity. It was nearly midnight, but Linda called Audrey anyway. She answered on the first ring.

"Mala was the girl from Texas," she said. "The one the old guy talked about."

"How do you know?"

"I've been searching newspapers online back a hundred years, the same thing I did for my family tree. I don't know why, Linda. I couldn't let it go."

"What did you find?"

"Her name. Misspelled, but I'm pretty sure it's her. It's this quarter page ad in a newspaper from fifteen years ago, some lawyer looking for her. He doesn't say why, there's just a phone number."

"What are you going to do?"

"Call and see if the number works. Ask if he'll tell me anything."

"I have a guest right now, but you'll let me know, right? As soon as you talk to him?"

"You'll be my first call."

As Linda hung up she glanced over to see Peter's body framed in the doorway. Dennis stood just behind him.

"Linda?" Peter said into the dark kitchen.

"Sorry," she said. "I'm here."

He flipped on the light. "Do you have Paige?"

"What?" she asked stupidly, blinking against the glare.

All she could see of his face were his eyes, the look of stark fear and helplessness. Before he could open his mouth to explain, she stepped back and shook her head, as if by doing so she could change what was about to happen.

"Call the police," Peter said to Dennis. "Linda, I checked the yard and the pool, check again. I'm going to drive around and look for her."

Even as Linda ran out the back door and went down on her knees by the illuminated pool, shouting Paige's name and scanning the still blue depths, she felt a sharp surge of pride at the way Peter had just spoken to Dennis, taking charge and instructing him as if he were a underling. His voice, his manner, everything about him had changed. In those three words he had finally showed Dennis who he was. She scoured the perimeter of the yard, scratching her arms as she searched behind bushes and in thorny corners, panic and guilt mingling with an incongruous feeling of comfort. For the first time since they had left New York, she believed her husband was actually going to make it.

Fifteen

Christine hated Paige, hated her with every cell of her being, and when she thought of her, no less than a thousand times a day, she wanted to throttle Peter and Linda, but not before she asked them exactly how a child could vanish from a second-floor bedroom on a perfectly ordinary evening without being seen. Were they that inconsiderate of others?

At first it appeared she had simply run away. All signs pointed to a melodramatic reaction to an argument with her stepmother, but then Peter discovered that Paige had taken nothing with her, not even her cell phone, and that the back door had been ajar for what might have been two hours before he realized she was gone. Worse still was the black ballet slipper spied by the beam of an officer's flashlight, sole-up on the curb twenty feet from Christine's house. It was as if Linda and Peter had planned it, carefully set the scene with tantalizing clues that would lead directly to Tim. They were too wrapped up in their own terror to notice their effect on anyone else, but if they had stopped spinning in frantic circles for one minute they might have seen the disaster they'd created. Tim had been on the verge of regaining his freedom simply because the resource-starved police could no longer pursue a fruitless lead, when the girl across the street conveniently vanished, and in doing so, pointed her finger right at him.

It wasn't that Christine didn't care about Paige or what might have happened to her. For the past two nights she had been kept awake by images of the little girl wandering alone in a harsh, Dickensian world, where fire burned in the streets and the sidewalks were slick from blood and fog. She saw her in a series of shocking and incongruous settings: walking in torn clothes through a culvert, staring out the back window of a stranger's car, buried under trash, an exposed bare foot the only clue to her fate. But Christine's mind always returned to what might have been if Paige weren't missing—life gradually returning to normal, Tim himself again, going to work every day, painting the baby's room at night—and before she could stop herself, she had wished everything terrible that could befall a person on Peter and Linda for their ineptness.

"Don't tell anybody what you just told me," Tim said when she revealed her feelings to him. "They'll have us both put away."

"You must have had the same thoughts," she said. They were in bed, the only place in the house where Christine didn't feel exposed. Even with the curtains drawn and the lights turned off, she wondered if the shadowy silhouette of her figure could be seen crossing the living room.

"No," he replied. "Not once."

"It doesn't make you angry that they just—lost her? You never let anybody off the hook. That's what frightens me. It's not like you at all."

"What's happening isn't their fault. God, Chrissie, Peter's daughter is missing."

"Something's wrong with me," she said, pressing her fingertips to her eyes until she saw white flashes. "All this stress. I don't know who to blame. I can't think straight anymore." She slid close to him. "At least we have the baby coming. That's something to hang on to, right?"

"Right," he said, laying a hand to her stomach. "Just concentrate on that."

The evening of the disappearance, Christine had been in session with her last client of the day while Tim staged a house that had languished on the market for a year. It was the part of his job he hated most. Using rented furniture and stiff plastic plants, he had tried his best to resurrect the once joyful spirits of the owners, who were on the verge of walking into the bank, throwing the keys at the nearest loan officer, and washing their hands of the whole thing. Of course, Tim had been at the house alone most of the time, decorating and arranging with an obsessive sort of desperation, and then he went to the grocery store, where no one remembered seeing him and the CCTV tapes had been accidentally erased. He seemed to be magically invisible everyplace he went except his own home, and then he didn't have a moment's peace.

Christine lay in bed with her husband asleep beside her, trying to picture a world in which he had killed not only a stranger but the neighbor's daughter, too. It seemed impossible, but wasn't that what every wife said? She lined up the chain of events in sequential order, creating a crude documentary in her mind. Tim would have staged the house in Fountain Valley, knowing he had months of hard luck and broken contracts stacked against him but going through the motions anyway. Optimistic to the end. Cheap prints hanging on the walls, miniblinds closed against a view of train tracks or a row of battered school buses. Polishing the front doorknob with his sleeve, he might have locked up and gotten into his car, praying for a strong turnout at the next day's open house. It would have made him feel pathetic to have such puny desires, when he used to breeze in to work an hour late because he'd been held up at the boat dealership. Tim had always been the brash, tooth-whitened, paisley-patterned shark, the person everyone envied, the one who let buyers' calls go to voicemail and claimed to lose track of how many houses he'd sold in a month. The life he had now felt, as he put it, a little like being dead except he had to get up and do things every day. He didn't even get to just lie there.

Maybe these thoughts had driven him crazy. Maybe he'd come home to change before going to the grocery store, a task he griped about and had largely managed to avoid until Christine opened her practice. These mundane domestic chores always made him feel like Audrey's husband Mark, a man Tim thought of as a cheery, jobless boor who pinned his hopes on snake oil and other people's ignorance. Mark could be seen driving his son to school and picking up the dry cleaning—for all intents and purposes, a eunuch in a Ford Taurus. That wouldn't happen to Tim, career problems wouldn't mess with *his* mind, turn him into an Age of Aquarius freak who lived off his wife's hard work and talked up total strangers about the acid balance in their blood. And it was even worse because Mark used to be a good guy, somebody Tim could relate to.

With Mark in mind, maybe Tim had decided to put off the grocery store until the morning. He might have been sitting by the front window enjoying the sudden absence of surveillance due to the state's amazingly convenient budget problem, when he'd seen Paige outside across the street, three driveways down. She was everything he wasn't—privileged, unhurt, with most of her disappointments still ahead of her. Looking at her in the clear glow of twilight, it would be easy to have black thoughts. Today was all that mattered to Paige; it was three times longer than days in her twenties would be, five times longer than days in her forties. Her luckiness might have seemed miserably unfair to Tim while he sat there, the surveillance finished but the damage done. Maybe she had hopscotched down the block toward the house, and he'd gone outside on impulse, with no plan in mind other than to appear in her line of sight, cast a six-foot-tall shadow over an otherwise perfect evening.

"Hi, Paige, how you doing?" Good-looking, a little jittery, his prematurely gray hair a silver shock against the darkening sky. All of his forty-two years concentrated on his head, making his face look oddly young and preserved.

"Fine. How are you?" Paige was a polite girl, demanding and sarcastic at home, Linda said, but well-mannered in public.

"Pretty good, except I could use your help with something."

Christine could see them talking as clearly as if she were watching from the dining room window. But after that her thoughts froze up and refused to go any further. The figures of Tim and Paige stopped mid-gesture, their faces illuminated by the last rays of sun, waiting for instructions Christine couldn't seem to give them. That her imagination couldn't go on was a good sign. Her husband couldn't have committed one and possibly two horrific crimes and not at least have given her a fleeting look of anguish over dinner. Or maybe he felt no anguish at all, only amazement that his wife was standing by him in spite of his presence at the center of every recent crisis.

The next morning she resolved to quell any lingering worries by discovering as much as she could about her husband. Being suspected of one crime was a fluke; two would disturb any woman, no matter how loyal or pregnant. It didn't mean she didn't love Tim, it meant the opposite. She loved and needed him so much, she was determined to erase all doubts about him.

She sat at the top of the stairs, listening to him make breakfast. Her phone vibrated on the carpet beside her—Audrey calling again.

The last Christine had heard, Audrey tried to contact a lawyer who'd placed an advertisement looking for Mala Rinehart, but the number was disconnected and a bit of research turned up his obituary from ten years ago. Beloved husband, father of three, etc. Now Audrey was trying to find someone in his family to see if they knew anything about his old cases, or how he had known Mala. Even if they found her—in a crypt, maybe, or withering in a nursing home—Christine knew there would likely be no antidote to the odd ritual she had performed in Audrey's backyard. By now she'd nearly convinced herself there was nothing to undo. No one had that much control over what happened. The more she repeated this refrain, the easier it became to believe. It didn't matter what she'd envisioned or arranged on a candlelit table, she still would not have miscarried, at least not yet. Paige would have disappeared. Tim would be downstairs, pouring coffee and closing drawers with too much force, their contents rattling in protest and going silent.

Maybe it was the act of eavesdropping without his knowledge, but every sound he made felt filled with portent. The metal whoosh and click of the toaster. Loafer heels on the travertine floor. The refrigerator opening and shutting, then opening again, staying open so long the door alarm began to beep. He wasn't being efficient. Tim had once valued efficiency above all else, a quality best revealed by his closet, where shirts hung in formation, strictly organized by type, function, and color. But now he was bumbling about like an old man, as if the events of the last few weeks had released a store of blinding plaques into his brain. Even from here she could hear a knife scraping raspberry jam onto toast. The same breakfast, every weekday since they got married. He muttered something unintelligible and dragged out a chair. There was silence for several minutes, then came the sound of water running and the sharp ring of china on granite. For years he had blared the radio in the morning—NPR or the local rock station—but it occurred to Christine now that the radio had been muzzled for days. He'd canceled the newspaper and stopped watching the local news because the name Jennifer Guthrie was like a razor blade dragging across his nerves.

Before Christine could stand up, Tim came into the hall and looked up the stairs. Startled, she pulled the deep V-neck of her nightgown together with one hand, as modest as if she were being leered at by a stranger.

"What?" he said.

She shrugged, an imitation of nonchalance. "Nothing."

"What are you doing?"

"Sitting here."

"Why?"

"I had a little dizzy spell, that's all. No big deal."

He paused, looking concerned but a little doubtful. "Are you all right?" he asked.

"I'm fine."

"How do you know?"

"Because it only lasted a second."

"And yet you're still sitting on the floor. Maybe you should call Dr. Marsh."

"What does that mean?"

"It means maybe you should call Dr. Marsh, Chris. Sometimes things are just that simple." He walked up the stairs, lightly touching her shoulder on his way into the bedroom.

When he left to go show a house, Christine threw on a sweatshirt and running pants and followed him. She was certain he would spot her immediately, pull over to the side of the road, lower his window, and yell out, "What the fuck? You, too?" But her silver Camry blended in with a million generic sedans just like it and she hid in plain sight behind him. He drove, as usual, as if on the way to the hospital with a shooting victim in the back, making tailing him nearly impossible. He cut off a truck filled with landscaping equipment and slid across two lanes, weaving in and out, honking his horn, and keeping his cruising speed between eighty and eighty-five. It was incredible that he didn't crash. Everyone on the road hated him, flipped him off, yelled silently behind rolled-up windows. Christine could see a freeze-frame of a man's wide-open, cursing mouth even after she looked back at the road. She knew she was endangering the child inside her, but following Tim felt like a compulsion, the biological imperative of a woman who suspects her husband has been supplanted by an imposter. She drove along with him as best she could, keeping back a car length and trying not to rear-end anyone.

Tim seemed to know the route by heart. He had said he was heading to Anaheim to show a bungalow that had been renovated to within an inch of its life, tarted up with Carrara marble and a backyard fountain that gushed from a satyr's mouth. It was too bad none of it could improve the once up-and-coming neighborhood, which was rapidly reverting back to a slum. But if Tim was going to Anaheim to try to convince a young couple that the decaying surroundings were an artsy haven offering lots to do, then he was taking a shortcut Christine had never seen before. Tailgating a delivery van that would have killed him instantly if it had braked suddenly, Tim got off the highway a few miles before the first Anaheim exit and turned right toward the ocean. "What are you doing, Tim?" she said aloud.

He stopped to get gas. Christine pulled into a parking lot next door and watched him get out, swipe his credit card, stick the nozzle into the tank. From where she sat, everything he did seemed incredibly familiar but peculiar, as if he were being played by someone who had spent months studying his movements. It was strange to think that he was a person she loved; he seemed so remote, so oddly ordinary.

She almost lost him after that. He raced through a light as it turned red and there was a cop sitting at the intersection, so she was forced to stop. But Tim had been held up by road work and was only three cars ahead by the time she caught up to him. She could practically hear him losing it, banging the steering wheel with the heel of his hand, bellowing, "No wonder the state's broke, paying you shitbags. For Christ's sake, move it." It was still possible that he was taking a back way to Anaheim, but also possible that he had something unthinkable to take care of. A blood-smeared towel to dump, a visit to an out-of-the-way car wash so he could scrub fingerprints off the windows and vacuum up strands of Paige's S-shaped hair. It would be a relief if he drove to a hotel and slept with another woman in a crappy room; after all, it was no different from what Audrey was doing, and her life was still intact. It could be a strengthening moment in their marriage, and best of all, there would be no way to argue that she was culpable for anything she had imagined or was doing right now.

"Please God," she said. "Please let him be screwing somebody."

He drove up a side street called Hilliard Lane, slowed down, and parked in the driveway of a small yellow house. Christine stopped at the curb two houses away and shut off the car. This wasn't Anaheim. There was no For Sale sign on the lawn. The house was obviously lived in; there were marigolds in the window boxes and a plastic table and chairs on the porch. Tim wouldn't try to discard evidence here, in a middle-class neighborhood at nine in the morning, the yards crawling with children and a phone line being repaired up the street. No matter what he was doing, it was better than if he'd driven down an isolated county road or pulled up to a dumpster in a ruined part of Los Angeles. Christine tried to hold on to this shred of consolation, but could find no reason to believe it and in a moment it was gone.

Tim got out of the car and walked up to the front door. Christine supposed he could be meeting with a homeowner to discuss putting the house on the market, but he had left his laptop and briefcase behind. So this was the setting for his affair, then, a humdrum little street with birds tweeting and toilet paper fluttering gently in someone's tree. This was what her husband had sunk to, utter mediocrity. Exceptional, go-getting, one-hundred-and-ten-percent Tim, transformed into a has-been with a has-been's conventional taste in distractions. It made her sick to her stomach, watching the door and waiting for it to open, but more than anything she couldn't wait to find out what was next. Exactly what sort of woman did Tim go for when he wasn't feigning fidelity? An easily impressed college girl? Somebody's sad, breast-implanted wife?

She glanced in the rearview mirror and saw a black car parked about twenty feet behind her. There was a man in the driver's seat staring straight ahead. He might have been waiting for someone, or talking on his phone, or he might have followed Tim all the way from Golden Hills Estates. Of course. It had to be the police, it was the only thing that made sense. They might be letting rapists out of prison because they were too pricey to keep locked up, but evidently Tim was a higher priority. Suburban real estate agent, European clothes, nice house—one look and the detectives had probably despised him. She could almost see it from their point of view. Cocky asshole, one of those scammers who helped destroy the value of everybody's home and now thinks he can outwit the guys who actually work for a living. They couldn't arrest him yet but they could rattle him, make him wet his pants every time he stood at his kitchen window or drove somewhere.

When Christine looked at the house again, all she saw was Tim's back and the door closing behind him. Five seconds of inattention and he had slipped from sight. Worse, though, she had missed the appearance of Tim's mystery woman, and might never again have the opportunity to be so perfectly and spectacularly outraged. Wasn't that what everyone waited for in life, to be completely right at least once?

"Goddamnit," she said, throwing her door open. Why didn't someone just arrest Tim and get it over with? She could do something then, either leave him to his fate or believe in him to the end.

She walked up to the other car and stood beside the tinted window. "Excuse me?" she said, her voice shaking.

The window lowered slowly. It wasn't the police, it was Peter. Now that she saw him, she wondered that she hadn't recognized his car.

"Peter?"

He didn't say anything; he didn't have to. His eyes were lost in pockets of puffy red tissue, as if he had spent half his life in tears. Christine's only experience of him had taken place at various dinner parties and cookouts, where he'd displayed nothing but a very limited set of upbeat and orderly emotions. She hadn't known he was capable of anything more.

"What are you doing here?"

He cleared his throat roughly. "What are *you* doing here?"

"Well . . . I'm not sure."

"You're not sure," he repeated.

"You don't think—"

"I don't think anything, Christine. I stopped thinking two days ago. My ex-wife and her husband are flying in tonight. Do you have any idea what a disaster this is?"

"Yes."

"The police are questioning Linda this morning," he said with an incredulous half smile. "I find that astounding."

"Why?"

"*Why?*"

"They don't really suspect her."

"Of course they do," he said, squinting at her. "They suspect me. They suspect your husband."

"They're doing their jobs. It doesn't mean they have evidence against him or anybody else."

"So Tim had nothing to do with this."

"Peter . . ."

"They were watching him for a reason, Christine. Why do you think I'm here? I don't know what else to do but drive around chasing whatever I can think of. Help me. You live with him, you're having his baby."

"What does that have to do with it?"

Peter gave her a look of stunned disappointment, as if she were too stupid to believe. "You know him!" he shouted. "Who the hell is he? Is he capable of hurting somebody or not? Would he take a child? Any ideas?" Across the street a curtain parted and an elderly female face appeared at a window.

"I'm not going to talk about this on the street."

"Then where should we talk about it? In that house? The one Tim just went into?" Peter slowly shook his head. "You have no idea what he's doing there, do you? Incredible. You're his wife and you're just as ignorant as I am."

Christine leaned close to him and lowered her voice. "Peter, Linda is a friend of mine, and I'm sure you're going through a lot right now, but what happens between me and my husband is my concern."

"The hell it is. It stopped being your 'concern' when a bunch of cops invaded the neighborhood and started keeping an eye on everybody. Now maybe that's fine with you and Tim, but I'm embarrassed to tell people where I live."

"So move."

He didn't answer. He was looking out the windshield, his lips pressed together and his chin quivering slightly.

Christine glanced over and saw Tim. He was standing at the gate of the house, staring up the street. His head was angled slightly to one side, and his hand lay carelessly on top of the gate as if he had forgotten it the moment he saw his wife. She had never seen him appear so utterly stunned and insulted.

"You should go now, Peter," she said.

"I didn't come here to find out nothing. I want to know what's going on." He unbuckled his seat belt and pulled the keys from the ignition. But before he could get out, Tim walked calmly to his car.

"Where's he going?" Peter said, hoarse from panic and desperation. "Stop him!" He pushed his door open and hit Christine in the leg.

"I can't."

"Why not?"

With a deep sense of weariness, she stood in the street and watched Tim drive off, his blinker flashing—so correct, so law-abiding—before he turned and disappeared. When she looked back at Peter, his foot was still on the pavement as if he were about to stand, but his eyes were closed. His blue dress shirt had irregular wet patches under the arms.

"I'm sorry," she said. "Really."

She went to her car and drove home to get dressed for work. She didn't call Tim, and he didn't call her. At the office, she focused her attention on each of her clients, the only remnant of the morning a well of tears lodged in her throat. But as soon as she drove back through the development gates, she realized she had no idea what would happen next or how she would handle it. This feeling was compounded by the disarray in the neighborhood: the police cars, the television vans, the searchers standing around looking awkward and impotent. Linda was down the street, tall and confident, her hands fluttering as she tried to direct some volunteers. Christine would have liked to go over and offer help, but her encounter with Peter stopped her. She assumed that her friendship with Linda would suffer or be finished. What happened to Paige would determine it.

Tim hadn't come home yet. Christine sat by the window with a glass of water, waiting for his car to drive into view. The living room felt stuffy and forlorn, as though it had heard what happened. She looked from wall to wall, seeing sadness in the stance of furniture and the folds of drapes. After an hour her legs got stiff and she stood up. Eventually she forced herself to eat, though she had no appetite. When she finally tried Tim's phone, there was no answer, just the same message he'd had for a year. "You know what to do and when to do it."

It was twilight when she went upstairs to change. The door to the closet was open, and the sky just bright enough that she could see an unfamiliar darkness on Tim's side, a gap she hadn't noticed before. Sensing that it would be a thing better felt than seen, she left the light off and stepped inside.

Her hand reached out for his shirts—always spaced an inch apart, stripes, solids, patterns, dress and casual—but touched only air. She knelt and felt for his suitcases, but both were gone. She turned on all the lights then and searched the house for a note, but found nothing.

On impulse, because it was the only thing she could think to do, she called her father for the first time since he'd refused to loan her money for a surrogate. She didn't have to tell him about Tim, she could just hear his voice and lean on the fact that she had a father somewhere, even if he wasn't a particularly involved one. After two rings he answered—"Hello?"—and she said, "Hi, Dad. I'm so glad you're there." But the voice rambled on and she realized she was talking to his voicemail. Feeling vaguely ashamed, she held onto the phone for a few moments after the tone sounded, but hung up when she couldn't think of anything to say.

Sixteen

$\mathcal{A}$udrey had been in bed with William when Paige disappeared, and that was the problem.

In his attempt to be helpful in those first dramatic hours, after he noticed a cruiser parked at Linda and Peter's house, assumed a health crisis, and rang the bell to offer the use of his home defibrillator—and after Linda told him everything in a tearful rush—Mark volunteered the information that his wife had left for a colleague's birthday party in Garden Grove around seven-thirty that evening, and might have seen Paige or something that would aid the investigation.

"You told them what?" Audrey said, standing in the foyer just before midnight, her purse still over her shoulder, her chin raw from William's stubble.

"A little girl is missing and that's all you can say?"

"Is Jonathan all right?"

"Of course he is. He's not the one who disappeared."

"I have to go to Linda's *now*?"

"I told the officers you would. You better hurry up before they leave."

And so Audrey ended up on Linda's front porch, one foot propped on the hedgehog shoe brush, lying to a policewoman. She knew she didn't sound convincing—she stuttered when she described driving down to the main road from her house, and twice said Cerritos instead of Garden Grove—but she assumed this would be perceived as stress rather than deception. One thing she said was true: she had seen nothing unusual, no wandering child, no strange person in the neighborhood. Someone might very well have been there, Paige could have been screaming and flailing under a kidnapper's arm, but Audrey had been too absorbed by anticipation and the thrilling scratch of lace underwear against her skin to see much past the hood of her car. She probably hadn't been fit to drive.

She had hoped to make love with William one last time and then, with great wisdom and good humor, tell him it was time he started dating women his own age. But as soon as she'd seen him, leaning in the doorway with his shirt unbuttoned and his eyes focused so completely on her that she felt real for the first time in days, it scared her that she'd even considered it. And that weakness, that inability to do what was right, might have resulted in a child's disappearance. If she had come back earlier, would she have seen Paige? Would Jonathan have been standing at his bedroom window, or Mark taking out the garbage, or would the simple fact that she was home have influenced the outcome? It seemed incredible that while a scarred young veteran was bringing her to orgasm and whispering Conway Twitty lyrics in her ear, a child was vanishing at the same moment. Why wasn't there a safeguard against the concurrence of events so at odds with each other?

No one would look at her and believe that sex would be her undoing. By now, three weeks into their affair, she had expected her desire for William to be on the wane, but to her astonishment it was only increasing. When she was home, she was restless, prowling the hallways and dropping dishes, needing to be told things twice. She didn't remember feeling the same sort of passion for Mark, though he hadn't been a lover in those early days as much as a safe house. She had needed him to shelter her from the first twenty years of her life and he happily obliged, and in the two decades since their wedding, they had been making love at what she thought was the ideal suburban pace. She had assumed that it would continue that way— two or three times a month, on the bed or in the shower—until they were too ugly or sick to bother anymore.

But Mark's fixation with everlasting life had recently twisted his outlook on sex as well as death. Now when he reached for her, he seemed to be surrendering to some primitive drive he wished he didn't have to waste time on. "*Science Daily* just published another study about exercise and aging," he'd said one night as he rolled off her body. "I wonder if this counts as cardio." He approached eating in the same way, as a weakness he hoped one day to overcome. In comparison, chain-smoking William, with his mangled calf and nightmares and ability to have sex twice in half an hour, was the picture of robust immortality, preserved by nicotine and loud commercials, pickled in cheap beer.

That night, Audrey had lingered at William's apartment for nearly three hours. She brought him a video game he wanted but couldn't afford, and they had sex twice—once in bed and once on the living room carpet in front of Anderson Cooper. Afterward they ate tortilla chips and canned jalapeno dip, a meal so brazenly unhealthy every swallow had given Audrey a little jolt of exhilaration. "Tell me about your parents," she said to William. She sat cross-legged beside him on the floor, the rough carpet imprinting the sides of her naked calves.

"What do you want to know?"

"Where are they? What are they like?" These were questions she had wanted to ask ever since she noticed the suspicious blankness of his client file. She knew the shape and feel of his scars and the slightly concave curve of his chest, but had no idea what sort of woman had given birth to him. His old country records were the only hint.

"My mom was okay, except she hooked up with a lot of losers. You wonder how somebody makes the same mistake over and over and never figures it out. She died a couple years ago when I was overseas. Heart attack, probably, but I didn't want somebody cutting her up, so I don't know for sure." As if to say the story was finished, he shrugged.

"That's all?" Audrey said.

"The summary of Mom," he said, his heavy-lidded eyes on the muted television. "Not much more to tell. Dad side of the equation's a little more complicated."

"How?"

"I hardly knew him. Last time I saw him I was about fourteen and he was on probation for drugs. And my sister's a whole 'nother story. She married this Cuban guy, some lawyer who stopped her from coming to see us. No idea where she is or what she's doing now."

"Oh, honey." Audrey leaned over and kissed his bare arm. His family sounded strikingly similar to hers, except that it might have the distinction of being worse for being so small. With only four people, there was no way to spread the adversity around. She leaned back against the sofa, feeling strangely lucky. What were the chances that she would find someone who knew what it was like, when asked about his relatives, to launch into a narrative that sounded like a police report? Feeling that he would understand anything she said,

Audrey told William the story of Mala's book. Cigarette burning down between his fingers, he watched her face in the half-dark as she described being given the book by Linda, the trip to Bakersfield, and yesterday, tracking down the daughter of a dead Texas lawyer and sending an email titled "Mala Rinehart." It had felt like her first real break, because there was only one Daphne Bortner on the Internet. It was as if the woman had been given an unusual name solely to make it easier for someone to find her.

"Why not?" William said. "One thing I learned overseas, you don't pretend to know what might happen."

Encouraged by his lack of cynicism and analysis, Audrey talked on without fear or embarrassment. She had always believed there was a world where the usual rules did not apply, and the book had given her proof of this. At least one person had thought as she did, that in the background of ordinary existence was a place where a balloon drifting in the sky meant something important. She might not know what, exactly, but the main thing was that nothing was insignificant. She had looked up the proverbs from the book, and actually found a few in circulation on the Internet. This hadn't taken away their power for Audrey, but made Mala seem eerily present, as if, with a little probing, her wisdom could be found beneath the surface of almost anything. Sixty years after the book was written, snippets of her were flowing through broadband lines and cropping up at garage sales, passing from neighbor to neighbor and altering their lives in ways they might never understand. It was almost as if she were begging to be found.

"I don't know why this book matters so much to me," she said.

"I do," William said, and they left it at that.

Two mornings later Audrey joined an impromptu search party, walking in a somber line with three other women—stay-at-home

mothers from the neighborhood, all wearing latex gloves and carrying plastic bags—through the empty fields behind U Street. It was
the area where two acres of grand homes had been planned—the
Orvieto, the Arezzo, the state-of-the-art Duomo—and then scut-
tled, leaving only metal stakes and pink flagging tape as evidence of
the developer's ambitions. The ground was rough and knotted with
crabgrass that remained defiantly green despite the lack of rain. Audrey shuddered in apprehension and relief as she walked, imagining
the horror of hunting for her son's body, while the other women
appeared almost glad to be out of their respective houses. They
combed the fields for nearly two hours, finding everything, it
seemed, but Paige: glassine envelopes powdery with drug residue,
paper coffee cups, the black remnants of a campfire, a warped pile
of engineering textbooks, finished to great satisfaction, maybe, or
thrown away in disgust. Up by the rarely used service road, Audrey
nearly stepped on a little pile of animal bones, all jumbled and broken, probably the remains of a mountain lion's meal.

"Poor thing," one of the women said.

"Whatever it was," another replied, peering closer.

Linda was talking to a detective when Audrey returned to the
house, so Audrey just shook her head, offered a quick, reassuring
smile, and mouthed, *Back later.* She groaned with relief as she drove
out of the neighborhood, which had begun to feel like the stage set
of a tragedy. She had given Mark strict instructions to drive Jonathan to school, pick him up in the afternoon, and have him in sight
at all times when he was home. The doors were to remain bolted and
the alarm turned on. If he wanted to buy a Taser, she would be delighted.

It was after lunch by the time she got to the office. None of her
colleagues even glanced up from their computers—a good sign, as
it meant they hadn't heard the news about Paige and wouldn't expect more than the usual bland interaction.

Audrey had just opened the file of a new client, finally managing to focus for a minute on the work at hand, when her cell phone rang. The number was blocked. She was about to ignore it when a thought—an instinct, really—lit up in her mind. *The police.* She felt her heart wither. No client except William had her personal number, and who but the police would need to block a call? In the few seconds it took her to answer—there was no avoiding something like this, no acting like it didn't exist—the whole sordid tale unspooled in front of her. Deceptions didn't come out the way you imagined they might. Your husband didn't follow you when you left to meet your lover, he didn't burst in and drag you from another man's bed. Instead, a friend's stepdaughter disappeared, and you invented a story to cover up another, lesser crime, but your car was seen in a Cerritos parking lot, perhaps by Paula, the alleged birthday girl— no, a neighbor had seen your car return from the north, not the south as it would have if you'd truly been in Garden Grove, and because Mark couldn't keep his mouth shut, everyone knew about the idiotic defibrillator incident and what she had told the police, and one of the women in the development, thinking of her life as a movie the way Audrey often did, noticed a tiny inconsistency, probably nothing, but she thought the authorities might want to know about it. And now an officer was calling to say you were considered not only a liar, but a suspect. Your husband would know everything within the hour.

It had sounded histrionic, or hormonal, when Christine said that her life had shifted off its axis, impossibilities piling up one after the other, the pin removed from the gear that turned things in a regular, organized way. But as Audrey opened her mouth to speak, she wondered if the same wasn't true for her. "Good Fortune from Bad" might mean anything at all. She simply had to look at Linda and Christine to know that something had gone wrong, all three of their lives in turmoil, the usual sorrows and defeats replaced with the god-awful and the unbelievable.

"Audrey Cronin," she said.

"Hello. This is Daphne Wallace."

Audrey sat back, uncomprehending, the silence stretching to seconds.

"Daphne Wallace from Texas?" the woman continued. "Bortner was my maiden name. You sent me an email."

Blood flooded Audrey's face and she breathed for what felt like the first time in minutes. "I'm sorry. I was expecting someone else."

"Am I interrupting something?"

Now Audrey heard the accent, a distinct twang different from her own suppressed southern drawl. "No, no, I'm glad to hear from you. Thank you for calling."

"Forgive me, but I have to ask. Who are you? How did you find me?"

Keeping her voice low, Audrey told Daphne everything, how Linda had found the book and passed it on, the clues, the futile research, the Bakersfield trip, the advertisement she'd found in the archives of the San Antonio newspaper, her disappointment at finding George Bortner's obituary. "He's the only link to Mala Rinehart I've been able to find," she said, "until you."

"We knew she spent some time in Bakersfield in the late forties," Daphne said, "but there's no sign of her after that, and we've never heard of any book."

"So you know who she is?"

"Not exactly. We know a little about her. She was from West Texas, part of a—Romani clan, I guess. Palm readers and migrant workers, that kind of thing. But we have no record of her, no Social Security number or work history, nothing that would help us trace her."

"When you say 'us,' who do you mean?"

"I'm a lawyer like my father. I took over his practice after he died."

"Why was he looking for her?"

"A client of his, of mine now—actually, he's not the client any-more, he's been dead a long time." She laughed, a low, raspy sound that ended suddenly.

"I don't understand. Who's your client?"

"If you aren't a relative, I can't give you any more information. All I can say is that we'd like to find her, or if she isn't alive, her daughter, but we don't even have a name. Honestly, I'm not opti-mistic. A private investigator looked into this years ago and found nothing. I assume because there's nothing to find."

"Wait a minute," Audrey said. "She had a daughter?"

"Would you be able to send the book to me? It could be very helpful in our search."

Audrey imagined sending the book off to a stuffy office, where it would spend its remaining days buried under dusty law manuals and empty soda cans. "I don't think I could part with it, honestly."

"A copy would work just as well."

"But what do you need it for?"

"Again, that's something I can't go into."

"Would you tell me if you found her? Please, I know it doesn't make sense and I'm a stranger to you, but if you could just tell me a little about her. Are there photographs? She must have been some-one, right, if you're looking for her?"

"I wish I could help you. If you come across anything in your research or can send us the book, I'd appreciate a call. It really is quite important."

"Why?"

"Goodbye, Ms. Cronin."

Audrey sat for several minutes, her eyes fixed on the phone in her hand. She had to tell Christine and Linda; together they needed to do something with this information, whatever it meant. But she didn't know how to make it seem important to them. How could she ask them to care about a development so disconnected from their lives and the crises of the last two days? In the end she left them nearly identical voicemail messages. *Just want to see how you're doing, if there's anything you need. I'm thinking of you.*

By the way, I've got news.

Seventeen

JUNE 16, 1948

Her second week in Bakersfield, Mala took to knocking on doors in her search for Ruth. It was difficult just to get somebody to listen. Those who did either couldn't help or sent her to neighborhoods that took half a day to reach. She kept at it, one long block at a time. Every street connected to another, each lined with dozens of houses, wavering in the sun and stretching all the way to the distant ridge of mountains. After a few days walking up and down porch steps and across train tracks, she decided that you don't know the size of a place until you try to talk to everyone who lives there. No matter how many people she met, there was always somebody else turning a corner or stepping onto a bus, and in the afternoon, crowds of faces flooded from buildings downtown in a bustling blur of hats and stockings. A thousand times Ruth appeared, only to become a suspicious stranger the moment Mala stepped up and reached for her.

If she had any strength left in the afternoons, she looked for work. She went back to the same places again and again, wearing people down and becoming familiar to them, hoping her face would turn ordinary with enough repetition. If nothing else, she would show she was persistent. Finally she was given a temporary job sweeping floors at the Emporium Western Store while the regular woman was out sick. By the end of the week she had enough money for a meal at a lunch counter and had saved enough to last maybe ten more days. Enough time to find Ruth or decide she couldn't be found. Mala hid the money in the back of her notebook, which she kept concealed behind a loose brick in a wall of the abandoned warehouse. Or as she thought of it, home.

She was on the edge of sleep one stifling midnight, kept company by the wind and the scuffle of rats, when the brick fell out of the wall and the book banged to the floor beside her head. It sent up a small cloud of dust when it landed, and the pages settled down one by one. The cover closed slowly, the way it would in a dream. As she lay looking at it, wondering how it had fallen and if it might be a message from Drina, she heard a distant footfall, a heel on pavement. Immediately awake, she slid on her pants and pulled a blouse over the undershirt she slept in. She got up and crept through the decaying doorway to the passage that led past other rooms to the street.

It was so empty and hollow in this part of the warehouse that even the scratch of her bare feet echoed. Through the broken windows, Mala could hear a car rumbling by and turning at the corner. She went from window to window expecting to see a dark figure, but there was only the brush of palm fronds against the wall. She was about to go back to the bed she'd made from fabric scraps and an old bedspread when she heard a single word come in on the wind. It was a man's voice coming from outside, maybe ten feet away. She froze, unable to move.

The heavy iron door scraped open and stuck against the cracked stone floor, leaving a gap barely a foot wide. By the time Mala heard a step, she was back in her hiding place, the cramped, protected nook that had once been part of a furnace room. The moon blazed through the splintered windows, illuminating the hallway. It was as light as afternoon, but with long shadows and wind whirling through holes in the walls.

"Mala?" A half whisper bounced off the stone and died abruptly.

She didn't have to see him to know who it was. Resting her forehead against the cool brick, she waited for him to speak again. It wasn't happiness she felt as much as an angry sort of relief. She had thought of him a thousand times over the last week, hadn't he thought of her? What had taken him so long? Maybe he'd just come for his money. In that case, she had almost all of it, three crumpled dollar bills and a pile of nickels and pennies. If that was what he wanted, he could have every cent.

"Mala?"

She stepped from the doorway. "Yes."

"You okay?"

"Of course I'm okay. I'm standing here, aren't I?"

He nodded, scuffed the toe of his boot against the floor. "How you been?"

"Fine. Never better."

"Well, you're in a mood."

"I was asleep," she said. "Did you come for your money?"

The moon was so bright she could see him frown. The buttons of his shirt glinted like coins. "I say anything about that?"

She shrugged. "What do you want, then?"

"Nothing. I have something to show you, is all."

"I don't know. It's the middle of the night."

"Sorry about that, but it can't be done any other time."

She folded her arms to show her reluctance.

"Get your shoes and come on," he said.

"To where?"

"Five minutes in the truck, seven tops. I promise."

"How do I know you're not taking me to the police station?"

"I would have done it the first night, wouldn't I? I've got no reason now."

She paused for as long as she could, making him wait. "What if I say no?"

"Then I'll keep coming back and aggravating you."

She turned suddenly and went back to her room. "Ridiculous," she muttered, pushing her dirty, callused heels into boots. "Almost one in the morning." She grabbed her book off the floor and shoved it into the hollow in the wall, trying three times to get the brick to fit before giving up and dropping the book in her bag.

She followed Elliot outside and around the building to the street. His truck was parked at the curb, windows down, its bed a mess of tools, straw, and oil-stained blankets. "Go on, get in," he said.

"You never told me where we're going."

"Just get *in*."

Mala got in. She squeezed herself up to the door and watched him as he drove. "I wish you'd tell me what this is all about."

"You'll know soon enough."

"Shouldn't you be at the farm asleep?"

"Yup."

His face glowed in the light from the dials as if there were a candle under his chin. Mala forced herself to look away from him and out the window. Elliot drove all the way through town—much longer than five minutes, in her estimation—to a neighborhood of simple houses, all of them silent with darkened windows. He was slowing down now, riding only a few inches from the cars parked at the curb.

"I think I've waited long enough," Mala said.

"Don't make a fuss about this, okay?"

"Why is it that when a woman asks a question, men call it making a fuss?"

"Give me a chance," he said, taking his eyes off the road long enough to look at her. "Believe it or not, I'm doing you a favor."

"Is that what it is? Because it feels like kidnapping."

His laugh was a rolling, husky sound even deeper than his voice. "You got in my truck on your own two feet."

"Well, I wish I hadn't."

Peering out his side window, he came to a stop. "I think this is it."

"You think this is what?"

He turned off the engine and got out. "Come with me."

Mala sat in the truck with her arms crossed. He looked at her through the windshield and raised his hands. After several seconds he came to her window and knocked on it. "You going to stay there all night?"

She opened the door forcefully and stepped out, her arms and back burning from a week sweeping floors. "What's going on?"

"Quiet. You'll wake the whole neighborhood." He grabbed her wrist and pulled her up the walk to a little white house with tapered porch columns and stained glass set into the door. As soon as he rang the bell, he dropped Mala's hand. "I have a friend," he said. "Kid who sorts letters at the post office."

"So?" she said, confused.

He reached out but stopped just short of touching her arm. "Listen, I got to get back. Good luck, okay?"

"You can't just leave me here," she said, starting after him, but stopped when she heard the door open behind her.

She knew before she turned to look, before her eyes could adjust to the sudden dazzle of a bare bulb overhead. She let herself turn slowly, because the moment would happen only once and had been so long in coming.

Ruth stood on the other side of the screen door, wearing a simple blue bathrobe and blinking against the light. She was smaller than Mala remembered, with sloping shoulders and hands that showed every rough knuckle and blue vein. Her pale red hair was shorter now and half gray, her forehead creased but her body still strong and stout.

At first she looked confused, even a little frightened, but then Mala stepped closer and said, "It's me."

There was a long silence before Ruth began to cry, a sudden wrenching of emotion that seemed to surprise her. Mala opened the screen door and grabbed Ruth's hands. "I'm sorry," she said.

"For what?"

"I don't know. So much time going by."

Ruth embraced her, shaking her head as she clutched Mala's back and shoulders. She pulled back, her eyes still glassy but the tears already dry. "What are you waiting for?" she said. "Come in."

Mala followed her inside. The air smelled faintly of cooking and the rug was like deep grass under her boots. "I didn't wake anyone else, did I?"

"There's no one else here. I live alone, have for the past five years. Where are you staying?"

"I've been sleeping in an old warehouse for a couple weeks while I looked for you."

"A warehouse! My God."

"It's not so bad."

Ruth led the way to the living room, keeping Mala's hand gripped in hers. It was the sort of kindness Mala had always hoped for from Ruth, back when she'd had to settle for the occasional smile or encouragement.

"Are you hungry?" Ruth asked.

"No," Mala said, although she was, and had been for nearly two days. It was an emptiness so deep and long-lasting one lunch counter meal wasn't enough to fill it.

"Who was that young man who brought you here?"

"Just somebody I met. He helped me find you."

"Well, I can't imagine why you're in Bakersfield," Ruth said, switching on lamps and illuminating a room filled with antique furniture, plants, and books. "Tell me."

"I got sent away for a year. I didn't know what else to do but look for you." Mala sat on the edge of a stiff red sofa, acutely conscious of her manners and appearance. She had been bathing as best she could from a rusty spigot's trickle in what had once been the warehouse boiler room, but black dust still clung to her fingernails and the grooves of her skin.

"Sent away?" Ruth said, sitting across from her. "What on earth for?"

"I got the blame for a lot of things, usually whatever went wrong."

"You're different, that's all. People don't know how to take it. They never have."

"It's more than that," Mala said. "They think I make things happen, and I guess I do. Tell you the truth, I don't really know."

"Oh, come on now. You don't believe in any of that, do you?"

"Sometimes, maybe."

"You know, the world would be a different place if we could just make things happen."

"Maybe it's what it is because we have."

She looked at Mala for several seconds before smiling. "Well, what I'm wondering is, where have you been all this time?"

"Oh, just about everywhere. Killeen, Round Rock. We even got as far south as Victoria once. I never went back to the ranch. We lost our store and moved on not long after you did."

"I heard that."

"How?"

"I have a friend at the ranch who writes from time to time." Ruth let out a breath that sounded like seven years of stored-up regret. "You weren't the reason I left, you know. There was a misunderstanding between Mrs. Nolan and me. I've always wanted to tell you that."

"What happened? I heard rumors but I never really knew."

"I'll tell you all about it someday, when it isn't so late. We should get to bed."

Mala stood up to go, already anticipating a long walk down dark and unfamiliar streets, but Ruth shook her head. "You're staying here with me," she said. "Most of the time I've rented this house my guest room has stood empty. I'd like it to get some use."

"I can't pay you for—" Mala began to protest, but Ruth waved her off.

"I don't tutor children with no interest in learning and save my money so you can sleep in a warehouse."

"You don't keep house anymore?"

"Only for myself, and that's enough. Upstairs now, Mala. I have a pupil in the morning and you need a bath and some sleep. You'll wear one of my nightgowns and tomorrow we'll work out the rest."

Half an hour later Mala was splayed in her first real bed, damp hair spread across a pillow, skin still tingling from a hard scrubbing. "You're dreaming," she said aloud. "Don't get used to it."

She rolled from side to side in the white moonlight, amazed at the sheer width of the mattress and smoothness of the sheets, but as soon as she wanted to sleep she found it impossible. There was such a thing, she realized, as too comfortable. No matter how she turned or stretched her legs, the bed gave way under her hips and shoulders, so soft it was like lying in midair. She expected any moment to plummet to the floor.

It was nearly three by the ticking clock when she got up, took the book from her bag, and wrote *found her* in the margin of a crowded page. Then she spread a blanket on the thin braided rug beside the bed. She lay down, welcoming the familiar hardness under her head and spine. Wrapped ankle to neck in white muslin, she dropped into the kind of sleep possible only in a house with a locked door.

Eighteen

*E*veryone expected Margaret to fall apart when she got to California. So far her reaction to her daughter's disappearance hadn't been encouraging. She screamed when Peter woke her with a 5:00 A.M. call, sobbed into her cell phone all the way to the airport, blamed Peter's company, the economy, and Paige's teachers, and was nearly arrested after swatting away the hands of the woman who patted her down at security. Luckily, Neil had brought Valium, and he managed to haul Margaret onto the plane and into her seat before she collapsed and fell asleep for the first time in thirty hours.

But by the time she arrived at Golden Hills Estates, she had become eerily serene and forgiving, making Linda appear practically hysterical by comparison. "You're not to blame," she told Linda as she got out of the rental car. "I am, for letting her come and live with you."

"I'm so sorry, Margaret," Linda said. She had cried so much that speaking was enough to bring it on again.

"I know," Margaret said, giving her two brief pats on the back. "We all are."

"This is what she does," Peter whispered to Linda as they walked into the house. "As soon as somebody else gets upset, she turns into the calm one. So keep it up, all right? It's the only reason she's able to function right now."

"What do you mean, keep it up?"

"You don't want to see the alternative. It won't help any of us."

Margaret stood in the middle of the foyer, appearing so out of context that Linda could hardly believe she wasn't having visions. The dress code of California had already seeped into Linda's subconscious, making Margaret appear flat-chested and severe with her dark bob, like a character from a cabaret. She was a few inches shorter than Linda, with an angular, somewhat equine face that had only recently begun to show signs of age. Though she looked completely conventional with her low heels and wide-legged wool slacks, Linda had always sensed something vaguely secretive about her, as if she swiped things from department stores or harbored sexual proclivities her neighbors would have trouble understanding. But from what Peter said, she wasn't anything out of the ordinary in bed, and had once called her insurance company to say she'd been undercharged. She had been born in Vermont to a family of well-off cheapskates, a background that explained her abiding refusal to raise the thermostat above sixty-five degrees, no matter how much her houseguests shivered. Two Christmas Eves ago she had draped a mothball-scented throw around Linda's shoulders and said, "It's a good thing you weren't a pilgrim, my dear. You'd have been dead in six months."

Margaret didn't want to hear about the minutiae of the investigation or anything else until after she had unpacked and seen the house. Heaping everything on her head at once wouldn't find Paige. She needed to take things one at a time, the way she did on ordinary days. "It's a shame my first visit has to be under these circumstances," she said. "Show me the kitchen."

It felt like a sacrilege to be giving Margaret the grand tour, but Linda was afraid to set her off by refusing or asking Peter to do it. "Uh-huh," she said, following Linda from room to room. "Okay. Wow." Only when Margaret stopped outside Paige's door did her emotions rise to the surface.

"Please tell me the police did this, looking for evidence."

"They looked around, but it's basically as it was," Linda replied.

"Well, the first thing she'll do when she gets home is hang up her clothes. I didn't teach her to make a mess in other people's homes."

"It's her home, too, I guess."

"Either way, Linda, there's underwear on the floor."

Margaret's final impression of the house wasn't surprising. "Lots of space," she announced when they reached the pergola in the backyard. "Not much charm, but I guess that's California."

"It isn't really my style," Linda said.

"Of course it isn't. Thank God."

Linda wasn't sure what a good mother looked like, so it was hard to tell where Margaret fell on the bell curve. During Margaret's first afternoon in California, Linda noticed that she spent most of the time talking about her emotions, which coping mechanisms her therapist had suggested, how the whole situation was affecting her sleep and digestion. Of course, she herself was a failure at being maternal by anyone's measure, so it was all the more shocking when she found herself feeling that her response was more appropriate, more motherly, than Margaret's.

She had done everything a person is supposed to do when a child goes missing. She'd stopped eating and showering, and cried every day until she gave herself a crushing headache. It seemed the least she could do, spend every night puffy and miserable, rubbing the base of her skull and sleeping in short snatches on a damp pillow. The biscuits incident came back to her again and again, in waves of graphic images that included Paige's toes, the splashing eggs, and the knife held high in the air.

"Did you and Paige have an argument?" was one of the first questions the police asked her that morning, after, "Is there anything you'd like to tell us before we get started?" She brought them out to the patio so Peter wouldn't have to overhear the same questions he'd already answered. She wouldn't have been nervous at all, certainly not about Paige, if she hadn't spent the last eighteen years anticipating a moment exactly like this one. It was remarkable how much the cast of characters aligned with her imagination: the obese detective in his fifties who wheezed and spat with every word, the woman in her late thirties whose friendly demeanor was undercut by something predatory in her eyes, the younger, handsome one who looked like he'd joined the force after one too many humiliating auditions. When he sat in the Adirondack chair across from her, the smell of his cologne wafted over like a gust of pesticide.

"We talked to Emily yesterday," he said. He set her up for it, seeming to enjoy her anxiety, asking how well she knew Emily and if she'd ever had an altercation with her.

"Of course not," Linda replied. "She's a fifth grader."

"She says you're hard on Paige. You make her do a lot of chores and go to bed without supper."

"That's coming from an eleven-year-old," Linda said. "It didn't happen that way."

"How did it happen?"

"She was helping me make biscuits for a dinner party." This sounded so painfully contrived that Linda hardly believed herself. Biscuits? Nothing she said came out right. She regretted bringing up the knife the moment she mentioned it, but there was no other way to explain the argument. "I didn't want her to cut herself. It was a sharp chef's knife. I was trying to protect her."

"Of course." This was Lisa Finnegan talking now, one overwhelmed modern woman to another. The men, apparently bored with the domestic line of questioning, were muttering to each other in quiet voices.

"She got upset and wanted to go swimming at Emily's house. When she came home she seemed fine."

"You didn't send her to bed without dinner? Emily got a text from Paige to that effect."

Linda inhaled with the intention of letting out a long, exasperated sigh, but thought better of it. "Of course not. She didn't have *our* dinner, but she didn't want that anyway. She had something else."

"No children of your own, Mrs. Fredrickson?"

She wanted to say, *What does that have to do with it?* but responded simply, "No." She said this sadly, as if it were a burden imposed on her by a cruel universe.

After an endless half hour the police left. Peter had gone out without leaving a note, but came back just before noon. "Where were you?" she asked. "I tried to call."

"I know." In an unsteady voice, he described following Tim and Christine to some far-flung neighborhood and getting lost on his way home, so lost he'd had to pull over at a gas station in a slum and ask for help. The car's navigation was worthless. He didn't know what Tim was doing and neither did Christine, which convinced him that Tim was up to something. Whether it had anything to do with Paige, he didn't know.

"You should tell the police," Linda said.

"Tell them what? That I followed a guy who did nothing illegal? He's married to your friend."

"That doesn't matter right now! He's already been questioned about a murder."

"No, no, you're right. I'll do it this afternoon."

Later she heard him on the phone with one of the detectives, saying, "I think you should check his trunk." He came into the kitchen after hanging up, his expression a study in injustice. "Can you believe it? They've got no evidence that would let them search his car."

"How are they supposed to get it if they don't do anything?"

"It's outrageous. I guess I'll have to do it."

"How, Peter? You can't just start breaking laws."

He stared at her with wild, helpless eyes. "I'm supposed to live with this guy doing whatever he wants? I'm not going to let it happen. I'll go crazy."

"Don't worry, okay?" Linda said. "We'll figure something out."

"What?" he asked.

It was a question neither of them could answer.

By the time Margaret woke on her second day in California, she was convinced that Paige had run away and would come back as soon as she got hungry enough. "I had a dream about it," she said, sitting at the kitchen table in her robe. "Paige is in a peach yogurt phase, right? That'll be pretty hard to satisfy if she's wandering the streets without any money." Margaret refused Linda's offer of breakfast with a barely perceptible jerk of her chin and continued. "You know, it can't be a coincidence that she complained to Emily about the dinner party a few hours before she vanished. It's only logical. We're going to be awfully embarrassed when she calls crying or comes home after scaring the hell out of us, which I personally think is her goal. We might even have to reimburse the police for all this. It's only fair that you pay the bill, Peter, considering you were the parent in charge."

Perhaps it was Linda's fault for gradually becoming calmer, but by noon Margaret had decided that the ballet slipper and the Jennifer Guthrie murder were facts too significant to explain away, and she would probably never see her daughter alive again. "I won't see her dead either," she said, still in her robe but now wearing patent leather loafers. "Nobody's going to force me to identify her. I won't do it."

"Slow down," Linda said. "We're a long way from that."

"We could be minutes from it," Margaret replied. She stood at the living room window, eyes fixed on the barren horizon, one hand full of clutched drapes. "Be straight, Linda. You have no way of knowing."

"Do you want some lunch? You haven't eaten since last night."

"Please don't ask me about food again, all right? It's like asking if I want to go on without her."

The serenity she'd demonstrated on arrival had boiled down to a tooth-grinding stoicism, punctuated with stifled waterworks behind a closed door every hour or so. "I'm sorry but I can't help with the search," she said, emerging from the bathroom later with a tissue pressed to her nose. "It would mean I'm looking for a body. I'll stay here in case Paige comes home. I can answer phone calls and make a bunch of those posters, if I can figure out Peter's asinine printer."

That afternoon's search in the fields near U Street yielded nothing, an outcome that gave them all a boost of optimism followed almost immediately by a feeling of despair. This was the way it might go for days, weeks, months. Neil spent the evening on the phone to Connecticut, talking to the other children and to his mother, who was acting as substitute parent in his absence. After a few hours of driving around neighboring towns and slowing down to look at every child over the age of five, Peter trudged upstairs to watch the news. Neither Margaret nor Linda could imagine going to bed yet, so they stayed up and had a glass of wine at the kitchen table. Any animosity Linda had harbored for Margaret—for sending Paige to California, for calling too much, even for the ugly size-ten shoes she had abandoned by the front door—could not be sustained in light of Paige's disappearance. To be irritated by something small would seem practically barbaric.

Margaret, suffering from jet lag and unaccustomed to the effects of alcohol, was drunk in twenty minutes. She had an explosion of tiny red spots under each eye from crying and the skin in her face had gone lax, making her look every inch her forty-six years and then some. But she wasn't a maudlin or sloppy drunk; in fact, she was one of those rare people who becomes more articulate and interesting when intoxicated. "I'll tell you the truth, Linda," she said, "I never pictured you living in such flashy surroundings."

Though Margaret's tone was light, anyone halfway observant could hear the subtext that flowed beneath her words like a fetid stream. "We had no choice but to move in here," Linda said. "Our apartment in New York looked nothing like this. You remember."

"Yes. Hard to believe this is all they have out here."

"In this area, at least. We looked at a Spanish-style house but it was worse. Formica and old windows. "

Margaret poured herself more wine. She already smelled powerfully of alcohol, as if her lungs were lined with it. She was going to be miserable in the morning, and maybe that was her intention: to pile on so many kinds of pain that she had trouble deciphering what was related to Paige and what wasn't.

She pulled her lips into a sorrowful smile. "You know what I felt when Peter called me?"

"Oh, God, I can only imagine," Linda said.

"Relief. Just for a second, until it all sank in. Isn't that terrible?"

"Why relief?"

"I don't know. I've always had this odd feeling of transience with her, like she was about to slip out of my hands. It's something I've sensed from the beginning. You know how that is, don't you?" Her eyes searched Linda's for some trace of understanding. "It was like the end of my marriage to Peter. I knew it was coming and I didn't want it to happen, but when it did I didn't have to fight anymore. I think that's why I let Paige come here. Because I knew I couldn't hang on to her, and I almost didn't want to. I didn't have the energy."

"Hm." It was all Linda could manage. She was so used to feeling like the most callous person in the room, the only one who would survive by herself in a bombed-out city or on a drifting ice floe, that listening to Margaret talk was like discovering something horrible and cold about humanity. It was easy to be heartless when you were surrounded by people who were soft and cowardly, but when you were surrounded by heartlessness, it only made you realize how weak and foolish you'd been all along.

"I guess I'm an awful mother," Margaret said. "I've earned the right to be, dealing with so many children. Kids bring out everything shameful in you, they really do. I've begun to think that's what they're there for. To make you confront yourself."

"Parenting is hard."

"How do you know? I mean, honestly?" Margaret seemed to be swallowing her manners along with her wine. A different and less predictable side of her was emerging. The next thing Linda knew she would be praising the built-in white lacquered clock that grew out of the living room mantel like a plastic tumor.

"I'm a stepmother," Linda said.

"Technically, I suppose you are."

"Actually, there's no denying that I am."

"Though you never wanted to be, and that's okay. I shouldn't judge you, Linda, not for anything. You know why? Because whatever you've done, I've done worse."

"What do you mean, what *I've* done?"

"You don't think I looked into you when you started dating my husband?"

There was that perverse sense of relief Margaret had spoken of—someone finally knew after all these years—but it was quickly followed by the kind of fury that couldn't be smothered over by good breeding, of which Linda had none, or a smile, which was usually easier to summon after two glasses of wine but not tonight.

"Why the hell would you look into me?"

"Not because I care what Peter does, God knows, but he did give me the house and he pays for the children's schools, and if Paige and her brother were going to come into the city and spend the night under your roof, I wanted to know who was tucking them in. I think that's perfectly reasonable."

"You wanted to make sure I wouldn't poison them."

"Exactly. But my point is not that you put your father in the worst state-run nursing home in New York and threw away the key, but that I'm not one to judge you. Don't you see what I'm getting at?"

Linda sat back and crossed her arms. "Not really, Margaret. No."

"I was glad Peter didn't marry one of those socialites he was always screwing around with, the desperate ones in their late forties with the scrawny necks and the eyebrows pulled up to here. He chose you, and after that I was able to stop feeling like the most flawed woman on earth. You and I have more in common than you realize."

"You know nothing about my father."

"I'm sure that's true, but it doesn't matter." Margaret was slurring slightly now. It would be difficult in the morning to believe that she'd actually meant any of this, or that it had even happened. Linda knew already that she would wake up wondering if something so absurd was possible.

"I think it matters a lot," she said.

"There's more to it than your father, or your brother, who signed the papers right along with you. I couldn't find out all the details, but you were arrested in your twenties, weren't you?"

"You've gone insane."

"From what I could tell, you didn't do anything violent, and New York was a pretty rough place back then, so I decided it wasn't worth mentioning to Peter. It only happened once, so you must have learned your lesson."

Linda took her wineglass and got up. "I'm not surprised you don't drink, considering what comes out of your mouth when you do."

"Sit down, Linda. You haven't heard the best part."

Linda dumped the rest of her wine in the sink. "I'm going to bed. We have a lot to do tomorrow morning."

"That's why none of this is really important. Sometimes you need something really bad to happen to make you realize the insignificance of everything else. For comparison's sake."

Linda filled a glass with water, drank it all, then filled it again. She shut off the lights one by one until Margaret was sitting in complete darkness with only the stove clock to keep her from running into a wall.

"He isn't her father," Margaret said quietly.

Linda stopped at the doorway, a breath frozen in her throat. Half a minute went by before she said. "I don't want to hear any more."

"I keep wondering, how would he feel if he knew that I'd had an affair with an old friend from high school? Paige looks exactly like him. What if I told Peter that? Would he still feel the same way about her or would there be a part of him that would care a little less?"

"You'll never find out because you're not going to tell him."

The base of Margaret's wineglass hit the table with a clumsy thud. "What if it would make him feel better, though, Linda? Think about that. It could really save his life."

"I promise you it wouldn't."

"How do you know?"

"Good night. And please leave the living room light on. In case Paige comes home."

...

Linda went upstairs to find Peter lying awake in the dark. "I was about to come find you," he said. "It's one in the morning."

"Margaret's drunk."

"She's drunk? It must be the first time in her life. Is she all right?"

"She's just rambling, that's all. Go back to sleep."

"I don't know if I can."

"You can."

Linda slid into bed and put her arms around him. It wasn't until the middle of the night, long after Peter had thrashed around and talked in his sleep and stretched horizontally across the bed with his long, thin legs under hers, that she heard Margaret come upstairs and shut the door to the guest room down the hall.

Nineteen

*T*wo days after moving out, Tim came to the house to pick up his tennis racquet and some clothes. He arrived after work, just as his email had said he would. He rang the front doorbell like a solicitor and waited for Christine to open it.

"Hi," he said. "I just have to grab a few things."

Wordlessly, she stood aside and let him pass. When he didn't stop to ask how she was or volunteer to talk, she followed him across the house and down the stairs to the basement. Tim had once had plans to turn it into a luxurious home theater, to build a bar and put in a pool table, but somewhere along the line it had become the second stomach of the house, where objects went to ferment for an undetermined length of time before being recovered and put to use or left to pile up.

He flipped on the light and started going through plastic storage bins of gym clothes and hiking gear.

"You're playing tennis again?" she said. "It's been years."

"Yeah, and I miss it." He inspected the bottom of a pair of sneakers and set them aside. "How are you feeling?" he asked without turning around.

"Do you really care?" she said with a short laugh. "I haven't heard from you in two days."

"Christine, come on."

"I'm pregnant, Tim. High risk, over forty. I'm here all alone."

He looked at her over his shoulder. "Who's fault is that?"

"What were you doing at that house the other day? Can't you at least try to explain it?"

"I've got nothing to hide." He shook out a pair of running shorts, found a tear, and dropped them to the floor in a silky blue heap. "God, we collected a lot of crap. Stuff that should have gone to the thrift store a long time ago."

The past tense—*collected*—gave Christine a nauseating feeling of finality, of being entirely helpless. Tim seemed to be saying that the decisions—whether to talk, stay married, be a father—were his alone.

"Have you seen that black gym bag?" he asked. "You know the one I mean, with the front pockets?"

"Where are you staying, Tim? You haven't even told me."

"Ask the cops, they know," he said. "They're watching me there, too."

"You're in a hotel?"

"No. An executive apartment in Irvine."

"Not with that woman who lives in the yellow house?"

He sat back on his heels. "You mean Sharon Proctor."

"Who's that?"

"Do I really have to explain this? She's one of the secretaries. Or was. She didn't last very long."

"You're—" Christine had to stop to take a breath. "You're sleeping with her?"

He closed his eyes, as if it took all of his strength not to start shouting. "Look," he said. "She got fired last week and she's all up in arms. I went there to try to smooth things over before she files a lawsuit or something. That's the last thing the brokerage needs."

It was such an absurdly simple explanation—and wholly possible, with the flaky cast of characters Tim worked with—that she didn't believe it. It was too neat. He must have spent the last two days inventing it.

"If that's all it was, why didn't you tell me?"

"Why bother? If there's no trust here, we've got nothing." After digging around behind a row of bursting boxes, he finally produced the black gym bag. "I don't see my racquet," he said, slinging the strap over his shoulder. "Is it in the garage?"

"It's right there, in the corner."

"Oh." He leaned across an old outdoor umbrella, grabbed the racquet, tested the strings against the heel of his hand. Then he actually swung it, casually slicing a forehand through the air with a low whipping sound.

"They haven't found Peter's daughter yet," Christine said pointedly.

"I figured. I would have heard about it otherwise."

She stepped closer, moving into his line of sight so he would be forced to look at her. "Why are you acting this way, Tim? I'm finally pregnant after so many years of trying and you just move out?"

"It's more complicated than that and you know it."

She waited for him to continue, but he didn't. He just stood there looking around as if the most important thing was not to forget his knee band.

"Please come home." There, she'd said it, and she immediately hated herself for it. She sounded exactly like her mother pleading with her father—*I can't be by myself, not after all these years.* As a teenager, she had always taken her mother's side in arguments, but after sitting in her bedroom that night listening to her mother's melodramatic whimpering and watching through the cracked door as she fell pathetically to her knees and clutched his shirt, she'd understood exactly why her father wanted to leave. She'd wished she could go with him.

"I want to come home," Tim said. "But look, lately it's been one shit storm after another. For years if you count the miscarriages. Maybe we should start paying attention to that."

Christine's mouth trembled and her vision blurred with tears. "Why don't you stay for dinner? Or we can eat out."

"Can't tonight. I'm having a drink with one of the new agents. Single guy, just moved here."

Already he was going on without her, having shrugged her off like an old skin. "How about tomorrow?" she said, struggling to keep the grating sound of tears out of her voice. "We have to talk sometime. In a little over six months we'll be parents."

"How about this. I'll see you Thursday after work. We can talk then." He started up the stairs. "I just need to get some stuff from my closet."

"I'll help you."

"That's okay."

He was almost to the stairs when he turned and saw her behind him. "You know what, I'll get the stuff tomorrow. Traffic was bad getting here and I don't want to be late meeting this guy." At the sight of her face, he looped his arm around her shoulders. "Don't worry so much," he said, shaking her gently. "We'll be all right."

"*We* will? Or . . ."

He kissed the top of her head and left.

...

Christine called Audrey the next morning from the office, wanting to spend the time before her first session discussing anything but pregnancy, Tim, or Paige's disappearance. Although Audrey was at work, she gladly obliged, taking her cell phone to a supply closet and talking about her affair, which was going well, and her search for Mala, which was not. After talking to some lawyer in Texas, she had begun to look for Mala's daughter. She'd called the old man in Bakersfield to see if he remembered seeing a child at the house across the street, but his granddaughter said he was in the hospital with pneumonia and his condition was deteriorating. Audrey's latest idea was to look through birth records for information, but there was no guarantee that Mala's daughter had been born in Bakersfield, if she'd been born at all. More discouraging still, she had probably been given the father's last name, and without a name, Audrey had nothing.

"You'll keep trying, though, won't you?" Christine asked.

"If there's something to try, I'll do it."

After the call, Christine went out to the waiting room to plump pillows and put out fresh magazines. The door behind her opened and she turned, expecting to see her ten o'clock client walking in early. It was Arso.

"Hello," he said. "You have a minute to talk?"

"About what? How did you find me here?"

"It was easy. You have a business, right?"

"Why didn't you call first?"

He was wearing the same uniform he'd worn during their meeting in Riverside, except this time he had on a cheap gray dress shirt. One side of the large pointed collar was tight to his neck, while the other flopped down over his collarbone, revealing a triangular patch of dark chest hair. "I was nearby. It seems better to talk in person."

"I'm listening." She leaned against the back of the sofa, her cell phone clutched in her hand. She didn't think she had reason to fear Arso, but just in case, she was prepared to dial 911, or if she didn't have time, to break the phone over his head.

"Well, first I say congratulations because you are pregnant."

"You know about that?"

"Your husband tells me, and this takes me to why I am here. He comes to my house again yesterday night. Did you know?"

"No, I didn't."

"Okay, please, I want him to go away."

"Why was he there?" she asked.

"He wants his money, of course. He comes three times and makes a lot of trouble for me, yelling in the street."

"I'm sorry about that."

Arso nodded. "He makes my wife afraid. It's not good for her. She is having in vitro now."

Suddenly the whole thing seemed so pointless, so avoidable. "I'm not making excuses for him, but have you ever thought about just giving him the money? It was a little unfair, keeping it the way you did."

He smiled in a condescending, European way that seemed to say she was naïve and stupid for suggesting he do anything but keep what was given to him in a moment of weakness. "It bothers me to keep the money, I don't want to do it. I want our agreement to happen, but you change your mind. What else can I do?"

"We didn't change our minds. I'm pregnant and that should have voided the agreement."

Arso shrugged as if her reasoning were so silly it wasn't worth a response. "I don't want to call the police and this is why I come here. Please talk to your husband."

"That was our money. You don't need it. You have this other couple paying you."

"I don't come to argue about the money, but to ask a favor. Is your decision what you do."

Just as she was about to show him the door and instruct him not to return, a thought occurred to her, an idea so calculating she was ashamed to consider it.

"Arso, I'm going to tell you something," she said. "For the protection of your wife and family."

He frowned slightly, but he was also smiling, as if he expected her to sputter more nonsense, or perhaps threaten him in a way that he would only find amusing.

"You've heard about the murder near here? About six weeks ago?"

It took several seconds, then his eyebrows went up. "The young woman, choked," he said, briefly wrapping a hand around his own throat.

"Yes. Awful." Christine fixed her eyes on Arso's so there would be no mistaking her sincerity. "I don't think you've heard. My husband is a suspect."

Arso paused and his lips parted. "A suspect. This means . . ."

She nodded slowly.

"Ah—*hah*," he said, his maddening composure finally slipping.

"He's been under surveillance. I'm only telling you because—I'm concerned. I don't know if he's guilty, even the police don't know. But the fact that he's coming to your house . . ."

"My wife would be very worried to know this."

For the first time in weeks Christine felt in control of a situation. That she was capable of steering Arso's emotions, pulling him this way and that after he'd boasted about his properties and kept the money, was particularly gratifying. "Let me help, Arso."

"How?"

"The most important thing now is to protect Sofija, right?"

"Yes, no question."

"Even if Tim is innocent, he's unpredictable. Do you know he moved out three days ago? I just came home one night and he was gone. The stress is too much for him."

"What do I do? He says he comes to the house every day until he has the money. He might be there now, with Sofija alone!" Arso's forehead had turned pink. Saliva was collecting at the corners of his mouth.

"Listen to me. Do you have your checkbook?"

"No, of course not, I don't take it everywhere," he said impatiently.

"Okay, is your bank nearby? Because there's only one way to stop this. Go withdraw the money and come back here. I have a client in fifteen minutes, but you can just stick it under my office door. I'll give it to Tim tonight and that will be the end of it."

Arso thought for a minute, rubbing his cheekbone with his fingers and staring at the floor. "It is unfair for me and my wife. We do nothing wrong."

"But you see how impulsive my husband is." Christine raised her hands, giving him a smile to show that she was on his side. "Is it worth three thousand dollars to have him at your house all the time going crazy?"

Reluctantly, Arso admitted that it wasn't, though he said twice more that he deserved to keep the money and any court in the country would agree with him. While he ranted behind her, Christine looked up his bank on her computer and found a branch a quarter of a mile away.

Half an hour later she was in session with a middle-aged lesbian couple when she heard the outer door open and shut. Her clients were so busy blaming each other for an argument, they didn't even notice an envelope slide silently under the door in front of them.

Three times that afternoon Christine picked up the phone to call Tim's brokerage and ask for Sharon Proctor, but she couldn't do it. She was afraid Tim would answer, which was possible if the other lines were busy, or that someone would recognize her voice. The fact that she couldn't call, couldn't verify what Tim had told her, brought back the impotent frustration she'd felt in the basement the day before. The Internet had been no help, returning dozens, maybe hundreds, of Sharon Proctors in California, and none on a Hilliard

Lane. Already she could feel herself succumbing, wanting to blame Tim for simplicity's sake. On the way to work she'd had a vivid fantasy of a clean break, an entirely different life. She imagined living with her child in a little house, bolts of dusty afternoon sunlight, a bed covered with quilts, a distant train whistle. It was a joke, obviously, a delusion requiring only a gingham dress and a well. No one lived that way anymore. But every time she glanced in her side mirror, the images were there.

As soon as she got home she went into Tim's office and began to go through his things. Before she had dinner with him on Thursday, she needed to find something, either damning or consoling. She started with his desk drawers, some so overfilled they were a struggle to open. Along with legal forms and various supplies, each contained fossils of the old Tim—canceled commission checks; an empty container of X-Labs protein powder; a hardcover copy of *Secrets of the Millionaire Mind*, given to him on his fortieth birthday by Audrey's husband; a half-smoked cigar, stuck back in its plastic case and forgotten. Christine gripped the edge of the drawer and closed her eyes, sick with nostalgia for the innocent days when Tim puffed foolishly on cigars and drank martinis at night, when every possession was a symbol of his mastery of life. It had been a wonderful, disposable world they'd lived in, back when they lit up the house like a landing strip every night because they could afford to and had something worth showing off.

She moved on to the junk drawer in the kitchen, the one that would break someone's foot if it ever fell onto the floor, but it contained nothing but tools and yellowed appliance manuals and expired coupons. If this was all she had to go on, she might have believed that hers was a model home, staged down to the smallest detail to make it look as if ordinary people spent their days there, letting their batteries run dry under piles of take-out menus. In fact, it was so lacking in any kind of distinguishing characteristic that she felt as though she were rummaging through the contents of a stranger's house. Where had all the rubber bands come from? Who had saved a pamphlet from the Unitarian church? Up close, everything looked meaningless and foreign: the scratch on the refrigerator, the legs of the chairs, the dried leaf tips of the violets on the windowsill. She would have given anything to find a love letter to another woman, something that proved Tim was possessed by passion, that he was a person she could understand.

Upstairs, his closet was a disturbing sight, the few remaining trousers and shirts still arranged in order, as if they'd been instructed not to move. On the top shelf was a row of rectangular wicker boxes that she could just reach if she stood on her toes. She pulled the first one down and removed the top, hoping to find lingerie or a half-drunk bottle of whiskey, anything that might jolt Tim into being honest, but was disappointed to see only a jumbled pile of photographs. This might have been a poignant discovery had they shown Tim as a child, or Christine while they were dating, but the pictures were mostly of Tim looking proud of himself on Caribbean beaches or in front of the silver Jaguar he'd been forced to turn in eight months before the lease was up. She appeared in only a few of them, usually tanned and off to the side.

The second box was more promising—it held ultrasound images from all of her failed pregnancies, though under these were several pirated DVDs, an old tube of lip balm, and the nose hair clippers that Tim had used once and then broken when he dropped them on the bathroom floor. Hardly a collection of sentimental keepsakes. The last box contained half a mangled tube of athlete's foot cream and Tim's old golf club ID, back before he'd sold his invitation-only membership to the highest bidder. There were some work papers that meant nothing to her, and it was while she was putting these back that she noticed one of his pre-iPhone calendars. She took it from the box and flipped through it, amazed at the chaos of writing inside. Every page was crammed with phone numbers, notes, directions to properties, things underlined and crossed out. For ten minutes she searched for a suspicious lunch date or the name of a hotel, but the only thing to catch her eye was a local number, nearly erased but still legible if she held it up to the light. There was a faint square drawn around it that went into points at the corners like a frame. Awfully elaborate for Tim.

She glanced up and saw herself in the full-length mirror on the closet's far wall, her face slightly warped in the glass and frighteningly unfamiliar. Usually she could avoid looking middle-aged by pursing her lips slightly, raising her eyebrows, and favoring the left side of her face, which so far had been spared the smile line and faint jowl of the right. Tonight, though, caught unaware, she saw herself exactly as Tim must see her, frantic, a bit deranged, with only traces of youth remaining in her cheeks. She reached over and flipped off the light, glad to be plunged into darkness. Leaving the calendar on the night stand, she went downstairs to the kitchen.

She was in the middle of eating dinner in her office when she set down her fork abruptly and went back upstairs. The calendar was still lying on the clock radio, warm to the touch. She picked up the phone and dialed. It seemed to take a long time for the call to connect, and the rings—three of them—sounded strange, as if they were echoing down a long marble hallway in a foreign country. It would be a disconnected number, or it would be answered by a mechanized voice that gave her no more information than she had now.

She was so certain of the outcome that when she heard a woman's voice, she nearly hung up in surprise. "Hello?" the woman said again, and waited.

Christine blurted the first thing that came to mind. "May I speak to Tim, please?"

There was a long pause. "My son Tim?"

My son Tim. Christine had the bizarre illusion that she'd called Tim's dead mother, who had answered from the grave.

"Uh, you have a son named Tim?"

The woman laughed. "Yes, but he's only four years old."

"Four?" Christine repeated dumbly.

"Yes, so I think you probably have the wrong number."

Christine didn't know what to say, so she said nothing. The meaning of it all, if there was one, was so muddled that there was no way to respond.

"Hello?" the woman said.

"Yes. Are you Sharon Proctor?"

"Who?" the woman asked, wariness creeping into her voice.

"Sharon Proctor."

"Like I said, you have the wrong number."

Christine was about to ask, *Do you live in a yellow house near Anaheim?* But the woman said, "I'm sorry," and hung up.

Christine sat on the edge of the bed, a hand resting absently on her still-flat stomach, trying to piece her thoughts together. Did the conversation point to anything other than coincidence? A little boy was named Tim, just like her husband, one of her father's friends, and her sociology teacher in college. It was an unsatisfactory explanation, but the alternative was a maze of speculation and conspiracy theories. She could only imagine Tim's reaction when she asked—this time directly, in a shrill, aggrieved voice—if he had another family in a neighboring town. In an attempt to silence the last of her curiosity, she went to her computer and looked up the number on the Internet. Her search returned nothing but reverse phone look-up websites and page after page of random digits, running endlessly down her screen like some sort of impenetrable code.

Only the angle of the moon alerted her to the time. She had an early session in the morning and a ransacked house to clean up. She dragged a chair from the corner of the bedroom and stood on it, arranging the wicker boxes and Tim's clothes as best she could. She couldn't remember now where she had found the calendar, there were so many things to put back and they were all out of order. As hard as she tried to position the boxes and T-shirts and sweaters, nothing was going back the way it had been, and she was sure Tim would know and it would be the final kick in the head to their marriage. So much said in the empty space between hangers and a calendar mistakenly put in the pile marked *2006*.

It was while she was replacing the last box that she saw the gun.

It lay, half hidden in shadow, in the back corner of the shelf on a folded hand towel. Even as her heart pounded and her head reeled from adrenaline, she cast around for a way to make a large, black pistol seem innocent, even reassuring. Tim was afraid of vigilantes. He had bought it to protect her and his unborn child. If he'd wanted to hide it, he wouldn't have left it in the closet like an old sock, and certainly wouldn't have told her in advance that he wanted to buy it. She stared at it for a minute before extending an arm and lightly touching the barrel with her index finger. Smooth and cool, it was pointed at her neck, as if aimed to kill in the event of discovery. Carefully, she directed it toward the wall, imagining as she did so the trajectory of the bullet, which would pierce the tile in the master bathroom and shatter the shower enclosure while she washed her hair or shaved her legs.

After staring at it for a minute, she gently picked it up and carried it downstairs, terrified of falling, feeling like an accessory to a crime she still didn't understand. She went to the basement and stood in the stark glare, looking around. The gun was a huge, blurry silhouette on the carpet. Scouting the room for a hiding place, she felt an uncomfortable stab of guilt and responsibility. But she wasn't trying to hide Tim's mistakes, not really. She was slowing him down, making it harder for him to destroy his life and hers. Sometimes, making things harder was enough.

After peering into most of the boxes against the wall, she finally buried the gun under a bunch of Tim's dead mother's possessions—stained linen napkins and old dish towels and the plain cotton nightgowns she'd worn at the hospice. The only things Christine knew for sure would make him stop and think.

Twenty

Two days after her call from Daphne Bortner, Audrey received an email from Bakersfield.

Dear Audrey,

My grandfather died yesterday morning at Bakersfield Memorial Hospital. Your visit brought back a lot of memories for him in the last week of his life. Thank you for that. His last afternoon at home, we looked through letters and pictures he hadn't seen in a long time. It made him very happy. Good luck with your search. I'm sorry we couldn't be of more help.

Beth Gray-Parks

Stunned with disappointment, Audrey reread the email three times. Sweet old man. Her only connection to Mala, the one person she knew who had actually seen her, was gone. And, as she'd expected, an Internet search of birth records had showed no Rinehart ever being born in Bakersfield. She turned off her computer and went to find Mark so she could gripe to him and ask for a hug, but before she could say anything, he saw her coming from across the kitchen and called out, "Hey! I just got my thirtieth follower on Twitter!"

His phone was stuck in the waistband of his shorts and he was up to his hair-sprinkled forearms in soba noodles. He had decided a few nights before that it would be a good idea to invite a bunch of people over for dinner, if one could call it that, only four days after Paige went missing. "A little light in all this darkness," as he referred to it. It felt unseemly to Audrey to host a get-together during a neighborhood crisis, especially one happening to a good friend and her husband. Almost worse than that, though, was the idea that all of Mark's guests were angling for eternal life, an idea that seemed downright inappropriate considering that Paige might not make it to eleven years old. Might have stopped at ten only a few minutes after vanishing off the street.

Audrey had been waiting for good fortune to come from bad, but so far all she could see were bad events coming of whatever good had existed before. Paige's arrival had been a wonderful opportunity for Linda to discover the joys of parenting, and now Paige was missing and quite possibly dead. Mark had decided to become an entrepreneur and pursue his dreams, but those dreams made other people frown and whisper and mention him in the same breath with Frank Moranto, who claimed to have spotted Bigfoot on a camping trip. Her search for Mala had turned up not a fascinating and wise old woman, but an intractable mystery that infused her days with smoldering frustration. Christine, in her gentle therapist's way, had suggested that it had become a substitute for things that Audrey had no control over, and that by itself it meant very little. Audrey disagreed.

Only a week ago she would have viewed these events through the gauzy shroud of her affair with William. Paige would have been a runaway, Mark a wonderful father, the hunt for Mala a diversion worth pursuing no matter how it turned out. But her regular trysts weren't having the same hypnotic effect anymore, and the rawness of things was returning in force. Not that her feelings for William had lost any intensity, but real life had recently begun to appear around the edges of their afternoons and strike her in the face the moment she put on her clothes. Her mind, once consumed almost entirely by her lover, was reverting back to its old habits of obsession and repetition, and her solution was not to see less of William but to see more of him. She spent her weekends looking for any excuse to run to the supermarket or the mall so she could stop at William's on her way.

Though Audrey was hardly in the mood for a party, Mark needed help making the red lentil burgers and an appetizer concoction involving a radish spread he would puree in the food processor, which he first tried to operate with the blade inserted upside down. "Not the best way to extend your life," she said, unplugging it and pushing him aside. Clearly, he couldn't be left alone. He had bought ten pounds of salad, which he considered washing in the bathtub until she shot him down, and he wanted to try sautéing broccoli sprouts on low heat to see if their flavor improved. The menu itself was like something dreamed up in the kitchen of a county detox. No alcohol would be served, and for dessert there would be a hastily chopped selection of in-season fruit. When Audrey suggested living a little and offering sorbet, Mark blew out a breath and said, "Haven't you been listening to me all these months?"

"Lighten up," she said. "It's a dinner party."

"It's *my* dinner party." The implication was that his party would be nothing like the one she would throw, with cocktails, grilled meat, and cheesecake à la mode. It wasn't meant to be an indulgent celebration of the senses, but a celebration of austerity and self-denial, which seemed to Audrey less a reason for scheduling a party and more a reason for canceling one.

As Mark reached across the counter for a knife, his sleeve slid up, revealing the glinting edge of a metal bracelet. "What's that?" Audrey asked.

"This?" he said, shaking his wrist. Bright spots flared on his cheeks. "Nothing. A cryonics bracelet."

"I don't know what that is."

He turned his back and began to whack at a pile of parsley. "It's so people will know to contact the cryonics lab if I die. So I can be frozen and brought back to life later."

Audrey stared at Mark's bent brown head. "You want to be *frozen* now?"

"If I die I do. There's this whole amazing process where they pump oxygen into your body until they have a chance to replace your blood with antifreeze. So no autopsy, all right, because that would ruin it. Just call Levacor and they'll take care of everything."

"Levacor—why didn't you tell me about this?"

"I was waiting for the right time. From the way you're reacting, I don't think this is it."

"I can't imagine that being frozen is, uh, a free process, is it?"

"No, it's not."

"How are we paying for this?"

"*I'm* paying for it with a little of the retirement I saved from all my years toiling in a corporate prison. I think I deserve it, don't you?" The parsley was flying around in tiny bits now.

"It's not a question of deserving it. You don't have a job."

The chopping stopped. "I have a job," Mark said, "it just doesn't pay yet. And I know you think it never will, but there's a word for people who step all over your ambitions. Dreamkillers." He said this without anger, as if regurgitating a phrase he'd swallowed whole at one of his seminars. It had the same gung ho, brainwashed ring as the titles of the books he left lying around.

"I'm not trying to kill your dreams, I'm trying to make the house payment."

"Sometimes I can't tell the difference."

Audrey thought of William and the expensive Italian underwear that lay hidden in the back of her sock drawer, and stayed silent. Whose secret, whose desire, was worse? The quest for eternal life had the benefit of being exhaustingly abstract, while adultery was as straightforward as it got. There was no rational debate about sleeping around, no pros and cons to discuss. She had only to think of the conversation they'd be having if her lies were the subject, the shouts and tears, Jonathan standing paralyzed halfway down the stairs.

She peeled the last of the beets and dropped them into a bowl with shredded cabbage. The dressing recipe, which Mark had scrawled on the back of a phone bill, called only for vinegar, lemon, and pepper.

"So you'll wake up two hundred years from now without me and your son," she said after a few minutes. "That doesn't bother you?"

"Is that was this is about?" Mark said. He came up behind her and put his cold, damp hands on her upper arms. "You know, there's nothing stopping us from doing this together."

"Yes, there is," she said, but the doorbell rang at the same time, and Mark never heard her reply.

Audrey had always considered herself a welcoming hostess. She was happy when Jonathan brought friends over, and couldn't wait until he started bringing girlfriends home ("Let's not define his sexuality for him, he could be gay and that's fine," Mark had recently said). But the straggly group that arrived between seven and seven-thirty made Audrey feel as if Mark had sent invitations to the eating disorders floor of the local psychiatric hospital. She had trouble covering up her sadness—and yes, her contempt—as she made the rounds of men and women nibbling suspiciously at vegetable sticks and smiling with all the vigor of the Donner party.

"Audrey, this is Karen Feinman," Mark said. "We met at that talk at the college I told you about."

"Talk at the college?" Audrey said, smiling and shaking the woman's surprisingly strong hand.

"My wife never listens to me," Mark said cheerfully, and he was right. Audrey couldn't remember how many times in recent months she had simply tuned him out while he was speaking. She could re-call only several late nights in bed, his head backlit by the yellow chemical glow of the lamp, his mouth like a moving shadow that made sounds but not much sense. It wasn't that her mind was some-where else, but that what interested him seemed to have nothing to do with her, or even with him anymore. Who was this man? Where was her husband? What were all these strange people doing in her house?

Mark had invited just eight slender guests, among them a pro-fessor of chemistry, a haiku poet, a neonatal nurse, and a man who made furniture from reclaimed walls and floors. He introduced her to everyone as his next convert, putting his arm around her, and saying, "I wouldn't want to live forever without her." This was an explanation, she supposed, for the forty extra pounds she carried on her hips and thighs. She had never felt fatter—not in the de-pressed, awkward way she usually felt in dressing rooms and doc-tors' offices, but in a practical sense, as if she were an unflinching realist while everyone else in the room was a dreamer with no con-nection to the substance of life. She wedged in between groups of people, using her size as an example of courage and acceptance of the inevitable. She had spent her life terrified of death—bargaining with it, dreading it—and she was the only one in the room not try-ing to outrun it.

"I started doing the hyperbaric chamber and the enemas on the same day, and I really think it's made a difference."

The silly gravity of the conversation made Audrey smile as she roved her living room offering runny hors d'oeuvres and wine-glasses filled with mineral water. As soon as her serving platter was empty, she abandoned it on a counter and escaped to the bathroom. With a feeling of being pursued by gaunt maniacs, she shut the door and leaned against it, winded just from hurrying down the hall. If only the window weren't too small to crawl out of, she could be at William's in ten minutes. She could be there in fifteen if she simply walked out the front door without a word.

Audrey combed her hair and smacked her cheeks. She went back to the party determined to enjoy herself and learn something, be-cause it would be wonderful to realize that Mark had been right about everything all along, and she could follow him to wherever it was he had gone over the last seven months. But there was already a dreariness to the gathering, as if it were past midnight, the food and drink long gone, the guests bored but not sure how to leave without appearing rude. It was only eight-thirty, and everyone seemed to be talking about Paige's disappearance. The evening light was throw-ing shadows on sunken cheeks and bony necks, giving Audrey the impression that her house was filled with chattering ghosts. Mark was unfailingly energetic as usual, but he looked tired.

"Are you all right?" she asked, intercepting him at the china hutch.

"Are you kidding?" he answered. "Baby, this is my tribe."

After leaving a stack of ravished plates in the kitchen, Audrey was heading back toward the distressing sound of voices when she swerved left and fled upstairs to check on Jonathan. He was in his room with a pilfered nonalcoholic lemon spritzer, sitting in a com-fortable slouch at his computer. "What are you doing?"

"Nothing," he said.

"You must be doing something. Breathing, at least."

"If you really want to know, I'm calculating the possibilities that Paige was kidnapped."

"Jonathan, that's terrible. It sounds like something a serial killer would do at your age."

"No, listen, I'm trying to help. I figured out the risks using the latest crime statistics for California, and if you look at it, chances are really good that she ran away."

"How does that help us find her?"

"Maybe it doesn't. I'm just saying, she's probably not tied up somewhere, and that's a good thing to know."

"You're not planning to leave the house, are you?"

"You wouldn't let me even if I wanted to."

"I have to run out for a little while. If your father asks where I am, tell him I went to see a friend."

"Don't you like the party?"

"The party's fine. See you soon, okay? Don't stay up too late."

Half an hour later she was in William's arms, feeling like a teenager in bed with a boy she'd been forbidden to see. After making love, when she lay attached to William's side like a sticky and satisfied frog, she found herself complaining about Mark for the first time, as if he had just appeared in her life out of the blue.

"We have nothing in common anymore," she said. "Nothing except Jonathan."

"So leave him," William said, smoke drifting out of his nose.

"And do what?"

"Move in here."

"I can't just leave him. He loves me."

"Yeah. So?"

It was a sign of William's youth that he could be so dismissive of a twenty-two-year marriage, but Audrey wondered if his reaction was the right one. If she put love and Jonathan and a long history aside, what was left of her marriage to Mark? Were the remains enough to hold them together?

"What do you want to happen when you die?" she asked. She wanted to ask what he saw in her and where their relationship was going, but death seemed like a less loaded topic.

"When I die?"

"I mean, do you want to be buried or cremated, or . . ."

He sent a thick smoke ring rippling toward the ceiling. "I haven't really thought about it. I figure after two tours I'm cheating death as it is. It almost doesn't matter."

"But if you had to decide right now. Fancy military funeral? Or maybe you'd want to be frozen so you could be brought back in the future."

"I don't think we'll be around for the future, the way things are going." He leaned over to stub out his cigarette. "As long as I get a few more years, I don't care what they do with my body. Hole in the ground, pine box, fine with me."

"I knew you'd say that," she said, squeezing him.

"So why'd you ask?"

"To make sure I was right."

She was driving home on the freeway when her phone rang— Mark, surely, wanting to know where she was at 10:45 on a Sunday night. She picked up the phone without looking at it and answered, "Everybody gone?"

"Audrey?" It was a strangely urgent female voice. She slowed down on instinct, bracing against terrible news.

"I'm sorry. Yes?"

"This is Beth Parks from Bakersfield. Aaron Gray's grand-daughter. I hope you weren't asleep?"

"No. I'm in my car."

"Good. Listen, I'm here with my brother. We've been going through my grandfather's things, those old letters I mentioned in my message?"

"I remember."

"I thought we'd looked at everything, but there was an envelope we must have missed. Anyway, I've just found a photograph I think you should see."

Twenty-one

JUNE 20, 1948

Mala retrieved her belongings from the warehouse, stashed them in an old wooden trunk, and moved into Ruth's spare bedroom. What followed were two weeks of a kind of peace and contentment she hadn't known was possible, and didn't trust to continue. This was the way other people lived, in a world of coffee smells and clean sheets, polished wood and corn brooms. Cast iron was scrubbed, apples were peeled, books were read aloud, baths were filled, and spiders were swept out of corners before they could spin webs. Nothing happened. Once in a while it rained. There was always milk on the doorstep and sugar in the cupboard. Ruth would leave in the morning to tutor her students, or they would come to the house, glum, spot-faced boys and girls between ten and sixteen. Mala had two new pairs of shoes, proper ones, soft black leather with low heels and silver buckles. She had quickly lost her need to sleep on the floor, and now had to be called four times before getting up. When she mentioned finding a job, Ruth shook her head and said, "Take time to get settled in first. Anyway, I need your help around here."

Though Mala was preoccupied with the pleasantries of habit, her thoughts were tainted by recurring images of Elliot. She would be collecting summer squash from the garden or scouring tea stains off a cup, when one part of him—his flat eyebrows, his slender left hand—would appear in her mind without warning. Washing dishes in Ruth's kitchen, she would hear his truck drive up and stop in front of the house, but as soon as she ran to the window it would turn into a distant train or a crop duster flying overhead. How the grinding of an engine could inspire such misery and excitement was a mystery she brooded over while hemming curtains or listening to Ruth read after supper. Later, she would sit by her open bedroom window in the dark, wondering if part of her would always be dissatisfied no matter how comfortable the circumstance.

How was it that she wasn't perfectly happy? She had everything a person could want. And there was the fact that he'd almost certainly forgotten about her. He didn't come to the house and she wouldn't go to see him. It made her cringe to think of finding the farm, one of a hundred in the area, getting manure on her new shoes and dirt on her dress as she knocked on doors and asked farmhands about the boy with the rusted truck. Foolish though it was, she planned it all out one afternoon, even thought of the story she would tell Ruth. She imagined stepping in front of Elliot with braided hair and clean fingernails, while he stood in a ramshackle barn surrounded by bales of hay, the sun lighting the dusty air above his head.

It would never happen. She had found Ruth, or been taken to

her, and luck like that didn't happen twice. Now she was nostalgic for something she'd never experienced, which made no sense at all. The life she had should be enough. But if she wasn't moving on or making plans or considering what lay ahead, she wasn't sure what she was supposed to do. You could think about wringing out a rag and scrubbing steps for only so long before you started to wonder what the next town looked like, or who you'd meet if you hitched a ride to another county. Mala's head was full of roads—tree-lined, salt desert, winding, rutted dirt—and she couldn't imagine giving them all up for the one that ran by Ruth's house. With time and effort, maybe she would get used to the view from a single window, to simple happiness and staying put.

It was nearly midnight on a Saturday when Mala heard the engine come back down the street on a rattling gust of wind. She sat up in bed and listened. The smell of an extinguished kerosene lamp hung in the air, the only dirty thing in a house of washed floors and starched curtains. The engine idled and stopped. For several minutes there was nothing but the sound of windows trembling against their sashes. She lay down again and closed her eyes, but her mind and legs were restless. She threw back the quilt and got up. In bare feet she went into the dark hallway and down the stairs, whose wooden creak was drowned out by the shaking of the house. She would go to the front window to teach herself a lesson. After she saw nothing, she would never notice that sound again.

She pulled back the curtains. A few yards past the house, just outside the pool of light from the streetlamp, was Elliot's truck. The rust and dents distinguished it from others like it, along with the bales of hay in the back. At first it was enough just to see it, and Mala believed that she could sustain months of living on that alone. But then the truck started up and it seemed the worst thing imaginable that it would drive off with no promise of returning. She unbolted the front door and ran across the dry grass to the sidewalk. Suddenly self-conscious and unsure, she hesitated, standing on the rough brick, the wind tearing at her nightgown. It was shameful, standing outside for Ruth and all the neighbors to see, but the impulse to go back to the house wasn't as powerful as the impulse to step into the street.

When Elliot saw Mala's face, he turned off the engine and sat back in his seat. In just two weeks he seemed to have grown years older. His hair was longer, his face solemn, and he wore what looked to be a new plaid shirt. After a few moments of staring at each other, he rolled down the window.

"Sorry," he said. "I don't know what to say."

"You could start with why you're here."

"I don't know that either. All I know is I got in my truck and drove to your house. I've done it about ten times now."

"And you don't know why?"

"You tell me why you're standing there wearing almost nothing."

Mala folded her arms across her chest. "I heard a noise, that's all."

"Oh, okay. That's all."

"You shouldn't be here," she said. "Ruth wouldn't like it."

"If you don't tell her, she won't know about it."

"I'm not in the habit of keeping things from her. It's not right."

"It wasn't right for you to get stuck in my head either. I don't like it at all but that's how it is." He opened his door and slid over, leaving room for her behind the steering wheel. "Come on. Someone'll see you."

She did as instructed and shut the door.

"You got no shoes on," he said. "You usually investigate noises at night in your bare feet?"

"Once in a while."

"You know what? I don't believe a word you say." He kissed her before she had a chance to think or pull away, and almost as soon as it started it was finished. Brief as it had been, it was something she could never take back. Wouldn't, even if she had the choice. For the rest of her life, Elliot would be the first man to kiss her. As hard as she'd tried to forget him, now she had no chance.

She returned to the house sometime after the clouds cleared, Elliot guessed around two or three. She didn't think about Beni or Ruth, or the fact of being an unmarried woman sitting in a truck with a man she hardly knew, until she was back inside turning the knob and slowly releasing it, shutting the door with a quiet click. Even then she could feel the cool pressure of Elliot's hands through her nightgown, and being unmarried seemed a trivial detail in comparison. The bolt lock shot into the door frame, loud enough to give her a start but probably too distant to rouse Ruth from sleep. She looked out the window just in time to see the truck slow at the intersection, then rumble off into the night.

The house had never seemed darker. As her eyes adjusted, the furniture swam out of the blackness, the sofa, chair, and side tables like faint spots on a map. She used them to navigate to the kitchen, touching each with her hand as she crept by. She drank water at the sink, the tap squeaking on and off, and then dried and replaced the glass, leaving no clue for Ruth to discover in the morning. The moon emerged as she passed the room where Ruth taught her students, laying a beam across the floor like a path to follow, which Mala did, up to the window beside the mahogany desk. It felt forbidden to be standing here, alone with no lamp burning. She was rarely invited into this room except to dust, and only after Ruth had put all of her stamps, pens, and stationery into drawers so they wouldn't be mixed up or swept onto the floor. Mala always took her time polishing the furniture and baseboards, stopping to enjoy the brightness of the air and the walls of windows before she returned to the rest of the house, dark-paneled and dim by comparison. She looked out now at the illuminated garden, the rows of sprouting lettuce, the tall, slender palms with their leaves drafting upward on the wind. She wished she could spend more afternoons here, at a desk of her own, practicing her spelling and the penmanship Ruth called too fussy, an artistic pursuit where none was needed. The point of words was not how they looked but what they meant.

Slowly, quietly, she pulled out Ruth's chair and sat. She stayed on the rounded edge as if she might have to leap to her feet, listening to the groans of old wood adjusting to unfamiliar weight at a strange time of day. The chair was no more comfortable than the bench in the ranch kitchen, which had given her a backache she'd assumed was a part of growing up until Ruth left and everything changed. No more backache, no more lessons, and soon after, two men had come to the storefront and taken every last scrap. Cash, a cracked crystal ball, dusty drapery. One of the men, Drina said, was the deputy sheriff's son, and it was this detail that galled the landlord, who wanted no part of it. Back on the road they'd gone, and the storefront was remembered as the kind of curse that comes with striving.

Mala lay her arms on the desk and put her head down, reliving every moment in Elliot's truck, murmurs and intakes of breath coming back to her in stomach-turning waves. Between thoughts she drifted into a momentary sleep, dreaming one moment, lucid the next. It was a sunlit morning, and then it was night again. She was looking out at the garden, but it was winter now, and the tomato vines were bare and twisted. She and Ruth were in the kitchen, and outside she could see Elliot leaning against the side of his truck. She began to speak to Ruth and the sound of her own voice jarred her awake. It seemed like the tail end of a dream when she raised her head and saw a letter, half covered by an envelope near her right elbow. Her mind still clouded, she read the words, shadowy letters, splinters of vague sentences: *here. weather. county board. Mala.*

She blinked against the moon, which shined in her eyes like sunlight. Pulling the page toward her, she began skimming it, struggling to find the meaning of her name in a letter from a stranger. No, not a stranger. Henry Nolan.

Please write more about Mala, her plans, how she looks as a grown woman. I must have sent five men out after her over the years, you remember. Any one of them could track a white steer in a snowstorm but couldn't find a teenage girl. I'm sending along something to cover your extra expenses, and I hope you know by now there's no point refusing it. I'm only repaying you, not just for the trouble my former wife and I caused you, but for watching over Mala then and now.

    Henry

With the feeling of having stumbled on a riddle, Mala dropped the letter and put her hands to her chest. There was no reason why a man like Henry Nolan would mention her name. He'd never taken interest in her, or in anything, really, but horses and cattle and buying land cheap. She remembered him as tall and quiet, not around much, the only person on the ranch who seemed flustered by the presence of a child. Sometimes she had seen him in the mornings, a broad-shouldered figure striding through the kitchen with a kind smile, but as soon as they looked at each other, a gulf opened, something like mutual shyness, or even fear. It wasn't that he disliked her, Mala thought, but that he didn't know what to do with her. She once tried to describe the feeling to Ruth, but Ruth said, "None of us would be here without Mr. Nolan. That's all you need to know about him."

Sensing a presence behind her, Mala turned her head to see Ruth standing in the dim doorway.

"Next time you go out during the night, bring your key and lock the door," she said. "I don't want some drifter coming in here, falling asleep on my sofa."

"I'm sorry," Mala said.

Taking in Mala's wild hair and dirt-smeared nightgown, she shook her head. "He must be quite something to send you out in all this wind."

"His name is Elliot. He's the one who found you."

"Yes. I recognized the sound of the truck. I'm sure my neighbors did, too."

Mala tried to move her feet to stand but they felt rooted to the floor. "I read part of a letter," she said. "Just now."

"I thought so."

"I shouldn't have done it, but I saw my name."

"Henry asks about you, and well he should. You practically grew up in his house, you know."

"I think it's more than that."

"Mala," Ruth said, pleading gently. "It was a long time ago. Let's leave things as they are."

"Things," Mala said, weeks of suspicion, years of rumors, suddenly shaking loose. "What things?"

"We can talk about it another time."

"I want to talk now."

The moon rose slowly in the sky behind Ruth's head. By the time she spoke again it had nearly cleared the crooked pine tree in the backyard. "Beni did his best for you, I'll say that. He can't be blamed for anything. Not with the way your mother treated him."

"My mother?" Mala said. "What do you mean?"

"Do you have any memories of her?"

"She and Beni argued a lot. I remember her funeral most of all. Why?"

"I won't speak badly of a dead woman. It wouldn't be right."

"How could you speak badly of her? You never knew her."

"I did in my own way," Ruth said. "I cleaned in the afternoons after she left the ranch. I swept up strands of her hair. I aired out the bedroom so no one would smell her perfume."

"My mother never stepped foot in that house."

"You weren't born yet, Mala. She used to come in the mornings after Mr. Nolan's wife had gone to town."

"She would never have done that."

"You said you wanted to know."

"I do."

"Here's the truth, then. When Mrs. Nolan went to visit family, your mother would stay for days. We all thought it would pass, but it lasted until you were almost four years old. I honestly believe he loved her."

Mala got up suddenly, striking the desk with her knee and rattling the cup of pens. "Where was my father all this time? He had to know something."

"Of course he knew, that's why he married her," Ruth said, responding to Mala's rising voice by lowering her own. "Henry was in no position to do it. She was pregnant by a married man and she needed help and Beni couldn't refuse her. It's a good thing, too. Look what happened to you, getting sent off on your own. Who knows what they'd have done to Zina."

"Beni's never been able to keep a secret," Mala said. "He wouldn't have waited nineteen years to tell me. He would have talked about it in his sleep."

"Mala. Listen to me."

"What does it matter, anyway? She's been dead most of my life." As hard as Mala tried to swallow down the tears, they came in a humiliating torrent, burning her throat and eyes. "I saw her go under the water. I thought she would come back if I waited long enough."

Ruth walked up behind Mala and put her hands on her shoulders.

"I stood and watched. I might be there now if somebody hadn't come along."

"You didn't know better."

"It still happened the way it did."

"There's more to it than that. You're old enough to hear it now."

"Tell me, then," Mala said.

Ruth turned her around and took her face in her hands. "Your mother didn't drown by accident and that's the truth. She killed herself when your father wouldn't see her anymore. It haunted him, it still does. Years after it happened his wife found one of Zina's rings in his desk drawer. Why do think she made me leave the ranch? Because I knew all that time and I never told her."

"What do you mean, my father?" Mala said in a whisper.

"The owner of the ranch, Henry Nolan. You're his only child, Mala. The only child that man has ever had."

Twenty-two

*A*fter the night in the kitchen with Margaret, Linda was no longer free to blame herself for her stepdaughter's disappearance. She couldn't bask in the sympathy and support of others, castigate herself over her exchanges with Paige, or take charge of what needed to be done, staying strong for Peter and briskly organizing the volunteers. The circumstance had changed from simple, albeit tragic, to something with so many layers and possibilities that she had to repeat it to herself every morning when she woke up just to keep it all straight. The ringing of a phone—Peter's, Margaret's, the one screwed to the wall in the kitchen—became like a knock at the door during the night. Either something had happened that was so wonderful it couldn't wait or terrible news was being delivered. There could be only one good outcome: Paige had been found alive, although this possibility dwindled with every hour that passed. Linda would hear ringing from four rooms away and stop to listen, hands knotted in front of her, until she found out who was calling and why.

"They have a lead," Peter said, hanging up his phone on the fourth day. "Nothing to get too excited about, but somebody might have seen her."

"Where?"

"Walking around Hollywood. Which would mean she either lost her mind or ran away." It was obvious that he wanted to get angry, couldn't wait to, in fact. What a pleasure it would be to yank his dirty and disheveled child out of the police station and march her to the car, squeezing a bruise into her arm and promising her a life of misery, chores, and homework.

"What do we do?"

"Nothing, for the time being. They'll see what else they can find out. It's not much but it'll get us through the next few hours."

Peter seemed to be stating the adage of their lives. Four days into the ordeal only a few people were still showing up with offers to help, but a few was better than none, Linda thought, considering their relatively recent arrival and the diseased state of the neighborhood. On Saturday morning she put five women and a teenage boy to work tacking up flyers before she locked herself in the bathroom and put her head between her knees.

It was late in the afternoon when a car pulled up outside and two men got out. Margaret was sitting on the couch, defiantly unfashionable in a long plaid skirt and a white blouse that might have gotten its start several decades earlier on the back of someone's asexual aunt. Neil was on the phone with his mother, who was taking care of the four remaining children in Connecticut and having a miserable time of it; they'd held her down like Gulliver when she tried to unplug the television, which they refused to turn off, and somehow got their hands on a fair amount of money and used it to buy fast food and a bloody comic book. Linda knew all this because Neil—rudely, un-self-consciously—had his mother on speaker, which blared along with him as he paced from room to room, holding the phone just far enough away from his mouth that he was forced to shout. She was two days from throwing him out of the house, maybe less.

"Oh, no," Margaret whimpered, parting the curtains as the men came up the walk. "What now?"

"Relax," Peter said. "Don't jump to conclusions, all right?"

"But they have those looks on their faces. Like the soldiers who come to your door to tell you your son was killed by a sniper."

"Please, Margaret," Peter muttered, "the drama." But his face went white and he stumbled over the carpet edge on his way to the foyer.

Looking at each other, Linda and Margaret strained to listen from the living room. "Honey!" Peter called a moment later.

Margaret slumped with relief against the back of the couch and glared at Linda. "Give me a break," she said, as if the whole thing were Linda's fault.

When Linda got to the door, she found that Peter had disappeared, leaving the men standing on the threshold by themselves.

"Yes?" she said.

"Got a few minutes, Mrs. Fredrickson?" one of them asked. His name was Detective Klein. He was about six feet tall—Peter's height—but so muscular and stubby-armed that he seemed much shorter. Linda hated him immediately.

"What for?" she said, not inviting them in. "I've already been questioned."

"This won't take long. Got a private place where we can talk?"

Deciding it would be better to show irritation than fear, she sighed heavily. "All right. Follow me."

The moment Linda sat down in the never-used "craft room," she thought of all the TV shows she had seen, the idiot characters who'd committed spectacular and brilliant crimes but blurted their offenses under the least bit of pressure. She would not make that mistake. Under intense questioning, even under threat of electrocution, she would go silent, lie in the face of a mountain of evidence, because surely if the evidence were that strong then no one would even bother to question her. They would simply come for her one day and take her with them.

But maybe that wasn't how it would happen. Maybe her smarts and her killer instinct and everything else useful had been whittled away by guilt, and she was collapsing of her own weight like a hollow tree. Confronted by someone strong and intimidating, she would crumble because there was nothing left to prop her up. Facing Detective Klein, she could feel her face flush and her hands shake, and there was nothing she could do about it.

"You were arrested some years ago for soliciting," he said.

She'd been so sure they would accuse her of murder that she nearly replied, "Is that the only thing you know about?" But an instant later her relief dwindled and her defenses flared. "The charges were dropped," she said. "It was all a mix-up."

"Was it? Maybe you can explain to us what happened." Detective Klein chewed gum with his mouth closed, as if that would hide the vulgarity of it. The other man seemed to have no purpose except to sit there and keep Linda from attacking anyone.

"It was a long time ago. I hardly remember."

"Something like that doesn't usually slip a person's mind."

"Well, it slipped mine."

"The charges *were* dropped, but only because the witness in the case didn't appear. Do you know anything about that? Why she didn't come to the hearing?"

Linda shook her head. She honestly didn't know. Besides avoiding capture for killing someone, it was perhaps the luckiest thing that had ever happened in her life.

"How long did you live in New York after that?"

"A long time. About seventeen years."

"Are you in contact with anyone from those days? Anybody who might want to interfere in your life?"

"I would have mentioned it the first time I was questioned."

"This upset you, Mrs. Fredrickson? You seem a little bothered."

"Of course I'm bothered. You should be out looking for my stepdaughter and instead you're sitting here drilling me."

Detective Klein took his time writing something on his pad of paper. He looked up, smiled briefly, and sniffed as if waiting for her to say more.

"We heard there was a lead on Paige," she said. "Is there any news?"

"Not yet. We'll let you know as soon as there is."

"Well, if that's all, I'll get back to trying to find her."

"Before you go, anything else we should know about your background?"

"Yes. I used to have a catering business, I met my husband at a party at the Gramercy Hotel, and my father's in a nursing home. Fascinating, isn't it?"

The detective leaned back in his chair, shifting his hips as if he found it extremely uncomfortable. "Speaking of your husband, he's gone through some troubles lately, hasn't he? Used to be one of those Wall Street guys?"

"He never worked on Wall Street. He's still with the same company, but in a different position."

"That must have been difficult, when his salary was cut."

"How do you know about that?"

Detective Klein shrugged with a look of mock innocence. "He told us."

Linda dropped her hands into her lap. "Why are you asking all these questions? Because we're not having a hard enough time with Paige missing? Just to see if you can make us crack? No wonder Tim Mahoney's acting like a lunatic."

"Excuse me?" said Detective Klein.

"The way you badger people, you've ruined his life. You're not going to ruin mine."

"We're just trying to help. All we want to do is find your step-daughter, and sometimes that leads us to painful places."

Linda stood up. "I have things to do. Do you mind?"

"Not a bit." Both men got to their feet.

"I'd appreciate it if you wouldn't mention any of this to my husband. He has enough to deal with right now. He doesn't need to hear about a misunderstanding from twenty years ago."

"Of course," Detective Klein said with a tight smile. "If you think of anything else we should know, I hope you'll give us a call."

It was a difficult and disappointing day. The lead resulted in the recovery of another wayward child, a fourteen-year-old girl who had already been arrested once for drug possession. There was no new information about Paige, although she was mentioned in a vaguely exploitative local news segment, which Margaret watched standing two feet from the television. "That's the picture they show?" she cried while everyone else sat in numb silence behind her. "It's a year and a half old! It doesn't even look like her!" Peter went for a walk at dusk and came back with thistles lodged in his shoelaces and dirt on the seat of his pants.

"Where did you go?" Linda asked, picking a scrap of leaf off his sleeve.

"I sat in somebody's yard and watched the birds. It was beautiful. I don't know why I've never done it before."

"You sat there for an hour?"

"I also went by Tim's house to try to break into his trunk, but I didn't see his car."

"Oh, Peter."

"What? All I did was check his driveway."

After a dinner that Linda spent two hours cooking but no one really ate, Margaret and Linda passed each other in the upstairs hall. It was the kind of awkward moment Linda had always guarded against with Paige, but it was worse with Margaret because she'd had wine again, and her social graces had been all but annihilated by worry. Her initial refusal to blame Linda had turned into a silent, put-upon superiority that gave her face an oddly pleased look. She wouldn't state the obvious, she would simply carry it around like something that could smash to the floor at any moment if she decided to let go.

"What did the police want?" she asked.

"Nothing. You know them. They have to ask the same questions four times."

"You're not concerned?"

"About what?" Linda asked.

"The way they might interpret things."

"I don't know what you mean," Linda said with a slight smile. "Honestly, sometimes I think you're speaking another language."

"To you, I guess I am." Margaret shrugged. "You know, the police talked to me once and that was enough."

"That's probably because you weren't here when Paige disappeared. You were on the other side of the country."

Margaret grimaced. "Disappeared. Can we put that another way, please? She didn't 'disappear.' We don't know what happened, she's just not here right now."

"It has the same meaning, doesn't it?"

"Are you arguing with me about this?" Margaret said, gaping at her. "I'm her mother and I'm asking you not to use the word 'disappear.'"

"Okay, I'm sorry," Linda said, raising a hand in surrender. "I won't say it again."

"Thank you. Now, what do you think about this Tim person? Peter's very suspicious of him, but I don't know if that's because he's just a convenient target."

"I don't see Tim doing anything violent but I could be wrong. I've known him less than a year."

"How trustworthy are your instincts?"

Suddenly Linda felt drained. "I don't know, Margaret. Why don't you decide."

As night closed in on the house, the atmosphere became raw and incompatible, and the four of them drifted in different directions. Peter sat in his office in the dark listening to Bach while Margaret stood in the kitchen talking to a friend in Connecticut who planned to fly out to offer support, and Neil went for a drive in the rental car "on the off chance," words that needed no further explanation. Linda looked up Detective Klein on the Internet and discovered that he had a wife and four children and had graduated from a military academy, no surprise there. Later, after Neil returned and Margaret followed him upstairs, Linda heard them arguing loudly in the guest room over Neil's mother and whether she was exaggerating the children's behavior so he would go home. "Paige isn't related to her so she doesn't care!" Margaret cried. After that, Linda put on her headphones and blocked out their voices the way Paige had with her. It was remarkably effective.

By eleven the house was quiet. Peter was asleep, thanks to double the recommended dosage of his sleeping pills. Linda watched his side rise and fall. It was hard to believe that the situation wouldn't continue like this indefinitely, time suspended, the ordinary rules of decorum and day-to-day life no longer in force. Running errands, thinking about the future, growing older, all had the feeling of luxuries they could no longer afford, activities that would never be resumed because there was no point to them.

Linda sat with her back against the headboard, letting the wood slats dig into her shoulder blades. Even as she sat there, events seemed to bend in an uncontrollable direction. Peter looked so in-nocent and pitiable lying beside her. It was a terrible thing she had done, disguising herself as a woman he might like to marry. She reached toward him, her hand filling the moonlit air above his right arm. She had a sudden, dangerous longing to wake him. It would be so easy to tell him everything while he was in a gentle, stupefied state, his usual perspectives shattered by catastrophe. Contrary to what she had always thought, it might actually make her feel better. Maybe that had been the purpose for Detective Klein's visit—to show her the way to an honest life. It would guarantee one thing: no matter what happened in the future, Peter would never be surprised by what his wife had done. If she used the right words—*self-defense, happened so quickly*—he might forgive her, even take her side of it.

She was so close to touching him her fingers tingled. First, she would softly nudge him awake and reassure him that there was no bad news. Then she would preface her story by making it sound worse than it was. If she succeeded, he might even feel relief when she finally told him the truth. *That's all? It was terrible but you had to do it. It was you or him, wasn't it?*

"I should have told you a long time ago," she would begin. "You'll want to leave me and I won't stop you." She was startled to hear herself whisper the words, but Peter didn't move. The air con-ditioner switched off and the bedroom was plunged into silence. Neil had stopped snoring in the bedroom next door, and for a few horrible seconds Linda was certain that Margaret had heard her through the wall.

She pulled her hand back and shot out of bed with a feeling of having scrambled back from the edge of a cliff. Had she completely lost control? Eighteen years of secrecy, nearly ruined by the lure of confessing to a man who couldn't bear another thing.

She crept down the stairs and into the living room, where the glowing lamp revealed the reassuring solidity of walls and furni-ture. It was the first trace of affection she had felt for the house since moving in. Neil had set up a miniature command center in the corner using his laptop, an end table, and a credenza, not so he could find Paige but so he could continue to trade stocks for his clients from thousands of miles away. He would be up in five hours with the opening bell.

The blue light on his laptop flickered rhythmically, a sign that it could be brought to life with a touch. Linda walked up to it and, almost without thinking, tapped the On button. The screen came up to a website showing photographs of missing children, none of whom was Paige. She looked toward the doorway, saw no one, and sat on the chair Neil had dragged in from the kitchen. A hundred times she had thought of using her computer or Peter's, or going to a library, but the urge to know had never lasted more than a minute. In the last few years it had faded altogether, but tonight it felt out of her hands, a thing with its own momentum.

The act of typing his name into the computer seemed to resurrect him: the lumbering body, bloated face, the small, angry eyes of a drunk man, so young—not more than twenty-two—that in the beginning she had mistaken him for someone shy and easy to manage.

She'd seen him once before in her five or six months "in the trade," a time of shocking desperation that she had since tried to put in the same category as a short-term heroin problem or nervous breakdown. He was memorable for being just out of college, and for telling her that she charged too much, though he grudgingly paid her five hundred dollars and left without another word. She forgot about him until he called her again, six weeks later. This time when he showed up, he'd been drinking and seemed upset about something he didn't want to discuss. She pretended to care, sitting down beside him on the bed and putting her hand on his slumped back, hoping he would just take his clothes off, get it over with, and leave her alone. She didn't care why he was unhappy. If anything, she felt that a man like him deserved to be.

There had to be something about him online. A memorial page, or an old obituary like the one Audrey had found in the Texas paper. How many times had she imagined his funeral? His mother sobbing, the casket closed to hide the swelling and disfiguring gashes. The lamp—an old one, probably from the fifties—had been incredibly heavy, like a tire iron. She wouldn't allow herself to think of how much damage it had done.

Linda waited until the page had loaded on the screen, then raised her eyes. A breathless scan of the first results revealed nothing—a marine biologist in Australia, a genealogy site listing a marriage from the late 1800s. But halfway down the page she saw four words that stopped her. *Manhattan Office. Our Team.*

It was the website of an international insurance company. His name was listed—why? She couldn't imagine. Unless . . . that was it. His father must have the same name. Ross Picard, Sr., a man with a tightly knotted tie and sad eyes. Maybe no one else recognized his haunted look, but she would.

Linda panned down the page, looking for the name, waiting for the photograph of an older man to appear. Once she had actually fantasized about sending an anonymous letter to his parents, explaining what their son had done to her and how much she'd wanted to live. Thinking of it now, she still couldn't remember the incident in a linear way. Her memories began at the end—with him lying on the carpet, his head gushing blood with every fading heartbeat—and went backward one violent close-up at a time to the beginning, when he slapped her twice, then dragged her into the bathroom and forced her to look at herself. For some reason, seeing her own face—her terror-stricken eyes, her bleeding lower lip—had been the most humiliating part of it. She didn't know what had set him off, she still didn't. Maybe he had heard the boredom in her voice, or sensed her revulsion as she lay under him thinking, This is the last time. Never again, never again. She didn't know how her brother would live or afford tuition, but she couldn't be Mom and Dad for him and for herself anymore, not like this.

"I'm sorry," she'd said again and again to her face in the mirror. That was the other humiliating part, that she apologized while he was hitting her. She had even apologized when he made the mistake of turning his back, lurching drunkenly toward the phone to rip the cord out of the wall, and she grabbed the first thing—the only thing—at hand, and killed him with it.

His face appeared on the screen and she flinched as if he had just stepped in front of her.

Ross Picard, Senior Investment Accountant. It was not his father, it was him. He was twenty years older, with a red, heavyset face and receding hairline, his smile professional and a little miserable-looking. There wasn't a visible scar on him. His bio said that he was married with two children, Madeleine and Ross, Jr.

How?

Her mind skipped through the possibilities. Someone had heard her cries and called the front desk. A maid had come to the room by chance and saved his life. He wasn't as badly injured as she'd thought. After she'd frantically gone through the room wiping away her blood and fingerprints with towels and a pillow case, he regained consciousness, got up and stumbled home.

She would never know. In eighteen years she never once imagined that he had survived. Now that she knew he had, she wasn't sure how to think about herself or her life. It was like discovering that all this time she had been someone else, someone better and more fortunate.

"Shorting the dollar?"

Linda looked up. Neil stood in the doorway in a T-shirt and shorts, smiling sleepily. He hadn't even finished speaking before she closed the browser, leaving only the missing children's website up on the screen.

"Sorry," she said. "I couldn't sleep."

"It must be contagious."

"I was just surfing around, hoping for—I don't know. News of some kind." Her relief was so great, years of it coursing through her at once, that she had trouble hiding it from him. She felt intensely grateful but also exhausted, the side effect, she supposed, of casting off a burden that had consumed half her life.

"Find anything?"

"Nothing relevant," she said.

He leaned back and looked up the stairs. "Listen," he said. "I want to apologize for Margaret. I'm afraid she hasn't been treating you very well."

"I don't take it personally. She's doing the best she can."

"Is she? I know it's the worst thing that can happen, that goes without saying. But I wonder if she's going to look back on this and realize that she wasn't a very good human being through it all."

Linda, who had always seen Neil as little more than Margaret's annoying and well-heeled appendage, was surprised by his sensitivity. She crossed the room and stopped in front of him. "Thanks. But I understand her."

"She won't say it but she thinks it's her fault."

"That's what I mean," Linda said. Then, on impulse, she hugged him. At first he was taken aback—an uncomfortable laugh escaped his throat, and he stood stiffly with his arms hanging at his sides—but after a few moments she felt his hands come to rest lightly on her back. Eventually she pulled away and patted his upper arm.

"See you in the morning," she said.

Twenty-three

The photograph was delivered to Audrey's house Thursday afternoon. Twenty minutes after arriving home and finding a manila envelope on the front porch, she knocked on Christine's door.

"You have it?" Christine asked.

Audrey held up the envelope. "Right here."

Christine had been waiting to see the photograph since Audrey told her about the call from Bakersfield, two days before. Though it was probably a false hope, it was better than surrendering every thought to Tim, whose only response to her discovery of the gun had been to say, "I told you I wanted one for protection and now you act like I lied about it. And you wonder why I need a break from this relationship." As for the phone number and the coincidentally named little boy, Tim was not to blame for what people called their children, nor did he have total recall. The number was one of perhaps thousands he'd written down and erased since becoming a realtor. That Christine was making something of it—that she had actually called the poor woman, probably a former client—made him concerned about her health and stability. No matter how she'd been treating him of late, he loved her. Had she been eating? Seeing the doctor as she was supposed to? "You have a responsibility to take care of our child, and yourself." They were meeting at a restaurant in a few hours to talk. Tim's invitation to dinner seemed to be a cryptic message of some sort, but Christine wasn't sure how to decipher it. She hoped she would know when she saw him.

Audrey, not usually at a loss for words, silently followed Christine into the house. They sat side by side in the dining room with the envelope between them. In addition to the photograph, Audrey had brought the book, which sat on the table like a bedraggled witness. She inhaled deeply and tore open the envelope as if she had just that instant worn out the last of her patience.

Slowly, she pulled out two pieces of cardboard that had been carefully taped together. She peeled off the tape and lifted one piece of cardboard to reveal the picture. Christine leaned closer to see it. It was a small black-and-white snapshot, wrinkled and missing the upper right corner, but otherwise intact. It showed the house they had visited, painted white with small stained-glass inserts in the door. The house was blurred at the edges, giving it the appearance of having moved just as the picture was taken. A ladder-backed chair on the porch looked like an object dropped in from a dream. Beside the walkway was a large tree with a heavily contrasted, metallic look. In front of the tree stood two women. One of them was about forty, pale-haired and slightly stocky with a stern nose and thin, smiling lips. She wore a polka-dotted dress with a narrow belt around the waist, and held a small bundle in her arms. A baby.

Next to her was a girl, a young woman, not more than twenty. Christine's first impression was of darkness—straight black shoulder-length hair, skin that looked lighter than brown but not much. The rest of the face, the wide cheekbones and strong, oval chin, was eclipsed by translucent light eyes that stared intently into the camera.

After several seconds of silence, Audrey said, "That's her."

"It must be."

"It's creepy. I almost feel like she can see us."

"Who knows. Somebody like that? Maybe she can."

"I bet the baby is the daughter the lawyer mentioned." Audrey turned over the photograph. *Our neighbor, Ruth Simon* was written on the back in smeared ballpoint pen. "The older woman must be Ruth."

"Why is she holding the baby?" Christine asked.

"Women hold each other's babies, I guess," Audrey said. "Unless she had one of her own. That's possible, too."

"I had no idea Mala would be so young, did you?"

"What was she doing there?" Audrey asked. "It's all so ordinary—the house, the yard, her clothes. I would have expected . . ."

"Jewelry, at least," Christine said. "Something more flamboyant."

"There *was* jewelry in the box at Susanna's, a bunch of old things. Linda let her throw it out. She didn't know what she had." Audrey set the photograph on the table between them. "The closer we get, the more bizarre it is."

"Why didn't Mr. Gray remember this? You'd think he'd remember taking a picture at that house, wouldn't you?"

"His granddaughter isn't sure he took it. It could have been anybody in the family, the grandmother or some other relative who lived there. To me, it looks like they just got back from a christening. It would make sense with the baby, wouldn't it? I don't know. We still don't have much to go on."

"We have another name," Christine said. "That's something."

"But what do we do with it? Keep looking? Who was this client the lawyer talked about? Why were they trying to find Mala?"

"Maybe this is where we stop. Maybe it's enough to know she was real." Christine could see Audrey turning this possibility over in her mind, then discarding it.

"I know myself. I'll stay up all night tonight trying to find this Ruth Simon woman. And when that doesn't pan out, I'll move on to something else."

"Why, though? How long do you keep doing this?"

"Would you stop reading a book thirty pages from the end? I want to know what happens. I can't jump ahead sixty years to see what comes of my life but I can do it for somebody else. I can try."

"But it's not really an ending," Christine said. "There's always too much we won't know."

"Maybe. But it's as much of an ending as we get."

Ironically, Tim had chosen to meet Christine at La Campagna, the Italian restaurant just down the road from where Jennifer Guthrie had been killed. It was as if he were daring the police and everyone else to say he didn't have a right to be there. When Christine walked in, she saw him sitting by the front window gazing out at the hill, a little refuge of trees and grass surrounded by miles of black asphalt. Tim had come to the restaurant directly from the gym and his hair was still wet. He seemed to have grown handsomer and more confident since moving out, or maybe this was just an illusion suffered by all discarded wives.

He turned as she approached, giving her the kind of smile she hadn't seen in three weeks. It was as if all his troubles were behind him. Or he was just enjoying his life without her. It couldn't possibly mean he was glad to see her.

But he was. As soon as the waiter brought their drinks, Tim took her hand across the table and said, "I owe you an apology."

"For what?"

"For this whole fucking mess. For not thanking you the other day for dealing with Arso. I don't know what you said to him, but I'm glad it's done. That pissed me off beyond belief."

"Why were you going to his house like that? Threatening to have him deported?" Tim was being warm enough that she felt she could afford to push him a little, to ask honest questions.

"Because I hate unfairness."

"To him it was harassment."

Tim gave her a quick little shrug. "Who cares what it was to him? It's a simple equation. Don't keep money that doesn't belong to you and nobody'll knock on your door. Did you deposit the check?"

"Yes," she said, though it was still zipped into a small pocket in her purse.

"Keep an eye on it. If it bounces, I want to know. This isn't over until the money's back in our account."

The waiter put down a basket of bread and a small white dish of olive oil. Christine took a piece of bread and broke off part of it before realizing she wasn't hungry. When she glanced up, she found Tim watching her. "Not feeling great?" he said.

"No."

"I can still read your mind, Chrissie. I've always been able to. That hasn't changed."

"It seems like everything's changed."

"Not really. When two people have gone through hell, you can't pull them apart. I've been thinking about it these last couple of days. You could do pretty much anything and I'd forgive you for it. Take away all the extraneous bullshit and we have a permanent bond."

"So—I don't understand. What do we do now?"

"I come home and we get through this. We come out the other side like we always do, and we do it together."

Christine's sense of relief and gratefulness was tainted by fury, though it was directed more at herself than Tim. Why did his behavior surprise her? She had always known he could be ruthless. All she had to do was think of the overpriced houses he had inflicted on trusting families while taking a six percent cut of their life savings, and the way he'd explained his apparent lack of conscience. "Welcome to life on the savannah. It's Darwinism 2.0. If you looked at everything through a moral lens you'd give all your money to orphans, and then you'd go bankrupt and starve. What's moral about that?" The whole episode—packing his suitcases and holing up in some apartment for four nights—seemed now like something he'd planned for maximum effect and control. He had taken a pregnant woman in stressful circumstances and shaken her sense of stability, given her a dark glimpse of life without him, knowing that if he upset her enough she would take any emotional crumb he doled out. At this moment, looking at his smiling face, she despised him.

"You seem like a different person from the other day," she said.

"Really?" he said, lifting his beer. "The cops have lightened up on me. Maybe that's what you're sensing. I walked outside this morning and there was nobody there, unless they're using satellites. Wouldn't be surprised. You know how the unions love to spend taxpayer money."

"What I mean is, you were ready to divorce me, and now it's like nothing happened. What were you trying to accomplish?"

"This isn't a therapy session, Chris," he said, tilting his head as if speaking to a child. "Let's not pick it apart. I just needed to step back and get a clear view of things. You understand that, right, considering what's been going on? It seems like something you'd be in favor of."

"Was it stepping back or jerking me around?"

"Truthfully, I'm glad it affected you so much. The way you've been acting, following me, I didn't think you cared anymore."

"You drive to a strange woman's house and *I* don't care? I care too much."

"Okay," he said, raising his palms. "Maybe this was premature. I thought you wanted me to come home but maybe you just want to make me pay. I guess I don't have room to be human."

"I don't understand you, Tim. You always talk everything to death. What's different this time?"

"Look at the last few weeks. Is it a surprise I'm sick of dealing with it?"

"How does your moving out have anything to—"

"Chrissie, stop. We're not doing this anymore. I'm not, anyway."

She saw how fine the line was. Accept his version of events and they could go home together and begin their life as a family. Push for an explanation and he would stay away until she was calling him in the middle of the night weeping, pleading to see him. "I don't want you to pay," she said. "I'm hurt."

"You're also irritable. Is it hormones?"

"No."

"How do you know?"

"I guess I don't." And with this contradiction she gave in, showing herself to be unreliable and silently telling both of them that she wouldn't argue any further.

After dinner they returned to the house together. Tim unpacked his suitcases, put on flannel pajama bottoms and sandals, and went to the kitchen for water as if he'd never left. "Where'd you put the gun?" he asked, ice clinking against the glass. "I want to make sure it's nearby, just in case. I'm everybody's scapegoat these days."

"In the basement, in the box with your mom's clothes."

"Why there?"

"I was afraid it might go off."

He smiled at her. "Guns don't shoot by themselves."

"I know nothing about guns," she said, and went upstairs.

He came into the bedroom a few minutes later and replaced the gun on the closet shelf. "Ready for anything," he said. "Seeing Mom's stuff just now? I got the feeling she'd be really proud of me. Protecting us and doing what I have to do."

Later, they sat in bed watching television, Tim on his side, Christine on hers. Without him the bedroom would have felt cavernous and vaguely accusatory, just as it had for the past several days. With him it felt tense and claustrophobic. Even during their worst arguments she had never felt this chasm between them. As the credits flashed on a show Christine had watched with unseeing eyes, Tim affectionately touched his calf to hers and said, "I missed this."

"So did I." Her stomach clenched even as she let out a contented sigh. She stared at the television, trying to examine her feeling, to herd it into a bright corner of her mind so she could name it. Repulsion, sadness, rage—nothing seemed right. Well, whatever it was, she would get over it. She had gotten over worse. In the history of her marriage to Tim, this would take its humble place alongside the surveillance and screaming arguments and her miscarriages, and might someday even be remembered as an important turning point. If they could survive the last three weeks, their relationship might be scarred but it would be practically indestructible. That thought, at least, gave Christine a reason to go on.

After Tim left for work the following morning, she went down to the basement and began the arduous task of organizing. The doctor had told her not to exercise strenuously but he said nothing about sifting through piles of clothes and baskets filled with useless stocking stuffers and old wires, which she could practically accomplish standing in one place. The clutter that had represented stability only a few weeks ago now felt smothering. She had awakened with an unexpected desire to purge everything that represented her old life, with its material excesses and depressing relics of optimism and naiveté. One four-foot area took her nearly all morning. Over the years, their belongings seemed to have formed a complex system of layers. Behind each bag and stack of old books was something else, a pencil box or a space heater, and under that was a rusted can of WD-40 or an unopened tin of nuts that should have been thrown out years ago. Nothing that she found inspired any particular feeling, even the CDs Tim had made for her while they were dating. She would keep them but she wasn't sure when she would listen to them again. They could go upstairs on the shelf with all the other music they'd loved, gotten used to, and put aside.

She was filling a box with clothes for the thrift store when she saw what looked to be a half-filled garbage bag crumpled near the expired treadmill. She tucked the bag under one arm, grabbed some premarriage photo albums, and headed up the stairs, kicking the door shut behind her with a sharp slam that sounded as if it might have loosened something in the wall.

While she was crossing the kitchen the bag slipped out from under her arm, and its contents—old papers, wadded tissue, a sticky tangle of masking tape—dumped onto the floor. She set the photo albums and box on the table and knelt down, aware of feeling winded and, for the first time, as if her body wasn't hers alone. Scattered across the marble tile, among the dirty paper towels and old receipts, were the remnants of a greeting card. It had been torn to pieces, but the fragments were still adorned with sparkles and the ruined purple figure of a cartoon animal, a dinosaur, maybe, or a bear. There was a large, round scrawl on some of the scraps, and the words *Birthday, Dad!* had somehow been left intact. It took her ten minutes to lay out all the pieces of the card, though many were missing or too small to connect with the rest. *Me to You. Celebrate.*

Wish! Special. Christine sat cross-legged on the floor, staring at the scraps as if at a language she'd once known but couldn't remember. Something about it should make sense to her, but what?

Eventually she gave up and put the fragments into an envelope. She brought the rest of the trash outside to the garbage bin and buried it under two large white bags. After scrubbing her hands roughly with dish soap and a nail brush, she went upstairs to her sock drawer. The calendar she'd discovered in Tim's closet was tucked behind an old pair of tights. She took it out, sat down on the bed and dialed the number again.

This time there was no answer. There was only a little boy's voice on an answering machine, speaking in a slow, careful monotone. "You've reached me and my mommy Diana. Please leave a message and one of us will call you back. Okay? 'Bye!"

Christine made four wrong turns and drove all the way through Anaheim and back before finally finding the right street. There were still remnants of toilet paper in the tree across the road, blowing lazily in the breeze like underwater moss. She stopped the car and got out. In the forty minutes it had taken her to drive to the house, someone had come home, evidenced by the open front door and the SUV in the driveway. Or maybe they had been home all along, screening calls. The idea that she'd had to drive all this way when a phone call would have sufficed irritated her, and she walked up onto the porch with the feeling of following a badly written script. *Drive to house. Go to front door. Ring bell. Confront woman. Leave Tim.*

She didn't have to ring the bell because the woman was standing on the other side of the screen door with a basket of laundry in her arms. She was a small, slim-hipped blonde with dark commas for eyebrows and a nose that managed to be both charming and too long.

She jumped when she saw Christine. "You startled me," she said with an apologetic smile. "I'm sorry. Can I help you?" It was the same voice Christine had heard on the phone when she'd dialed the number four days earlier.

"Hi, Diana?"

"If you're from the census, I already sent in my forms."

Christine nearly laughed. If only she were on such a harmless bureaucratic errand. "No, I'm not. I'm just—do you have a son named Tim?"

Diana's expression remained open and unsuspecting. "You're from the school?"

"What school?" Christine asked.

"My son's school."

"So you have a little boy named Tim." She forced herself to repeat it so there would be absolutely no confusion.

"Yes. That's what you're asking, isn't it?" Diana looked flustered, as if Christine were playing a verbal game she couldn't follow.

"Yes. Is Tim's father at home?"

"He doesn't—why are you asking?" Diana asked, leery now.

"No reason. That's all I needed to know."

"What do you mean?"

Christine started unhurriedly down the steps. It was strange to think that Tim's infidelity would exonerate him in at least one way with the police. She might not be able to tell them anything about Paige or Jennifer Guthrie, but she could tell them that the child in the car with him that night had been his own son.

"Wait a minute, who are you?" Diana shouted after her. "Did you call me the other day?"

Without turning around, Christine got into her car and drove away.

Twenty-four

$\mathcal{A}$ little after eleven on the night she received the photograph, Audrey found Ruth Simon's headstone. A photograph had been posted on a grave website three years earlier by a person who had left only their initials: zms. While there were many Ruth Simons buried in cemeteries throughout the country, there was just one listed in Bakersfield. After clicking on her name, Audrey had been so afraid of disappointment that she paced the room while the page loaded, sitting down only when the picture filled the screen in front of her. It had been taken in the same cemetery that she, Christine, and Linda had visited, but in a section of newer plots, mostly neglected upright and flat granite markers set in a treeless expanse of grass. Ruth's grave, though, was one of the few that looked recently visited, at least then. There were fresh yellow roses in a vase at the base of the headstone, along with a small kneeling angel. A slim wooden stake had been stuck into the ground and hung with wind chimes. Above Ruth's name was inscribed the word MOTHER, but the birth and death dates were too small to read.

So Ruth had a child, maybe the one she'd held in her arms in the photograph. That child, or someone else, was keeping up the grave. Audrey felt so intensely hopeful, she had to remind herself that the picture of the grave was three years old, and represented one day out of hundreds that had passed since Ruth died. In the intervening years her son or daughter—or maybe she had more than one child—might have moved or passed away, making the headstone just another tantalizing but futile lead. And there was no reason to believe that this person had known Mala or could help her find her, though there was always a chance. It was that chance Audrey couldn't let go of.

In the morning she called the cemetery and got the manager, a man with a gruff way of speaking. She gave him her name and asked if, by chance, he could tell her who came to visit the grave of a woman named Ruth Simon.

He waited so long to answer, Audrey thought they'd been disconnected. "Now, how am I supposed to know a thing like that?" he asked.

"I'd imagine you *would* know, since the grave is so well-kept. Considering the state of most of your headstones, it should stick out like a sore thumb."

Instead of hanging up on her, he clucked his tongue and blew out a breath. "Hold on, maybe Martin knows. He's out there all day gabbing with everybody."

"Who's Martin?"

"Groundskeeper." He put the phone down with a deafening rustle and a thunk. Audrey heard a chair creak and after that the line went silent.

She waited for nearly ten minutes before the rustling started again and a breathless, higher-pitched male voice said, "Hello? You still there?"

"Yes," Audrey said. "Is this Martin?"

"Yeah, what did you want?" he asked, though his tone was more curious than unfriendly. "Phil wasn't too clear."

"I'm looking for a person, maybe more than one, who visits a grave at your cemetery. Ruth Simon's. Do you know which stone I mean?"

"'Course I know," he said without hesitation. "You ride a mower around here for four years you feel like you know 'em."

"So you know who comes to see her?"

"An older lady, her daughter, I think. She comes pretty often. Not for about a month now."

"Have you ever talked to her?"

"Few times. Nice, but she doesn't say too much."

"Do you know her name?"

"Ah . . . hm. Don't think she ever formally introduced herself, and if they don't volunteer, I don't ask. Hey, why do you want to know all this? She in trouble or something?"

"No, we just—know people in common. I'd like to meet her, that's all."

"Well, she's usually here on a weekend. I haven't seen her in a while, though."

"What time?"

"Oh, she mostly shows up mid-afternoon. Drives in from somewhere, I can tell you that."

"When does she come? Holidays? Birthdays?"

"I'm not here on holidays so I don't know. Birthdays, for sure."

"Do you know when Ruth Simon's birthday is?"

"Haven't memorized it, of course, but give me your number and I'll check and call you back."

Twenty minutes later Audrey's phone rang.

"June eighteenth," Martin said without preamble.

"Really? That's—" Audrey looked at her watch. "Next week, isn't it?"

"I don't know if the daughter'll be here on a Tuesday but you're welcome to take your chances."

"Martin," Audrey said, already knowing she would call in sick that day and make the trip, "you've been a big help. I can't thank you enough."

"Okay!" he said, and hung up in her ear.

"Brake lights ahead," William said.

He sat in the passenger seat of Audrey's car with his leg stretched out in front of him and his seatbelt dangling uselessly by the door. He seemed to have made the leap from sick to healthy when she wasn't looking. Suddenly, his shoulders were broad and straight and his chest was filled out, as if he had gained twenty pounds in a few days. His face was a burnt tan from sitting in the one corner of his patio that got sunlight. At some point he had stopped using his cane and simply begun limping around. Audrey couldn't say when because he hadn't mentioned it and it had escaped her attention. She felt selfish and insensitive for being less interested in his recovery than the way he made her feel.

Although she had given him only a day's notice, he was ready and standing in the parking lot near his car when she went to pick him up. Since getting in next to her, he had hardly stopped talking. He had a Humvee driver's awareness of his surroundings, which revealed itself in a continuous patter of nervous, backseat observations. "Guy coming up behind you pretty fast. Stupid girl texting on your right."

"I've been driving since before you were born," Audrey said.

"I know. Just think of me as your copilot."

They had left for Bakersfield at ten-thirty, giving them what Audrey thought would be ample time to arrive at the cemetery and wait for Ruth's daughter to appear in the afternoon. In addition to sodas and snacks, Audrey had brought the book, the photograph, and a bouquet of white lilies, which had immediately scattered pollen across the backseat and given the car a sickly, funereal stench. "Lucky for me, my sense of smell is half-gone," William said after Audrey sneezed for the third time. She rolled down her window but the wind rattled the plastic wrapping and sent yellow dust flying around the inside of the car. At the first rest stop, she got out and dropped the flowers into the trunk.

Two miles later she saw a line of red lights ahead of her. "Oh, God," she said, slowing suddenly. "What's this?"

"Road work, maybe," William said. "An accident."

The traffic inched forward for several minutes, then came to a stop. In her side mirror Audrey could see three lanes of cars behind her, stalled in a shimmering haze of gas fumes. "We'll get there, right? We have plenty of time."

But by noon they'd made it only to Santa Clarita. She didn't want to give up and turn around, but the decision to continue would mean sitting in traffic for as long as it took. "This is awful," she said. "I'm really sorry."

"So we'll talk. That'll pass the time." William put his hand on her thigh and left it there until they got to the cemetery, nearly three hours later than planned.

Audrey pulled into the parking lot and turned off her car's exhausted engine. She still had the sensation of moving forward, starting and stopping, the motor vibrating through her seat. Now that she was here, she felt overwhelmed to the point of tears. Should she try the manager's office or look for the grave? Stay here so she wouldn't miss Ruth's daughter when she drove in?

"I can stay in the car if you want," William said. "I don't know what she looks like, though."

"Neither do I."

He opened his door and, with a barely visible wince, extended his leg and rested the heel of his sneaker on the pavement. "All that matters is who leaves, right? If she's coming, you'll see her. There's almost nobody around. If I see a woman walking back and getting into a car, I'll let you know. Got your phone?"

"Yes." She kissed him quickly and was about to get out of the car when she stopped. "Thank you."

"I'll wait right here."

The cemetery was large and the afternoon hot and dry, but at least she knew where to start: not in the old section where she had imagined Mala would be buried, but among the newer and uglier headstones close to the road. She felt old and out of shape, hustling across the spiky grass in a skirt and sandals, the sun searing the back of her neck. In the distance she could see a mower spinning around and around, weaving among the graves and going surprisingly quickly. As she got closer she could make out the figure of the driver, a small, black-haired man wearing khaki green pants and heavy boots. She was only a few yards away when the mower stopped and the man began wiping his forehead with a blue handkerchief.

"Are you Martin?" she asked, shielding her eyes from the sun.

"Yup."

"I'm Audrey Cronin. We talked on the phone yesterday."

Looking at her blankly, he unscrewed the top of a water bottle, drank several swallows, and wiped his mouth with the back of a finger.

"About Ruth Simon," she continued. "You said her daughter comes to visit her grave?"

"Oh!" he said. "That was you? 'Course I remember. You seen the grave yet? It's right over there." He turned in his seat and pointed a few rows behind him.

"Thank you. It would have taken me an hour to find it."

"Bad news, though. The daughter already came and went."

"When?" Audrey asked with a feeling of crushing disappointment. "This morning?"

"About an hour ago. She only stayed a few minutes. I barely had time to say hello to her."

Too tired and discouraged to be concerned about decorum, Audrey sat on the edge of the nearest headstone and rested her purse on her knees. "I can't believe it. After driving all this way."

"Too bad, huh?"

"Martin, I have the worst luck of anyone I know. My life—you can't imagine. I just don't enjoy living it most of the time."

"Isn't that how things go? What you don't want always comes easy." He laughed as if this depressing aphorism were somehow funny.

"Well, I don't know what to do now. I live a hundred and fifty miles away. I can't keep driving back here."

"Nope. You can't. Wouldn't make sense." He crossed his arms and, looking around at the trees and grass, sighed contentedly. "Nice out today, huh?"

"Hot. I'm sweltering."

"I like it hot."

"You're used to it."

"Well, maybe you'll see her the next time you come out. You really need to talk to this lady?"

"Yes, or find her somehow."

"I don't know if it'll help, but your phone call got me thinking. I talk to her a couple times a month and don't know what her name is. So this morning I just asked."

"And she told you?"

"She did, and it isn't easy to remember so I hope I don't mess it up."

Audrey fumbled in her purse. "Will you write it down for me?"

He took a pen and torn scrap of envelope from her and, using his knee, wrote the name carefully. "Might have spelled it wrong."

"That's okay."

She took the piece of paper back from him and held it in her hand. It wasn't until Martin drove off on his mower in a blast of exhaust that she let herself read the name.

Twenty-five

*A*ny person, Mala reasoned, with a new life laid out for them, would have trouble not considering the possibilities.

It didn't mean she was happy with the twisted circumstances of her birth and her mother's death. For days she'd been venomously angry with Beni, had hated him for condemning her to a life she wasn't meant to lead. Henry Nolan had wanted to find her, sent men out searching years ago. To think she might have gone to school, worn perfume, slept in a room of her own. She had always been a stranger in her family, and for nearly twenty years Beni had known why. He could have told her earlier and given her a different destiny, but even when he'd finally been honest he'd hidden the truth of it, letting her wander into the night with a bag of old books. Had he been afraid of losing her, or was his memory so damaged from liquor and bad luck that he couldn't remember who had made love to his wife and given her a child? No matter the excuse, Mala was determined never to forgive him.

"He had his reasons," Ruth said. "He took care of you by himself for fifteen years. That says everything."

"It says he was selfish. He didn't want to be lonely."

"You can choose to see it that way if you want," Ruth said, and went back to seeding tomatoes.

It took some time for Mala to realize it, but of course Ruth was right. She could curse Beni for holding on to her, or she could imagine what might have happened—abandonment, growing up under Drina's roof—and thank him for preventing it. She could lament the foreign blood in her veins or begin thinking about life as a young woman of privilege. It was deferred but maybe not too late. Her father, Ruth said, wrote about her in every letter and hoped to see her. Wanted nothing more than to be reunited with his only child.

Mala began to spend long hours daydreaming, envisioning what this alternate future might look like. It would be, like any other future, a combination of intention and accident. Once she decided to become the daughter of an important man, events would unfold in a different pattern, transforming every moment that followed. Even alone in a room, she would know she hadn't come from nothing, and that would change the way she carried herself and saw the world. Freedom wouldn't be a bitter effect of banishment, but the result of means and accomplishment. Her father would no longer be a drunk, but a successful businessman and landowner. That fact would forever change the way people looked at her.

She would get married. But first she would spend a year being known as the most eligible girl in West Texas. The housekeeper would turn away hordes of young men, who would come to the house two or three at a time in shiny automobiles. Because a story like that could defy distance and social isolation, even Drina would hear about it. She would talk about her in hushed, envious tones, and every person in camp would regret the way they'd treated her. Her name would be mentioned in the local newspaper in the same sentence with charities and restaurants, and it would be rumored that the son of an oilman had pursued her only to be rejected without explanation. And after all that was done, she would surprise everyone by marrying a poor farm boy, who would run the ranch alongside her father as if he were born for it. There would be a lot of children and trips to interesting cities. Dying would feel a long way off.

But at the end of these reveries there was always Beni. Even in a world of the imagination, something had to be done about him. As soon as Mala grew tired of hating him, she went back to missing him desperately. After nineteen years of sleeping across the trailer from her, he had hold of her mind. There would be no bringing him along into this new life, but not because she wouldn't try. No matter what luxuries might be waiting for him, Beni wouldn't give up quietly. He would be damned if he'd live like a pet dog in another man's home—his pride wouldn't permit it even if her real father would— and so he would continue wandering from canyon to flood plain, scrounging for pennies along railroad tracks and showing up drunk in the middle of the night with tears streaming down his face. For this reason it was a relief in some small measure when Mala decided that none of her visions would ever come true.

Elliot began driving by the house every night. This continued for a week before Mala summoned the courage to get out of bed again and go outside, knowing she might wake Ruth, but the situation had the feeling of something that would take place no matter what. This time she put on shoes, a dress, and one of Ruth's hand-knit sweaters.

"Thought you'd never come out," he said as soon as she opened the door of the truck, and for an hour those were the only words they exchanged. When he finally spoke again, he said, "I know it's soon but I think we should get married."

Mala slid away from him and stared him down. "You're crazy."

"You may be right about that."

"Please don't say it again."

He grabbed her hands. "Let's get married. I'm not kidding around."

"You hardly know me. You've got no idea what you'd be marrying into. What sort of family, I mean."

"I don't care. You don't say much about where you come from, but I can see you're not like everybody else. Okay by me, my folks are nothing to crow about and my brother's been slow since he was born. He still lives at home and gets himself in all kinds of trouble."

"Where you come from isn't my business."

"Same way I feel. Matter of fact, I think eloping would be a good idea. You'll come live on the farm with me. My uncle won't like it but there's not much he can do about it. He's got no son of his own and he needs me. That farm'll be mine someday, and yours, too."

It was tempting to admit how closely his vision of the future hewed to her own, except to do so would make both ideas seem like real possibilities. "I'm going home next year. I can't stay here."

"Why not?" he asked. He was almost crushing her hands between his.

"I've got people to get home to."

"We'll go visit them. Hell, we'll move them out here."

Mala could almost imagine it—Beni getting off the bus, looking around with a bewildered expression as if he'd just been left on the moon. She could show him to his room, a real place to sleep with an electric light and a new wool blanket, which he would appreciate for about a week before he got fidgety and began to complain. "Whole place is closing in on me," he would say at breakfast. "Can't you feel it? I need to do something besides sit here and wait to die." And then he would ask if there was whiskey to go with his eggs. He would pace around the house at night and go missing for hours or days at a time, coming back one morning with a deep scratch on his nose and eight dollars in single bills in his pocket.

It would never work. It would be near impossible to keep Beni in one place, until he went in the ground, anyway. Sitting there in the truck, she realized she'd been considering Beni her father and it hadn't even occurred to her to do otherwise.

"I'll think it over," she told Elliot.

Two days later Ruth went to visit her brother, who had left Bakersfield three years before for a job in San Francisco. It was as if she were encouraging Mala to make an impetuous decision that would stay with her the rest of her life.

"I'll be back next week," she said when the taxi stopped outside the house. "I trust you to do what needs to be done. There's soup on the stove for your supper. Don't forget to lock up at night."

Mala stood by the window and watched the taxi drive toward the bus station. It was the first time she'd been alone when she wasn't either on the run or at the river, avoiding going back to camp. She went about her usual routine, the chores and the gardening and the ironing, aware every moment of being alone and what that meant. The freedom it gave her.

As if he knew he would be asked in, Elliot came to the house at ten o'clock that night. Mala was ready for him, wearing her better shoes and a dress that Ruth had sewn from navy blue cotton. With clumsy hands, she had tried on a smear of Ruth's red lipstick, but wiped it off after seeing her clownish reflection in the mirror. Her eyes were decoration enough, now that her skin was pale again and her hair growing toward her shoulders.

She hadn't considered the neighbors until she led Elliot up the walk and onto the front porch. A curtain dropped as soon as she looked across the yard at the next house, and somewhere nearby a screen door creaked shut. Everyone was bound to notice the truck at the curb while Ruth was out of town. It was a godsend that she hadn't heard whispers about it appearing after dark almost every night, or maybe she had. Maybe she'd decided that, in the interest of harmony, it was best not to mention it.

Mala nearly crumpled to the floor from nerves when she shut the door behind Elliot. "Take off your boots," she said. "We can't have hay tracked in here."

He left his boots by the door, removed his hat, and walked the perimeter of the living room in thin dark socks. "I haven't been in a real house in a long time," he said. "It's nice."

"What about your uncle's house?" she asked, perching awkwardly on the arm of a chair.

"It's kind of an extension of the farm. The smells, the dirt, all the chicken feathers. My aunt does her best but there's always men going in and out." He leaned over the mantel and looked at Ruth's photographs. "She have a husband?"

"No. Far as I know she's never been married."

"I wonder why."

"Not every woman gets married, you know."

"And some that do wish they hadn't. My mother being one. My father's a traveling salesman and he's home about five days a month." He smiled and sat down, his sprawling legs stretching so far across the carpet his foot almost touched hers.

Just then Mala remembered that she hadn't offered Elliot anything to eat or drink. Ruth would have said it showed that she'd grown up like a wild animal. "What can I bring you?" she asked, jumping up. "Coffee? I'll make a pot."

"Nothing," he said.

"Are you sure?" She went to the kitchen and turned on the light. When she turned, he was behind her. They stood at the counter talking, their fingers laced, the coffee forgotten and minutes vanishing at twice their normal rate. Then they were walking up the stairs toward her bedroom, and any thought of it being unwise was eclipsed by her belief that the opportunity wouldn't come again. That alone made it right. Her bed squeaked loudly as Elliot sat down on the edge in the dark. She stood in the doorway, pleased to see him in a room where so much thinking about him had been done.

"Come here," he said.

"All right." She sat beside him but he didn't touch her.

"We can wait if you want," he said.

"Is that why you came here, to wait?"

"I came here to see you, that's all."

But then he kissed her and she pushed her shoes off with her toes, letting each one drop to the floor. The door was bolted, the moon already down, and when Elliot reached for the buttons on her dress, she didn't try to stop him.

It was a little after five in the morning when she woke to a hazy white sky and a situation that couldn't be reversed. She felt too heavy to move, not from regret but from a feeling she couldn't name because she'd never had it before. She knew only that everything that came before it—the trial, the ride west, her capture at the farm, finding Ruth—were ingredients of something more important.

Elliot lay on his back in the light, his mouth closed and a thin hand resting on his sternum. She watched him, trying to draw out every moment, but each moment tumbled away from her as soon as it approached. A car passed and Elliot woke suddenly, sitting bolt upright, looking at the clock and scrambling into his pants. Mala sat in bed with the sheet pulled up, smiling as he hunted on all fours for his shirt. "Sorry to hurry off," he said, buckling his belt and kissing her shoulder. "I'll come by tonight."

He did as promised, coming that night and every night that followed except for the last before Ruth returned from San Francisco. Mala had been rushing to prepare a special dinner, because everything they'd eaten the rest of the week—sandwiches and a hastily roasted chicken—had felt like an afterthought. But this night, their last together for who knew how long, would be different. She would pick lettuce from the garden and lemons from the tree in the backyard, and they would have pork chops from the butcher, who knew Mala and greeted her by name.

Late that afternoon Elliot came to the house, running up the walk with wild eyes and a heaving chest. Mala stood at the open door like a woman hearing bad news, and bad news it was. Elliot was on his way out of town, driving five hundred miles to Nevada, all night if he had to. His mother had telephoned to say that his brother was in jail, and with his father on the road, Elliot was needed at home right away. He didn't like leaving this way but he promised to write and hoped Mala wouldn't be gone before he got back. Whenever that was.

He pulled a tiny yellow flower from the bed along the walk and handed it to her. Then he hugged her, long and hard. "I hope you're thinking about the question I asked," he said. He drove away grinning, the sun glinting off his truck and leaving a white impression on Mala's vision. Every time she blinked, she saw him go one more time.

She didn't wait for the flower to wilt. Though it was still bright, practically still growing, she took it to her room and pressed it in the back of the notebook. Then she went downstairs and took the place settings off the table. She put away the wineglasses and wrapped up the pork chops, which she and Ruth could have tomorrow. Eating dinner alone in the waning light, she wondered what might have happened had Elliot stayed, and decided that it didn't much matter. Eventually, once he had left and the house was silent, she would have felt the same certainty she felt now. She wouldn't be going back to Texas anytime soon because events would intervene. Though she couldn't see them clearly, she could sense them building like thunderheads, not bringing trouble, necessarily, but bringing change.

This wasn't a future she could turn away from, it was inevitable. There if she went north, there if she went south.

She sat at the table watching the sun set, which tonight felt like the saddest thing in the world. If she'd thought it would be a long time until she saw Beni again, well, it was going to be even longer than that.

Twenty-six

It wasn't long after Paige's disappearance when Peter and Margaret resumed their bad marriage, picking up where they left off but with new spouses to call in as reinforcements and intermediaries. As soon as the shrieks and insults began, Linda and Neil became like AWOL soldiers from different armies, escaping together to the far reaches of the house where they would be difficult to find.

"I don't know why she won't go to a hotel," Neil said, shutting the door of the laundry room. "I keep asking her but she doesn't want to hear it."

"She wants to be here in case something happens," Linda said from her perch on top of the dryer. "You know, if Paige calls or walks through the door. I'd feel the same way."

"I'm not getting involved anymore. I'm here to find Paige and be a shoulder to cry on, and that's where my responsibility stops." He glanced up at the ceiling as a door on the second floor slammed, followed shortly by the sound of something hitting a wall. "God Almighty, she's nuts sometimes."

"They're under a lot of stress," Linda said, though she knew things couldn't continue this way. The crisis was changing shape, transitioning to a phase that felt depressingly static and drawn out. It was no longer an emergency, but a situation that had developed a history and structure of its own.

It was after one of these arguments, when the house had settled into an uneasy silence and Linda had sought asylum in the kitchen, that Peter came up behind her and said, "Let's talk."

"About what?" she asked, shaking the hair out of her eyes.

"Upstairs, okay?" His voice was cold. It was going to be about Margaret.

"I thought you were making an appearance at work this afternoon," she said, walking ahead of him down the hall. "You need a break from all this."

"I'm leaving in an hour."

"Are you ready?"

"No."

She went into the bedroom, waited for Peter to follow, and shut the door. "Let me just say, we need to have compassion for her."

"Who?" Peter asked. He sat on the brown velvet cube by the window, his sneakers planted side by side on the carpet.

"Margaret. She has to make us the enemy so she can get through this."

He looked at Linda with what she first believed was deep exhaustion, but as soon as he spoke she realized it was pity.

"Why didn't you tell me?" he said.

Linda turned to her dresser, whose top was inconveniently empty. Nothing to arrange, nothing to dust or put away. "I hope she won't hate us when it's all over. We all need to stick together for Paige's sake."

"I just talked to Detective Klein."

She stared at the wall, a perfectly white patch of blankness. "Oh. Why?"

"Would you mind looking at me?"

"Sure, uh-huh," she said, turning to face him. "Absolutely."

"I wanted to know why he was giving you such a hard time. I don't like these guys showing up without calling and cornering you."

"I don't need protecting, Peter."

"He wasn't going to tell me but I insisted. He said you denied everything. I need you to be honest, is it true?"

She wanted to try, one more time. *You must be joking.* But she couldn't. She managed a shrug and even that took more strength than she had.

"You're not going to answer me?"

His voice sounded distant. Her heartbeat was so heavy her ears felt plugged and her skin damp. "Let's not draw this out. Just say what you have to say."

It seemed to take him a long time to collect his thoughts, and when he did, he spoke carefully. "I don't care what you did when you were younger."

"If you didn't care we wouldn't be talking."

"You don't think I know what your life was like, with a father like yours? You had to survive somehow."

"You know what I've told you. It was a lot worse than that."

"I guess I wouldn't know, would I? I'm just the fool you're married to. I believe whatever you tell me."

"Well—I'm sorry. I'm sorry I did awful, unforgivable things

and didn't tell you all about it when we first met, but I don't think you would have stayed if I had. God, Peter, it was almost twenty years ago. The only thing I want in life is to get away from it."

"You're not listening to me. It isn't what happened then, it's what happened yesterday in this house!" His eyes revealed a new kind of pain, one Linda had never seen before. "You didn't say a word after the police left. You didn't even look upset. It's so ruthless, hiding something like that."

"With everything that's going on, why would I want to burden you?"

"If you had to lie to me for seven years, at least be honest now. You didn't care about burdening me, you didn't want me to know."

"You're right. I didn't." This admission seemed to throw him, and he stayed silent. Lowering her voice to a half whisper, she said, "Margaret found out. She had somebody investigate me before we got married."

"Jesus Christ, are you serious? What does she know?"

"That I was arrested. That's all. She brought it up the other night when she was drunk."

"Something else I wish you'd told me." He looked out the window, his face gray and worn-out in the late morning glare. A bird flew by and his eyes tracked it, moving up and to the side, before it disappeared.

"I only did it for a few months," she said. "If that makes it better."

"I love you either way but I don't think you see that. It just makes me really sad, Linda."

He got up and went to get dressed for work. Linda returned to the kitchen, listening like an animal for sounds and voices, straightening her back when she heard leather shoes squeaking down the hall.

"I'm leaving," Peter said, leaning into the kitchen. "Call me if anything happens today."

"Of course I will. Good luck."

Instead of walking out, he stayed in the doorway looking at her. She turned, holding up cilantro-flecked hands.

"I can't talk about it anymore, all right? Some other time, but not now."

"We don't have to talk about it at all. It's over."

"Then why are you standing there?"

His smile was slight but there was an intimacy about it, as though he'd made love to her upstairs after confronting her. "I was just going to—I don't know how to say it. With everything I've had to deal with this year, I'm almost glad to find out you're not this perfect being who's never made mistakes."

"I can't believe you ever thought I was," Linda said.

"One more conversation for another time. Now, is there anything else I should know? While we're on the subject?" He had a slightly amused and forgiving expression, as if he were already sure of her answer. Sure that, though her mistake had been grave, there'd been only one of them.

"Peter . . ." She thought of Margaret's affair and of Ross Picard, risen from the imaginary dead, living in New York with his wife and kids. Some things weren't secrets to share, they were burdens you passed on, images that infected the mind. Keeping them silent was an act of love.

"No," she said. "Nothing."

That afternoon, while Margaret called Detective Klein to berate him for what she referred to as "a shoddy and unproductive investigation," Neil and Linda left to meet volunteers at Hop Prescott Wilderness State Park. Another young girl had been found at the same park the year before, buried in a shallow grave under a scrub oak tree on a remote hillside. As soon as Linda heard this, she could not imagine finding Paige alive. The other murder seemed like a precedent, a pattern that all young missing girls would follow no matter how different their circumstances. She wondered if that conviction originated in the same part of her brain that had spent eighteen years convinced she'd killed someone. Maybe it was the same sort of assumption, nothing but too little information combined with a congenitally dark disposition. Clearly, she could not be counted on to see things clearly, even when they happened right in front of her.

They drove south toward San Diego—Neil talking on his phone to one colleague after another, Linda thinking how boring his job sounded—and arrived just before one o'clock. Christine and Audrey had offered to take the day off to help, but they'd already done so much that Linda refused. It was strange to think that these two women, whom she hadn't expected to feel particularly connected to or interested in, had proven to be such faithful friends. In the beginning, she had assumed they were chirpy housewives who would find her sarcastic and closed off. But rather than get offended when she called the development "an internment camp for bleached blondes," they had laughed, and then Christine asked her to join the book club. Almost with embarrassment, Linda remembered the relief she had felt, that two of her neighbors would accept her even if they didn't quite understand her.

"What a turnout," Neil said. "There must be thirty people here."

"Good. It's a big park."

A young policewoman named Maria helped Linda and Neil organize everyone, hand out gloves and plastic bags and trail maps, and send people off to search in small groups.

"We like to be around for these things in case any suspects show up," she told Linda. "Sometimes they're the most helpful volunteers of all. They can't stay away."

She and Linda were the last to start out, taking the trail that led east toward the desert, and eventually, Linda thought, New York. It was steep and sunny, and after about ten minutes, she had to stop for breath. "I know I should be looking around, but I'm afraid," she said. "I don't want to see anything, even if it's there."

"Just remember why you're here, Mrs. Fredrickson," Maria said. "To eliminate it as a possibility, at least today."

After two hours of searching, climbing off the trail through brambles and underbrush to examine every bit of garbage in case it might be a scrap of Paige's clothing, Linda returned to the parking lot near tears. Most of the volunteers were still out looking, and so far no one had found anything. She had that to cling to. The thought of calling Peter with bad news was so repellent she no longer permitted it into her mind.

Linda got back to her car and nearly finished her bottle of water, reserving a little to pour into her hand and rub over her face, which she dried with an extra shirt. Her vanity and concern for dirt and germs were gone. Through dry, filmy eyes she saw a red hatchback at the far end of the dirt parking lot. She wouldn't have noticed it except it was sitting at an odd angle, as if it had been parked in a hurry. There was a woman inside, just sitting in the driver's seat. Maybe she was there to hike or had driven one of the volunteers, but Linda wanted to be sure. As she got closer to the car, she could hear the engine idling. All of the windows were rolled up and the woman appeared to be talking to herself.

Linda tapped lightly on the window, and the woman turned, startled. Her mouth was large and loose and her teeth were filled with dark gaps. She was about forty, slight and deeply tanned, with a fan of wrinkles above her upper lip. She had on a wide leather bracelet and a halter top that revealed skinny, freckled shoulders. There but for the grace of God, thought Linda.

"Here for the search?" she asked as the woman rolled down her window.

"Well, yeah. Sort of."

"What's your name?"

"Patricia."

"Thanks very much for coming, Patricia, but we've already sent everybody out."

"Oh," she said. "I wasn't sure when it started, but . . . Are you Linda?"

"Yes. How did you know that?"

"I saw you on the news. You look really good on camera."

A cold feeling filled Linda's chest, but she smiled in spite of it. "Did you really think so? I hate being interviewed, especially under these circumstances."

"I bet." Patricia had large, startled eyes and a nervous way of moving her hands. She was repeatedly rolling something over in her lap—a pink cigarette lighter, Linda realized.

"You find anything up there?" Patricia asked.

"Not yet, but the search isn't over," Linda said, holding up her cell phone and two-way radio. "We just hope we find her alive."

"Of course you do. I can't imagine."

Patricia coughed into a palm, oddly ladylike. "Listen, I don't want to make trouble, but I drove all the way up from San Diego and I'd be pretty pissed at myself if I left without saying it."

"Saying what?" Linda had the feeling—common over the last ten days—of not knowing how the next few minutes would transpire. She was terribly agitated but also curious. What was happening? How would it end?

"Well, I'm not here for the search. I mean, not because I don't care, but I came because I wanted to talk to you."

"Oh. Okay."

"I took a whole day off work to do this—I'm a home health aide and I love it—but sometimes you get a feeling. Do you know what I mean?"

Linda squatted down, resting her forearms on the hot metal of the window frame. "I know exactly what you mean."

"Really?"

"Of course. Absolutely."

"Then you understand what it's like. For a whole week I was going over it and I couldn't figure out why, and I'm saying to my husband, 'I've really lost it this time,' but then last night you're on the news again, and I thought to myself, Sandy."

"Sandy?"

"My grandfather's sister. She lives near here, about five miles that way. Or wait. That way. I get all spun around out here." Suddenly, she looked past Linda's head toward the trailhead. "There's a cop here?"

Maria was across the parking lot, putting unused gloves and gear into the trunk of the police car. "She's just here to help with the volunteers," Linda said, reassuringly, on Patricia's side. "I can't do it all alone."

"Use all the help you can get, huh?"

"Exactly. So tell me about Sandy. Why did I make you think of her?"

Instantly, Patricia got very serious. "She's not doing too well, first off. She shouldn't be driving. I tried to take her keys away but she about killed me. She won't even talk to me after that."

"Is she sick?"

"She had a couple of strokes and her mind is going. I deal with this stuff all the time, on a professional basis. She lives alone and she won't let anybody help. Her neighbors are awesome, though, they try and keep an eye on her and that's why I'm here. Because one of them calls me last week and tells me he saw a little girl over there."

It took a moment for the words to register, and then came the delayed flooding of physical response, the thudding heart and sick stomach. "A little girl?"

"Not *really* little, about eight or so. And Sandy doesn't know anybody that age, and I don't think there's a mom in the world who would let her kid stay there by herself."

"Do you think it's—"

"I sure wish I could say. I tried to go over myself but nobody answered the door, which is strange if you ask me. I don't want to get your hopes up because the girl could be anybody or it could all be some big misunderstanding. I just think it's funny, that's all. Worth checking out."

"Can you bring me there, right now?"

"Um, I guess so. In my car?"

"I'll follow you in mine." She reached in and grabbed Patricia's hand. "Thank you. Wait here, okay? I'll be right back. Thirty seconds."

Later, she would remember the next several minutes only in brief, jumbled snatches: Maria on her car radio, Neil jogging stoutly off the trail, her own fingers dialing Peter's number and hanging up before he could answer. Neil thanking the volunteers. Cars being started and backed out and driven away.

And she would remember being too exhausted to argue with Maria when she asked Linda to go home and wait. There were too many unknowns. It could be another child. The situation might be too dangerous. "Of course," Linda said. She had never been so glad to be told what to do.

She and Neil drove out to the main road through the dust from Maria's tires. Patricia and Maria turned one way, Linda the other. "Are you going to call Margaret?" she asked, accelerating toward the freeway.

"Not yet," Neil said. "Did you call Peter?"

"I couldn't."

"Maybe it's better that we don't," he said. "For now."

Twenty-seven

Christine could see Tim give up. It was like a sudden deflation of his body. At the sound of the name "Diana," his cheeks hollowed and his shoulders dropped forward, as if his whole being were collapsing along with his arguments.

"I wanted a child," he said in a soft, pleading voice. "I didn't want to die without leaving a piece of myself behind."

Christine had expected, at least, to scream. She had thought she would hit him and turn over a table full of dishes, but whatever she was feeling couldn't be reduced to simple displays of violence to her household. She sat in stone silence across from him.

"It was after your second miscarriage," Tim said. "I was fucking beside myself. Our life together just seemed so depressing, nothing but death and doctors all the time. My mom had had her first cancer surgery around then, and I needed to get away from it, you know? I was only thirty-six."

If he was going to pick and choose places to lie, this would not go well. It wouldn't go well even if he told the truth. "Get your facts straight. Your mother wasn't diagnosed with cancer until you were thirty-eight."

"So the miscarriages weren't enough? Men grieve, too, Chris."

"Sleeping with somebody else isn't grieving!"

He drew back a little, hung his head. He was sitting on the sofa in the living room, still wearing his work clothes, his car keys clutched in his hand. "You're right, absolutely. I was being a coward."

"So, what? You decided it would be a good thing to do, have a baby with some woman you met in a bar?"

"First of all, it was an accident, a one-night thing. I never thought she'd get pregnant. She tracked me down on the Internet and called me at work one morning. I couldn't believe it. At first I told her never to call me again, but then I kept thinking how much I wanted a child. It was about the baby, Chris, that's all. I know how it sounds but I thought it would an easy thing. You know, victimless."

"Victimless," Christine repeated.

"I didn't want to pressure you anymore. I knew you'd had more than you could take, and I thought this would solve the problem for both of us. I could be a father for a few hours every week and we could go about our lives, maybe get pregnant ourselves if we were lucky." He leaned forward, put his elbows on his knees and opened his hands toward her. "I was going to tell you, when we were past all the fertility stuff. I thought you might actually be okay with it someday. Maybe I was kidding myself."

"You know what bothers me the most?" she said.

"What?"

"When you told me you'd gone to talk to one of the secretaries out of a harassment suit—you almost sold me."

"I was protecting you, Chrissie. Don't you see? That's what this whole thing is about. I love you more than anything in the world, and if I had to cut my wrists to keep from hurting you anymore, I would."

"Keeping your sperm out of some stranger's uterus would have been simpler. I'm surprised you didn't think of it." She got up from her chair and walked toward the kitchen. "I want you gone. Tonight."

Tim refused to leave. He followed her from room to room even when she stopped responding, trying new arguments and using twisted logic while she prepared a salad she didn't want to eat. More than anything, his revelations made her feel obtuse. Of all the impossibilities that might have—that had—occurred, infidelity should have been the one she saw coming. Tim had slept with so many women before their marriage that his behavior under stress had been predictable. If only she had opened her eyes.

Midnight came and went and still Tim kept talking. He seemed so convinced that this was just a temporary blip in their marriage that he became impossible to reason with. It was like talking to someone in a coma. No matter what Christine said, his mind could not be changed. Brushing aside her silence and contempt, he plowed on with the single-mindedness of a zealot. It was a stupid, meaningless affair, he said. People had lived through much worse: epidemics, poverty, genocide. Compared to that, they were dealing with one small piece of the wrath the universe was capable of. He knew he'd screwed up, but he had done it from love, from a biological urge so instinctual he had been powerless to fight it.

"Was it so terrible to want to bring a child into the world, to keep you from going through more miscarriages?"

Christine spit toothpaste into the sink and sipped a palmful of water. It tasted of the tears she absolutely refused to cry. "I wanted a child myself," she said, drying her mouth.

"So you're saying that if you couldn't have a child, I couldn't either?"

She didn't answer.

"And that doesn't seem a little selfish to you?"

Christine flipped off the light, brushed past Tim, and climbed into bed. He followed and sat in the leather recliner.

"I want you to know I never went with her to the doctor. I wasn't there during labor. We had no more contact until he was born."

"Why would I care about that?"

"Because I don't want you to think that I've already done it all. Having our child will be just as new and exciting for me as it will be for you."

When this didn't elicit a response, Tim changed tactics. He began to castigate himself, rip his own personality to shreds. He knew that, in the ways that really mattered, he had failed. He was a shit provider and didn't know how to adapt to the new economy. His bad habits—the spending, the cockiness, being bossy and insistent and hard to please—he saw them all clearly and he was finished with them. He was a different man now, and would spend the rest of his life making it up to her, because she was the only thing that had ever mattered to him. And it might sound far-fetched, but she was going to love little Tim. He was sure of it.

"I know it will take time," he said. "But once you get over the obvious weirdness of it and you put it all in context, you'll see he's a just sweet, innocent little boy. And I think you'll like Diana. She's a regular person, nice but not half as smart or beautiful as you are. I swear you won't feel threatened at all."

"Do you support her financially?" Christine finally asked, because she was curious how far Tim had gone. "I mean, what's the arrangement here?"

At the sound of her voice, Tim's face took on a hopeful look that

Christine found pitiful. "I've never given her a dime. I buy Christmas and birthday presents for Tim. He gives me cards. That's all." He got up and approached her until she held up her hand, stopping him in mid-stride. "Listen, Chrissie. We can work this out."

"No, we can't," Christine said. "Now, are you going to pack a suitcase and go to a hotel or am I?"

In the end Tim was the one who left. He swore it would not be permanent. He was doing it as a favor to his wife and as an acknowledgment of his many deficiencies as a husband, but he would fight to the end for his marriage and his child. Christine had no idea how devoted he was, the lengths he would go to.

"The time to prove that is over," she said, opening the front door for him, practically pushing him onto the porch. "Tell me where you're staying so I know where to send divorce papers."

She went to the window, pulled back the drapes, and watched as another impossibility unfolded before her eyes. Not that her husband was leaving, but that she was so relieved to see him go.

She had just arrived at her office the next morning when the phone rang. It was Diana, Tim's lover and the mother of his child.

"Please don't hang up," she said. "Though I wouldn't blame you if you did."

"Did Tim tell you to call me?" Christine asked.

"No. He made me promise not to. Ever."

"Then what are you doing?"

"No idea, I just—" She groaned and took a deep breath. "I want to say I'm sorry. That's all. I didn't know he was married until I was four months pregnant."

"You know what? I don't give a shit. Don't call me again."

"Wait, please?" There was an urgency in her voice that made Christine pause. "I have to explain something to you."

And explain she did. For ten minutes she hardly took a breath between apologies and pleas for understanding. "I didn't know what I was getting into, honest I didn't. Not until the whole thing was done, and by then it was too late. I totally panicked."

"I bet you did," Christine said. It was only the second sentence she had managed to fit in.

"Tim loves you, Christine. After the baby was born he was so worried you'd find out and leave him, he almost lost it. Now I wish I'd picked a different name, but at the time it was really important to Tim to pass on that piece of himself. I'll never be able to say it again without thinking of a guy who cheats on his wife."

"I really have to go," Christine said.

"Okay, but . . . I need to ask you one question." She stopped, evidently reassuring herself that Christine hadn't hung up, and continued. "After the baby was born I had a hard time. Obviously Tim wasn't around much, and I was taking time off from my job, so I felt really alone. He was interested in the baby but almost in a way that didn't involve me, if that makes sense. Like I was just this random person who'd given him the son he always wanted. Anyway, I was living off my savings until I could go back to work, and the baby was so colicky I wasn't sleeping more than two hours a night, max. So my mom decides that before I jump out a window she's going to get me some help for a few months."

Christine rolled her eyes. It felt like Tim's final act of humiliation, to inflict such a person on her. "Is this leading somewhere?"

"I'm almost finished. So, the girl who came to help was great. She wasn't judgmental about me having a baby on my own, or even about Tim being married. I told her everything. She was like a good friend, you know? Tim didn't like her at first, they only saw each other three or four times, but he didn't trust her. She came from this kind of redneck family and he was afraid she'd try to get money out of him or call you up one night. She joked about it once and he was beyond mad. I told him he was being paranoid, she would never do that, but it just goes to show that he was always thinking about you.

And of course nothing happened and she went to work for another family after four months. But she didn't like it there. I don't think they paid her very well."

The words had hardly taken hold in Christine's mind before she got light-headed, the same faint way she felt before getting sick. "That's too bad."

"It's awful, though, you heard about her, didn't you? Jennifer Guthrie. She was the one who got killed about a month ago. I cried for a week straight when I found out. And then I started thinking about the things Tim said and I was petrified. I thought, how well do I know this guy? I didn't see him that much, but when I did I'd talk about Jennifer and how I felt. That always made him really jumpy. He said it was because it happened so close to his house and he didn't want little Tim knowing about it, but that freaked me out. Please don't hate me, Christine, but one morning I broke down and called the cops."

Christine covered her eyes. "You did what?"

"I left an anonymous message that they might want to look into him. I didn't say why. I know, maybe it was ridiculous, but I was so upset I kept thinking he did it. Who else would kill her? Who had a reason? I didn't know Jennifer's boyfriend but she said she loved him. He was back home in Nevada. He was always worried she was going to break up with him, he was that in love with her." She paused for several seconds. "Hello?"

Diana's words were rushing by so quickly and in such a grating whine Christine had trouble comprehending them. When she spoke, her voice was hoarse and unfamiliar. "Yes."

"I felt guilty when Tim told me they questioned him, but the way he acted sometimes made me nervous. I didn't want to let him in my house anymore, but I was so afraid to piss him off. I had no idea what would happen if I asked him about it. If the cops weren't arresting him, then maybe I should give him the benefit of the doubt. There was all this evidence against him, but then he would come visit and everything would seem so normal. And that's what I can't stop thinking about. Do you think he could do that? Kill a girl because he thought she might wreck his marriage? One minute I feel so bad for suspecting him—you know, my son's *father*—and then I get so scared all over again—"

"Listen to me," Christine broke in, her voice breaking but her mind suddenly lucid. "You should have done more. You should have told the police everything you knew."

"But I thought if there was a connection, they'd find out."

"You just stood by and now my neighbor's stepdaughter is missing. If Tim is responsible, then so are you. You're almost as guilty as he is."

"That isn't fair, I—"

Christine hung up the phone. For a long time—ten minutes, maybe twenty—she was unable to move. She felt numb, crushed by her own ignorance. You could only know so much. That was the problem with being married, and with living. You couldn't do either one as well as you wanted because there was always too much you didn't know.

Her first action, and one she would always remember, was to check her purse for Arso's check. It was still there in the zippered pocket. Three thousand dollars wasn't much but it would give her time. She was making her own money now and could survive and raise her child by herself. The house on M Street—an innocent by-stander, a sad child of divorce—might need to be sold for a pittance, pawned off on people who would never sense anything in its walls and drapes, no connection or emotion. It would go back to being just a house.

Then she called Detective Warner. Christine had been so rude to her the previous week, it seemed only right that she should be the first one to hear the news.

Twenty-eight

"Is it someone else?" Audrey asked through tears. She wiped her cheeks and her fingertips came away black with dissolved mascara.

"No. It's nothing like that."

"Then I don't understand. Where did this come from? All this time I thought we were happy."

"We are. I mean, we were."

Mark sat cross-legged on the bed in loose drawstring pants, looking like an evil swami. For days she had been considering telling him about William, even saying she wanted to move out, but she never would have done it in such a cold, clinical way, with "separate interests" as the reason.

"You're leaving me for a diet," she said.

"It's an alternative lifestyle. A way of perceiving the world."

"It's a fantasy. Do you know that human beings aren't even going to last much longer? Look at the state of the planet. Wake up."

"You see? You're doing it right now. You're discounting my passion, the one thing that gets me going every day."

"I'm being realistic."

"Your reality and mine are two different things."

"There's only one reality!"

"You keep making my point, Audrey."

The worst part of it was his calmness, the cool, detached manner, as if he was so damned *enlightened* and she nothing but an earthbound pessimist. Somehow, Mark had turned her into death's defender, the advocate of its right to neutralize even the healthiest and most enterprising person. Part of her wanted to try killing her husband right now, just to see if it was possible.

"You never told me we had to feel the same way about everything," she said. "That's something you worry about in the beginning. I thought we'd been together so long it didn't matter anymore." She blew her nose loudly and hiccupped. Hurt as she was, she knew it was ludicrous to be upset under the circumstances. Being dumped by Mark made everything easier for her, didn't it? He and Jonathan would never have to know how she'd betrayed and lied to them, and because she was the injured party, she might even be able to keep the house and ask William to move in. What an ending. It would have been the event of the year if she'd been living in Georgia. It almost seemed a shame to waste it on Golden Hills Estates.

"I want you to imagine something," Mark said, leaning forward, looking earnest.

"Okay."

"It's 1972 and we're living in South Africa."

"What?"

"We're both white. You're from an old Afrikaner family and you like things the way they are."

"Mark."

"Hear me out. I think the black population is getting a raw deal and I want to help them gain political power."

"What the hell are you talking about?"

"Don't you get it? It's the same thing we're going through now. We have completely different values. I don't understand your priorities and vice versa. The only thing we have in common is our son."

"I'm not a racist," Audrey said, affronted.

Mark sighed. "I know. That's not the point."

"Well, it was a ridiculous example. And speaking of our son, what do you propose to do about him? How will this decision of yours affect him?"

"You don't think he already knows? He's been sensing the disconnect between us for a long time. Look, call me selfish, but if I want to study in India for six months or develop a motivational speaking program, I need to have that option. Jonathan can spend half the time with me, or more if he wants to. He's interested in what I'm trying to accomplish. I could teach him a lot."

To give Jonathan a chance to adjust, Mark proposed moving out gradually. He would spend less and less time at home, moving boxes out at the rate of one or two a day until there was nothing left. Then he would show Jonathan his temporary place, a cool little garage apartment on the estate of an Internet entrepreneur who took 150 supplements a day and had just returned from a trip on a Russian shuttle as a space tourist. He had come across Mark's blog late one night when he was up researching cryonics, and was interested enough to call Mark the next day and offer him a position as his health consultant. They would try it out for six months and see how it went. The pay wouldn't be great, but Mark would have a place to crash and lots of time to pursue his life's work.

The thought of their son bouncing back and forth between households, a displaced statistic with an unhinged father, made Audrey's stomach contract. "His grades will slip," she said.

"No they won't. We won't let them."

"You seem to think you have control over everything! What's the matter with you? Where did you pick up these insane illusions?"

"What about you and your omens?" Mark asked. "Your family curse? You've spent the last month obsessing over some old book like it's the key to everything. Look at all the energy you've put into it. The research and the trips to Bakersfield. Isn't that an insane illusion, too?"

That he would cheapen the book and her search with an erroneous comparison was infuriating. "It's different." But even as she said it, she struggled to figure out exactly how.

He unfolded his long, slender legs and got up. "I think we've talked about this enough, don't you? Nobody's to blame here. Sometimes relationships just run their course."

"But at your party you said you didn't want to live forever without me," Audrey cried, scrambling to her knees, the mattress throwing off her balance so she nearly fell into him.

"I did say that," he said, touching her shoulder with a gentle hand. "You know, babe, I guess it just wasn't meant to be."

If she hadn't been so angry, so terrified and confused, Audrey might never have found Henry Nolan.

After a family conference during which her husband and son wept and hugged each other like survivors of a shipwreck, and Audrey, mute and all cried out, sat there almost in awe of her stunning bad luck, Mark and Jonathan went to bed and she took refuge in her computer. That morning—when her life was still a solid thing resistant to the marriage-ending effects of affairs and eccentric hobbies—she had found Ruth Simon's daughter, Zina Simon, on the Internet. She was living near the Sierras, a teacher of some kind, but of course there was no phone number. Audrey would have to drive all the way up to see her, wait outside her house, ambush her, and hope she would divulge personal information to a stranger. Audrey had already made a promise to herself— however it turned out, this would be her last attempt to find Mala. She would not become obsessed the way Mark had, she would know when to accept the limitations of being human. If she had learned nothing else in recent months, she had learned this: a lot of things would remain a mystery. There would be no ending and no answer. Signs, prayers, and spells would not save her from this simple truth.

Because there was no one else to look for, and her own family tree now bored her, Audrey went back to George Bortner, the dead lawyer from Texas. There was more information on him than on anyone else she had investigated. Typing in his name brought up a trove of court cases, legal opinion, quotes in various dull journals, and textbooks written when he was a professor at a law school. There was so much to go through, it would keep her occupied for hours, which was her goal. Mindless trolling, incomprehensible details, history. Nothing that had anything to do with today. As long as she was looking back she wasn't looking forward, and that would do.

Sometime after the street had gone dark, after Audrey had seen Tim's car drive slowly away from Christine's house, and after a half-moon had made a brief, forlorn appearance at the window and vanished, Audrey found a digital clip from a college paper, an article she had overlooked during her search a few weeks before. More erudite law particulars—except that it wasn't. After skimming the first line, she started over and read all the way through.

...

San Antonio, June 20, 1997

On a normal day, local attorney and professor George Bortner is busy teaching constitutional law at St. Mary's University Law School and running a private practice from the same Durango Boulevard office he opened after passing the bar exam in 1958. But for the past two years he's taken on another role, one he has no particular training or affinity for: amateur sleuth. Between his duties at the school and his work as an attorney specializing in wills and estates, Professor Bortner doesn't have much free time. When he does, he spends it trying to find the daughter of one of his late clients, Pecos County rancher and town selectman Henry Nolan. Professor Bortner's fiduciary duties prevent him from divulging her name, which makes his task even more difficult. But he's hoping that a little publicity will help him locate a woman even the area's best private detective was unable to find.

"She was Mr. Nolan's only child, and she was illegitimate," he says. "We have her name and nothing else. We know she went to California in the late 1940s and came back to Texas a few years later, but after that, the trail goes cold." He has searched Social Security, tax, and even criminal records in his search, calling more city halls and pursuing more leads than he can count. While several women over the years have claimed to be Mr. Nolan's daughter, DNA tests have proved all of these claims to be false. Why is Professor Bortner so eager to find the illegitimate daughter of a man who passed away in 1989? Because as owner of the eighty-thousand-acre Equinox Cattle Ranch, Henry Nolan amassed a considerable fortune, and he left it all to her.

"The ranch was sold twelve years ago and the money's been sitting in a trust ever since," Professor Bortner says.

"The will stipulates that it be distributed only to his daughter or her heirs. I know the chances of finding her are slim, but we'll keep looking until I'm gone, and probably after that."

Audrey sat back in her chair and shut her eyes. Two days ago such a discovery would have kept her awake until morning, but tonight it had the opposite effect. Suddenly, she was very tired. She didn't reread the article or leave excited messages for Linda and Christine, she just turned off her computer and went to the futon sofa against the wall. She lay down, pulling her grandmother's frayed afghan over her legs. For the first time in many years she had no plan. Staring into the cool dark, she searched for a place for her thoughts to land, but found nothing. There was something sort of comforting about not hoping for anything, just saying, "This is it. Everything I've got."

She fell asleep and didn't wake until the birds were singing, and by then all of her old hopes had returned, resurrected by nothing more than the light.

Twenty-nine

It took three months for Mala to realize she was pregnant, and even longer for her to tell Ruth.

She had known weeks earlier, but kept this knowledge wedged in the back of her head where it wouldn't interfere with sleep and the work of living. There was too much to do. On weekends she'd been going with Ruth to call on neighbors, to tend to sick old women and lonely old men, and she couldn't afford to be distracted while spooning soup into toothless mouths and telling stories both true and greatly exaggerated. Even just sitting in airless sick rooms with strangers, it was a luxury to speak freely. She could fill an hour with her voice and no one objected. If anyone noticed something unusual about her, they were too kind or infirm to mention it. She was beside the point, anyway, as all anyone wanted to hear about was the outside world. Whether blind, crippled, or four days from dead, every person Ruth and Mala visited had time for another story. Mala took care never to repeat herself. One day she might tell the tale of the deadly storm of '41, the next, the lost little boy she and Beni had found in Texas Hill Country, sitting quietly by himself on the banks of the Sabinal River. Because she thought it might raise eyebrows, she omitted the part about dropping the child at a police station and squealing away in a borrowed car for fear they'd be arrested for kidnapping.

"How much of that really happened?" Ruth asked that afternoon when they were walking home.

"Oh, enough," Mala said.

Every week there was another letter from E. Weaver in Nevada. It was the first and only correspondence Mala had ever received, and she treated each one like a gift, gently slitting open the envelope with Ruth's dagger-shaped letter opener, unfolding the pages carefully and saving everything in an old hat box on the top shelf of her closet. Receiving a new letter was an excuse to lie in bed and reread them all. Elliot was not an eloquent writer but he never missed a week, and in a few words he could describe just about anything.

> *Dad can't get home for two more weeks and then he goes to Montana so that's not much help. This wasn't my brother's first fight it turns out. I guess jail serves him right but when I go visit him he cries and wants me to take him home. I told you he was slow and that's the worst part. He doesn't understand and I can't explain it. I wish I could leave soon but it doesn't look likely. My mother hopes I'll stay for good but I'm trying to get her used to the idea of me going back. I think she'll come around and if she doesn't I'm going anyway.*

Ruth always let Mala read in private, and never asked what Elliot's letters contained. She was good at appearing uninterested, averting her eyes or leaving the room, even if her worry was transmitted in the brisk way she shut her bedroom door or in the inflection of her words. "Ready for supper?" could mean, "Ready for supper?" or it could mean, "Are you finished daydreaming about a boy you hardly know?" Mala heard the difference but she never let on, answering, "I'll set the table," every time.

"I don't want to see you brokenhearted," Ruth said one night, and for a while it was the only candid words she spoke on the subject.

By early autumn Mala was having trouble staying awake. Ruth would come home to find her slumped in a chair with the broom lying over her knees, or sitting at the kitchen table with her head in her arms, a bowl of unpeeled potatoes at her elbow. She would sit among the pumpkins in the vegetable garden, shears in hand, staring vacantly at the brilliant afternoon sky without a thought in her head. And when she finally was able to sleep, it was something she got lost in for ten hours at a time.

"This can't go on," Ruth said on a morning in late October, throwing back the sheets and pulling Mala to her feet. "Other girls your age are making something of themselves. Are you bored here? Is that the trouble?"

"What makes you think there's trouble?"

"I think it's time we started lessons again. You have too much potential to lie around pining, feeling sorry for yourself."

"I'm not pining," Mala said. "I'm worn-out."

"How can you be worn-out after half a day in bed?"

Mala groaned and sat down on the mattress. "I don't know."

"You don't tell me what's going on, I'll call the doctor. I don't think you want that."

"Please," Mala said. "No doctors."

Mala had never seen a doctor, unless she counted Drina, who had pulled her molars with the help of metal pincers and a bitter gray powder she'd made her sniff. Drina treated stomach ailments with bark teas, chest complaints with red clover, flus with peppermint oil, horseradish, and garlic. Despite her skill with everyday conditions, she was not an expert in delivering babies. The job had fallen to her because nobody else had a prayer. Childbirth was nerve-racking for everyone in the camp, as it was one of the rare situations when nothing could go wrong but something almost always did. Many times a rusted car had roared off into the sagebrush with a laboring mother in back, headed for a hospital that might be a hundred miles away if it could be found at all. Mala could remember the funerals of five women and twice as many babies, and there were probably more that Beni had kept from her. She had vague memories of a red-haired girl of about seventeen, pregnant one day and buried the next, no explanation, just a young husband who didn't emerge from his trailer for months. A succession of older women going in carrying food, coming out shaking their heads.

Mala struggled to stand and get dressed. She got through the rest of the day, the muffin-baking and hem-sewing, by imagining what a doctor might say after one quick look at her. "This young woman's expecting a child." And Ruth's disappointment, all of Mala's so-called potential used up in nine months with no man to stop it from being a scandal. The only thing Mala regretted was that she had done exactly what the world expected of her, just gone ahead like she'd been dared to do it.

To make up for a lessonless summer, Ruth set Mala to work immediately after supper that night with an old book of math equations, the same fractions and decimals she had last looked at when she was twelve. "Take two days to review. Algebra starts Friday morning." Mala worked at the dining room table until ten o'clock, stifling her despair and marking problems she needed help with. Every time she was tempted to mourn the lost seven years of learning, she reminded herself of the chances that she would be here at all.

She waited until the fire was lit and Ruth was sitting in her chair with a book. The room smelled of fall: wool, black tea, apples, wood smoke. It was cooler at night now, but it was a desert chill, a bone-dry snap in the air that didn't appear until a few hours after sunset. By nine in the morning the sun was warm and the flowers were opening again, and the garden kept growing as if frost would never come. "Another month and it'll be here," Ruth said. "The closest to winter we ever get in this valley."

Mala put it off for nearly an hour, but finally got up from the table and sat on the ottoman at Ruth's feet.

Ruth slid a mother-of-pearl marker between the pages of her book. "Finished?"

"Almost. I have some questions."

"We'll go over those before bed."

Unable to look at Ruth, Mala dropped her eyes to the tile hearth. A cinder popped against the screen, burned, and went black.

"I need to tell you something," she said.

She opened her mouth but strangled on the words and began to cry instead. Ruth looked baffled at first, even a little exasperated, but it took her only a minute to put tears and exhaustion and an absent young man together. She let out a sigh so long and heavy Mala wondered if it would ever end.

"Have you told him?" she asked.

"No. I just figured it out myself."

"Well, it isn't the worst that can happen."

"It's not? What is?"

"I'm not sure," Ruth said. "I suppose we know when we see it."

"What do I do?"

"What every woman does in these circumstances. You wait."

...

Though Ruth had never had a child of her own, she had aided enough women—hysterical housemaids, wealthy young ladies, matrons horrified to find themselves in the family way at forty—that another pregnancy was like another room to sweep. Just a little bit more to do. The doctor came once, twice, and said he'd be back in a month. Mala wasn't much help around the house anymore, so Ruth put her to work with English primers, math lessons, and history books.

"Geometry by Thanksgiving," she said. "Dickens by the new year."

Mala studied as if to prove that more could come of the situation than a child. Time could be used for more than one purpose; you could memorize the capital of every state and carry a child and miss the man who'd raised you all at once. You could write letters that skirted the truth and send them off to a town in Nevada you'd never heard of, and when you were done, there was still time to watch your birthday, Christmas, and two full seasons pass by. Months vanished in an unbroken series of harvests and completed workbooks. By spring Mala's year of banishment was almost up, but returning to Texas was out of the question. It was strange. Every day she grew heavier made the place seem more distant. It was as if she were watching it move across the map in her geography book, slide slowly to the south under her gaze. At some point her thinking about Texas had changed. It was no longer a question of when she would go back, but if it was possible anymore.

Mala went into labor on a Friday and gave birth early on a Sunday morning in mid-March. She'd made Ruth promise not to take her to the hospital. She would rather bleed to death in her bed than be wheeled down an antiseptic hallway, past flapping doors into a terrifying tunnel of bright lights.

"You want a midwife instead of the doctor?" Ruth asked. "You're sure?"

What Mala wanted, if she was honest with herself, was Drina, self-taught anesthetist and illiterate medic, and the only reason any new mother at the camp survived. Instead, she would settle for the kind gray-haired woman who arrived an hour after her water broke, and who, in two whole days of screams and sweat, didn't mention the hospital once.

"She'll probably be your last," the midwife told Mala matter-of-factly, clipping the umbilical cord. "So much blood, I'm surprised you're still conscious. But you're alive."

Mala lay on her fourth set of soaked sheets, her teeth rattling and her vision dim. The baby sprawled on her chest asleep, a bit of crying and then the most serene rest imaginable. Mala slept, woke to feed the baby, and slept again.

Days went by in the same primal rhythm. Ruth brought trays of food, the sun rose and set. When Ruth had students, the midwife came. Again and again Mala dreamed of the *chiriklo* painted on her mother's wagon, its wings raised and its curved beak open. Beni appeared, young and foolish and wearing his old felt hat, the one that had blown off and disappeared over the San Angelo feed store. On the fourth day Beni and the *chiriklo* disappeared, and from then on every dream was about Elliot.

A week passed before Mala was strong enough to sit up. "You have to tell him," Ruth said, opening the curtains on a pale spring sky. "Soon."

"He'll find out when I see him," Mala said. She looked down at her fingers, so white and thin they looked like birch sticks.

"Why wait?"

"I want him to come back because he wants to."

"Sounds like pride, Mala."

"It is."

The baby had spent her whole short life being called "her" and "she." That morning Mala started calling her Zina. Not because her mother was someone to emulate, but because it was the only way to give a woman like that a second chance.

In June, Ruth received a letter and congratulations from Texas. "I hope it's all right I told him," she said. "I couldn't keep it to myself."

It wasn't all right, but Mala didn't say so. She believed that Beni would have learned to read and found a stable address if he'd known who would hear the news first.

"What if he came to visit us?" Ruth asked.

"Who?" Mala asked, still thinking of Beni.

"Henry's wife left two years ago. He's all alone now."

"He has a house full of people."

"They're not family."

"Neither am I."

Several minutes passed before Ruth said, "Maybe you'll go to see him, then."

"I don't think so." Mala slowly rocked the baby, who had cream-colored skin and a thin cap of blond hair. All Nolan and Weaver and no Rinehart, on the outside at least. "I wouldn't re-member how to get there anyhow."

"Go get that notebook you're always writing in."

"It's full but for one page. Why?"

"I'm going to draw you a map. Just in case you ever change your mind."

As often as Ruth brought up the subject, Mala would not bend. Being a mother had given her something, she felt, a right to her own opinion. But being stubborn on the subject of Henry Nolan didn't mean she never thought of him. There were threads she had to tie up in Texas, and going there was the only way to do it. Something else was happening, too, a craving to feel a road under her feet, go to sleep in one state, wake up in another. But there was no reason to mention it now, so many months ahead of time. When Zina was old enough to stay with Ruth, Mala would go back to Pecos County, stopping in Nevada on the return trip if Elliot was still there. August or September, after the worst of the heat had passed but before the cold came and the butterfly weed stopped blooming.

One part of her couldn't stand the thought of leaving, but another was already counting the days, packing her bag in her head and hitching a ride as far east as the driver would go.

Thirty

$\mathcal{M}$argaret collapsed like a character from a Victorian novel when she got the news about Paige, dropping to the couch in the living room and shrieking at everyone to go away and give her some air. After a few minutes during which Linda, Neil, and Peter retreated, whispering, to the kitchen, Margaret wiped her tears and assumed the imperious look of a mother who has been wronged from the moment her child burst out of the womb, leaving a raft of ugly stretch marks in its wake. She wasn't too relieved to be angry; quite the opposite. She had given her entire being to her daughter and had nothing left. Now that she knew Paige was all right, she didn't know if she could live under the same roof with a girl so manipulative and selfish that she would risk destroying her parents with her reckless behavior. She would see her, spend a day or two with her, and then she and Neil would return to Connecticut. The future was something they would think about once Paige had come to terms with what she had done.

What Paige had done, according to Detective Klein, was follow a cat through the neighborhood. The moment the police found her, watching television on an unmade pull-out couch, she told them everything in precise detail. Lured from her bedroom by distant meowing, she had crept out the back door, walked around the house to the sidewalk, and followed an elusive white form down the hill and across a field. Eventually the cat vanished, but Paige, afraid to go home for fear of being found out and reprimanded, continued toward the main road. As she walked she decided to invent a story about rescuing a lost cat and returning it to its owners, hoping that a good deed would prevent her from being punished. She had just turned back toward M Street when an old woman claiming to be her grandmother drove up in a car. She said she'd been looking all over for Paige and needed to take her home right away.

"Her grandmother?" Margaret said, interrupting Peter. "How could she fall for something like that?"

"She thought it was Gram at first."

"My mother?" Margaret said. "Paige doesn't even remember her."

"Exactly," Peter said. "I guess she thought it might be possible."

"That what? Gram would come back from the dead?"

"She's ten years old, Margaret," Linda said.

"I don't care. There were Egyptian kings younger than that."

"It doesn't mean they were ready for it, anymore than Paige was ready for what she's gone through the last few years."

Margaret looked at Linda for the first time in at least an hour. "Are you blaming *me* now?"

"Why shouldn't we blame ourselves?" Peter said. "Isn't it our fault it happened?"

"How? Tell me exactly how we caused our daughter to slip out of the house, walk halfway to a major road, and get in a car driven by an old lady with holes in her brain."

"We divorced when Paige was three."

"Everybody gets divorced. I don't see other children from broken homes trying to kill their parents."

"Did she try to kill us? I wasn't here for that." Peter wasn't usually sarcastic, and his words shattered any stoicism Margaret had left.

"What do you know about her?" she asked.

"A lot. I've helped raise her."

"On weekends. When you got around to it. She's been with me most of the time while you've been off living your life and working too much! She was trying to get attention. It's as simple as that."

Neil cleared his throat. "You know what? We got some wonderful news today. Paige will be here in a few minutes. We should be celebrating, not arguing."

"*We're* not arguing, Neil," Margaret said. "Peter and I are."

"Do you think Paige would like something to eat when she gets home?" Linda piped up.

"Is that why she wanted to come out here?" Peter asked Margaret. "Because you were doing such a great job with her?"

"I do my best, you know. I have five kids now."

"By choice. You didn't have to marry Neil."

"Now, wait a minute," Neil said. "How did I get dragged into this?"

Linda decided she would grill a breast of chicken and heat up leftover mashed potatoes, and if Paige wasn't hungry for that, there was lots of peach yogurt. For a week Linda had avoided looking at the bright plastic containers in the back of the refrigerator, little receptacles of sorrow stacked in twos behind the eggs. Only in the last hour had they turned back into something innocuous.

"You don't know your own wife, let alone your daughter," Margaret said. "Do you have any idea what kind of life she used to lead?"

Linda and Peter looked at each other across the corner of the granite island. Under the edge of the counter, he gave her hand a brief squeeze. "By the way," he said under his breath, "thanks for not telling me about Paige until you knew for sure."

She leaned her cheek against the outer curve of his shoulder. When she straightened her head, she saw Margaret frowning at both of them.

"What the hell is going on?" she asked.

"Do you have anything she can take?" Peter asked Neil. "Some of that tranquilizer you gave her on the plane?"

"Don't talk about me in the third person," Margaret said. "I'm sitting right in front of you."

"Paige is here," Neil said, looking out the window. "If anyone cares."

Margaret flew out of her chair with a sharp cry. The rest of them followed her to the porch. Watching Paige climb out of the police car, Linda couldn't help but think that it would have been better if she had been kidnapped. There was something unseemly about her casual and unconcerned pace and her expression, as if she were finally getting the sort of recognition she deserved.

"Look at her," Margaret said, incredulous. "Not a goddamn care in the world."

But as Paige came closer, Linda saw that she was still the same bewildered and strangely adrift girl who had walked to Emily's house to swim. She glanced around with apprehensive eyes, as if she were being foisted off on relatives who had never heard of her but now, through the forces of propriety and guilt, were forced to open their doors to her. The flip-flops on her feet were two sizes too big. Her ponytail was lopsided and she wore a man's T-shirt over the same dress she had worn the day she disappeared. She might have worn it the entire time she was gone.

After a moment of restraint, Margaret ran down the steps and grabbed Paige in her arms. "Oh, my poor little girl. We missed you so much."

"I'm really sorry," Paige said against her shoulder.

"Are you?"

Paige pulled back and looked at her mother, then began to cry bitterly. Linda walked up and knelt beside her.

"I lost my shoe," Paige said.

"I know," Linda said. "We found it in the flowers. How did that happen?"

"I guess I dropped it. I was holding them in my hand."

"What were you thinking?" Margaret asked. "Can you tell me that?"

Paige shrugged, tears dripping from her jaw. "She said I was her granddaughter, then she drove all over and took me to her house and I didn't know how to get home. I couldn't remember anybody's number, and anyway, her phone didn't work. She hardly had anything to eat. I wanted to leave but she told me it was too dangerous. I was afraid to go out because of what happened to that girl on our hill."

"Why did you get in her car?"

"I don't know, I thought it would be fun. I was going to call you from Gram's house and surprise you."

"I think it was more than that," Margaret said, her voice growing quieter. "You wanted to be the only child for a little while. That's why you came out here in the first place, am I right?"

The emotions on Paige's face—defiance, shame, relief, disappointment in the outcome of a grand, naïve plan—seemed to express every possible incarnation of childhood. "I wanted to see Dad."

"Of course you did," Linda said. "And he wanted to see you."

"Then I'm not sure why you ran away and made him worry like

that," Margaret said. "Do you know what you've done to everybody?"

Paige looked at Linda as if hoping she would answer the question. Linda took her hand and smiled. "We make mistakes, honey. We think things will turn out differently than they do."

"I should have brought my phone," Paige told her. "That was really dumb."

"It doesn't matter now. Not a bit. What matters is that you're here."

"You're not mad?" She looked at both of them, her eyes shifting from one mother to the other.

Margaret stood up. "Nobody's mad. But you're going to stay here with your father and Linda for a little while. If that's okay with you."

Paige didn't answer, she just ran up the walk ahead of Linda and threw herself into her father's arms.

Thirty-one

*I*n the hours after Tim was arrested for the murder of Jennifer Guthrie, Christine found herself wishing that he had died. A dignity-preserving car accident or an understandable heart attack. A falling brick, terrorism, something unavoidable, even bizarre. Anything he hadn't caused himself with his insanity and paranoia. She imagined—in the same yearning way she had once imagined getting married and having children—sitting in the front row at his wake, racked with grief, the wonderful innocence of mourning a man taken too young, through no fault of his own. If the impossible had to happen, let him be an innocent victim, annihilated in clear conscience while following the rules.

He had been gone only two days, and evidence of him—remotes, magazines, shoes—still lay scattered around the house as if waiting for his return. "He's not coming back," Christine said aloud, half expecting objects to begin a slow exodus toward the kitchen, where one by one they would throw themselves away. She wandered through rooms, trailing her fingers along the furniture, picking up knickknacks from one table and leaving them mindlessly on another, trying to reacquaint herself with a place she had lived in for six years. For a long time she stood at the living room window and stared at the street, as if watching a very slow, plotless film. It was Saturday afternoon, warm and sunny. Twenty-four hours after Paige had been found, the only visible remnants of the recent neighborhood upheavals were three television vans and a group of reporters hoping for a glimpse of the kidnap victim or the killer's wife. She pictured Tim as well as her father and mother, and how they were filling each moment, and wondered if their moments were as long as hers or if the circumstances of their lives had somehow contracted time. Surely Tim would not want the future to arrive, knowing what lay ahead. There were so many impossibilities still to come, evidence, a trial, gruesome facts that she would never be able to unlearn. For a few minutes, leaning against the frame of the window, she honestly believed that the pain of her marriage to Tim would outlast everything. In some cruel quirk of physical laws, she would live forever in order to keep enduring it.

When her phone rang she thought it would be her father, responding to the message she hadn't left. She almost looked forward to telling him the news, jerking him from his annoying good humor and feigned poverty, raining on his evergreen parade in the Canadian woods with his compost pile and his outhouse. And while he chopped wood and flirted with hippie neighbors, her seventy-year-old mother was on eHarmony every night in Florida, frantically trying to find a husband. Maybe she would tell her father first that she was pregnant and then describe in frank and unnecessary detail the last month of living with Tim, whom he had always liked. If his phone didn't die and cut her off first, she could make the lead-up last an hour.

"Mrs. Mahoney," came a voice on the other end. "Detective Warner."

Christine said nothing.

"I have something to tell you."

Christine closed her eyes, but the sun was in her face now and, instead of soothing darkness, she saw a patchwork of orange blood vessels.

"Hello?"

"Yes," Christine replied. Maybe Tim had killed himself, climbing under the blankets in his cell and pulling a contraband plastic bag over his head. She was so sure of this, she could feel the scream prepare to tear from her throat.

"I thought you'd like to know that we're releasing your husband."

When Christine opened her eyes, the sun was bisected by Linda's chimney, light-years from where it had been just moments ago. "I'm sorry?"

"Yes. We're processing his discharge right now."

"To another prison, or—"

"No. He's a free man."

The phone slipped from Christine's weakened fingers, dropping lower into her palm. Only the pressure of her jaw prevented it from falling to the floor. "I don't understand what you're telling me."

"We've just had a confession from Jennifer Guthrie's former boyfriend. Apparently he told a friend about the killing a month ago. This friend came forward when he heard Tim had been arrested."

"You have evidence?"

"Against the boyfriend? Yes. That's as much as I can say right now."

"What about Tim's gun?"

"I'm waiting for the final report, but it looks like it's never been fired."

"He's completely innocent, then."

"It would appear so."

In the background Christine could hear the harsh clatter of the police station—deafening male voices, distant clanging, a crying child. She tried to imagine anyone there caring about her or Tim or their fractured lives, and couldn't. "So—what was all that for?" she asked.

"Excuse me?"

"I'm asking you honestly. Why did this happen to us? What was the purpose?"

"First of all, I want to personally apologize. You and your husband have been through a lot, and we genuinely regret that." Detective Warner stuttered over some halfhearted explanation about the complexities of murder investigations and the difficult duties of police officers, but she wasn't answering the larger questions, the ones Christine had really asked.

Why had the impossible happened and come undone just as quickly? What was she supposed to do now?

"Where's he going to go?" Christine interrupted.

"They'll be discharging him any minute now."

"And then?"

"He's free to go home any time after that."

"No," Christine said. "He isn't."

She hung up, went to the master bedroom, and began to pack Tim's clothes. She paused in the middle of sweeping his toiletries into a paper bag to text him and tell him to find somewhere else to live. When she was finished loading duffel bags and suitcases and lugging them out to the foyer, she called Diana, who answered sounding so proud of herself, so justified in her actions, that Christine almost hated to ruin it. "He's out," she said. "He's all yours, if you want him."

...

Two days later—or maybe three, Christine seemed unable to keep track anymore—Linda knocked on the door.

"Can I come in?" she asked. It was the first time they had seen each other since Paige had come home.

"I don't have much to say to anybody."

"That's okay. Neither do I."

They went into the living room and sat across from each other.

"How do you feel?" Linda asked. "Physically, I mean."

"I'm starting to get my appetite back. For ice cream, anyway." She tried to smile but it still felt strained, like something grown rusty from disuse.

"I'm sorry," Linda said.

"What are *you* sorry for?"

"For keeping you at a distance those first few days, after Peter followed you. He was out of his mind."

"I know. Everybody was."

"Thank you for all the time you put in, looking for her. Peter's going to come over later and thank you, too. He's all right, but it's going to take him a while to recover."

"But you had a happy ending. I'm glad."

"Oh, you know. Things will keep happening and they'll keep going wrong."

"Something you and I know very well, I guess."

Linda opened her mouth twice before asking, "So Tim moved out?"

"He picked up everything yesterday."

"You seem okay, though."

"I'm glad I know what happened. That's all."

Christine wanted to thank Linda for being there, for forgiving her for handling things badly with Peter, but wasn't sure how to form the words. "Audrey drove to someplace near the Sierras today, to find Zina Simon," she said.

"She told me. I wanted to go with her but the timing was off."

"Yes, it was. I wonder what she'll find when she gets there."

"I'm sure she'll tell us. Did you hear about the article she found?"

"Of course I did. She called and woke me up at six in the morning." Christine hesitated, feeling her fears gather and spill over. "Listen, do you think . . . ?"

"No," Linda said firmly. "I don't."

"But look at what happened. This disaster that went on for a month. Longer, now."

"When did they first start suspecting Tim?" Linda asked.

Christine sat back, sighing. "I don't know. May sometime."

"And when did you sit in Audrey's backyard and light some candles? A few days later?"

"Yes, late May."

"So, whatever happened, it was set in motion before you'd ever heard of the book. Before *I'd* heard of it. The only thing that's changed is that you're pregnant and you know who your husband really is. Both good things, I think."

"You don't know what it's like," Christine said. "All you did was give the book to Audrey."

Linda shook her head. "I wished that Paige wouldn't come to live in my house, and look what happened. Not exactly everything as it should be."

"But you didn't want her to disappear, did you? And anyway, you're happy to have her home. It's as it should be now."

"And you're going to be a mother in six months. You thought it was impossible, didn't you?"

"I thought losing Tim was, too. After this, I don't think anything's impossible anymore."

"It wasn't to begin with. Nothing's really changed."

Except everything, Christine almost said, but she let Linda have the last word.

They talked about what Christine could do with the house, although she had already made up her mind to keep it. Tim had always wanted to get out from under the mortgage and the responsibility, but it was her decision now, her home as long as she could afford it. She didn't think she'd have any trouble. Even if her practice had been suffering in the short term after Tim's arrest and release, clients would come back and her career would go on. Her phone had already started to ring again, now that Tim wasn't in the news anymore and the Guthrie case had been solved.

You could always count on people forgetting. It seemed to be the one thing everybody was good at.

Thirty-two

SEPTEMBER 13, 1949

$\mathcal{M}$ala stood in front of the bus station's ticket window, baby in one arm and bag in the other, as close to crying as she could get without tears. It was September, as blazing as midsummer. A fan stirred weakly overhead.

"If it's going to tear at you, take her," Ruth said.

Mala looked down and touched Zina's cheek, so thin and white the veins showed through. "She's not strong enough for a journey like that. She had a fever two weeks ago."

"Be grateful she's a little sickly. It means she's alive, and that was hardly a sure thing."

"It doesn't make leaving easier," Mala said.

"I'm not sure why you're going, then."

"Because I won't have her start out life wandering. She gets raised like everybody else. I don't want her to be different."

The baby stirred, whimpering in a way that made both leaving and staying feel impossible. With a hard sigh, Mala sat on a bench and shook her head. "Nothing I do is right."

"Wait a while," Ruth said, sitting beside her. "What's the hurry?"

"Beni's looking for a reason to give up, and me not coming back is a good one."

"You might not find him, Mala. You have to be prepared for that."

"But I know him. If there's a hope in heaven, he'll be there."

"Then it seems to me you've already made up your mind."

"I guess I have," Mala said, but with no conviction at all.

With Zina asleep in her arms, she waited to buy her ticket, glad for a long, slow line in front of her. Afterward she and Ruth sat on the bench, shoulders touching, not talking. Ruth fanned herself with a bus schedule. Mala didn't so much hear the bus start up as feel it, a low vibration through the station floor. She got up and gently handed her daughter to Ruth. "If anything happens—" she began.

"It won't."

"She stays with you until Elliot comes for her. Nobody else."

"Some things don't need saying."

Ruth followed her to the bus, kissed her, and watched her walk to the top of the steps. "Think about going by the ranch," she said. "Henry knows you'll be there."

"Then he knows more than I do." Mala went down the aisle toward the back and slid up to a fingerprint-smeared window to look at Zina. She hoped Zina would open her eyes, look up and say in some unspoken way that going was all right, but she slept on. Ruth's smile from the curb said, "Three weeks until I see you, maybe four." She walked away with the baby in her arms, her shoulders rigid, not looking back. A woman without misgivings would have stopped and turned to wave. She'd have stood on the sidewalk, holding up the baby's hand until the bus drove out of sight.

The next station was an hour away. Mala was sure she would get off and board the first bus back to Bakersfield, but her worry for Beni was a weight pressing her into her seat, a paralyzing drowsiness that lasted all the way to the California border. When she finally woke, it was nighttime and she could see Arizona, a low line of lights in the distance. She hadn't been awake long when she thought of the notebook, forgotten in the closet where she'd left her jewelry and old clothes. The closet seemed so distant now, a dark shadow behind a closed door in another world. After a moment of despair, she came to the only conclusion she could under the circumstances: she didn't need the book anyway. She had looked at Ruth's map so many times, she'd memorized every swinging stoplight and railroad crossing between the lodgepole gates of Henry Nolan's ranch and Fort Stockton, one day ahead.

She stepped off the bus in Pecos County at two in the afternoon on the fourteenth of September. The sky was a bright blue dome, the streets still wet from a storm that had stayed just ahead of the bus, dumping hail as it swept east across the interstate. Mala had no suitcase to wait for, just the bag over her shoulder and seventy-two dollars in her shoe. "Make it last," Ruth had said. Mala walked to the end of town, happy that things looked no different. Sometimes, time could pass and leave no mark. From there it was easy to get a ride in the direction of the ranch, so easy that she wondered if there was some significance to it. But she got dropped off too early and had to walk three miles toward a blinding sun, squinting through the dust for road signs, her dress whipping against her legs. She didn't reach the ranch gates until after sunset and by then the wind had turned gritty and cold. In between gusts, the air was silent.

She stepped onto the cattle guard, sliding her leather soles gingerly across the bars until she reached hard dirt on the other side. The driveway was the same as ever—gently curved, bordered by split-rail fences and three stubborn pecan trees. After ten minutes of walking, the house loomed up out of the dark, a wide, rambling silhouette on the flattest stretch of land ever made. Seeing it at night, Mala could hardly believe she wasn't dreaming. Two rockers on the porch swayed back and forth, their runners creaking quietly. Though it was still early, all of the windows were black except one on the second story. It was wide-open and tall as a door, and lit from inside by a pale yellow light. Long curtains swept in and out, revealing a man's figure sitting in a chair. Mala recognized him at once: the strong head shaped like a bull's, the iron-gray hair, the straight, elegant nose, the round chin exactly like hers. An oddly familiar stranger, but a stranger all the same.

Henry stood up, swept the curtains aside, and reached out for the window latch. Mala took a single step toward the darkness, but he had seen her. He stopped, his hand extended, touching nothing. Neither of them moved.

They remained that way while the wind cycled through, rattling the underbrush and slamming a corral gate. Her eyes on her father, she imagined walking inside and standing at the bottom of the mahogany staircase she'd never been allowed to climb. She pictured the oak floors pocked with tiny nail heads, the carved marble fireplace, the stern relatives in picture frames, staring across the hall at other relatives, all long dead. She tried to anticipate what would begin when she opened the front door, but all she could see was a life unlived. There was nothing to predict, just a step forward or back.

She raised her hand before letting it fall to her side. At this gesture, Henry left the window, but by the time he reached the door Mala was fifty feet away behind a fence post. She heard him calling her name, then a truck started and drove off slowly toward the main road. She raised her head just in time to see taillights vanish in the direction of San Angelo.

Afraid he'd come back, she walked along the edge of a pasture for a few miles before jumping across a shallow gulley to the highway. She was lucky to get a ride from a cowhand in the first hour, but he couldn't take her far and she waited most of the night at a desolate junction. It rained, stopped, rained again. The coyotes cried, close by at first, then more and more distant until they eventually disappeared. An old couple getting a head start on a drive to New Orleans picked her up about four in the morning. By the time she reached camp the sky was clear and it was nearly dawn. She walked up the gravel road toward the river, past a ruptured shoe and a length of rolled barbed wire with a tumbleweed stuck in its jaws.

The camp was deserted. Mala stood at the edge of the empty field that had once been filled with trailers and bonfires, listening to the song of the first birds. She couldn't see the river, but she could hear it a hundred yards away, running low after a long dry summer. From the looks of the ground, it had been many months since anyone had lived here. Even the black scars of the fire pits had been erased by clumps of spurge and nutgrass.

They could be anywhere. There was nobody to ask, no trail to follow. They might have drifted away from each other, scattered across different counties and states, so she could search for years and never find them. She sat on a rock against the base of a tree and tried to pick out the spot where she and Beni used to camp, but there were no trailers to guide her memory. What had once been home was now just an abandoned field, with nothing particular about it except what had stuck in her head. The way it turned into a shallow, muddy bowl after a rain. The tiny sharp stones that hid in the brush. The crunch of live oak leaves after a frost.

She leaned against the mesquite trunk and slept. When she woke up, the sun was barely at the horizon, a small orange glow through the trees near the river. For a moment she imagined that her mother's wagon had been left behind to smolder forever at the edge of the field. She wouldn't be surprised to find that it had never stopped burning. It had taken nearly a full day for the fire to go out, and even then the blackened frame remained standing like something indestructible, like rock. The men had hacked it apart with axes as if it were something they couldn't afford to let be, because of the woman it had belonged to.

Mala watched the orange light for a long time. Only when a huge fireball rose in the sky behind her did she realize that she hadn't been watching the sun, but the glowing window of a trailer that had stayed behind, waiting for her return. Now she saw the outline of it through the branches, the familiar rusted curve of the roof and the pitted aluminum shell, four worn steps leading to the door. A lamp flickered inside as if to show the way, and she got up and followed its path across the grass and into the trees.

Nothing inside the trailer was different, except for Beni. Mala thought he was sick from loneliness and isolation and would recover. Except for the rare odd job or journey to town for supplies, he had been alone since the clan broke camp the year before, abandoning him like a boat run aground.

"I waited here until May and you still didn't come," he said. "Started to die not long after."

"Well, I'm here now so you can stop," she said.

"It's the kind of thing you can't quit."

Beni was feverish and damp, his hair stringy and the skin across his cheeks like bloodshot parchment. Though it hurt to breathe and blink his eyes, he had never appeared so cheerful. He wanted constantly to hear about his blond, white-skinned granddaughter, never tiring of the story of her birth.

"I can't have any more," Mala told him.

"One's enough," he said. "Believe me."

He was so happy to see her that he stopped sleeping, preferring to lie awake and stare at her by candlelight until a dream took him by force. Her third night back, she woke to find him sitting up in bed with a blanket around his shoulders.

"Ruth told you about him, didn't she?" he asked.

"Yes," Mala said.

"And you came anyway." He lay down a minute later and never mentioned the subject again.

He coughed one afternoon until he felt a rib crack, but flatly refused to see a doctor. He'd spent every cent on kerosene, burning the lamp all day and night for more than a year. "Would have kept it burning, too," he said, "as long as necessary." Even when Mala said she could pay to bring the doctor to him, Beni groaned and flopped onto his bed. "Find your aunt. She'll take care of me."

"I just got done with a journey like that," Mala said. "Did she say where they were going?"

"How could she if they didn't know?"

For weeks Mala nursed him, massaging his swollen hands, making him inhale steam through an open mouth, scrubbing his shirts and draping them over leafless branches to dry, hitchhiking back and forth to town for flour, vegetables, and rice. The trailer and roads were the same, but they didn't feel like home, and neither did Bakersfield. Maybe there was no changing it, and no sense trying anymore. If you didn't learn to grow roots when you were young, maybe your outlook never recovered, like a broken bone that wasn't set right. You believed home was the next horizon. You planned to settle down someplace you'd heard of but would never see.

All well here, don't worry, Ruth said in her telegram. *No sign of Elliot yet, except in your little girl.* Every week at the post office, she picked up a letter from general delivery and sent one off to Nevada. As weeks went by, Elliot's letters got longer, hers shorter. He had a lot to say about his meddling mother and his brother's plight, but there was nothing much for Mala to write except she missed him. In every letter she almost mentioned Zina. Not quite.

One month passed, then two. Beni, if not better, was holding steady. Whenever Mala mentioned California, he would put his hands over his ears and shake his head. "You were born in this trailer, I ain't leaving it."

"What about Zina?"

"Bring her here, there's plenty of room."

"This isn't like you. You hate seeing the same thing day after day. You were fed up with this field two years ago."

"I'm old now. Things change."

But it wasn't just his decaying trailer or consumptive lungs keeping Beni stuck in one place. He had been given a ride the previous year by a preacher who took him to church three times, gave him a Bible he couldn't read, and even offered to dunk his head underwater to make sure he didn't go to hell. If he had someone to accompany him, Beni said, he'd be at church every day. He'd been thinking about it, and maybe Jesus Christ was one thing the folks in town were doing right. No, you couldn't see him and there wasn't what you'd call proof, but it was no different from anything else he'd put stock in, the philters and superstitions that all added up to nothing. Now he had an explanation for a life so like Job's it gave him a twisted sense of pride. Other men had suffered the way he did. Others had had it worse. People from different clans felt the same way, too, ruddy-skinned, bony-nosed strangers and acquaintances he'd seen in the pews, swaying with closed eyes and moving their mouths without speaking.

Beni and Mala became regulars at the Sunday morning service. She sighed and yawned while he sat stock-still with the Bible upside down in his lap, dabbing his forehead, listening to the preacher's every word and not once opening his mouth to argue. Beni would argue over the color of the sky.

"Peaceful, sitting here," he said one morning before the sermon. "This town could be a good place for you and Zina to live. Back with her own people."

"What people?" Mala whispered. "We're the only ones left."

"They'll be near enough. Only so many places around here to go."

"Zina doesn't look like us. She won't grow up the way I did."

"Blood is what matters. She'll know where she comes from."

"She won't if I don't teach her. Sometimes I wonder if I should."

He kept staring straight ahead but the muscles around his eyes drooped. "The world changed you, Mala."

"All right, but it changed you, too. Look where we're sitting."

"Nothing wrong with it, is there?" he said hoarsely. "Once in my life, I don't want to stick out. I want to do like everybody else."

"Then why don't you shave? Wear the new suit of clothes I bought you."

He opened his Bible and dropped his eyes to the page as if he understood every word. "Fool girl. You need these sermons more than me."

Mala stopped trying to reason with Beni and started packing things in the trailer on her own, writing to Ruth and asking permission to bring him to Bakersfield. *He's free to come,* she wrote back, *as long as he sees a doctor. You don't know what he's got and we've got Zina to consider.*

Beni gave in soon after, submitted to the idea of traveling because Mala made it sound like a romantic notion, a way to be young and free again. It took two days of tale-spinning to convince him, but when he fell, he fell completely. He got out of bed at midnight and combed his hair, found his suspenders, cleaned out his coffee-pot. He would miss his church but he would find another one in this new world his daughter described in such heart-wringing language. He was ready to go right now, by the light of the moon. The trailer had done nothing but sprout rust holes anyway, so let it rot by itself on the banks of a shit-colored river. Most of the memories he'd made here weren't worth the trouble, and the one that mattered most he was taking with him.

The flurry of packing and excitement lasted until morning, when Beni collapsed in an overstrung heap outside the trailer. He was too weak to resist going to the doctor, who diagnosed him with tubercu-losis and gave him two months to live.

Mala didn't tell Beni, but he seemed to know. On the way home in a taxi, he didn't say a word, not even about the money the ride was costing or the car's fancy seats. Back at the trailer, he slept for twelve hours straight. He spent the whole next day in bed staring out the window, his head resting on the hard cover of his Bible. When he finally sat up to eat a little corn soup, there was a scrolled impression on his left temple.

He didn't ask what was wrong with him and he didn't complain, he just seemed to fold up a little more every day, an old spider pull-ing its legs in one by one. For a few weeks he regained his appetite, and Mala began to hope the doctor was wrong—all doctors were, if you believed Drina—but by December he was managing only a few bites a day and struggling with that. Through a parishioner who knew somebody who knew somebody in a clan up near Abilene, Drina heard about Beni's condition and showed up without warning one afternoon, bow-legged and coral-haired, driving a battered produce truck from the thirties and carrying an old suitcase. "Where you been?" Beni said, not bothering to roll over and face her.

"Same kinda place as always, just a couple hours north. Now

she's back, I don't know why you don't move up. Things are going good as you can see." Drina tilted her head toward the truck outside. "I'm busier than I even want to be, and a couple of the boys got work on a highway crew."

"I wouldn't go anyway," Mala said. "I made a life for myself somewhere else."

"Well, you sure haven't changed." Drina set her case on the end of the bed and opened it, revealing vials of colored powders and bits of muslin stuffed with dried herbs. "What you been giving him?"

"Everything I could think of," Mala said.

"Since when do you poison a man with drugstore cough syrup?" she asked, nudging the empty bottle on the floor with her shoe.

"Since he started coughing up blood."

Mala walked out and banged the door behind her, glad for once to see the field deserted. She lugged a bucket to the old pump near the road and pumped rusty water until her shoulder burned, hauling it back to the trailer and sitting on the steps to wait out her aunt's visit. Drina came out a while later with a blunt look on her face.

"He ain't good," she said.

"Did you help him?"

"I doubt it."

"You at least gave him hope."

"I didn't do that either. I known him too long to lie to him."

She stood in front of Mala, case in hand, as if expecting her to say something important. When she didn't, Drina said, "We tried to take him with us. He wouldn't budge."

"I guess that's my fault, too."

"It's somebody's. That's how things work. A person does something and something else comes to pass."

"It doesn't mean they planned it that way."

"No, and I didn't say that. Personally, I never believed you caused all that trouble, but you were always there when it happened. It's hard to see the difference."

"Well, I didn't kill my mother."

"You didn't save her either. I wasn't right to blame you but it was a weakness I couldn't help. Think hard and see if there's not somebody you're blaming for what they didn't do." She took a look around the field and made a face that said she was through with it. No nostalgia, no regret. "I'm glad you made it home. We all been wondering about you."

"I'm not staying."

"So you say."

She patted Mala's shoulder and drove away in her truck, and for an hour afterward the field smelled like burning oil.

"I don't want nobody else to know," Beni said that night, clutching the edge of the flattened wool pad he slept on. "Don't let Ruth or any of them come here and make it worse."

"You don't want to see your granddaughter?"

"I ain't safe around her. I ain't safe around you."

"I'm all right." But after that Mala tied a handkerchief around her face the way the doctor had told her to. Beni didn't mind; he said in some funny way it made him feel properly tended to.

Elliot wrote that he was coming to Texas after the new year for as long as he could get away, family problems or no. *My father's sick and doesn't have long,* Mala wrote back, and this time she told him everything. No dancing around it, just the facts. Reading over her letter, she didn't feel any of the pride of months back, only regret that she hadn't told him sooner. There was no telling how she'd changed things keeping the news to herself, but no doubt things had changed. She'd never know how.

Three ladies from church heard about Beni's illness and started driving out every day to help, kind white Christian women bumping up the gravel road in a groaning Chevrolet, their hats grazing the ceiling. They brought new blankets and pillows and pots and pans, all the things Beni hadn't let Mala buy but accepted now with humility. They'd have been there the last night but thought Beni had more time. It was only a few hours before the end when Mala realized he didn't.

Flushed and bright-eyed, his forehead flaming, Beni gathered his breath between fits of coughing to recount memories so colorful and unreliable they had to be coming from his imagination. Wars he'd fought, bulls he'd ridden, a sister he'd forgotten all about. Sitting on the floor by his bed, Mala pretended to remember along with him until his words scattered and he started hallucinating. He was going to tell her a great secret, he kept saying, but around dawn he slipped into silence. His last breaths were so shallow that Mala missed his dying moment, realizing he was gone only when his hand stiffened in hers.

As if they'd been summoned, the ladies drove up about midmorning, finding Mala dry-eyed but speechless, staring through the scratched window by her bed. "She's in shock," she heard a voice say. "Don't startle her." While the others dressed Beni and washed his face and hands, one of the women sat with her heavy, perfumed arm around Mala, saying soothing things Mala was too stricken to make sense of. Soon the coroner came in a long black car, carrying Beni from the trailer he'd been fixed to for twelve years. Two days later, using money collected from the congregation, Beni's pastor gave him a Christian burial in the East Hill Cemetery, laying him to rest between a train conductor and a young child. Seven members of the church attended. It was the most dignified thing that had happened to Beni, Mala thought, and better too late than never.

The woman who'd sat with Mala offered her a room until the worst of her grieving had passed. Mala thanked her but returned to the field, intending to leave for California as soon as she felt strong enough. Her skin seethed and her legs ached, as if Beni had left behind his fevers when he died. The night of the funeral, she lay awake, listening on instinct for his breathing and reliving his passing when she heard nothing. She slept all the next day, rising at dusk to eat what the pastor's wife had brought before sleeping again. She was dimly aware of time passing. In the middle of the third or fourth night, she sat up, out of breath and fully awake. One side of her throat was throbbing and her whole skull hurt, not from sickness but shame. She'd let Beni die in his trailer and leave life without his belongings, just tossed his wandering spirit to a religion he barely understood. She hadn't covered the wall mirror or laid a coin on his coffin, and even as she scoffed at the idea of him buying his way into heaven, she could see him standing penniless outside the gates, a beggar in life and death.

Sunrise was a few hours off but she got up anyway. Shuddering from fear and cold, she packed in a rush, sensing Beni's offended soul behind her no matter where she looked. She thought she heard music and stopped, heart pounding in her ears, but it was wind whistling through the cracked aluminum floor. Though she knew there was no sense arranging his few possessions, she pulled his blankets over sweat-stained sheets, touching the faint outline of his body and smoothing his still-indented pillow, gently but with the devil at her heels.

Bag over her shoulder, she looked around one more time, knowing she'd stayed too long. She stepped outside and left the door wide-open. The air was barely lit by stars. At the corner of the trailer, she knelt down and swept dead leaves and twigs into a pile. It would be quick—she had matches and kerosene and it hadn't rained in a month. One or two trees might ignite but there wasn't much around but sand and rocks and the river. Cupping her hand, she lit four matches before one took, crackling needles and sending up a whoosh when it found the fuel. In less than a minute Beni's trailer was on fire, metal buckling and windows cracking, the steps he'd made from treated wood throwing out long blue flames. Halfway across the field she stopped to look, feeling heavy with sadness but ready to go.

The barbed wire tangle snagged her ankle on the dirt road, and by the time she got to the tar she was bleeding. Dawn was a thin gray haze on the horizon, studded with distant ridges. She'd gone maybe half a mile when her legs refused to carry her and she sat down to wait.

Hours passed. Above her head the sky shimmered, huge and white. Trucks went by but they felt distant and unreachable, and even when one stopped a little up the road, she realized she couldn't walk to it. After a minute it drove off. It must have been after noon when a car slid to a stop in front of her, so close she could touch the hot metal of the door handle.

"Come on," said a woman's voice through the lowered window. "You want a ride or not?"

"Yes, I do." Standing unsteadily, Mala found just enough strength to slip into the backseat and pull her bag in after her. The ceiling seemed to swim above her head.

"Going far?" the voice asked.

Mala had to think a moment. "I'm going to California. Maybe Nevada first."

"We can get you to Fort Stockton."

"That'll do." She smiled and laid her head back. A ride to Fort Stockton would give her time to sleep. And when she woke up, her head would be clear, her parents' ghosts lulled by the smoke still rising from the field. Closing her eyes, she could see the way ahead, the winter skies and cracked desert roads, the destination clouded but just in front of her. Almost as if she'd already arrived.

Thirty-three

OCTOBER 21, 1950

*R*uth's letter came months after Elliot's last trip to Texas, from which he'd returned glum and empty-handed, his face sunburnt, his appetite poor and his mood unbearable. It didn't matter what Helen said or cooked for him, she couldn't drag him out of it. "No trace," he kept saying. "I'm telling you, she disappeared."

"That's what girls do," Helen replied.

"Not this girl."

Helen said nothing, letting her son sit with his contradictions. Eventually he would see it: Mala had run off with somebody else or the state of Texas had swallowed her up. Either way, she wasn't coming back.

Helen wasn't careless enough to keep Mala's final letter—that kind of thing had a way of making itself known, springing up through the soil where it was buried, emerging from drawer or floorboard decades on. She'd taken it from the mailman's hand with the most maternal of intentions. Elliot had never been a very forthcoming boy, and how could she guide him if he wouldn't let her? The way he moped around, always staring out windows and asking, "When? Why?" As if life in his parents' house was an affliction. Feeling genuinely sorry for the girl, Helen had read the letter twice and burned it out in the dark backyard while Elliot slept and his brother sat in jail awaiting sentencing and her husband sold household items to lonely women in Utah and Idaho. Only two things could take her son away for good: a woman or a child. No way to know if he was the father, anyway. Maybe she would tell him about it when he was established, too rooted to abandon his family on a lark like that farm business with his uncle.

She'd expected other letters but none had come. It was tempting to believe God had a hand in it, making an appearance in her life for the first time. Even as Elliot roamed around Texas and wrote to a woman in Bakersfield hoping for news of his girl, Helen had faith. Everything would turn out in the end because something had to. Nobody could go their whole life with not a single thing turning out.

But here was another letter all these months later, when Elliot seemed, if not over his misery, then settled into it, going to his job every morning and working with the lawyer on his brother's appeal. This time it wasn't Mala writing, but Ruth, the Bakersfield woman who had the baby. Helen held the envelope in her hand, trying to discern the contents. No mother wanted to break her son's trust twice, but she didn't want his life ruined either. He was driving down to visit his brother and wouldn't be home for hours. It couldn't hurt to steam it open, just to see.

Reading at the kitchen table, it was as Helen feared, the baby story all over again with a sweet picture slipped inside. Ruth said she could have given the girl to the grandfather, some rich rancher, and in truth they'd fought over her, with Ruth taking the child back to California and moving away before he could follow. She'd promised Mala she would raise the child until Elliot came for her, and she planned to do it. The girl wouldn't grow up a motherless orphan, nor would she know she was different. That story had already been told. If Elliot couldn't be a father to her, she understood. Zina had a home with her whether Mala came back or she didn't. Ruth left a phone number and an address in San Francisco and signed it with just her initial, as if she'd known Elliot for a long time.

Helen sat across from her son at dinner that night and for weeks afterward, the words bottled up in her throat. In early winter somebody at a Texas hospital wrote saying there was a young woman who'd come in maybe a year ago, sounded like the one he was looking for. No identification on her and she'd died of polio two days later. She'd been cremated when nobody claimed her, but that was all the information they had. It took Elliot days to emerge from his bedroom, and when he did, something in his eyes had hardened and gone dead. He wrote to Ruth and told her but the letter came back, no forwarding address. This was the sign Helen had hoped for, the ending she wanted and the one she was going to get.

Elliot wasn't happy these days, but he was a man. He'd endured some difficult things that made him appreciate what he had, family included. He was gentler with his mother, no longer treating her like something in his way. She knew he would move out in time, but those dreams of going off to a big city or another state felt like a boy's ideas now. He said so on one of the few afternoons when his father was home, and his father put an arm around his shoulders and told him how proud he was.

Once in a while Helen remembered those two letters burned in the yard, their ashes fertilizing the cottonwood tree that shaded her son's window, and thought that there are many routes to happiness.

Most of them, she'd discovered, you make yourself. If you surrendered to what life gave you, you wouldn't get anything. She'd fought for her son and now she had him, his footsteps on her stairs and his presence in her house when nobody else was there. No one could tell her it hadn't been worth it, even if what she'd done wasn't right.

There was no denying that part of it, and she didn't try.

Thirty-four

The car had been sitting in front of the house all morning, parked across the curbless asphalt strip torn up from years of frost heaves and dry heat, one of those forgotten county roads that never should have been one in the first place. Too remote even for the hopelessly lost. It was a straight shot through a sparsely inhabited valley on the backside of the southern Sierras, not far as the crow flies from lakes and sequoias but a long way off by every other measure. It had been a jolt to retire and move here, not for the lack of people as much as the silence, which Zina had quickly realized was just a different kind of noise, a low rushing like a stream under the floor. Even after six years living in this house, she sometimes had the desire to take a flashlight to the basement and search for signs of water.

She went upstairs to vacuum and make the bed in the wallpapered noontime heat, but when she came down the car was still there, a woman in the driver's seat, her brassy head turned toward Zina's front door. One of her husband's old girlfriends maybe, widowed or divorced, coming all this way on the off chance Warren had no wife. Waste of a trip. Or maybe she just wanted to paint the view—Zina had seen a few lovers of the high desert on roadsides with easels set up, weeds to their knees—but amateur artists didn't usually come this far. The scenery was better in a thousand other spots and a lot easier to get to.

She was at the side of the house unwinding the leaky hose when she heard footsteps on the flagstones. The blond woman stood at the gate, too young to be one of Warren's ex-lovers but not to be an inconvenience. From five feet off, Zina could tell she planned to ask a lot of questions.

"Help you?" she said, going back to the hose. She knew how she looked: gray braid halfway down her back, dark sunglasses, rough bare feet—the kind of person who might pay the electric bill on the grow room with a Social Security check. The truth was a lot less interesting than that.

The woman cleared her throat. "I'm looking for someone."

"Who are you?"

"My name is Audrey. Does Zina Simon live here?"

"Are you from the IRS, Audrey? Because we're almost caught up on this place. Contrary to what you may have heard, a teacher's pension doesn't go very far."

"No, I'm not."

Zina noticed a book in the woman's hand and shook her head. No corner of the world was too distant to try to convert. "Then if you'll excuse me, I have tomatoes to water." She dragged the hissing hose, her legs and skirt taking most of the spray.

"Wait—just a second? Please."

Zina stopped but kept her back turned.

"I'm trying to find information about Mala Rinehart."

At first the name was meaningless, a bunch of random letters just thrown together. Then something inside Zina cracked open, a tiny chink in the wall between now and a long time ago. "Is that why you've been sitting outside my house?"

"Yes. I was afraid I'd be disappointed."

"Well, I'm sorry but I didn't know her."

"You know the name, though."

Zina sighed and turned around. "I know the name." At the sight of the woman's face—heavy on the eyeliner, her thin lips trembly and nervous—Zina said more than she wanted to. "She was a friend of my mother's, disappeared around 1950. I have no idea what happened to her. Do you?"

"I was hoping you could tell me."

"Are you a journalist or something?"

"No. I've just got this." She held out the book, not a Bible at all, but an old gray journal filled with yellowed pages.

Zina hesitated, not wanting to encourage the woman but not wanting to wonder later either. She cranked off the hose and took the book across the top of the gate. It was a baffling thing, creepy and fantastic, like looking into the heart of a churning spirit. She knew Mala's handwriting—the exaggerated loops and swirls—from old letters stuck in storage with the rest of Ruth's things. There was something else Zina found vaguely familiar—not the words, but the need to read what was coming in a dream or a cloud formation. There was sadness in it, too, as if writing all this down had been meant to make a difference.

"Where'd you get this?" she asked.

"It showed up at a garage sale. Somebody found it in the house where you lived in Bakersfield."

"You probably know more about her than I do. I've never even seen a picture of her. I used to think my mother was making her up."

"I guess this proves she didn't."

"I'd heard Mala had kind of a bohemian background but I didn't know she wrote any of that stuff. How'd you connect it to me?"

"I tracked down your mother's grave. A guy at the cemetery told me your name."

Zina handed back the book and began snapping the dead heads off a rosebush. "He shouldn't have."

She couldn't be making it any plainer, but Audrey made no move to go. "So you never even met her," she said, her voice thick with disappointment. Zina hoped to God she wouldn't start to cry.

"My mother talked about her. She looked for her for thirty years. For the fiancé, too."

"I didn't know about a fiancé. There's nothing about him in the book."

"Then how would you? I looked him up on the computer a while ago. If it's the same guy, he's a retired judge in Denver. I never called. No point in bothering him after all these years."

Audrey swallowed and fanned her face, which had turned dark pink in the sun. "Listen, I don't mean to ask favors but I didn't know you lived so far out and I haven't had anything to drink in hours. Can I trouble you for some water?"

Knowing it was probably a mistake, Zina reached for the gate latch. "All right. Come on."

They sat with clinking glasses at the wrought-iron patio table, its legs uneven on the stones, top tilting every time one of them leaned an elbow.

"Did your mother ever mention if Mala had a child?" Audrey asked.

"Nope, but my mother didn't mention a lot of things." There was something about Audrey's open face that made it too easy to talk. If she wasn't careful the woman would ask to stay for dinner.

"You go to visit her grave a lot."

"I go to try to figure things out," Zina said.

"What do you mean?"

"I'll just say this—fifty-nine years I thought she was my mother. She's not." There was no reason to go into it, how getting her first passport had torn up her life and dropped it at her feet in an unrecognizable state. She and Warren had planned that anniversary trip for four years. If she hadn't wanted to leave the country, she'd never have known. She wouldn't have ordered the birth certificate, the "delayed certificate of birth," which probably meant she'd been born at home. Not much of a surprise, until it came in the mail plainly marked *Adopted*. That had explained a lot—an absent father, a mother she didn't resemble—but not enough. Not why. Not the reason for keeping it secret.

"I even asked her about it once," Zina said. "She could have told me the truth and she didn't."

"Things were different then."

"Not really. A lie was still a lie."

"She loved you, though, didn't she?"

"Maybe too much, I don't know. I try not to ask questions that don't have answers."

Audrey asked if she'd looked for her birth mother, an idea that always gave Zina the feeling of standing in the middle of a huge, roadless plain. "No," Zina said. "She's probably dead anyway."

"Just knowing might help," Audrey said.

But knowing wasn't a solution to everything. Zina had thought about it, and every time decided she'd have been better off ignorant. Stir things up and sometimes they never settled back down. Of course she craved civilization. Some mornings she looked at the mountains hemming the land to the west and felt like a penned horse. But Warren loved this house, every day walking the same narrow hallways he'd run through as a kid, the nostalgia of the gouged wood floors and wavy windows, as if buying his parents' old place could help him stall time. He liked commuting to the one-story town hall and taking people's property tax checks, easing the sting with a funny remark. There was no reason to tell him how much she missed the city, the noise and garbage blowing in the gutters and run-down little restaurants. For thirty years he'd wanted to come back here, and they couldn't afford to live in two places. It was no more complicated than that.

"I don't think looking would help," she told Audrey. "They didn't keep the same kind of records in those days."

"I got this far on almost no records at all."

"And we still don't know what happened to Mala."

"Maybe her fiancé does."

"Then why didn't he ever let Ruth know?"

"All sorts of things could have happened."

"And they surely did." Zina sat back, exhausted from talking, or maybe it was the subject she had no more tolerance for. Some people could go on endlessly about the past, not realizing the present was disappearing right in front of them.

A cloud passed over the sun, the first bit of shade in four days. Zina took off her sunglasses and leaned her head back, blinking at a hawk riding thermals a mile up. Squinting, she looked back at Audrey, who stared at her, no attempt to be polite or look away.

"When were you born?" Audrey asked after a while of saying nothing.

"Nineteen forty-nine."

"Around the time Mala left?"

"Just before she went back to Texas to take care of her father. He died there. She probably did, too."

"Texas," Audrey repeated, the word blowing away on a bit of wind.

"That's where my mother met her. She used to keep house on a ranch where Mala's father worked. My mother taught Mala to read. One of the few of her kind who knew how back then."

"A ranch in Texas. Of all things." Audrey didn't say much more after that. She asked questions about the house and garden, though Zina could see her mind was on something else. The long drive back to the suburbs, probably. It was barely mid-afternoon when she got up, offering to leave the book with Zina but not arguing when she refused. It wasn't that Zina didn't want it—she didn't want what came with it. Unanswered questions in her house, the kind of thing that could ruin the peace of a place like this, where peace was the point.

"I hope you'll call the man in Denver," Audrey said at the gate.

"Why?" Zina asked.

"I think he'd like hearing from you, that's all."

"You know how to get to the highway all right? I can draw you a map."

"It doesn't matter," Audrey said, halfway down the path. "Tell you the truth, I don't think I'd mind getting lost for a while."

Zina wanted to ask what she meant but didn't. She went inside, thinking that after all these years she'd finally turned into a local. People from the city didn't make a whole lot of sense to her anymore.

The package was delivered the following week. Brown paper, packing tape, the return address a town called Rancho Alegre. It was so tightly wrapped it took scissors to tear into it. Zina sat at the kitchen table, not surprised to see Mala's old notebook, just confused. There was no note. She didn't open the book, just slid it away and looked at it. There was an impression of letters on the cover, name and year. She hadn't noticed that before and Audrey hadn't mentioned it. Lying next to the salt shaker, the book seemed no different from the old cast iron stove in the basement or the 1970 Pam Am calendar curling upstairs on a closet wall. It was sad, proof of her age and other lives gone by, but nothing that would keep her awake at night wondering.

She drove twenty-seven miles to the nearest town and back, put groceries away, went out to the yard and filled a bowl with the first ripe tomatoes. She washed them at the sink and set them to dry on a dish towel. The sun was lower now, slanting across the kitchen and revealing things she hadn't seen two days before. A spiderweb stretched across the corner of a countertop. Fingerprints on the freezer handle, hers and Warren's, overlapping. The slim white edge of something inside Mala's book on the table. In a different light, it might have stayed hidden for years.

She pulled it free with damp fingertips and turned it faceup. It was a photograph of Zina and her mother standing in front of an old house, her mother holding something in her arms. A baby, she supposed. Nothing unusual about it except it gave her the feeling of being off-kilter. Everything was familiar but all wrong, the way a house is still familiar when it's half burned down. She had never worn that dress or had hair that dark, her mother had never been so young, and the eyes that looked at her out of the photograph—clear green even in black and white—had been someone else's before they were hers.

She put her hand over the face but it was there when she pulled her fingers away, more alive than most things living. Mala, just as her mother had described her, leaving out the features Zina shared. No explanation, no way to get to the truth. With Ruth and Mala gone, there was nobody left to ask but the old man in Denver. She had his phone number somewhere, scribbled on a receipt she hadn't quite managed to throw away.

She sat at the table until the kitchen was filled with shadows. When she finally opened the book, a folded slip of paper dropped onto her lap. It was an article from fifteen years ago, about a lawyer's search for a woman he wouldn't name. She skimmed it, not understanding at first, thinking it a mistake. Something Audrey hadn't meant to send. By the last sentence she had no breath left and her palms were slick. She could see it all now, what had been then and what was to come.

When Warren came home, she was out back in the herb garden with a trowel in her hand. She heard the familiar rhythm of his steps and leaned back on her heels.

"What's that inside on the counter?" he asked, reaching down to touch the back of her neck.

"Nothing that can't wait for the sun to go down. I'll tell you about it later."

He shaded his eyes and looked west. "It's going to be a good one with those clouds. I'll be right back."

"No hurry. It won't set for fifteen minutes." Even though this was true, Zina stopped what she was doing and watched the mountains slowly swallow up the light and turn darker.

She remembered what she'd felt earlier sitting at the table—an arrival, the end of a long journey. But right now, watching the sky, it was nothing like that. She knelt in the dirt and looked back at the simple house with its crumbling chimney and sun-bleached shingles, a hundred and thirty years on the same dry ground. It was a place where anything could happen, even to a woman like her. She could be sixty-three and starting all over again. She could glance in the mirror on a summer afternoon toward the end of her life and see herself for the first time.

Acknowledgments

Many thanks to Caitlin Alexander and Kerri Buckley, Kim Witherspoon, Allison Hunter, Alison Masciovecchio, Amy Sherman, Rosalyn Feldberg, Andy, Lori, and Jordan Harris, my mother and father, and especially Paul, Mo, and Ruby.

And finally, thanks to my late grandfather, Thomas Milton MacDowell, whose discovery at seventy-eight that he was adopted helped inspire parts of this story.

ABOUT THE AUTHOR

ROSE MACDOWELL is the co-author of the novel *Turning Tables*. She lives in Boston and New Hampshire's White Mountains.